THE HEIR OF SWANSGROVE

K. J. PRITCHETT

CONTENTS

To anyone who's ever felt like they didn't belong.

Chapter One

THE END OF AN ERA

Silent Springs, Pennsylvania

The woman peered pensively into the dark abyss outside, her brilliant red tresses flowing in the cold winter air. Only hours ago, the night sky had been illuminated by magical activity as forces of darkness struggled to solidify their reign over the country. Fortunately, they had *not* been successful. Regardless, Dervla suspected that the next time, darkness would triumph, particularly in a magical hotspot like Silent Springs.

Magic attracted magic, the stronger the magic, the stronger the attraction. Dervla accomplished what was necessary to protect the modern magical world, but the time had come for her to focus her efforts on protecting her family, even if it meant leaving that world behind.

Dervla didn't need magic to sense the approach of her closest friend, Cecelia Swiatkowski. From the moment Dervla and Cecelia met in kindergarten, they were inseparable, helping each other through the awkward years of adolescence, studying together at the university in V'riglia, the magical capital of the United States, and even finding love and settling down in the small rural town of Silent Springs, Pennsylvania. Where one went, the other was always close by. Until now.

"Well, there you are," Cecelia said, sitting beside her. The petite woman was a few inches shorter than Dervla's own five feet six inches and more delicately built. "Everyone's been looking all over for you. One might think you wouldn't be sulking around during the celebrations."

Dervla turned to face her best friend. "The celebrations? Seems odd everyone is so happy with all the lives that were lost."

Cecelia shot her a challenging look with sharp blue eyes. "I'm sorry about your brother, Dervla. War is something I wouldn't wish upon anyone. But what would have happened if we didn't rise against them? We've all lost loved ones, and we must preserve their memories. But to do that, we must move on with our own lives and live, to ensure that their sacrifices weren't in vain."

Well, this *should go well,* Dervla thought, steeling herself for the impending dispute. "Celia, that's exactly what I wanted to talk to you about," she confessed, looking up into the moonlit sky.

Cecelia knit her pale brows, her expression calculating. Joseph, Cecelia's husband, had the ability to Sniff magic; Cecelia had always been able to sniff out dishonesty. "Oh?"

Dervla turned to face her friend. "Well, Celia, I am moving on. And away."

Cecelia's blue eyes widened with shock at Dervla's words. "Excuse me? After you've fought *so* hard to bring about an end to the terror, the death, the destruction . . . you're running away?"

Dervla wasn't surprised her friend was upset at her announcement; throughout the years, they had never been separated by more than a few miles at a time. What surprised her was the fact Cecelia was letting her emotions show. Her best friend had never been one to wear her emotions on her sleeve, and for this reason had been one of the Resistance's most talented spies.

"It's all right, Celia," she promised, placing her hand on her friend's shoulder. "I'll keep in touch."

Cecelia wiped the tears from her eyes, her expression equal parts anger and sadness. "No, you won't. You just want to forget that all this ever happened! You want to forget about this war, our friendship . . . even magic! And what, because you don't want to deal with the consequences of war?"

"Come on, Celia," Dervla said, as kindly as possible. Consolation had never been one of her strengths. "You're not alone. You have a wonderful family—a loving husband, three beautiful children—"

Cecelia turned to face her, blue eyes blazing with the intensity of someone unaccustomed to losing. "Yes, Dervla, I'm fortunate enough to have a happy family. But why can't I have my best friend too?" The woman rubbed her forehead feverishly. "You want to keep your heritage from your children, don't you? If you learn one thing from me, let it be this: you can't *tell* magic what to do. You can tell yourself whatever you want. If you put space between your family and what happened, it'll all go away. But you're a Swansgrove, Dervla, and history has shown that Swansgroves can't avoid magic. Maybe *you* won't be pulled back in, but your children will be."

There *was* some truth to what Cecelia was saying, but Dervla had already made the necessary travel arrangements and was unwilling to change her mind. She and her family were moving to the other side of the country, and only then would she be able to keep them safe. "I will miss you, Celia," Dervla admitted. "In spite of all this, you're my best friend."

"Then don't leave."

Dervla sighed. Cecelia was still the difficult, stubborn girl she had met in kindergarten. "Look. Why don't we both just go and enjoy one last party together with all our friends? You'll have fun if you let yourself."

Cecelia swallowed, though her saliva or her pride, Dervla couldn't be sure. "All right, let's go. I just hope you know what you're doing."

She wouldn't admit it, but Dervla shared the same concern.

Chapter Two

New Girl

Silent Springs, 10 years later

Fourteen-year-old Acacia Wheatley glared daggers into her oatmeal, wishing she could make it spontaneously combust.

"Eat up, dear. You'll be late for your first day." Her mother, Dervla, turned the page of her newspaper.

Acacia stabbed her breakfast with her spoon. "Fine with me. This isn't my school."

Her mother sighed. "Acacia, it's not exactly a secret you're angry about moving here. Pennsylvania wasn't my first choice either. But your grandmother isn't getting any younger and Daddy wants to be closer in case something happens." Dervla folded the newspaper, laid it on the table, and stood. "And the move gave your father a fantastic opportunity to open his own practice here."

"Yeah, I know. And all my fantastic friends are back home in Sacramento."

Dervla rolled her eyes at her eldest daughter, not amused whatsoever. "One day, you'll meet a wonderful man and get married, and you'll have a little girl who'll be *exactly* like you."

"Mom!"

Her mother smiled and ran a hand through Acacia's long coppery tresses, which extended down her back. "Hurry up, dear. You don't want detention on your first day, do you?"

Acacia scowled into her oatmeal but ate.

***

Twenty minutes later, Acacia was ready to go, wearing a long-sleeve black T-shirt, beige shorts, and sneakers, with her hair tied back into a single long braid. Her older brother David was watching a motocross race on the television as she headed for the door.

"Have fun in detention," Acacia said. "Some impression you're going to make."

"Driver's license, Achy." David shot her a bored glance. "Don't have to leave for another ten minutes."

Acacia arched her coppery brows. "Why can't you take me? I swear, you can drop me a block or two away! Please!"

"And show up to school carting my baby sister around?" Dave laughed. "Thanks, but I'll pass."

Acacia folded her arms across her chest and glared at her brother. "Mom!" she hollered. "Dave won't give me a ride!"

Sarison, Acacia's eleven-year-old sister, poked her head in the room. "Average, annoying Acacia. It's not like you had any real friends in California."

"Sari, shut up!" Acacia yelled. A few sparks of green light appeared at Acacia's fingertips, and Sari bolted immediately from the room. Acacia blinked, trying to figure out what had happened, but when she looked at her hand again, no trace of the green light remained.

"Weird," Dave commented, echoing Acacia's thoughts. "Better move, booger. I'll bet you can still make it on that piece of junk you call a bike."

Acacia glared one last time at her brother. "Whatever, Dave." She threw her bookbag over her shoulder and grabbed her helmet as she headed out the front door. Her brother made some smart retort, but she slammed the door and mounted her bike, pedaling as fast as possible.

***

Silent Springs was vastly different from Sacramento. Where Sacramento had been flat and dry, Silent Springs was hilly, wet, and minuscule. The trip from her new home to the high school took less time than expected, and Acacia realized she wouldn't have to leave the house as early tomorrow morning.

The school, too, was strikingly different from what Acacia was accustomed to. Silent Springs High looked like an old castle, constructed of red brick. Surveying the scene, Acacia pulled her bike lock out of her bookbag and secured her bike to the closest rack.

A handful of students were lingering in front of the main entrance, talking with friends, and reminiscing about their summer vacations. Acacia leaned against the brick wall on the side of the stairs leading to the entrance, content to watch the crowd. Out of the corner of her eye, she saw a few sparks of blue light, not unlike the green sparks she'd seen earlier that morning. Her curiosity piqued, Acacia looked and saw two boys about her age, both with dirty blond hair, gray eyes, and freckles. Upon closer inspection, Acacia realized they were identical twins, the only difference being the darkness of their eyes.

"I'm telling you, high school is *bound* to be better than middle school," the boy with the lighter eyes was saying in a cheerful tone. "Like, eighth grade was the actual worst, but that doesn't mean high school will be too."

The boy with the darker eyes shook his head and looked toward the school with a face full of worry. "I don't know, Zander. It's been a couple months, but what if people are still talking about it?"

Acacia had never minded the academic component of school, although she didn't love the homework. But the gossip and drama—those were another issue entirely. Something could have happened in first grade, and if you attended the same school, people would still bully you about it years later. *I guess that's the* one *nice thing about being new. No one knows about the embarrassing things you did when you were younger.*

The boy with the lighter eyes put his arm around his brother's shoulders. "People are not still going to be talking about it. I'll bet over the summer so many other things happened that no one's going to remember eighth grade drama."

Acacia took a deep breath and walked over to where the twins were standing. She had been a soccer fanatic at her old school, her intensity chasing away many a potential friend. There was no reason for her to fall into the same habits here.

"Hi," she said, scratching the back of her head. "Is this your first day here too? I'm . . . new."

The twins exchanged curious glances and looked back to her. The one with the lighter eyes removed his arm from his brother's shoulder and extended his hand to her. "I'm Alex, Alex Swiatkowski," he said as Acacia shook his hand. "And yeah, we're both freshmen, me and my brother AJ. AJ's worried high school is going to be awful, but I think it's going to be okay. Percy said the other day, you just have to make sure you fall in with the right people."

"Percy is hardly the expert on high school life," the boy with the darker eyes, AJ, replied. He turned, casting a curious look in Acacia's direction. While his brother's eyes were friendly, AJ's were searching, almost suspicious. "I'm AJ, the less charming twin. Welcome to Silent Springs. . ." He paused, waiting for Acacia to introduce herself.

"My name's Acacia Wheatley," she said with a grin, feeling her face redden in embarrassment. Maybe she could do this, maybe she could make friends and not be the scary redhead all over again. "My first name is kind of weird, but it's like the plant, uh-kay-shuh."

Alex grinned as a bell rang from inside the school, beckoning the students forward. "Nice to meet you, Acacia," he said as the three of them followed the crowd into the front door. "Maybe we'll see you later."

Acacia smiled back, hoping they would.

***

After a heated argument with the guidance counselor, who tried to convince her that her name was Allison, and an invigorating search for classroom 112, an exhausted Acacia arrived at her first period English class.

"Fantastic," she said to herself. "And now it's time for a lecture about boring books written by dead people."

"That's what I said," a familiar voice agreed.

Acacia spun around. One of the twins from earlier had appeared behind her.

"Oh, sorry." The boy blinked. "Didn't mean to spy on you. It's just nice to meet someone that's equally bored of sitting around listening to what a dusty old book's supposed to represent."

Acacia blinked. *Now what were their names again? Alex, I think, and AJ. But which one is this?*

"There's plenty of stuff I like to learn about," the twin said. "Things you can use to help people. My dad ran this shelter for runaway kids down in West Virginia for a while. And you have to know a lot to do stuff like that. But you don't learn them from reading old books."

Acacia looked in wonder at the talkative boy. "Alex, right? I met you and your brother outside this morning?"

"Well, supposedly we're twins, but I think Andrew's adopted," Alex replied with an infectious smile. "I mean, who can take the square root of whatever but doesn't know what a red card is?"

"You play soccer?" Acacia felt her mood lightening by the moment. Soccer was one of her favorite things in the world, right after oatmeal raisin cookies.

Alex nodded. "Since I could walk. I'm not too bad either. I beat out a couple of older guys to make the JV team."

"I guess I missed tryouts," she said, feeling a disappointed frown settle across her face. "Bummer."

Alex patted her on the shoulder. "Don't sweat it. That means you have all year to get ready! You should join us at lunch, unless you've got someone else to sit with. Just watch out for Mattes. He's AJ's friend, but he always has something to say, even when you're minding your own business."

"Thanks for the invite." Acacia was beginning to like Alex more by the minute. "I'll be there!"

"Awesome," her new friend said, and the two of them entered the classroom, taking seats in the middle of the room.

***

A few hours later, Acacia approached her last class before her lunch period, biology. Silent Springs was a small school, and while this time Alex wasn't in her class, his brother was. Try as she might, Acacia couldn't get a good read on AJ to tell if he wanted to be friends or if he was just being nice because Alex liked her. Acacia figured that this was an issue for later and took a seat at a lab table next to him. Part of Acacia wanted to ask him about what he and Alex had been talking about earlier in the morning, but she suspected he was more likely to tell her to pay attention to Mr. Portland's explanation of the syllabus than divulge any personal information.

Truthfully, today *was* turning out to be a much better day than she'd expected. Acacia had never transferred schools before, but she had heard horror stories from students who had. It was bad enough to start high school in the same place where you grew up, never mind to start all over in a new school where you knew no one. Acacia had turned herself against the town of Silent Springs from the moment they got off the plane in Philadelphia, but she'd already been able to make at least one friend. Maybe a less awkward person could have made more, but Acacia always preferred quality over quantity.

Acacia realized she had been in a deep reverie and shook her head, jolting herself back to reality. Seconds later, she became aware of a strange pulling sensation in her chest. She wasn't quite sure how to explain it, but it almost felt like something deep inside her body was awakening. It was like she had an alternate bloodstream, though instead of being filled with blood, it was full of energy she'd never noticed before. Either that, or her excitement at having a better day than expected had caused her to temporarily lose her sanity.

Acacia caught a glimpse of something green from the corners of her eyes. She glanced down to the table and, to her surprise, saw a cluster of sparks, much like those she had seen earlier that day, gathered at her fingertips.

"Wha—!" Acacia exclaimed, trying to shake the sparks off. As she did, the entire class turned to stare at her as if she had grown a second head.

"Miss Wheatley?" Mr. Portland had a stern voice, which was even more serious given Acacia's sudden outburst. "Is there something you'd like to share with the class?"

Yeah, Acacia thought. *I keep seeing weird sparks everywhere and I think I'm crazy.*

"No sir," she said instead. "I . . . just think I saw a spider."

The teacher shook his head. "My dear," he began, picking up the class syllabus with a flourish, "I'm not sure if you are aware, but we *are* in rural Pennsylvania. If you are not comfortable with the occasional spider, you might want to consider relocating."

The bell rang, much to Acacia's relief. She turned to collect her things and found AJ staring at her with a rather uncanny expression on his face.

Acacia jammed her hands into her pockets in case the green sparks reappeared. "What's up?"

"You didn't see a spider," he remarked flatly. A flash of blue light seemed to appear in his gaze.

He knows, Acacia realized with a start. *I have no idea* how *he knows, but he knows.*

AJ got up swiftly, picking up his bookbag. "I have to go take care of something," he said in a dazed voice. "Alex said you're sitting with us at lunch. The cafeteria's not too hard to find. Go all the way down the steps and you'll walk right into it. Just don't go to the boiler room by accident."

Acacia was starting to feel a bit suspicious of the boy, but since she didn't want to get into an argument with him, she nodded and led the way out of the classroom. She headed in the direction of the staircase but glanced backward to see where he'd gone. Oddly enough, no trace of AJ Swiatkowski remained, as if he had disappeared off the face of the earth.

***

When Acacia arrived at the cafeteria, she was immediately shocked at how small it was. In general, Silent Springs High School was tiny compared to any of the schools in Sacramento, but since she'd only met a grand total of two people, Acacia didn't mind. Within a few minutes, she found Alex, or more accurately he found her, and they got in line to buy their lunches. While waiting, they talked about their favorite soccer teams and speculated about the next World Cup. For the first time since arriving in Pennsylvania, Acacia felt joy, as she'd managed to not only make a friend on her first day, but a friend who shared her love of soccer. They picked up their food and paid, and Alex gestured for Acacia to follow him to the lunch table.

"Here we are." The boy stopped at the table on the far side of the cafeteria closest to the windows. Acacia recognized AJ, who'd emerged from whatever task he had to take care of, but she didn't recognize the other two. One, sitting at the end closest to where Acacia and Alex stood, was a boy she guessed was the twins' older brother, with blond hair and bright blue eyes. Next to him was a boy with messy chestnut brown hair and amused hazel eyes, who Acacia assumed to be Mattes, AJ's friend who Alex had warned her about.

"Well," Alex began, motioning first to the blond boy. "This is our cousin Percy Golec. He's a junior this year. And that's Matthias Knight, but we all call him Mattes. And, well, you met my brother." He paused and gestured toward Acacia. "Everyone, this is Acacia."

Both Percy and Mattes said hello, and Acacia realized that for the first time of her school career, she was the lone girl at a table of boys. With the introductions out of the way, Alex took the seat across from Percy and Acacia sat down adjacent to him.

"Did Alex manage to scare you off the cafeteria food?" Percy asked with a polite smile. "He had some bad fish sticks back in elementary school. And to be honest, we never knew if it was the fish sticks or the number of fish sticks that made him sick."

"Enough, Percy!" Alex's face was turning a deep shade of crimson. "Do you *have* to tell everybody that I got sick one time when I was seven?"

Percy laughed brightly and began to eat his lunch. Even from the brief interaction, Acacia could tell the twins' cousin was not easily offended.

"Feel free to laugh at Alex," Mattes remarked, reaching out and brushing his fingers against the top of Acacia's hand as if asking her to a dance. "It's a good, consistent source of entertainment for everyone. But anyway, you've got to be tired. After all, you've been running through my mind all day."

Acacia laughed nervously, unsure of how to respond. She thought the boy was joking, as no one ever flirted with soccer fanatic Acacia Wheatley, but she still wasn't sure how to react to even joking flirtatious advances. Alex opened his mouth to speak, but his brother beat him to it.

"Charming as always, Mattes, but since you just met her, that pick-up line doesn't make sense." AJ flashed his friend a challenging look with eyes the shade of storm clouds. "And besides, I didn't think you *came* to school on the first day."

Mattes ran a hand through his unkempt hair. "I usually don't. But I decided to make an exception. I thought you'd be pleased, Captain Pretentious."

AJ shook his head and let out a long sigh. When he faced Acacia, she noticed his expression shifted from annoyed to calm in a matter of seconds. "Acacia," he began in one of the friendliest tones he had used all day. "I meant to apologize for earlier."

"What did you *do*?" Alex looked as if he were going to jump out of his seat to throttle his brother.

"Would you relax, Alex?" AJ shot his brother a serious glance before turning back to Acacia. "Anyway, I'm sorry for ditching you after class. I wasn't feeling too well after smelling . . . some of those chemicals Portland keeps locked up in the lab. My nose is a little on the sensitive side."

"Oh, it's okay," Acacia responded, trying to remember if she'd noticed an overwhelming odor during biology. Maybe at last she was going to find out what the sparks were about! "But what were those things? I've been seeing them all day, and I don't have a clue what they are."

The boy raised his pale brows at her, a challenge hidden behind a passive smile. "Of course, you do. It was a daddy-long-legger."

Acacia's mouth dropped open. It had seemed like the boy was trying to make amends for his strange behavior, but that was proving not to be the case.

"What do you mean?" Acacia asked. "The first thing you said after class was 'You didn't see a spider.' I know you saw—"

"A daddy-long-legger. Not a spider. They have longer legs than regular spiders, thus the 'long-legger' bit." Acacia knew the boy was lying, but he spoke in a factual manner.

"Hey, AJ, do you have to be a know-it-all?" Alex asked. "Or at least such an annoying one."

AJ got up from his seat, picking up his empty sandwich bag and used napkin. "I have to throw this out," he said, heading toward the garbage receptacles. "Be back in a minute."

Looks like it's time I get to the bottom of this, Acacia thought, getting up and grabbing Percy's leftover trash, much to the older boy's surprise. *Andrew Swiatkowski, you've got a lot to learn if you think you can trick* me*!*

"Hey, hold up!" she called, following the twin. "I've got something to throw out too."

As she walked across the cafeteria, Acacia couldn't help but feel like she was crossing a battlefield, although a much different battlefield than the historic ones she'd toured with her family on vacation. AJ was the one hitch in her perfect first day, the one person who was treating her like an outsider and playing mind games with her. Acacia didn't particularly care if people didn't like her, but she saw no reason for being sneaky and two-faced. *Well,* she thought as they disposed of their garbage in the bins. *Let's do this.*

The garbage bins were in a small hallway outside the cafeteria, making it easier for students to throw things out as they left for their afternoon classes. This feature also made it easier for Acacia to grab her companion by the wrist before he could return to the table without attracting the attention of any of the teachers on lunch duty.

"Okay," she began. "What was *that* all about? I know you knew what I was talking about."

"Of course, I did." AJ arched his brows at her. "The real question here is whether *you* know what you're talking about."

"And what's *that* supposed to mean?"

AJ rolled his eyes. "Do I look stupid to you?" he asked, a touch of quiet anger creeping into his tone. "You can't honestly expect me to believe you have no idea what it is you're seeing."

"Aha!" Acacia exclaimed, feeling the excitement rise in her body. No matter how contrary AJ was being, he'd confessed to seeing the little blips of light as well. And judging by his comments, it was obvious the twin knew what was happening, or at least, knew much more than Acacia did. "So, you do know what I'm talking about! Can't you take pity on the new kid and help me out?"

AJ blinked, wrenching his wrist free of Acacia's grasp, and inspected her, as if he wasn't exactly sure what she was. For whatever reason, it seemed AJ was afraid of her, though Acacia couldn't remember doing or saying anything rude or mean to him.

"Okay, fine, "the twin said after a moment of silence. "Let's pretend you don't know what's going on and you do need some guidance."

"How many times do I have to tell you?" Acacia felt her patience fraying by the moment. "I have no idea what's going on here! And you're not helping with all these roundabout answers!"

Despite bearing such a strong resemblance to his brother, AJ's speech patterns differed greatly from Alex's. Where Alex spoke with a bright chattiness that drew others into the conversation, AJ was quiet and thoughtful, speaking only after he measured his words with caution.

"Here's the deal," AJ began in a calm, almost emotionless voice. "I'll tell you everything you want to know if you can tell me what those sparks are that you've been seeing and why you've been seeing them."

Acacia studied the boy, unsure if she was more angry or more confused. "And why is it, Mr. Swiatkowski, that you can't just tell me? Seems like that'd be the easiest thing for both of us."

"To be quite honest, Acacia," AJ said, rubbing his temples, "because I don't trust you. Things have been calm around here, but since *you* showed up, that appears to be changing quite drastically. So, forgive my rudeness, but I'm not about to take any unnecessary chances, even if you *are* the new kid."

What could he possibly mean 'things have been calm around here' but now they're changing? Acacia thought, her mind reeling with confusion. *What is that even supposed to mean? And why would he think* I'm *responsible for whatever's changing when I don't know what's changing?*

"Look." Acacia placed her hands on her hips. "What's your problem? I've done nothing to you, and what? Now you're accusing me of changing the natural order?"

AJ shrugged, showing no sign of being offended by her remark. "I have an iron deficiency," he said in a flat tone. "It tends to make me cranky. And I'm sorry for accusing you, even if you don't believe me. But if you are innocent in all of this, you shouldn't have any trouble getting to the bottom of this little mystery."

"And who are you to be deciding who's innocent or not?" Acacia demanded, losing her temper. "You're the one who lied about the spider thing in the first place!"

"I wasn't lying," he said. "Since you were the one who insisted it was only a spider you saw. I only improvised."

"You still weren't telling the truth, were you?"

"Not the whole truth, maybe," AJ said. "But not technically a lie, since the entire school is crawling with daddy-long-leggers and there could have been one in the biology classroom."

Acacia had always possessed a rather short temper, and she knew her patience was dwindling with each passing moment. Who did this boy think he was accusing her of having some nefarious plot when she was just trying to adjust to life at a new school? She folded her arms across her chest and shot him her finest glare.

The twin blinked, his expression suspicious but not intimidated. "Well, have you decided to take advantage of my offer or not?"

"Well," Acacia said. "Mr. Swiatkowski, let me be the first to inform you that as fascinating as your offer sounds, I won't need it. If there's something going on in this town, I'll find out without your help, thank you."

AJ arched his pale brows at her, his gaze stormy. "Interesting. Especially since you were just begging me to tell you what's going on."

And there they were again, those pesky green sparks, this time lingering by the rack stacked high with lunch trays. *I swear!* Acacia thought. *Even the stupid sparks are mocking me!*

But at that moment, the entire rack jerked forward and launched itself, trays and all, at AJ. The twin gasped and moved quickly, trying to get out of the way. He tripped over a stray milk carton and fell, banging his chin roughly on the hard tile floor. The rack toppled over a mere few inches in front of him, and the trays went flying in all directions, creating an explosion of sound as they fell to the ground.

The cafeteria had fallen eerily quiet. Acacia imagined many of the students were now looking in their direction, curious to see what had happened to make an entire rack of trays fall over. *Great,* Acacia thought. *Now everyone's going to think I'm a weirdo. Just what I needed on my first day.*

"Miss Wheatley, Mr. Swiatkowski." One of the teachers on lunch duty hurried over to them. "Can you please tell me what's going on here?"

AJ pushed himself to his feet with almost catlike reflexes. "Oh nothing, Mr. Watkins. I just, uh, lost my balance for a minute."

What?

Mr. Watkins shook his head, looking rather disappointed. "All right, Swiatkowski, starting cleaning up this mess. Wheatley, it doesn't seem like *you* have anything to do with this. On your way."

Acacia nodded as the teacher walked away. Once he was out of sight, she turned on the twin, who had managed to push the rack upright and was stacking the trays back on it.

"And what was that about?" Acacia demanded. "I don't know what happened there, but you definitely didn't lose your balance!"

AJ shot her a crooked grin as he placed another tray in the rack. "I'd tell you, Acacia, but if you'll recall, you don't need my help. Though you might want to hurry up with your powers of deduction. It would appear those sparks of yours are becoming quite impatient. You might want to act before they get a hold of something a bit more lethal than a stack of trays."

"You're not very nice, you know that?" Acacia fired back. "It's a wonder no one's managed to permanently shove your head down a toilet."

AJ rolled his eyes at her and shook his head. *At least watch what you're doing, Red. The next time you might flatten someone you like.*

Acacia scrutinized the boy carefully. She had *definitely* heard AJ's sarcastic voice, but it seemed to have come from inside her mind instead of out of the boy's mouth. *Or maybe I'm just losing it,* she considered.

"Have fun with those trays," Acacia commented in an acidic tone. "I'd be careful not to lose my balance again, if I were you."

She turned on her heel and returned to the table before AJ could respond with another one of his snippy comments.

CHAPTER THREE

TRIAL BY FIRE

In no time, Acacia was rushing to the last period of the day. As she approached the classroom, she noticed she was once more in the same class as Alex Swiatkowski, her first true friend in Silent Springs. Which probably had more to do with the school's small size as opposed to some cosmic coincidence. Feeling the grin settle on her face, Acacia waved at Alex as they entered class and took seats toward the middle of the room. Maybe it was her imagination, but Acacia thought Alex looked as happy to see her again as she was to see him.

Acacia *had* given serious thought to the matter of the mysterious green sparks, but she felt as far away from solving the mystery as she'd been during lunch. All Acacia knew was that somehow, she needed to figure it out, and sooner rather than later. It irritated her to know something was going on and she hadn't a clue what it was. Like she was the butt of a bizarre joke, the joke of the school within hours of her arrival.

Mr. George, their history teacher, was reviewing the classroom rules, but Acacia's mind was elsewhere. AJ was obviously in on it, but who else was? Percy, the polite older cousin? Mattes, the charismatic friend who gave the impression of being far more complex than he let on? Alex, the friendliest boy she had met in her life?

And what *was* the joke? A scientific experiment gone wrong? Or maybe they did have some sort of special powers? It would explain why the sparks seemed to make an appearance whenever Acacia experienced very strong emotions. . .

About halfway through class, Acacia noticed she'd developed a headache. At first, it was a dull, nagging pain, but the more she tried to ignore it, the more it intensified. She massaged her head, and when that didn't help, clutched it, until she heard a booming, loud noise.

"Miss Wheatley!" Mr. George hollered. "Young lady, are you all right?"

Acacia winced at the sound of his loud voice. "Yeah. I'm fine, it's . . . just a headache."

"You don't look fine," Mr. George said, his eyes widening in concern. "Mr. Swiatkowski, please escort Miss Wheatley to the infirmary."

Alex nodded and rose from his seat, waiting for Acacia to do the same. Not wanting to make a scene, Acacia stood and followed him out the door.

"I'm okay, Alex," she said, once they were in the hallway. "I get headaches sometimes. It's no big deal."

The boy put a strong hand on Acacia's shoulder and continued to guide her down the corridor. "No. You're going to the nurse."

Acacia sighed. Her usual response would have been to argue it to the death, but now, her head was pulsing too much for this to be a viable option. Giving up, she allowed Alex to lead her to the infirmary.

When they arrived at the nurse's office, the small waiting room was empty. Alex walked up to the desk and rang the bell, and moments later, the nurse emerged from the back room.

"Hello," she said. "What can I help you with?"

Alex nudged Acacia lightly with his elbow.

"Oh, erm." Acacia's pain made it difficult to organize her thoughts. "I got a bit of a headache last period. It's no big—"

"Don't be silly," the nurse said. "Come back here and I'll find something for you."

Acacia followed the woman to the back room, which had a large cabinet stocked with non-prescription medicine, a sink, two cots, and a separate door containing a bathroom. The nurse pulled open the cabinet door, moments later producing a small plastic bottle.

"I'll give you acetaminophen for now," she offered. "And if you want, you can lie down for a while."

Acacia accepted a glass of water from the nurse, swallowed the pill, and sat down on a vacant cot. "Thank you, um—"

"Ms. Keyne. I'll be in the office if you need anything."

Ms. Keyne strode back into the waiting room to send Alex back to class, and Acacia was left alone. She flopped down on her back and sighed, hoping the medication would relieve her discomfort.

But life was never that simple, was it?

Before Acacia could begin to gather her thoughts, the sharpest, most intense jolt of pain shot through her skull, making her question if her head would split open then and there. Clenching her teeth together, Acacia watched as bright flashes of green light passed over her eyes, lingering over her pupils. Acacia jammed her eyes shut, hoping to escape the light, but even then, the bright green flooded her vision. The pain, too, seemed to be spreading from her forehead to every imaginable part of her body, growing in intensity as it did. Unable to hold it in any longer, Acacia flipped herself over, buried her face in the lumpy pillow, and screamed in agony.

She heard a rapid shuffling of feet as Ms. Keyne and Alex rushed into the room. Acacia could hear the nurse's voice in the background but, distracted by the intense throbbing in her skull, couldn't make out the words. After some time, Acacia flipped herself back over and forced her eyes open in time to see a green orb of light materialize from her own hand and fly, ultimately crashing into the medicine cabinet, sending several bottles crashing to the floor.

Don't worry, Alex assured her. His voice was as clear as if he were speaking in her ear, but the words seemed to resonate inside her mind. *I'll take care of it.*

More green flashes flew from her body, each causing their own variety of chaos. Some blasted into the walls, leaving burn marks on the aging beige paint, while others flew into the various objects and pieces of furniture in the room. Acacia's attention was still focused on the agony ensconced in her head, but she made out the sound of the bell and an additional set of footsteps on the wooden floor in the waiting area. Curious despite her pain, Acacia forced herself to listen and was surprised to hear AJ's voice.

"Ms. Keyne!" the boy exclaimed. "You have to come quickly! There's an emergency on the track! Someone broke into Coach Walter's locker and took the javelins."

The nurse had sprinted to the waiting area to attend to her latest student, and spoke with a rushed tone. "Mr. Swiatkowski, this is *not* the time for jokes. Unless you can't tell, I have an emergency in here!"

"It's not a joke, Ms. Keyne." AJ's voice was convincing, though Acacia suspected his statement about the javelins was less than factual. "There's a lot of blood. The principal told me to get you right away because Mike Romano took the javelins and—"

Acacia wasn't sure who Mike Romano was, but the mention of his name was enough to change the nurse's attitude within seconds. "That boy will be the *death* of me. What will it take for administration to get rid of that menace?"

"Acacia just has a bad migraine." Alex's voice was surprisingly persuasive. "AJ and I can wait with her so you can deal with whatever's happened outside. We won't go anywhere, I promise."

The nurse let out an exasperated, yet relieved sigh. "It *is* true what they say of you two. Wherever one goes, the other's not far behind." She jotted a number a piece of paper and handed it to AJ with a flourish. "This is my cell number. You call me immediately if her condition worsens, do you understand? I wouldn't usually leave a patient, but if Mr. Romano is involved with this incident, it can't be good." With that, Ms. Keyne stormed out of the infirmary, the door clicking shut behind her.

AJ depressed the lock on the inside of the office door and dashed into the back room, lurching to a stop next to his brother. "Okay, what's the—" He ducked as a glass bottle came flying at his head. It missed and crashed into the wall, coating it with a pink, syrupy medicine. Another flash shot from Acacia's hand and hit the sink faucet with full force, knocking it off, and causing water to spurt wildly from the pipes.

Alex rushed over to block the spurting water. Tendrils of blue light flowed from his hands, one forming a bubble around the leaking pipes and blocking the water, the other chasing the green flashes and capturing them, preventing them from causing greater damage.

"Why are you still standing there, AJ?" Alex hollered, turning to his brother. "Do something!"

AJ took a deep breath and turned to Acacia with apprehensive eyes. He opened his mouth to speak, but no sound came out. Looking annoyed, he drew back and raised his left arm, sending a blue tendril of his own at Acacia. She tried to brace herself for more agony but was surprised when the light swept over her like a pleasant breeze, cool against her hot skin. It rendered her immobile but soothed her pain.

Acacia still felt cloaked with confusion over what was happening, but *this* was certainly an improvement.

But before Acacia had time to enjoy her reprieve, a green lightning bolt shot out from her hand. It snaked along the blue tendril and circled around AJ, pulling itself tight around his arms. It was clear the green bolt had the opposite effect on AJ than his blue tendril had on Acacia, as a pained expression settled across his face from the moment the green power touched him.

Damn it, why am I doing this? I'm hurting him, maybe badly. What is wrong with me?

Acacia! Alex again spoke inside her head. *It's not your fault. Some people's magic is like this when it's been pent up too long.*

Slowly, the pieces fell into place. The voices Acacia was hearing in her mind were some kind of telepathy, and the lights she had been seeing had been a sign of . . . magic. She'd figured out the mystery, though it was possibly too late to stop these newfound powers from destroying her and two of her classmates.

Alex is right, Acacia. Judging from the strained quality of his voice, AJ was in pain. *Just relax and we'll get everything under control.*

Acacia looked him in the eyes and nodded reluctantly.

Well, Alex said, reeling the loose objects in with his blue magic. *What are you going to do now, AJ, let it zap you until you pass out?*

AJ glared at his brother with stormy gray eyes. *Do you want to switch places, since you know it all?*

No. But if you're half as smart as you say you are, you should be able to figure something out!

At his words, the green bolt flared in both brightness and intensity and wrapped itself even tighter around AJ's slight frame. Acacia expected him to cry out, as the bolt *did* seem to be zapping him as if real lightning. Then again, AJ didn't strike Acacia as someone prone to public displays of emotion. Instead, the boy steeled himself for action, his eyes as dark as storm clouds. Judging from his face, he had a plan, though Acacia wasn't sure of the quality of said plan.

Before either Acacia or Alex could ask what he was planning, AJ exhaled sharply and jammed his left arm against the green bolt.

"Idiot, what the hell are you're doing?" Alex shouted. "Are you *trying* to get yourself killed?"

"Yeah, Alex," AJ said, his voice more strained than it had been moments earlier. "I thought it'd be fun."

Alex looked and sounded every bit as distressed as Acacia felt. "Andrew, stop it! This was *not* what I meant by figuring something out!"

But AJ had tuned out everything except his own thoughts. He shot a blue flash from his left hand, which had a greater range of motion now that it was farther away from his body, directly at the green bolt. It hit its target, and Acacia's magic recoiled from the attack, releasing the boy from its grasp.

"You idiot!" Alex yelled. "What was that about?"

Acacia's power reared and charged again.

"No!" she cried, willing the bolt to stop. But AJ was prepared for the strike this time. As the bolt rushed forward, he sent a wave of blue magic at Acacia's with a wave of his right arm. Slowly, the blue wave overpowered the bolt and forced it back into Acacia's body. Somehow, the magic didn't hurt on its way in. The other bursts of green too, still being controlled by Alex, fled back into Acacia's chest and, finally, the pain ceased.

As if it had never existed in the first place.

Acacia sat up in the cot with trepidation, half expecting more green bolts to come shooting from her fingers.

"Acacia, you're okay!" Alex smothering her in the strongest hug of her life. "I can't believe you made it—well no, how could you not—but I'm so glad you did! I don't know what I'd do if—"

"Alex!" Acacia struggled to speak with her trachea crushed. "Can't breathe!"

Alex gave a little "oh" and let go of her.

She grinned and turned to the other twin. "AJ, I . . ." she began, not quite sure what to say. Up to this point, the boy hadn't been exactly friendly, so she hadn't been expecting him to rescue her from the assault of green flashes. Had he done what he did as penance for treating her in a less than amiable manner at lunch? Or had he helped her because Alex would have killed him if he didn't? Or maybe he did help because he didn't want to see Acacia get hurt? The boy was a bit standoffish and, for whatever reason, seemed to want to engage in a battle of wits with her. But everyone deserved a second chance, especially if said person had saved your life.

"Excuse me," AJ murmured, his expression still distressed. He rushed over to the bathroom and closed the door behind him.

"So, *that* was something?" Acacia asked Alex, trying to ignore the retching sounds coming from behind the door.

"I'll say," he agreed. "And I hate to say it, but we'd probably still be there if it wasn't for him." He jerked his thumb at the bathroom. "He's clever enough when he wants to be. Needs some motivation sometimes, but he'll always figure something out."

Acacia laughed nervously. "But Alex? What . . . happened just now?"

"I'd like to tell you, but . . ." Alex shrugged. "AJ can probably explain it better. I'm sorry, Acacia, but if I tried to explain it, I'd confuse you more. I don't exactly know what happened at lunch today, but whatever my brother said to you, don't be too hard on him. He's obnoxious sometimes—well, no, all the time—but he's not a bad person. I know about your . . . conversation by the garbage cans."

Acacia arched her brows. "Um, how did you know? Did AJ—"

"Tell me? No." Alex tapped his head with the tip of his index finger. "We're twins, though. There's the whole mind-speaking thing, but . . . we can read each other's minds sometimes. He didn't want me to know, but he was too distracted by other stuff to keep me out. I wanted to tell you about it myself, but I figured you'd think I was crazy."

Alex said all this very quickly and showed no sign of either stopping or slowing down.

"But now that you've got your powers too, maybe you can come train with me sometime! I can't believe how awesome this is. I mean, don't get me wrong, I still would have thought you were awesome even if you weren't . . . like us, but it's nice to not have to hide who you are."

A loud flushing sound resonated from the bathroom. Shortly after, AJ emerged, shaky and ashen faced. He met Acacia's gaze directly, but this time, his gray eyes were wide with anxiety.

"A-Acacia, I'm s-so sorry," he began, averting his eyes. "I d-didn't think it would—" He gagged briefly but fended off any additional heaves.

"It's okay," Acacia replied. Even if she wasn't sure what she thought of the boy yet, she had no intention of sending him into an anxiety attack. "I'm fine."

And it was true. Although she felt exhausted and drained of all energy, the pain had disappeared and she didn't seem injured.

"But what about you guys?" she asked. "I'm sorry about all this, whatever it was."

"Don't be silly," Alex said. "You just got your full powers. We've both had ours for a while, so we'll recover fast."

So *that* was what this had all been, getting her 'full' powers? All the pain and destruction, for some magic she might not be able to control? Would she lose control over it again, as she had today?

Somewhere in the distance, the last bell of the day rang.

"Ugh." Alex turned to his brother. "Hey, could you make sure Acacia gets home? I would, but I can't miss the first day of practice."

AJ nodded, a hint of reluctance flashing across his face. "Okay."

Alex turned back to Acacia, a large grin forming on his lips. "I'll see you tomorrow! I'm sorry to run, but I have to go! Bye!"

"See you," Acacia replied as Alex sprinted out of the room. Groaning, she pushed herself out of the cot and turned to face AJ, feeling the gravity of the conversation to come. The boy was studying her carefully, almost as if he expected her to attack.

"Hey, um, Acacia?" For the first time since she'd met him, AJ sounded . . . rather awkward, uncertain.

"Yeah?" There was no condescending glare this time, not even a sarcastic smirk.

AJ turned from her, his face reddening with embarrassment. "I'm sorry for being such a jerk before. I wouldn't blame you if can't forgive me, but we're going to be seeing a lot of each other since my brother likes you, and . . . well, I hope we could at least tolerate each other."

Acacia rolled her eyes. "If you think I'm going to hate you forever because of that, I guess you're not as smart as you think you are. Maybe I still don't know what I'm talking about, but I'm pretty sure you saved my life."

"You don't need to thank me. I didn't do anything that any other mage wouldn't have done." AJ yawned and stretched his arms toward the ceiling. As he lifted his arm, Acacia noticed that a section of his left sleeve had been burned off.

"Wait, what happened?" Acacia grabbed the boy's wrist and pulled his arm closer. Where the cloth had been burned off, AJ's skin was a vibrant red. "Did *I* do that?"

The twin let out a sigh of exasperation and yanked his wrist free of her grasp. "It's just a burn. I've hurt myself worse by accident."

"Well, excuse me! I didn't realize I wasn't allowed to be concerned for you when I almost killed you!"

"Almost killed me?" AJ repeated, raising his pale brows at her. "Do you really think I'm that fragile that a little lightning spell would kill me?"

"It didn't *look* like such a little spell when it was zapping you!" The image of the green lightning bolt pinning AJ's arms to his sides was still burned into Acacia's memory. "And besides, if it was no big deal, why were you over there puking your guts out?"

Her last comment had struck a nerve. "You think I was 'puking my guts out' because of a lightning spell?" AJ demanded in a stiff tone. "Have *you* ever tried to control someone else's magic, in this case, magic that's been repressed for who knows how long, to keep it from destroying everything in sight? "

"Well." Acacia was almost surprised by the anger in her voice. "You didn't do it without help, now, did you?"

"Of course not," the twin responded, his voice dripping in exasperation. "But what I did and what my brother did are two completely different things. There's a big difference between stopping magic from wrecking a room and keeping it from destroying a person." AJ shook his head and stared up at the ceiling. "I'm sorry, I'm being a jerk again. Go ahead and yell at me, I deserve it."

Acacia studied the with curious eyes boy. Moments ago, he seemed almost friendly, ready to be more honest about what had happened. But now, when Acacia expressed concern for his injury, AJ reverted to his previous standoffish self. "What's going on, AJ? Are you afraid I'm going to tell everyone you're not perfect or what?" A lightbulb went on in Acacia's mind at the sound of her own words. "That's *it*, isn't it? You still don't trust me. What is it you think I'm going to do, blow up the town? I'm not evil, you know!"

AJ flinched and drew back, as if Acacia had struck him. "I'm *sorry*, I—"

"Would you stop apologizing?" Acacia interrupted. "You seem like a smart guy, so I'm sure there's a reason why you're so paranoid. So instead of apologizing for not trusting me, why don't you just tell me why?"

"Um, well. . ." AJ's dark eyes darted around the room. "It's more complicated than I want to get into right now."

Acacia could feel the beginnings of a headache form again, though this time thankfully not of a magical nature. "And how is being so paranoid too complicated to explain? Somehow, I think it's more than just not wanting people to think you're weak."

"It is," the twin confessed, avoiding Acacia's gaze. "But since you're so persistent, to make a long story really short, let's just say my family has a history of getting into trouble when certain things weren't kept secret."

"I don't understand you," Acacia complained. "Or any of this."

"Well, I don't think I can help you understand my warped person-ality." AJ spoke in a considerably brighter tone. "But I think I can help you with the other stuff. I *have* to if you don't have someone at home who can teach you." He paused and tilted his head in thought. "You're absolutely sure neither of your parents are mages? It's been years since a mage was completely unaware of the existence of magic."

Acacia shook her head. "Definitely not. My dad is a psychologist, and my mom is the most normal person I've ever met. She wouldn't let us watch any fantasy movies until last year, and she freaked when I did some stupid card trick over the summer. There's no way she's secretly a . . . mage." She blinked and studied AJ again with new eyes. "Hold on. So, *you're* going to teach me magic?"

"Normally, mages are trained by an immediate family member upon receiving their full powers," AJ explained with a nod. "Except in cases where a family member isn't able, or willing, to do the training. The standard protocol in situations like this is that another mage who's completed their training is expected to do said training. Alex hasn't finished his yet, so you're stuck with me. Unless of course you want to go to the Council—our government—and get lost in the system."

Acacia felt her mouth drop open in surprise. Could this be true? If she wasn't the only person this had happened to, there *was* hope for her! And besides, any kind of training would help her, even if it was coming from another teenager.

And something told her AJ wasn't a typical teenager.

"*You've* finished your training?" Acacia asked. "How is that possible if you and Alex are the same age?"

"I got my full powers a long time ago." AJ shrugged. "It might not be ideal, but we'll make it work. But we can talk about that later. In honor of your getting your full powers without blowing up the school, we're going on a field trip downstairs."

Acacia's jaw almost hit the floor. "I thought you were taking me home. What's so special about downstairs, anyway? It's just the cafeteria."

"Come on and you'll find out," AJ called, already halfway through the door. "What are you waiting for? The custodians to come in and see the mess you've made?"

Acacia sighed and followed him out, feeling more uncertain with each step.

Chapter Four

DARK HISTORY

After the two teenagers exited the infirmary, they took a flight of stairs down to the cafeteria, and walked through the vast, empty room. From there, they continued down a long, narrow hallway.

AJ walked *fast,* much faster than someone who'd just survived a strange lightning spell had any right to.

"Before we go on this mystical field trip," Acacia said. "Are we going to talk about what happened with Ms. Keyne?"

"I told you already." AJ shot Acacia an annoyed glance without breaking his pace. How dare she try to slow his stride with questions, right? "That was you getting your full powers."

Acacia let out an exasperated sigh of her own. "That's not what I meant, AJ."

"Then what *did* you mean? If something else happened in there, I was a bit distracted by the repressed magic trying to destroy everything in sight."

"I meant you running in and telling her something about the javelins going missing and some medical emergency on the track," Acacia fired back. While she didn't enjoy the constant banter, as the middle child of the family, she was accustomed to it. "Did you make it all up to get the nurse out of the way?"

AJ met her gaze, his dark eyes serious. "Well, I had to tell her *something*. Could you imagine the chaos if we'd been trying to control your magic with a screaming non-magical in the background?" He paused, a rather guilty expression settling on his face. "Plus, it would have caused a headache for the Department of Non-Magical Affairs if she saw all of that."

"But she *did* see it, my magic at least," Acacia felt her stomach plummet as the gravity of what had happened struck her. She *knew* she'd seen Ms. Keyne run into the room just as the green magic had started to fly amok. "Oh no... is this all going to end up on the local news?"

AJ laughed, the most light-hearted sound he'd made all day. "As if. Whatever Ms. Keyne saw, she's going to convince herself she imagined it. If anything, she'll be mad at me for sending her on a wild-goose chase, but that's hardly an apocalyptic scenario. The worst that'll come of it will be an angry phone call home."

Acacia shook her head but let out a sigh of relief. She didn't know much about this world of magic and mayhem, but it would've been a shame if she'd been thrown in prison or something equally terrible for exposing the existence of magic.

"Also," AJ said, gesturing toward the wall in front of them. "We're here."

Acacia wasn't sure what she'd expected, a shining magical portal perhaps, or a reinforced iron gate hinting at danger and treasure within. What she *wasn't* expecting was for their voyage to come to an abrupt halt at a solid wall of red brick no more mystical than any other wall in the school.

"This is your field trip?" Acacia asked, staring at the wall. "This is a dead end!"

"You would say that, wouldn't you?"

"And what's that supposed to—"

Before Acacia could finish her thought, her companion made a circular motion with his wrist, conjuring a blue orb of light into his hand. He raised his hand, causing the magic to float from his hand to a spot on the wall about even with Acacia's hip. A few seconds later, the orb shifted shape and transformed into a makeshift doorknob.

Acacia stared at the translucent knob. "Of course," she said, her voice laced with sarcasm. "Magical doorknobs. Why didn't *I* think of that?"

"You're new," AJ replied, making a quick waving motion with his right hand. As if on cue, the blue doorknob turned as if by an invisible hand, revealing a dark, stone corridor. "Just give it time. Something tells me you're a quick learner."

The twin held his right hand in front of him, and another small blue orb appeared in the center of his palm. "So, to answer your question," he said, taking a step into the corridor, "you remember Mattes, the boy who tried to hit on you at lunch today? He's a mage too, but Mattes is an orphan of sorts. But due to . . . circumstances out of his control, he lives in what we call the 'Underground,' which I'll explain in a minute. We won't stay long, but I want to make sure everything's all right. So that's where we're going."

"Sounds good." Part of Acacia longed more than anything to return home, but her exhaustion was far outweighed by her curiosity, so she followed her companion down the dark corridor, their path lit only by the orb of blue light nestled in AJ's hand.

"So lesson number one is that magic exists and that you have it," the boy explained, holding the blue orb higher to cast more light on their path. "And from *that* encounter, your magic appears to be powerful."

Acacia nodded. *Great. Because why wouldn't my magic be powerful and difficult to control?*

"Magic is an aura we have, a type of energy that lives within our bodies until we summon it," AJ continued. "It's a hereditary trait, just like eye and hair color, and it's passed down from one generation to the next. Magic can be used for many different purposes, attacking, healing, and controlling objects among other things." He paused for a minute, his eyes fixed on Acacia's, almost as if he was worried she would run away. "The first thing you must learn is that magic has a psychological component, which means you have to possess strong self-control over your thoughts and emotions. Getting your full powers is an unconscious process so you don't have any control over what your magic does. After that, you have to learn to control it with conscious effort and practice."

Acacia nodded, letting the boy's explanation seep into her mind. A dedicated soccer player for years, Acacia was no stranger to hard work and perseverance. "But you can teach me how to control it?"

"It'll be a lot of work," AJ replied, his gray eyes searching. "But I think you have the makings of a great mage, if you can learn to conquer yourself. In our world, magic is power, and power can corrupt when used for the wrong reasons. Unfortunately, we all found that out the hard way."

It was Acacia's turn to study her companion's expression. The silence that followed AJ's last comment was filled with mystery, hinting at a thorough explanation to follow.

"It all started about ten years ago," AJ began, his voice measured and determined. "There was a mage called Henry Moore, whose life experiences led him down a dark path, the path of dark magic. Dark magic is what we call the power of the occult, derived from what people generally consider to be evil. Dark mages have abilities that regular mages would never want to use, spells that drain life forces to make one's own power stronger, summoning creatures of darkness, necromancy. Moore began recruiting followers to seize control of the country. I don't know how long it took, but he gathered his forces and launched his assault on the magical world."

Acacia blinked. *So not only does magic and dark magic exist, but a war was going on between the forces of good and evil. Or I've lost my mind. At this point, I'm not sure which is worse.* "I'm guessing there was a war. But the good side won, right?"

"There was." Maybe it was the poor lighting, but AJ looked *almost* impressed by her question. "Early on, Moore took on the name Sisyphus. Sisyphus was the name of a legendary king in Greek mythology who tricked the gods, and as punishment, they made him push a gigantic boulder up a mountain in the Underworld for all eternity. Anyway, our Sisyphus pretty much accomplished what he set out to do, and the Council had just about given up."

This was the second time AJ had mentioned the Council. What had he said before? It was the magical government?

"Well, that's not good."

"No, it wasn't," AJ agreed. "Sisyphus had consolidated his power in the Northeast when he was . . . obstructed."

Acacia's eyes widened in surprise. *That* had not been what she'd been expecting to hear. "Obstructed? Like defeated?"

"Hardly." Her companion's voice was pleasant but distant. "A faction of the resistance rose against him on Halloween night. My parents were there, my aunt and uncle, and one of the Swansgroves. I know you probably don't know too much about magical history, but the

Swansgroves had some of the most powerful magic around. Anyway, they managed to seal Sisyphus, along with a couple of his henchmen, in a vacuum spell we call 'Bloody Meadow' a few miles outside town. A vacuum spell is seriously powerful magic; you create a type of vortex and convert your adversary into pure energy and trap them inside the vortex. If it wasn't for that Swansgrove woman, they probably wouldn't have been able to manage it. Sisyphus and his people have been trapped in that vacuum for the past ten years."

"That's . . . impressive," Acacia said, feeling relieved at the outcome of the tale. "Good guys win, bad guys lose."

AJ glanced at her with a knowledgeable grin. "Not quite."

"But if Sissy Puss is all locked up—"

"Locked up, Acacia," he reminded her. "Not defeated. And his name isn't 'Sissy Puss.'"

Acacia quirked her coppery brows at him. *He's got to be joking. Locked up, defeated, what's the big difference?* "What are you talking about? If he's locked up. . ."

The boy turned and looked at her with a solemn gaze. "I understand what you're saying, Acacia, but you can't afford to be so naïve."

"But—"

"Acacia." AJ halted and bored into Acacia's green eyes with his stormy gray ones. "After *Sisyphus* was sealed in that spell, everyone thought the war was over too, that he was as good as dead, his followers disbanded and scattered, never to rise again. Two weeks later, one of Sisyphus's agents showed up outside our house. My father could . . . could tell something was amiss, so he went outside to investigate. This mage, Dionera, well, she killed him, no more than three yards from our house. The fact that Sisyphus was locked up doesn't make him any less dead."

Even if Acacia hadn't already stopped in her tracks, she would've come to a halt. Had AJ really divulged sensitive personal information on his own free will? From the first moment she'd met him, Acacia hadn't taken the boy as someone willing to share much, and until now, her assessment had proven accurate. But for him to tell her about the death of his father, AJ must have thought it was necessary for her to know.

"I am. . ." She fumbled for the right words to say. What did her father tell her that he did with clients who came for bereavement counseling? *Validation,* she remembered. *Validate feelings and empathize.* "I'm so sorry, AJ. I had no idea. Do you want to talk about it?"

"No, I don't want to talk about it!" Even in the poor lighting, Acacia could tell the boy's face had paled with discomfort. "I didn't tell you about it to get your pity, Acacia. I told you because it doesn't seem to me like you have a good grasp of the gravity of the situation and why we can't afford to take chances."

"Okay, stop," Acacia said in the most commanding voice she could muster. "What is it you're afraid is going to happen? That Dionera's going to come back?"

AJ turned to look up toward the ceiling. "Yes and no," he began in a somber tone. "Sure, Dionera might come back, but more importantly, Sisyphus and his comrades have had more than enough time to work out an escape plan. They're going to break out, and given the recent changes in the aura of Silent Springs, it's going to be sooner rather than later."

Once again, Acacia lacked the slightest idea of how to respond. In different circumstances, she might have argued, but considering how grave the conversation had turned, it seemed a far better decision to remain quiet, at least for now. They continued walking in silence for another ten minutes until reaching the end of the passageway and a single, sturdy oak door, secured from the outside by several iron bars. A much smaller path snaked off to the right and went up a sizable hill.

"Is this it, then?" Acacia asked, approaching the door and resisting the urge to give it a solid push. "The Underground?"

AJ looked up at the massive door, inspecting it with caution as if he expected it to move on its own accord. "The front entrance, yes. But we're not going in that way."

Of course not. Going in the front door would make sense. Why would we do something that made sense?

"You see, Acacia, the Underground is one of the Council's creations that doesn't make a lot of sense," AJ said, scratching his head. "The magical world operates many prisons to hold prisoners before and after they're tried and convicted of crimes. But sometimes, the Council decides *not* to put them in prison and exiles them to the Underground instead. It's its own world, self-governed by the leader of all the exiles, the Underground Lord. The Underground Lord is responsible for keeping the peace, though many Lords have abused their power and subjugated the less powerful." The boy paused to glance at Acacia. "The current Underground Lord is Matthias Knight."

Acacia's mouth dropped open in shock. AJ was sarcastic, but this time, he didn't appear to be joking. "Do you expect me to believe that? That there's some sort of exiled magical prison under the school? And a fifteen-year-old boy is the king of the exiles?"

"It's no more ridiculous than anything else I've told you so far today."

Acacia shook her head, trying to make sense of everything AJ had said. "So, say this is where all the leftover criminals are sent. What is Mattes doing down here?"

"I'm not comfortable telling other people's pasts," AJ replied. "I'd wager you could get him to tell you, especially if you play along with his flirting game. The only thing I'll tell you is that Mattes isn't a criminal."

The twin followed the path to the right from the door and hiked up the hill.

"Hold on a second," Acacia said. "How are we going to get inside? That door was the way—"

"Not exactly." AJ didn't as much as look up from the rocky path.

They continued onward until they reached the top of the hill. Acacia peered over the other side of the incline but saw nothing but darkness. AJ turned to the side where the door had been and moved a large rock using another wave of his magic. The rock's absence revealed a wooden trapdoor.

"Ladies first." AJ lifted the trapdoor, revealing a black abyss below.

"You think I'm just going to jump in there?" Acacia asked. "Into the land of magical criminals—"

"Who never go in the attic of the Underground," AJ responded. "All that's there are old records. You know *I'm* a bit of a worrywart, and I'm telling you there's nothing to worry about."

Acacia arched her coppery brows at her companion. Did she really want to do this? Jump into a sealed haven crawling with magical criminals at the request of someone she'd just begun to trust?

"All right," AJ said. "I'll tell you what. I'll go first so you can see it's safe, if you promise you won't run away."

"Are you . . . afraid to be there by yourself?" Acacia asked. "I didn't figure you for a coward."

"More afraid you'll run off and get lost trying to find your way back up to the school." AJ shot her a challenging glance and dropped into the hole.

Acacia scowled, took a deep breath, and leaped into the darkness. Her stomach didn't even have time to drop like it did when she went on amusement park rides. Within seconds, she hit the ground, hard.

"I told you you'd survive," AJ said, offering Acacia a hand.

Acacia accepted the help to her feet and surveyed her surroundings. They were in a small, dark room, with a sturdy floor. The trapdoor above had closed behind them, cutting off the only source of light in the room besides AJ's small blue orb.

"You know." Acacia twirled a strand of loose hair between her fingers. "For a big, scary, magic not-prison, this doesn't seem like much."

"Well," AJ said, his dark eyes mischievous. "Are you ready to move along, or would you rather further criticize the attic?"

Acacia let out a long sigh of exasperation. "Y'know, I'm starting to see why Alex is the charming twin."

"Took you that long, did it?" AJ said, shooting her a crooked grin. "Then again, I suppose you're not the most perceptive one around."

"I'm perceptive enough to see through your nonsense, aren't I?"

"That remains to be seen," he replied in what Acacia thought was a joking tone. "But on a serious note, we do need to get moving."

"What's the rush? There's no one around."

AJ raised his pale brows challengingly. "No one around? In our world, there's always someone around."

"Do us *all* a favor, Drew," a familiar voice spoke from above their heads. "And shut the hell up."

Acacia looked up in time to see a lithe figure leap from the rafters overhead and land with catlike reflexes a foot away from where she stood.

"Mattes," AJ remarked in a calm, even tone.

A quite different-looking Matthias Knight glared back at the twin. Of course, he still had the same effortless good looks, but he had traded in his relaxed charm for a no-nonsense demeanor. His hazel eyes were no longer playful and amused, but rather seemed austere and almost penetrating.

"Drew," Mattes replied in a tense, clipped tone. "I trust you have a reason for being here, besides giving me a migraine, which, by the way, you've already accomplished."

"What, can't I come visit my good friend Mattes anymore?" AJ asked. "You did this the last time too, remember? Always too busy even for one chess match—"

"I know damn well you're not here for some lousy chess match." Mattes ran a hand through his unkempt dark hair. "So, what, you haven't had your butt handed to you in a few days, so you figured why not take a run through the Underground and see what happens?"

"Hey there," Acacia said, waving her hand in the air. "You guys do realize you sound like a married couple, right?"

Mattes turned to Acacia, inspecting her with his hazel eyes. "Oh, how positively rude of me," he remarked, walking over to her and taking her hand. "Acacia, let me be the first to congratulate you on your full powers."

"Um . . . thanks?" Acacia blinked, feeling quite awkward. For the second time in six hours, Mattes's odd behavior had stolen the words from her mouth. She glanced over at AJ, who shrugged.

"Sorry, Matthias, but Alex beat you to it," he said. "You're off your game."

"So, Acacia." Mattes stroked the top of Acacia's hand in a flirtatious manner. "Maybe you belong in the Underground too. After all, you've stolen my heart."

This time, it was Acacia's turn to shake her head. *Wow, I'm not hit on once in fourteen years, then we move across the country and I'm hit on twice in the same day. Maybe I* am *losing my mind.*

"Would you ease up on the pickup lines?" AJ asked, a bit of the serious attitude reemerging. "The girl only got her full powers not even an hour ago. I believe hitting on her now would be considered taking advantage of her confused mental state."

"Hey!" Acacia yelled, finding her voice again. "I do not have a 'confused mental state'! It's not my fault you can't manage a straightforward answer to anything!"

Mattes laughed in amusement at Acacia's outburst. AJ returned her gaze and shrugged, an indifferent expression on his face. The twin seemed to possess a strong control of his emotions and wasn't quick to anger, unless adequately provoked. Acacia, on the other hand, had always been scolded by both family members and friends for her temper.

"Well, this should be interesting all right." Mattes's hazel eyes danced with entertainment. "Not only is she a novice, but she's also a loose cannon. I do hope *you're* not planning on training her, Drew."

"Well, she doesn't have any relatives who can. So that's *exactly* what I'm planning on doing."

If Mattes had been amused by Acacia's outburst, he was even more amused by AJ's plan to teach her. The boy laughed again, almost uncontrollably, and Acacia wondered if he was having a psychotic break.

"You have *got* to be kidding me," Mattes said. "You've never taught anyone before, and you think you can take on a student who's been repressed for years, and who just so happens to be a redhead? Maybe *you're* the one with the confused mental state!"

"And what's wrong with redheads?" Acacia demanded, annoyed at being left out of the loop. She looked at each of the boys in turn, unsure which one was more frustrating. "What? Doesn't anyone in this town answer questions?"

"Firecracker, this one," Mattes commented. "Wheatley, right? I guess no one's told you your new teacher is convinced all redheads are homicidal psychopaths. That tends to not come up in casual conversation, but in your case, it should, since Drew's going to be the one teaching you."

Acacia turned to face AJ, feeling her temper rise even more. "And what is your problem with redheads, Mr. Swiatkowski? Are you another one of those people who run around saying 'gingers have no souls'? Because I'll have you know—"

"Enough." AJ turned to Mattes and raised his pale brows. "I didn't come here for you to feed Acacia garbage."

"Ah, I see." Mattes's hazel eyes appeared to flash with yellow light. "So, you think she wants to hear the horror stories of the Underground. Or maybe get a nice little tour of the facilities? Going for the 'shock and awe' strategy, are we?"

AJ sighed. "I came here to make sure *you* were all right. I've never known you to show up to school on time on the first day of all days. It makes me wonder if there's something you needed to get away from."

"I guess you'll just have to keep wondering then," Mattes retorted, his hazel eyes not giving much away. "After all, that is one of your talents. Wondering and hypothesizing . . . making things worse than they are. . ."

Acacia couldn't help but laugh. Mattes's words had echoed her own thoughts of the twin. *Maybe Mattes isn't as bad as Alex made him out to be,* she thought with a grin. *If nothing else, he does seem to be able to keep AJ in line, and I wasn't sure that was possible!*

"But speaking of your talents," Mattes said, stretching his arms in front of his torso. "I recall that getting beat at chess is another one of them. Specifically getting beat by me." The boy cracked his neck and grinned, exposing a set of very white, very straight teeth. "It appears that I do in fact have enough time for a quick match. Are you still game?"

"Not today, I'm afraid," AJ replied in an exhausted tone. Acacia couldn't help but wonder whether the boy's iron deficiency was surfacing and he was either unable to hide it or didn't care enough to do so. "I told Alex I would take her home a while ago, so I should do that before he finds out we came here instead."

"You don't have to take me home," Acacia protested. "Just back to the school. I can bike home."

Mattes laughed again. "Not tired yet? If it's been an hour, the adrenaline will be wearing off. Meaning going for a little bike ride might not be the best idea. Remember, gorgeous, just because Drew is your teacher doesn't mean you have to have the same kind of awful ideas as he does."

"And yet," AJ said through gritted teeth. "My ideas aren't quite so awful that they don't work."

"Sure, they don't."

Acacia realized that if she ever had a boyfriend and their arguments sounded like this, she would worry.

"Well, let's go," AJ said, offering his hand to her. Acacia gave him a befuddled expression. "Now, come on, stop looking at me like that. It's not that I want to hold your hand, but we're going to take the elevator, and that always works best when physical contact has been established."

Acacia blinked. *The elevator? What could he possibly be talking about?*

"Well, this should be interesting." Mattes watched them with amused eyes. "You sure you want to do that, Drew? She might throw up . . . on you."

"Why is it that everyone never tells me anything?" Acacia cried in anguish. "Is it fun for you to rub all this in my face?"

AJ rolled his dark gray eyes and grabbed hold of Acacia's left hand with a surprisingly strong grasp. "Let's get this over with," he said, spirals of blue light materializing around the two of them until they were completely enveloped in a wall of his magic.

"It'll be fun, Acacia," Mattes's voice quipped somewhere outside the spell. "Kind of like a roller coaster. Only faster. And you go upside down."

Acacia opened her mouth to speak but was unable to as the attic of the Underground swirled around them until it was unrecognizable. And then she realized she had forgotten to ask Mattes why he lived in the Underground in the first place.

Chapter Five

TRAINING BEGINS

Whatever world Acacia entered was *not* like a Tilt-A Whirl. She could tell she was spinning, though whether it was her entire being or just her head, Acacia wasn't certain. No matter how hard she tried, she couldn't make out anything except a mass of blue light so intense it burned her eyes. The only thing Acacia was certain of was AJ's presence, and that was because he still had her hand in an iron grasp.

Suddenly, the magic faded and the two of them were thrown to the ground, though it was softer than Acacia expected. Before opening her eyes, she probed the earth with her fingertips, encountering a soft, grassy surface.

Acacia sat up and opened her eyes, curious to see what awaited her. To her surprise, the magic had thrown them in a small field in what looked to be the middle of the forest. AJ knelt several feet away from her, looking worse for wear, supporting himself with one hand on the ground.

"Where are we?" Acacia asked. "This better not be another—"

"Relax, would you," AJ said, pushing himself to his feet. "We're only about a five-minute walk from the school. It's not usually a good idea to teleport somewhere where there's a chance of being seen by non-magicals. And besides, you should take it easy in case you have side effects from the spell. Most mages have some queasiness when they have their first experience with a teleportation spell."

Ignoring his advice, Acacia rose to her feet. "I don't know why everyone's so worried about me. I'm fine."

"Good for you. That's one of us, at least."

Acacia examined the boy closely. AJ didn't look terrible, compared to how he'd looked after the incident in the nurse's office, but his skin was paler than before, and his dark eyes looked slightly out of focus.

"But you're not looking so great," Acacia said. "Maybe *you* should sit back down. I'm strong, but I don't think I could carry you if you pass out."

"That won't be necessary." He held his hands out in front of him as if to regain his sense of balance. "Though it would give you an interesting story to tell Alex later. Anyway, if you're feeling all right, we should get back before it gets dark."

Her companion began walking across the meadow, his gait a little unsteady. Not wanting to be left behind, Acacia followed.

"Can I ask you about something?" Acacia asked, relieved to see the school astronomy tower ahead. AJ hadn't been lying when he'd told her that he had teleported them only a short distance from the school. "What's the Council like? Like, what type of government is it?"

AJ raised his pale brows at her. "You're inquisitive. That's good, you'll learn more that way. Especially since you got a late start."

Acacia started to protest but decided against it. If what he'd told her was true, they would be back at school in another couple of minutes, and she she'd soon have a reprieve from his sarcastic comments.

"The Council of Mages isn't too different from the non-magical government you're accustomed to," AJ explained, his gaze cast upward. "It's a federal system, and we all fall under the jurisdiction of the local branch, called the Minor Council. The Minor Council reports to the High Council of Mages in V'riglia, which is our national capital, outside Maryland. And no, you wouldn't have ever heard of V'riglia before, since as hard as the government works to keep the existence of magic a secret, they work extra hard to keep the existence of V'riglia secret. The major difference between the non-magical and magical governments is that ours doesn't have all the different branches. It's a Council, a group of elected officials who meet to make all political decisions. Because no one person is in charge, there's a lot of deliberation, and they must arrive at a consensus whenever they have to make a decision."

"So, is there like . . . a police force?" Acacia asked, fascinated. "Or an army?

"A number of bureaus exist on both a national and local level." Now that he was convinced Acacia wasn't conspiring against the magical world, AJ didn't seem to have any qualms with educating her about the world she'd stumbled into. "Investigation handles the law enforcement, Non-magical Affairs deals with our interaction with non-magicals, Defense controls military and intelligence operations, Education manages our universities, and then you have the more obvious ones: Treasury, Transportation, International Affairs, and Inter-species Affairs." He let out a long yawn. "And that's our government."

And with that, they emerged from the woods. Acacia hadn't grasped until then just how rural the town of Silent Springs was. No matter where in town a person happened to be, they were never more than a few yards from the forest. *Well, it'll take some getting used to. Though I suppose that's the least of my worries right now.*

Her companion yawned again and stepped out into the road to cross the street. Just as an old, battered Jeep barreled toward him.

"AJ, watch out!" Acacia grabbed the back of the boy's shirt and yanked him onto the curb. He was lighter than she expected, and Acacia realized she *would* have been able to drag him to the school if he'd fainted.

"What were you thinking?" she hollered, her hands shaking in alarm. "Do you realize you almost got run over?"

AJ dropped to the ground, his body quivering. Acacia opened her mouth to yell again as a small, dilapidated blue sedan pulled over where they were standing.

"Relax, Acacia." The driver's side window was rolled down, revealing a familiar teenager with blond hair and blue eyes. "I got the jerk's license plate number. At worst we get him for running a stop sign."

Her anger abating, Acacia turned to look at the speaker. Percy, the twins' cousin, looked back at her, his face marked with concern.

"Did you *see* the car coming, AJ?" Percy inquired in a much gentler tone than the one Acacia had used.

"N-n-not exactly," AJ admitted, his voice trembling.

"How do you not see a car coming at sixty miles—"

"Acacia, relax. Everything's fine, thanks to those lightning reflexes of yours, so don't worry about it." Percy was clearly the type of person who would make you feel like everything would work out, even when the world was on fire.

"But—"

Percy put the car into park and studied Acacia and AJ with focused eyes. "You both look beat. Get in and I'll give you a lift home."

"No thanks," Acacia replied, feeling her rage subside. Percy seemed nice, but she didn't think she knew him well enough to get in a car with him. After all, she couldn't say they'd exchanged more than a few words in passing at lunch. "I've got my bike. And my house is probably out of the way."

The older boy looked as if Acacia had suggested she run a quick marathon before returning home. "Acacia, you just got your full powers today. You should be resting, not getting teleported around by someone with pica."

AJ cleared his throat, his face flooded with incredulity. "Excuse me, Perce, but I do *not* have pica!"

"What's pica?" Acacia demanded. "I thought you were anemic!"

"Yeah," the twin acknowledged. "I mean, I *had* pica . . . but not since at least sixth grade!"

"But what the heck is— "

"It means he eats paper." Percy scratched the back of his neck. "Along with other things that aren't digestible by the human body. Now, both of you stop bickering and get in the car."

"I do *not* eat— "

Percy made a sweeping gesture with his right hand, causing the back door of the car to fly open. As if on cue, Acacia and AJ were swept into the back seat and the door closed behind them. The vehicle was obviously a hand-me-down, its fabric seats well-worn and grease spots visible on the steering wheel.

"Hey! What are you— " Acacia was cut off as Percy cleared traffic to his rear and pulled into the street. "No, stop! My bike!"

"Sorry," Percy apologized. "I don't like to manhandle people, but I was supposed to pick up my sister five minutes ago. I wouldn't worry too much about your bike if you locked it up this morning. Of all the things Silent Springs is famous for, theft isn't one of them."

They pulled up to a yellow traffic light and took a sudden left turn, swerving past a long line of cars in the process.

"Oh, you should buckle up," Percy said as his passengers collided into each other. "Hey, Acacia, where do you live anyway? I forgot. I don't know where I'm going."

"F-fifteen oh four." Acacia peered out the window with wide eyes, wondering if she would ever set foot on land again. "L-Linden Street."

"Cool." Percy shifted gears again and popped a high-speed right turn. "We'll be there in five minutes."

"Percy!" AJ exclaimed, grasping the back of Percy's seat so hard his knuckles turned white. "This is a one-way street!"

"Oh." The older boy swerved to the right and pulled into a narrow alley. "Sorry about that. I'm not familiar with this area."

"Are you sure you have your license?"

Percy laughed playfully. "Yes, Andrew, I'm sure. Now tell me, which way is it to Linden Street again?"

A few minutes later, Percy screeched to a stop in front of Acacia's house.

"Th-thanks for the ride," Acacia said, stumbling out of the car. She'd been crouched so anxiously she almost tumbled right from her seat onto the hard cement of the sidewalk.

"Be careful," Percy warned, a few seconds too late. "You'll be tired enough from getting your powers, you don't need a concussion too."

Acacia shook her head, thinking back to her poor, abandoned bike. She still felt confused about the world she had just been introduced to, but she'd have to worry about it later. Mattes and Percy were right, a deep exhaustion had begun to settle in, and Acacia foresaw an early bedtime.

"I'll see you guys at school," she remarked, waving back to her friends. "Have a good night!"

"Later, Acacia." Percy shifted gears again and waved back at her. "Rest well."

"See you," AJ added. "We'll start your real training tomorrow."

Acacia couldn't help but wonder what 'real training' would entail. "Sounds good. Thanks again for the ride, Percy!"

She waved and watched the blue car speed away before heading inside. If nothing else, it hadbeen a first day to remember.

***

Acacia ran through the woods, her path visible only by the shallow green light emitted by her own body. She did not, however, know why she was running or where she was going. After some time, Acacia came to a small clearing, where AJ was waiting for her. This didn't bother her. What she was struggling with was the fact he was a small gray fox.

Did you find the staff? Somehow being turned into a fox didn't prevent AJ from communicating telepathically.

"Onawa was supposed to help me," Acacia said, though how she knew this or who this person was, she had no idea. "But I couldn't find her either."

The fox rolled his yellow eyes at her.

"Don't give me that look," Acacia warned, shaking an index finger at him. "It's not *my* fault people decide to go chasing after some lizard instead of helping a friend save the world. I can't do everything myself."

Fine. AJ flicked his tail. *We can stand around pointing fingers until we're all dead.*

"Ha, well you can't," Acacia pointed out. "Since you don't have any fingers."

"Acacia!" Alex's voice called, as if he were locked in an airtight box. "Kill the snake!"

Acacia glanced over her shoulder and saw a gigantic black serpent soaring through the air directly toward her head. She ducked out of the way, and the creature missed, colliding into a tree.

I don't think that's what he meant by 'kill the snake,' AJ said.

"Oh, shut up," Acacia retorted, as the snake reared its ugly head and launched itself into the sky above. "It's gone, isn't it?"

An enormous flying lizard, a dragon perhaps, appeared out of nowhere and swooped down to carry the fox off into the night.

"Well, that's not good," Acacia said, as the serpent dove into the ground in front of her. "I've never seen a snake do that before."

Me neither, Mattes agreed. *Makes it more fun though, doesn't it?*

"Fun? Are you serious?"

Relax. Percy's voice was as calm as ever. *It's no worse than the last time.*

She sighed as the snake emerged from the ground, and she was enveloped in the darkness.

***

Acacia screamed and fell to the floor. Confused, she tossed and turned, kicking with both feet until she untangled her legs from her blankets. Opening her eyes, she noticed she'd fallen, but only from her bed to the floor, a much better alternative than a great abyss.

"What kind of staff are you looking for?" a familiar voice asked. "One that you use for sheep or one like those guys were fighting with in that karate movie we saw in May?"

Acacia sat up and glared at her younger sister from across the room. "How should *I* know? It was just a stupid dream."

"It didn't sound so stupid when you were screaming about it." Sari was staring at her with wide brown eyes as if Acacia had uninvited her from a party.

"*I* wasn't screaming about it." Acacia stood up and searched for something to wear. Over the years, she had found that denial worked best with her sister. If she denied something enough, Sari would eventually lose interest and give up.

"Yes, you were."

"No, I wasn't."

"Yes, you were!"

Acacia stuck out her tongue. "Whatever, Sarison. Why don't you just go play with your dolls?"

"I don't play with—"

Acacia tossed a pillow at the girl and pulled on the purple shirt her grandmother had given her for her birthday.

"Sure, Sari," she said, pulling on her jeans and heading out the door. "Whatever you say."

***

Acacia's second day at Silent Springs was much better than the first for several reasons. First, she found her way around much easier and by a stroke of luck had fallen into a small friend group. Second, ever since AJ had forced her magic back into her body, Acacia hadn't had to worry about the pesky green sparks running amok. While the experience hadn't been an enjoyable one, now she possessed more control over her magic than it had over her. In addition, Acacia was pleasantly surprised by the new feeling of power that flowed through her body. Yesterday she'd felt like she was trapped in a slump she couldn't escape from, disappointments heaped on disappointments. Today she was brimming with vigor and vitality.

"You're in a good mood," Alex noted, as the two took their seats in English class. "Silent Springs growing on you?"

Acacia grinned. This small town was much more appealing to her, now that she had a few friends and was more familiar with her surroundings. Even so, she couldn't say that was the main reason for her mood. Her attitude seemed to stem from the feeling of power racing through her veins and the fact that the mystery of the green sparks had been resolved.

"I guess you could say that." Acacia tucked a lock of wavy red hair that had escaped her braid behind her ear. "Your weather's going take getting used to though. I'm not used to these cool mornings."

Alex giggled, a twinkle of amusement in his light eyes. "Wait until fall. You do know the temperature drops below fifty degrees here, right?"

"Oh no," she said, smirking back at her friend. "Not below fifty degrees! I'll have to get out my winter coat."

"Do you even own a winter coat?"

"Touché," Acacia conceded. "You win this round, Mr. Swiatkowski."

Alex shot her a gloating look but didn't have the chance to respond as their teacher rose from his desk and began the day's lesson. Shaking her head, Acacia sighed and took out her own book, doing her best to feign interest in Shakespearean drama.

***

Before Acacia knew it, it was time for lunch. Upon arriving at the cafeteria, Acacia found Alex with relative ease, and the two of them got in the never-ending lunch line.

"It's 'chicken' patty on a roll today," Alex said, gesturing toward the front of the cafeteria.

Acacia glanced at her friend quizzically. "Is that a good thing or a bad thing?" Something about the way Alex said 'chicken' made her question the integrity of the meat.

"Neither, I guess," Alex replied with a shrug. "It's not really chicken, but if it's the same as in the middle school, it's not bad as long as you don't look at it too hard."

Acacia shook her head. "You'd think they were serving witches' brew and swamp water, listening to you talk about the food here."

"He's been like that since he was little. You should have heard him the first time Mother tried feeding him gołąbki," a girl's voice said. The two turned toward a tall girl standing behind them in the line, who had quirked her brows at her. "Cabbage stuffed with meat and rice. *You're* clearly not from around here."

Acacia blinked as she studied the girl's appearance. With the same gray eyes, thin freckled nose, dirty blonde hair, and slight build as the twins, she had to be an older sister or cousin.

"I don't like cabbage," Alex protested, recoiling from her comment. "It smells weird and tastes as weird as it smells."

"If you spent as much time practicing as you do coming up with excuses, you'd be the best mage in town," the girl said icily before turning to Acacia. "*You* must be the new mage. I'm Ivy Swiatkowski,

Cecelia's oldest. Our mother's been quite busy since starting her job at the research center, so I'm teaching my lackwit brother."

It was obvious she wasn't talking about AJ.

"I'm not a lackwit, Ivy," Alex complained, his face as red as Acacia's hair. "It's not my fault you guys are better than I am at . . . well, you know."

"Hm." Ivy stuck her thin nose up in the air. "Even so, you should be able to prevent me from blasting you through an entire meadow."

"Ivy!" Alex hissed, looking quite scandalized. "Do you have to embarrass me in front of—"

"In front of who?" Ivy demanded. "Your little girlfriend? Please. And besides, Lex, don't worry about me embarrassing you. You accomplish that well enough on your own."

Alex glowered at her and fell silent. After what seemed an eternity, they picked up their food and he and Acacia parted ways with Ivy and headed for their table.

"What's the matter with you, Smiley?" Matthias Knight asked as Alex dumped his tray down.

Alex glared at the boy, his eyes every bit as stormy as AJ's. "Why do *you* care?"

"Alexander, I'm hurt." Mattes drew back in his seat, looking quite affronted. "Here I am, concerned about your emotional health—"

"Mattes, cool it," AJ spoke in a quiet yet forceful voice. Acacia appreciated the twin was trying to help the situation, but even from her limited interactions with Mattes she realized that if the boy had something to say, little could be done to prevent him from saying it.

"*You*," Alex rounded on his brother. "Why do you have to be so perfect?"

AJ blinked, looking puzzled. "Me? What are you talking about?"

"Whatever." Alex's mood seemed to be plummeting by the second. "Forget it."

Glancing between the Swiatkowski twins, Acacia could feel the figurative storm coming.

AJ let out a single forced laugh. "Okay, so let me get this straight. You're mad at me because you think I'm perfect, even though you know that's not true."

"Just shut up."

"What did I do?" AJ asked, throwing his hands up. Exchanging glances with Acacia, he added, "To *you*."

"Just shut up, AJ. You don't have to deal with Ivy like I do. So just leave me alone!"

AJ straightened in his chair and tented his fingers in front of his face. "Really? *That's* what this is about?"

"For the last time, Andrew, shut the hell up!" Alex exclaimed. "Don't try to reason with me, don't try to talk to her, just shut the hell up and stay out of my business!"

Paying no heed to his brother's warning, AJ rose from his seat. "Zander, we share ninety-nine percent of our DNA. Your business is my business."

"Don't you think about picking a fight with Ivy!" Alex warned. "I don't need you fighting my battles."

AJ shot him a stormy, no-nonsense glare. "Well, someone has to. And it doesn't seem like it's going to be you."

"Andrew!"

"I'll be back in a minute." And with that, AJ walked off in search of his older sister.

"Funny how he's not so quiet when it suits him," Mattes said, poking his sandwich aggressively.

Alex rolled his eyes but offered no verbal response.

"Oh, poor Alexander the Not So Great." Mattes's tone held more than a trace of an edge this time. "Can't deal with the Big Bad Ivy Wolf himself, so he sends in his younger brother—"

"Back off, would you, buddy?" Alex retorted, rising from his seat. "You don't know— You don't have the right to say any—"

"Can I seriously not leave you unattended for five minutes?" AJ asked, reappearing abruptly from behind. Acacia wondered if he had teleported back to their table but realized it was unlikely he would use an obvious display of magic in the middle of the cafeteria.

Alex arched his brows at his brother. "Well, that didn't take long. Got your fill of our lovely sister already?"

"I can't figure out why you're so convinced Ivy is such a monster," AJ said, a hint of challenge in his voice. "I mean, she's not the nicest person in the world, but it's not like she has three heads."

No, she doesn't have three heads, Acacia thought, watching the scene unfold in front of her. *But she doesn't have any manners either.*

"In your dear brother's defense," Mattes began, turning to AJ. "I'm not certain you're the best to decide who the 'nicest person in the world' is. After all, your idea of welcoming the new girl is threatening her in the cafeteria on her first day."

"Excuse me, Matthias, but I did not threaten her," AJ argued. "I think I know the difference between making a threat and having a conversation."

"Yes, but you also think you can beat me at chess." Mattes stood up rather dramatically and shook his head. "Which you have yet to accomplish. Face it, you're delusional."

AJ rolled his stormy gray eyes at his friend. "Me, delusional? If we're going to talk about delusional, how about we discuss the fact—"

Mattes responded with a fake-sounding cough. "Oh. I see. Here I am trying to help you in your obvious state of anxiety, and how do you respond? Why, by taking out your anger on me and pushing me away, isolating yourself to that terrifying place you call your mind."

"Matthias." Percy's voice was every bit as apprehensive as his expression. "Enough."

Mattes blinked innocently and smiled back at the older boy. "Enough? I'm sorry, but I have no idea what you're talking about."

Percy opened his mouth to say something further, but AJ spoke first.

"It's okay, Perce," he remarked in a nonchalant tone. "This is relatively normal for a Tuesday."

Both boys took their seats once again.

Acacia turned curiously to Percy. "Do they always fight like this?" she asked. "Or did I just show up at a really bad time?"

Percy chuckled, taking a glimpse at the two friends. "Oh no, AJ's right, this is pretty normal." The older boy's usual serenity had returned much quicker than Acacia would have thought possible. "But the important thing is when they do need each other, all that bickering goes right out the window."

Acacia shot the boy an incredulous look. "I'll believe it when I see it."

"Suit yourself," Percy replied. "Just be warned, stranger things have happened."

Mattes and AJ exchanged smug glances.

"Why indeed they have," Mattes said. "And will in all likelihood continue to happen."

Acacia let out a long sigh. "Again, I'll believe it when I see it. Seems to me you two are more likely to kill each other than protect each other."

"We're too similar is all," AJ said, massaging his forehead. "In my opinion, most of the bickering comes from conflicting egos."

"Too bad no one *cares* about your opinion." Mattes combed through his hair with his fingertips, as if to prove his point.

"Too bad no one cares about your hair."

"Oh, Drew," Mattes retorted. "If only that were true. You know as well as I do that plenty of people care about the health and vitality of my hair."

"Well, look what we have here," a familiar voice said. "The kiddie table."

Acacia whirled around and noticed that Ivy Swiatkowski had come to stand behind their table, arms crossed in front of her chest, looking like a woman on a mission.

"Was there something else you wanted to say, sister?" AJ asked in a serious tone. "I didn't think our previous conversation left anything open to interpretation."

Alex kicked him from underneath the table, from the sound of it, hard.

"You have a lot of nerve, Number Two," Ivy informed him, smirking at her brother. Tossing a lock of blonde hair over her shoulder, she added, "You'd do well to watch that tongue of yours before someone pulls it out."

"Fortunately, I don't think anyone here is in the market for an extra tongue."

Ivy exhaled sharply and took a long look at her brothers in turn. "You're really no fun to play with, AJ. I get more entertainment from watching the golf channel."

AJ shrugged, his body posture rather rigid. "Are you going to tell me why you ventured all the way to the kiddie table? Or should we just assume you're in the mood for mind games and your friends don't give you enough of a challenge?"

Acacia couldn't help but notice the twitch in Ivy's jaw with the mention of the phrase 'mind games.'

"Mind games?" Ivy repeated, a sarcastic grin on her face. "And what exactly do you mean by that?"

"Isn't 'mind-game' an appropriate term for when someone manipulates others' emotions to get what they want?"

Ivy laughed, her voice a bit caustic. "You're mistaken, all right, to think I would find the kiddie table more of a challenge than my own classmates. Besides, we never finished our little contest this summer. I hope you know I was about to devastate you, baby brother. You just got lucky."

AJ rolled his eyes and shook his head. He didn't seem to want to engage in a battle of wits with his sister, which surprised Acacia given most of what she had seen AJ do in the past twenty-four hours was engage in battles of wits with whoever was in sight.

"But since you're so concerned," Ivy said after an awkward pause. "I didn't feel like our conversation ended on the right note, so I decided to come and remedy it." Her gaze lingered on Alex for a few moments before shifting and settling upon Acacia. "New girl, you don't *look* like much, and you seem to be attached to my brother's hip, which makes me question not only your magical talents, but your intelligence as well. After all, birds of a feather do tend to flock together."

"Excuse me?" Acacia demanded, rising from her seat. "And what's that supposed to—"

Don't yell at her, AJ mind-spoke in a clipped tone. *You're falling into her game.*

Well, I'm not about to sit around and let her insult me and Alex! She doesn't even know me!

"It *means* what it sounds like." A haughty smile settled across Ivy's face. "It means your best buddy Alex is, as I said, a lackwit, and your 'teacher' isn't qualified to teach a rock. In other words, if you have any self-respect, you might want to look for some new friends."

Acacia opened her mouth to reply, but AJ was faster.

"Ivy, seriously, what happened to you?" the twin questioned, his face draining of color. "I don't even know who you are anymore."

Smiling dangerously, Ivy grabbed hold of AJ's wrist, pulled him toward her with a strength Acacia hadn't expected, and whispered something in his ear. A flash of darkness passed through the twin's face, and within seconds the two siblings were locked into a glaring contest.

"*Okay,* you two, that's quite enough," Percy said, coming to his feet, an alarmed expression plastered across his face. "We don't need any more outbursts for one day. Let's not forget where we are."

Ivy laughed and let go of her brother. "Oh, Percival," she began, her dark eyes amused. "Always the worrywart. But don't worry. No one here is worth my time anyway." And with that, she departed without as much as a glance over her shoulder.

Once Ivy was out of sight, Percy let out a sigh of relief and took his seat again. "You shouldn't goad her, Andrew," he said. "She's dangerous when agitated."

AJ shrugged and rubbed his wrist where Ivy had grabbed him. "Tell me something I don't already know."

"Then why do you fight with her?" Alex insisted in an irritated tone. "Doesn't seem like something you would do if you knew what was going to happen."

The twins appeared to be locked in a staring contest, and Acacia wondered if they weren't communicating telepathically.

"Because, Alex, just because you're afraid of something doesn't mean you always run away." With that, AJ picked up his bookbag and stormed off.

"Okay," Acacia said, her mind reeling from the events of the past hour. "What just happened here?"

Alex let out a sigh of exasperation. "Y'know, I'm not hungry anymore. Acacia, see you in history class."

"Alex!" Acacia called. "Wait, where are you—"

But the twin appeared not to have heard her, as he gathered his things and went to throw his food away. Percy shook his head and looked at Acacia with calm blue eyes.

"I apologize for my cousins' behavior," he said in a rueful tone. "The three of them have . . . an odd relationship."

Mattes let out an irritated sigh, running a hand through his hair. "More like Alex's afraid to give Ivy a piece of his mind, and Drew isn't. Honestly, you'd think that girl was the Loch Ness Monster by the way he acts around her."

"Maybe," Percy remarked. "But then again, don't forget, Andrew got his powers about the same time Ivy did, and Alex only got his last spring. It might not seem like much, but when you think about it, the power differential is considerable."

Whoa, Acacia thought. *So, AJ got his powers the same time Ivy did, even though she's two or three years older? Just from a glance, I'd have to say Ivy is a powerful mage and could probably kick my butt to California and back. Does that mean AJ's that good too?* She scratched her head, trying to absorb what had just transpired. *But what was all that about? What did AJ go to talk to her about in the first place? And why does Ivy insult everyone in sight?*

"I guess," Mattes conceded. "But seriously, that girl is out of control. The only thing we can hope for is that someday somebody manages to knock her down a few notches." After a brief pause, Mattes rose from his seat and picked up his book bag. "Well, after that lively lunch, I think it's time to simmer down with some good old-fashioned British literature. See you all later."

Percy shook his head as Mattes strode out of the cafeteria. "Well, I suppose it's just you and me now," he said in a tired tone. Glancing at Acacia's untouched food, he continued, "Make sure you eat up, Acacia. You've got a long afternoon ahead of you."

"Great," Acacia replied, picking up her sandwich reluctantly. She took a cautious bite and shot Percy a wary glance. "You're not leaving till I finish, are you?"

Percy smiled. "Not a chance. Now, eat up."

Acacia scowled at him and ate her chicken sandwich.

***

The rest of the day flew by. Once again, Acacia found herself only half paying attention to her classes as she attempted to process everything that had transpired during lunch. She overcame her anger from Ivy's insults fast enough, but try as she might, she didn't understand why the girl had been so rude without provocation. No matter how talented she was, Ivy didn't have the right to insult Acacia, someone she had just met, or her brothers for that matter. Maybe Alex lacked training, but from what Acacia understood, it was Ivy who was supposed to be training him. As for AJ, Acacia had come to learn that the boy could be accused of many things, but being a feeble mage was not one of them.

The bell rang, signaling the end of the school day. As students rushed to leave the room, Mr. George gave them their homework assignment due the next day. Acacia grimaced, realizing she would have to do quite a bit of work that evening to make up for her early bedtime last night.

Having gathered her books, Acacia looked at Alex, who hadn't moved since taking his seat at the beginning of class. His posture was rigid, as if bracing himself for some kind of collision, and his gray eyes were pensive.

"Alex?" Acacia asked. "Everything all right?"

"Sorry?" He looked at her as if she had woken him from a deep sleep. "What did you say, Acacia?"

"I asked if you were okay." Acacia adjusted her bag so it was even on both shoulders. "You looked a little . . . out of it."

Alex let out a short laugh and shoved his books into his bag. "I'm fine, I was just"—he glanced around as if to make sure no one was in earshot—"talking to AJ."

Acacia's eyes widened. "Oh? What's on his mind?"

"There's always lots of things on my brother's mind." Alex shrugged. "We're cool about what happened at lunch, but he says he's not going to stop messing in my business, especially with this Ivy thing. He's convinced she's not as awful as she's acting, which I don't get, but hey, who am I to tell my genius brother what to think?"

Acacia laughed, imagining the impossible task of trying to tell AJ something he didn't want to hear. "So, what are you up to now? Soccer practice?" AJ had said her magical training would start today, but Acacia almost wondered if the boy had forgotten about it with the current Swiatkowski family feud.

Alex frowned, picking up his bag. "No, actually," he said, biting his lower lip. "I'm kind of . . . skipping. Ivy told me if I don't show up for our training session today, I'm going to have to find someone else to finish teaching me."

"What?" Acacia's mouth dropped open in shock. Who did this girl think she was? "Alex, she can't just—"

"Oh, but she can." Alex stood up and threw his bag over his shoulder. "I mean, she might be bluffing, but she might not be. I don't want to find out. So, I'm going to take one for the team."

"But Alex!" Acacia ran into the hallway after her friend. "You could get kicked off the team if you don't show up for practice! Ivy might be your teacher, but she can't control your life!"

Alex shot her a curious look as he opened his locker. "Look, Acacia, I get that this all is weird. But sometimes, we have to do things we wouldn't have to do if we were regular people. Going to school during the day and spending our free time learning magic and figuring out where we fit in all of this." He stopped for a moment, his face set in concentration. "But you'll figure it all out in no time, I'm sure. Don't let Ivy scare you. My brother knows what he's doing. With magic anyway. And speaking of AJ, he asked me to tell you to stick with me. He said he's finishing something up right now, but he'll come get you soon."

Acacia let out a long sigh, unsure whether to be relieved or disappointed. "Am I ever going to know what's going on?"

"Not if you hang out with us enough," Alex replied with a crooked smile. "Trust me, I've known about this stuff for my whole life, and I still don't know what's going on."

Acacia grinned as they left the school and headed toward the forest where AJ's transportation spell had dumped them the day before. When they arrived at a large, well-hidden meadow, Acacia glanced around, searching for any sign of either Ivy or AJ.

"Well, where are they?" she asked. "They were supposed to meet us here, right?"

"Only here a day and you already think you should run the place, don't you?" a silvery voice whispered near Acacia's ear.

Acacia whirled around, half expecting a magical attack to come flying at her face. Ivy stood roughly a foot in front of her and Alex, her arms folded in front of her chest. The older girl glared at them, her dark gray eyes as piercing as a set of daggers.

"Well, Alex, I see you brought company," Ivy said as she took another step toward them. "Maybe we can see if you can get over your stage fright enough to manage a simple shield spell."

Alex turned from his sister, his face bright red with embarrassment. "C'mon, Ivy, I'm not that bad. I just—"

"You just? You just what? You just . . . are devoid of all talent whatsoever and must rely on your younger brother to stick up for you?"

"We're twins, Ivy! And it's not my fault he's better at magic than I am, okay? And he's had his way longer!"

A brilliant flash of blue appeared to Acacia's left, giving way to AJ's slim form within moments. Clearly AJ had finished whatever he'd needed to take care of, and used the same teleportation spell to meet them in the meadow.

"Well, look who decided to show up," Alex murmured under his breath. "Some great teacher you are."

AJ shot his brother a rather challenging glance but remained silent.

"I hope you don't think you're about to use this space for your pathetic little lesson." Ivy twirled a lock of dirty blonde hair between her fingers, her lips curling upwards in a smirk. "In case you haven't noticed, it's taken. Perhaps if you got your priorities in order, your student wouldn't be quite so doomed for failure." She paused and took a glimpse at Acacia, a haughty look on her face. "And what precisely have you managed to teach her? By the way, magic exists?"

"Acacia, let's go," AJ said in a calm tone, as if Ivy had been talking about nothing more serious than a quiz they had to take. "Ivy's right, it is a little crowded here."

Without another word, he walked off into the woods, gesturing for Acacia to follow. She glanced once more in Alex's direction, frowned, and took a few large strides to catch up.

"What's this?" Ivy laughed as they departed. "Turns out you are afraid of me after all!"

It took all of Acacia's willpower to ignore the girl, since even she didn't think it wise to argue with someone with years of experience on her. Once she caught up with AJ, she cleared her throat and reached out to grab him by the sleeve. "Hold on. I know you like to be sneaky and all, but—"

I think the word you're looking for is 'discrete,' AJ's voice said in her mind. Judging from his intense stare, Acacia realized he wanted her to communicate telepathically as well.

Fine, we'll do it your way. As much as Acacia thought AJ was being unnecessarily dramatic, she didn't want to push him too far. *So, what's her deal? Did you dump milk and cereal on her this morning or what?*

Piece of advice, Acacia, AJ replied, leading the way down a grassy trail. *If you're going to talk about people, even if you are doing it telepathically, you need to block your thoughts. Meaning you have to use your power to create a mental barrier between you and whoever's around. If you don't, anyone with a touch of magic can hear what you're saying. Including my dear sister.*

Acacia let out a sigh of exasperation. She was *trying* to get used to having magical powers, but it was hard enough to do without being constantly reprimanded for what she was doing wrong.

Okay, oh knowledgeable one, she said. *So, Ivy can hear me. Does she care what I'm saying?*

Yes. But she'll forget about us once we're far enough away.

Doesn't she have more important things to worry about? Acacia asked. *Like training Alex?*

The twin glared at her, his gray eyes stormier than usual. *Acacia, I do not have a problem with the fact that you don't know how to block your thoughts yet. What I have a problem with is that you're insisting on talking about my sister even though I just told you that she can hear every word you're saying.*

In other words, when I know how to block my thoughts and she can't hear everything I say, I can talk about her all I want?

AJ let out a long sigh. *I wasn't going to do this, you know.*

You weren't going to do wh—

Acacia wasn't able to finish her thought, as he grabbed her hand, and they were swept up once more in the blue of his teleportation spell.

Chapter Six

SHOCK AND AWE

Within seconds, the teleportation spell faded, and Acacia and AJ emerged in a spacious, open field.

"I must be getting used to that." Acacia heard the confidence in her voice, felt it in her body posture. "I don't feel sick this time!"

"We only traveled a few yards." Annoyance marked AJ's face, though Acacia couldn't tell if he was annoyed at her or something else. "Like I said, I wasn't going to do that, but you gave me no choice."

"What's that supposed to mean? I was just asking what your sister's got shoved up her butt—"

AJ let out an exasperated sigh, cutting Acacia off midsentence. "Enough," he commanded, his pale brows twitching. "What my sister has—as you so eloquently put it—shoved up her butt is not your concern. Besides, don't you realize the more you annoy Ivy, the more she's going to take it out on Alex?"

"What?" Acacia exclaimed. "What are you talking about? Ivy can't—"

"Acacia," AJ said, his tone clipped and authoritative. "You've *met* my sister, haven't you? You should be able to tell she doesn't exactly have the sweetest temperament. But one thing you might not know is that she doesn't appreciate being challenged, especially by someone she considers to be less powerful than she is."

Acacia tried to blink away her confusion. AJ's statement wasn't that surprising; she *had* gathered that Ivy didn't like being defied from their brief encounter at lunch. However, Acacia didn't expect to hear that Alex, who never challenged Ivy, would be the victim of her aggression.

"Why Alex?" Acacia asked. "Why wouldn't she take it out on me if I've annoyed her so much?"

"Because you're off limits," AJ replied, his dark eyes serious. Acacia was beginning to understand for as much as the twin wasn't quick to anger, he did have a silent fury when provoked, a fury when combined with his well-controlled magic would probably allow him to obliterate any obstacles in his path. "Don't forget, you're my student, not hers. If she messes with you, she knows she'll have me to deal with. And no matter how arrogant Ivy may be, it doesn't seem she's comfortable doing that."

Could AJ really be stronger than Ivy? Acacia wondered. *That's kind of hard for me to believe. Then again, AJ seems to have more secrets than he lets on. Maybe he* is *that good.*

"If by secrets you mean I'm not as frail as I look, you'd be correct," AJ replied, having heard her thoughts. "But we're not here to talk about *my* skills. We're here so you can get the training you need before Sisyphus and his minions escape."

It was Acacia's turn to sigh. "Mr. Swiatkowski, if Sissy Puss was so powerful, don't you think he would have found a way out by now? Ten years is a long time for someone with so much power to be sitting around."

"I'll advise you for the last time, Sisyphus might not react so kindly to your 'mispronunciation' of his name."

"Good thing, he's not here," Acacia said, folding her arms in front of her chest.

The twin quirked one of his pale brows at her, pointing towards the sky with his right index finger. "How sure are you about that?"

Confused, Acacia glanced upward, following the direction of the boy's outstretched finger.

There, higher than the furthest clouds, she could see a myriad of colors—green, red, yellow, orange, some intertwined, some clashing into each other, but all moving in some way or another. Acacia could feel a great power above, a magic strong enough to throw her and whoever else was around into oblivion.

"What. . ." Acacia struggled to form complete sentences, her mind reeling from the shock of whatever storm was crashing above her. Was it a magical storm? A portal of some kind? A creature being summoned. "What the *hell* is that?"

"That was precisely the reaction I was hoping it would have on you," AJ said, a self assured smile working its way across his face. "Sometimes seeing is believing."

Acacia shook her head to regain her composure. "Well, are you going to explain what that is, or are you just going to gloat about how ignorant I am?"

If AJ was at all bothered by her comment, his face didn't show it. "What that is, is the vacuum spell I told you about yesterday. We call it the Bloody Meadow because of all the blood spilled in the final battle."

Acacia stared up into the colorful mess, trying to imagine what kind of advanced magic would be required to—what was it AJ had said—convert multiple dark mages into energy and seal them in a spell in the sky. The way the colors, the auras, thrashed around led her to believe the prisoners were not only alive, but impatient.

"They've been getting stronger with every passing day since you arrived," AJ told her. "I know this because Mattes and I take turns taking energy readings on the site, so we won't be blindsided when something happens. You got here around August twentieth, right? That's when I picked up your aura and when the energy fields started flaring up. The only logical explanation is that you have something to do with it."

"You think I came here to mess with the vacuum thing." Acacia rolled her eyes. "You have got to be the most paranoid—"

"At first, I thought you were a second-generation spy," AJ said, silencing her with an intense glare. "But that's not the case since it doesn't seem you'd know who to spy *on* in the first place. For now, I'm going with there's something special about you that none of us know about yet."

Acacia blinked. Something special about her? She'd already found out she had magical powers she hadn't known about for fourteen years, and that these powers were undeniably strong. What more could she *not* know about herself?

"I don't know what it is yet," the twin said, studying her with a cautious gaze. "But we'll figure it out. I have a feeling something's going to happen this year, but hopefully there'll be time to get you well trained before it does."

"You think Sissy Puss and company are going to escape, and we're going to have to fight them," Acacia said, feeling a ball of anxiety forming in the pit of her stomach. Could this really be happening? Was she being dragged into some kind of war the first week of high school? "AJ, we're *kids*! How are we supposed to take on a bunch of evil geniuses if they *do* escape? Don't get me wrong, obviously you're good at this. But that doesn't mean you can go around—"

AJ let out a quiet laugh and smiled, looking for once the fourteen-year-old boy that he was. "Believe me, Acacia, I don't plan on starting any magical wars," he assured her, much more light-hearted than he had been moments earlier. "All I'm trying to do is figure out what's so different about you that could affect the aura field so much. And try to get you ready in case Sisyphus does escape. But there is one thing I'd like you to promise me."

"Oh?" she asked. "Would this promise be don't go opening any aerial vacuum spells?"

"Basically, yes." The twin paused, studying Acacia's face as if searching for something. "For whatever reason, the auras up there are excited you're here, which means it's not a good idea for you to be here. It's possible that if you were to come here by yourself, Sisyphus and the others may be able to latch upon your magic and find a way to use you to escape. So, I'd feel a lot better if I knew you weren't running around here by yourself."

Acacia sighed. "So what? I'm going to be this powerful mage, but I need a chaperone?"

"It's not you I don't trust. Besides." He shot her an amused expression that made Acacia think he was secretly laughing at her. "Maybe you will be a powerful mage someday, but you're not there yet. We've got a lot of work ahead of us."

Oh joy, Acacia thought, grimacing. *Because I didn't have enough to worry about.*

"Fine, I promise I won't come here by myself running around doing stupid things," she conceded reluctantly. "Maybe then at least you can stop worrying about one thing."

"I was hoping you would say that," AJ remarked, relief flooding his face. "Now let's get out of here. This place gives me the creeps, and we have more work to do before we can call your crash course in the magical arts over."

***

They strode away from the meadow at a rapid pace, or more accurately, AJ strode away from the meadow at a rapid pace and Acacia struggled to keep up.

"Hey!" she said after a few minutes, panting. "Is there a reason we're running?"

AJ paused to cast a rather smug expression in Acacia's direction. "Once you start your real training, you'll be doing a lot more strenuous physical activity. And besides, I told you we have more work to do today. I'm not about to be a negligent teacher."

"That's fine," Acacia said, catching her breath. "But I have a question for you."

"Oh?"

"What's your issue with redheads?" Acacia inquired, pushing her coppery bangs out of her eyes. "When we were in the Underground, Mattes said you think all redheads are homicidal psychopaths."

AJ's pale brows shot up in surprise. Of all the questions he'd been expecting, *that* clearly hadn't been one of them. "Well, if you must know," he said in a way Acacia couldn't be certain was annoyed or amused. "One of the few redheads I've come into contact with *was* a homicidal psychopath."

"So, you assume we all are?"

AJ shrugged. "Let's just say that some things are harder to get rid of when they've been lurking around in your head since you were four. But that's also not why we're here. All you need to know is I'm making a conscious effort to not assume all of you are homicidal."

"That's all I can ask for." Acacia grinned, sticking her tongue out at him.

They had arrived in another meadow, adorned with high grasses and wildflowers. This one was small in comparison to both the meeting place where they had split from Alex and Ivy, as well as the Bloody Meadow. AJ motioned for her to remain where she was and walked toward the middle of the clearing, putting about three feet between them.

"Now," he said, turning to face her. "It's time for your real training to start."

"Meaning?"

"Magic isn't something you can always learn from a book," the boy explained, shaking the tension out of his hands. "Of course, you can read about it if you have access to a quality library. But at this point, it's more important for you to work on the practical stuff."

"The practical stuff?"

AJ blinked several times, looking quite dazed. "You *do* know what practical means, don't you, Acacia? Practical as in how to use your magic. After you understand how to use your magic, we can consider supplementing your training with research."

Acacia rolled her eyes. She didn't mind reading, but she didn't think she'd have time for magical homework in addition to all her schoolwork once the school year picked up.

"You're going to have to do some reading at some point or another," AJ shot her a piercing glance reminiscent of his sister's. "Like I've told you, there's something different about your magic, and even *you* will want to find out what that is."

"Okay, all right," Acacia retorted, working to control her facial expressions. Of all the things she was in the mood for, another lecture wasn't one of them. "Are you going to show me how to do stuff?"

AJ nodded. "That's the plan. Although I think yours is going to be different from mine, at least in how you're going to have to summon it."

"'How I'm going to have to summon it?'" Acacia repeated. "What's that supposed to mean?"

For a moment, AJ looked as if he was going to give her a scolding. Instead, he let out a brief sigh and raised both his hands up, elbows bent, so they were a few inches away from his face. "Magic is a form of energy that we're born with which manifests in a particular color." He made a slow, circular motion with his right wrist, and as he completed the circle, AJ held his hand out palm up in front of him. An orb, much like the one he'd used as a light source when they'd ventured into the Underground appeared directly above his hand. "My magic is blue, as is Alex's, Ivy's, Percy's, and everyone else's in my family. Mattes's is yellow, and yours appears to be green."

Acacia nodded. After her experience yesterday, she would've guessed the same.

"For your purposes, it might help to think of your magic kind of like chi," AJ explained. "In a couple of Asian philosophies, your chi is your life energy, an energy that flows through your body like your blood does. The only difference is that your magic can be channeled through your body and can be used to do different things, while it's better for your blood to stay in your body."

"So, what kinds of things can we use magic for?" Acacia asked with a thoughtful nod. "I mean . . . yesterday you and Alex used your magic to control mine. You used magic to teleport us back outside the school."

"Both excellent observations." AJ nodded. "But obviously we won't be starting you with any of those spells. They all require the mage to possess mastery over his or her mind and emotions, and a strong level of concentration, which you don't have yet. You'll get there, but I wouldn't want you to try any of those without more training."

Acacia frowned. AJ might understand the finer details of how magic operated, but he wasn't so skilled at giving direct answers.

"The first thing we're going to work on is a simple shield spell," the boy told her. "Once you've managed that, we'll work on an attack. This way, we'll cover your two bases, offensive and defensive magic. There's a lot of things you can do with magic—creating and opening magically sealed entrances and exits, invisibility charms, teleportation—but those will come in time. For now, your mission is to raise a shield and launch an attack."

"Sounds like a plan," Acacia said. "But that doesn't give me an idea of how I can do any of that."

Her companion nodded and brought both arms across his body in a smooth, flowing motion, causing a wave of blue magic to appear in the air. The magic flashed for a moment, and then disappeared.

"Many of us practice martial arts when we're beginning to learn magic," AJ informed her. "It's helpful because it allows you to learn self-discipline, and the best way to summon your magic. It's not necessary, but not a bad thing to try out if you have the time. But everyone's magic isn't the same; some respond to quick, abrupt movements, while others require more expressive, flowing motions. As you can see, mine falls under the second category."

"Okay, that's cool and all," Acacia interjected. "But how am I going to figure out how *my* magic works?"

The twin shrugged. "Trial and error. By now you should be able to better feel your magic, like a warm energy in your body. Mimic the same movement I did and try to conjure a little bit of your magic to the surface. For now, it doesn't have to be anything powerful. Just enough so you can get an idea of what it means to control your power."

As much as Acacia hated to admit it, AJ was right; since she had woken up that morning, she did feel an energy coursing through her body, an energy she hadn't noticed before. Of course, she *had* noticed the magic yesterday, as it leaped from her body with a power she'd never dreamed possible, but this was different. The power of yesterday was angry and violent, bent on the destruction of whatever was in its path. This power was still powerful but seemed to want to help her.

Acacia nodded and carefully imitated the motion AJ had shown her, bringing her arms up and across her torso. As she did, she could feel that energy move through her body, originating in her heart and moving up through her arms, until finally a few sparks appeared at the center of her right palm.

"Not bad for a first try," AJ said as the sparks vanished after a few seconds. "Now do it again, but this time put more power into it."

Acacia did as he asked, alternating hands. She was right-handed so she wasn't surprised her magic responded better to movements made with her right arm. After about ten tries, she managed to create a thin sheet of green magic, which remained in the air for a minute before disappearing.

"Okay, that's good. I think we can move on now." AJ gave her an appreciative nod, his gray eyes brighter than they'd been all day. "With practice, that could be a decent shield charm, effective for deflecting attacks that someone else might send your way. We'll try some attacks before we call it a day. That movement I had you do is like a block in some martial arts, and since it's on the slow side, more similar to tai chi. In my opinion, you look like someone who responds better to more aggressive movements like you'd find in karate." Turning away from her, AJ stood with his right foot in front, and his arms again raised in front of his body. In one swift motion, he made another circular movement with his hand, causing a small burst of blue magic to materialize in the air. He then thrust his arm forward and rotated his hand so it was upright, sending a blast of blue energy through the meadow. "Do that and try to hit me with it. That way we can find out how well you can follow through with your spells."

"But. . ." Acacia said, thinking of the painful bursts of magic that had come flying out of her yesterday. The other magic she had conjured hadn't been too difficult, but it had also been a defensive maneuver. Acacia figured it was her aggressive magic that was the threat, and she wasn't sure she wanted to risk another incident. "I don't want to attack you."

"And why's that?"

"Oh, I don't know," Acacia replied, feeling her face redden. "Maybe because I don't want to hurt you like I did yesterday?"

"Acacia, that's not going to happen." AJ ran a hand through his hair in an almost Mattes-like gesture. "There's a huge difference between first getting your powers and then using them afterward. Getting them is a trial to see if you're strong enough to withstand them at their strongest, like a test to make sure you'll be able to control them. And we both survived, so it's fine."

Acacia gave him a long hard glare, trying to ignore the pounding in her chest. "There's absolutely no reason for me to attack you, so I'm not doing it. I'm not a monster like your sister."

"So . . . you're saying you can't do it?" AJ quirked his pale brows at her again and tilted his head. "Though given your powers of perception, I suppose I shouldn't be surprised."

The boy turned and began to saunter away. Logically, Acacia knew AJ was trying to goad her into action, but his words stung just the same. She tried desperately to peer into the boy's mind to see what he was thinking, but each attempt had the same effect as running into a solid brick wall.

"And you criticized Ivy for her mind games!" Acacia accused. "As if that's not exactly what you're doing right now!"

"But I suppose you've never been perceptive," AJ continued, glancing over his shoulder at her. "Having all those supernatural phenomena take place around you for fourteen years and never giving them a second thought? And then this year your family just so happens to relocate across the country? Perhaps they know more about our world than you think, but they'd rather watch you struggle."

With that, Acacia felt her self-restraint dissolve as she took off after the twin, channeling her power up through her arms and finally launching bursts of green magic at him through her palms.

AJ was fast, unnaturally fast. He spun around, swinging his right arm in a semicircle, in the process leaving a light blue wall around his body. Acacia's green bursts hit AJ's shield with considerable force, but then dissolved and disappeared.

"Good work, Acacia," the boy said, looking impressed. "Though I'm not sure why you were so hesitant to attack in the first place."

"Well then, let me show you just how hesitant I am!" Acacia bellowed, channeling more power to her palms.

"So, student challenges teacher," AJ commented, watching her approach with fascination. "I was almost hoping you would."

"Well, here's your wish!" Acacia channeled another rush of energy, this time in the form of a long, green lightning bolt. She gripped it at its base and ferociously flung its other end at her companion. But AJ had completely disappeared as if into thin air. Acacia scanned left and right, reabsorbing the bolt into her arm, but no matter where she looked, she couldn't locate him.

"You and my brother need to work on blocking your thoughts," AJ's voice said from above and behind the spot where Acacia was standing. She whirled around as quickly as possible to see the boy floating in a cross-legged sitting position about a foot above her head. "I'm not trying to be a nag, but you should have been able to hit me with that. But if you'd had your mind more closed off, I wouldn't have seen it coming, and you'd have me driven into that tree over there." AJ dropped to the ground and tilted his head thoughtfully. "I'm sorry I said those things to you. I didn't want to have to agitate you, but you were being difficult."

Acacia took a giant step backward and placed her hands on her hips. "*I* was being difficult? I'll remind you, Mr. Swiatkowski, it was you who started with the whole 'attack me now!' thing!"

AJ shrugged, his gray eyes indifferent. "Like I said, I'm sorry for saying those things, but I wasn't sure how else to get you to cooperate. And it *was* successful. Though I'm surprised you were so opposed to attacking me in the first place. Neither you nor your magic had a problem attacking me yesterday."

Feeling her anger abating, Acacia took a deep, long breath. Her energy, her magic, had needed to get out, this time of her own accord. And while she didn't approve of AJ's methods for motivating her to do so, she did feel better with some of the negative energy released from her system.

"You're talented, you know," AJ continued, shooting her an appreciative look. "Not many novice mages would have been able to cast a lightning spell. Strength clearly isn't going to be your problem. You have a good deal of raw talent to begin with, and with practice, you'll develop the skills you need. But anyway," he remarked, beginning to walk off. "I guess it's my responsibility to welcome you to the real Silent Springs. It might not mean much to you now, but I think you'll be in good company, even if I only kind of know what I'm doing."

Acacia shook her head. "I don't know, AJ. It seems to me like you know darn well what you're—"

A flash of blue materialized to AJ's left, and within a few more seconds, Alex emerged from the light, a broad grin on his face.

"Ivy, I found them!" Alex hollered, playfully tousling his brother's hair.

You look like you've been busy, Alex mind-spoke, audible to both Acacia and AJ. *I hope you haven't been up to anything too bad.*

AJ returned Alex's grin and attempted to straighten his now messy hair. *Nice teleportation spell,* he replied in what Acacia perceived to be a genuine tone. *You've been practicing.*

Another flash of blue appeared in the clearing, revealing a surprised-looking Ivy.

"Alex, that was. . ." The girl's voice trailed off. "Not awful. I feel like we may have accomplished something today, believe it or not. I hope we don't have a blizzard tomorrow."

The older girl turned to glance at Acacia and AJ, raising her pale brows questioningly. "I do hope you two managed to accomplish something as well. Perhaps something beyond 'oh, by the way, magic exists.'"

Acacia opened her mouth to respond, but AJ was quicker.

"Love you too, sister dearest," he said, looking quite facetious. "But surely you have more important things on your mind than what I taught Acacia."

Acacia was beginning to wonder what she would do if the siblings started fighting, right as Ivy let out a hearty laugh and looked down her nose at her brother.

"For your information, squirt, tonight, I have a date with Jared. So, in other words, I do." Ivy's expression seemed to communicate an additional *so there*. "So, you little brats have fun, but don't get too comfortable. After all, you never know when the next challenge will arrive."

Without another word, Ivy disappeared in what Acacia recognized to be a teleportation spell.

Letting out a sigh of relief, Alex walked over to greet Acacia. "Well, Ivy's gone, and that's never a bad thing," he said. "So did my brother treat you okay? Sometimes I wonder if he's any better than her."

"Hey Alex." AJ shot his twin a mild glare. "I'm standing right here, remember? Do you think you could wait to talk about me behind my back until I'm at least out of physical earshot?"

Both Alex and Acacia laughed. *Maybe I got lucky making the friends I did,* Acacia considered. *Everyone in this family seems to be super talented at magic.*

"Nope," AJ told her, having heard her thoughts again. "You just need to meet some more mages."

"Ignore him," Alex said, paying no attention to his brother. "Acacia, I'm sure whatever you did, you worked up an appetite. Do you want to come over for dinner?"

A bolt of surprise made its way down Acacia's spine. She had expected Alex to offer to take her home, not to invite her to a family dinner. Did Alex want her to meet his mother? That gesture seemed to be something boyfriends and girlfriends did when they were relatively serious. Or was it a friendly, no-strings-attached invitation?

She probably could have spent several minutes debating the reason behind Alex's invitation, but she could tell from the look on his face she didn't have the time. And besides, she didn't want to offend him.

"Um, well, sure, I'd love to!" she said, shaking the hesitation out of her body." I mean, I don't want to impose. . ."

Her friend beamed. "Oh, no, not at all! We haven't had anyone over in ages, have we, AJ? And Ivy won't be there! You'll love our mom, she's chill, and the house is clean."

Acacia couldn't help but notice that AJ was looking at them with great interest, a quizzical look on his face. But as much as Acacia tried to probe into his mind, as he so frequently did to her, she again found herself facing down a solid brick wall.

"Well, since we're having company, *I'd* better get home to help Mother with dinner," AJ said after some time, his dark gray eyes amused. "Pierogi don't make themselves, you know. And besides, *you two* look like you haven't seen each other for weeks. Though, I'm not sure how that's even possible since you only met yesterday."

"Always have something to say, don't you?" In just a matter of seconds, Alex's face had turned bright red. "And what do you mean, we look like we haven't seen each other in weeks?"

"It means what it sounds like." AJ laughed as blue magic encircled him. "I'll see you back at the house." And with that, AJ too disappeared, leaving Acacia and Alex to their own devices.

"I used up a lot of magic today," Alex said, as if worried Acacia would ask him to teleport them as well. "Is it okay if we walk?"

"That's fine with me." Acacia silently marveled at the stark differences in the personalities of the three siblings. "I'd better ask my parents first, though. Are you sure it'll be okay with your mom?"

"Oh yeah," he replied. "Like I said, she's laid back. She has to be with the three of us. She works a lot and isn't home all the time, so we help with all the chores. AJ does a lot of the cooking, which is fine because he's pretty good at it. So, if they're both making pierogi, you know it's going to be a good dinner."

Acacia returned Alex's grin and pulled her phone from her pocket. "Good to know," she said, recalling that this would be the second day in a row she was coming home late. "Let me ask my mom before she freaks."

Chapter Seven

PIEROGI

After Acacia had received permission from her parents, she set out with Alex on an abbreviated tour through Silent Springs, past the high school and through the small downtown filled with shops and cafés. It was endearing, quaint in comparison to Sacramento.

"The downtown is the boundary between the magical and non-magical parts of town," Alex was saying. "This exact spot is supposed to be the original dividing line." The boy gestured at the crack in the pavement right in front of them. "Back in the day the mages figured it would be easier if they isolated themselves from the non-magicals. Nowadays it doesn't mean a lot since everyone goes wherever they want, and we all go to the same school."

"Interesting," Acacia said. "But I'm guessing the non-magicals don't know about us?"

Alex laughed. "No, or I hope not. Sometimes one of them will see something, or overhear people talking about magic, but most times they'll convince themselves they heard wrong. And plus, there's a whole committee on the Council whose job is to cover up things like that. So, it's not something we worry about as long as we're careful."

Acacia nodded, thinking back to what AJ had told her yesterday when she asked about the nurse's presence when she'd received her full powers. "That makes sense. I guess most non-mages would be afraid of people thinking they're crazy if they told someone what they saw."

They passed the former dividing line and turned onto one of the smaller streets, leading into the residential part of town, filled with old townhouses. "What's the deal with your siblings? They do *not* get along."

Alex shrugged. "They're too similar. They both got their powers around the same time. I think AJ's came like a week or so after Ivy's. So they've always had this competition thing going on, like who's the most powerful or whatever. Though Ivy's the one who cares about it. AJ's always too worried about something else to care too much." He looked at Acacia and grinned. "And then there's me. I'm not as smart or good with magic as either of them, but I also don't have a hero complex either. Like AJ for example, always worrying the stupid vacuum spell is going to open. The way I look at it, we've all got better things to do than worry about what might happen."

"That's a healthy outlook," Acacia said, agreeing with Alex more by the minute. "He told me all about that . . . prison as part of my lesson. He seems kind of obsessed with it."

They had left the heart of the town for its more bucolic outskirts. The homes here were farther away from each other, separated by large grassy yards.

"I just don't like to drive myself crazy with stuff out of my control," Alex said. "And I mean, my brother's intentions are good, but . . . I don't know. He and Mattes are always plotting something, and I think they both put themselves in a lot of bad situations. If I worry about anything, it's that one of them will get into trouble they won't be able to get out of."

"And your sister's intentions?" Acacia asked, raising her coppery brows.

The twin let out a nervous laugh. "That I'm not so sure about," he replied, walking up to the front door of a quaint, two-level home surrounded by a wild-looking yard. Alex opened the door and called, "Mom! AJ! We're here!"

"In the kitchen, Alex!" a woman's voice said over the clanging of pots and pans. "The pierogi just need to finish boiling, so be a dear and set the table."

Alex stepped past the entryway, motioning for Acacia to follow. "Mom, this is Acacia," Alex said, taking her hand and poking his head into the kitchen. "She's in a couple of my classes at school. It's okay she stays for dinner, right?"

As soon as Acacia saw the woman, she immediately knew she was the twins' and Ivy's mother. All members of the Swiatkowski family had the same slight build, light complexion, and dirty blond hair. In fact, Ivy appeared to be the spitting image of her mother except for her eyes. Where the twins' and their sister's eyes were differing shades of gray, their mother's were a bright blue.

Mrs. Swiatkowski was rolling up the last of what looked to be some kind of potato dumplings on a large wooden board, but she looked up when Alex spoke. From both her appearance and the attitude she emanated, Mrs. Swiatkowski appeared to be a friendly soccer mom, intense but approachable and nurturing.

"So, you're the famous Acacia Wheatley," the woman said, as she dusted the flour from her hands and greeted Acacia with a strong hug. "Alex here has been talking about you nonstop."

"Mom!" Alex hollered, his face beet red. "Don't—"

"Oh, hello there," a familiar voice commented. AJ stood watch over a pot of boiling water, which was filled with the same little dumplings

Mrs. Swiatkowski had been pinching together. The boy shot them both a glance that seemed to communicate that he knew what they had been up to, despite the fact that they hadn't been up to anything at all. "Acacia, Alex must have taught you the ever-popular skill of showing up when the food's ready."

Mrs. Swiatkowski grinned earlier before turning back to AJ and shooting him a rather intense glare.

"Andrew! don't be rude to our guest!" she ordered in a voice that was both soft and forceful. "Pay a bit more attention to making sure the pierogi don't stick together and a little less to tormenting your brother." Mrs. Swiatkowski turned to the newcomers. "Well, Alex, I did ask you to set the table. You don't want to make a bad impression, do you?"

Alex followed his mother's request, pulling four sets of light blue plates and silverware from a cabinet and setting them on a wooden table in the dining room. *C'mon Acacia,* he mind-spoke when he was finished, winking at her. *Looks like we're just about ready. Want to see our room before we eat? It'll only take a second.*

Grinning in return, Acacia nodded and followed Alex out of the room, sticking her tongue out at AJ as they passed the kitchen. She wasn't sure why, but her teacher had become quite smug following her and Alex's reunion in the meadow, almost as if he were accusing them of something. After her first full day of training, Acacia wasn't in the mood for attitude, particularly upon realizing she would have to tell her parents every detail about her dinner out.

Without another word, Acacia followed Alex through a small living room equipped with a piano, TV, and couch, and up a spindly staircase. They passed a bathroom and a bedroom painted bright yellow before they reached their destination.

"I mean it's not anything special, but it's home, y'know?" Alex said as he walked inside.

It was a small room, maybe only about three-quarters of the room Acacia shared with Sarison, with bunk beds, two desks, a closet, and a dresser. Acacia could easily guess which parts of the room were Alex's and which were AJ's, as certain sections were orderly to a fault, while others were a bit messy. The room had one large bookcase that looked as if its owner couldn't decide which types of books he enjoyed more and had decided upon all of them. There were some political science and sociology books, some devoted to philosophy and science, and finally a considerable number that seemed to deal with different magical themes: potion-making, defensive maneuvers, and so on.

Three guesses who those belong to, Acacia thought, picking up a book about something called circles of protection.

"Take anything you want," Alex offered, noticing her interest in the book. "My brother has more books than he knows what to do with."

Acacia grinned and put it back, looking at another magical text, *Sniffing: Reclaiming the Lost Art.* She opened it and flipped through its pages in interest. *Wow, I had no idea there were so many books like this around,* she thought. *I mean, maybe it shows how ignorant I am, but still. There's so much out there I have to learn.*

"Do you always take things that don't belong to you?" AJ asked, appearing abruptly in the doorway. Though his tone wasn't unfriendly, his gray eyes were stormy, fixed on the book in Acacia's hands.

A small black cat with a white spot on its nose had followed AJ upstairs, nuzzling its head against its owner's leg. It too, seemed to be glaring at Acacia, questioning how she had the audacity to enter its space.

Alex let out an exasperated sigh and turned on his brother "Didn't you hear what Mom said? That bit about not being rude to our guest? Or did you not remember why you got yelled at?"

AJ's gaze hadn't shifted from Acacia's grasp on his book. *There must be something about this that he doesn't want me to see. What, does he have his super magical secrets hidden in here somehow?* But she decided not to push it and placed the text back where she'd found it.

"Nice cat," Acacia said, pointing at the creature hiding behind AJ's leg. "What's its name? Midnight?"

"Merlin." AJ's anxiety seemed to have all but disappeared as soon as the book was returned to its rightful place. "But you two are late for dinner. Now come on, I had to sacrifice my jeans to the flour gods to make these pierogi."

"Children!" Mrs. Swiatkowski's voice sounded. "Dinner!"

Without another word, the three of them descended onto the main floor of the house.

***

Dinner with the Swiatkowski's was very pleasant; the twins' mother was constantly asking Acacia about herself, how she liked Silent Springs, and if she liked the pierogi. Acacia did her best to keep up with Mrs. Swiatkowski's questions but had no idea how to answer those about her family. Were her parents mages? How was it she hadn't known about the existence of magic until yesterday when her powers arrived in full force? Why was AJ teaching her instead of an older family member?

"Not that I don't think you're capable, dear, but it's better with someone a bit older," Mrs. Swiatkowski said. "Things just seem to work out better that way. We could always . . . go to the Council and request they appoint someone to teach her."

AJ swallowed a small piece of broccoli and cleared his throat. "You know how well getting the Council involved tends to work out, Mom." Meeting Acacia's gaze, the twin added, "Besides, I can handle it. All of this is new to Acacia, so there's no reason to overwhelm her even more with Council procedures and politics."

Mrs. Swiatkowski glanced in Acacia's direction. "I don't disagree with that bit, but I'm concerned about all of you. I think it's a rough time, going into a new school and then having to worry about all this. I just don't want anyone"—she glanced at her youngest son—"overextending themselves."

For the rest of the dinner, the conversation shifted back to the first two days of school, how classes were going, and what Acacia thought of Silent Springs so far.

"I'm glad you could join us," Mrs. Swiatkowski remarked several minutes later as the twins carried the dishes to the sink. "You're welcome here anytime. Now, come on, I'll give you a ride home. I wouldn't want to worry your parents."

"Oh, okay, thanks!" Acacia replied. "Everything was great. Are you sure I can't do anything to clean up?"

Alex snickered. "Don't worry about it," he started, the sarcasm evident in his voice. "Washing dishes is good for AJ's compulsions."

AJ rolled his stormy gray eyes but let the remark slide, instead focusing on filling the sink with water.

Mrs. Swiatkowski dug her keys out of her purse and headed toward the door. "One more question, dear," she began. "Your mother wouldn't happen to be Dervla Wheatley, would she?"

Acacia felt slightly taken aback. Picking up her bookbag, she replied, "Um, yes, actually. Do you know her?"

The twins' mother grinned. "You could say that. I've been trying to get in contact with her since you all moved back here. Come now, it *is* a school night, and I'd love to spend a few minutes catching up with your mother before it gets too late."

With that, Acacia followed her out to the car, wondering how this caring and cheerful woman knew her mother and why she had referenced the Wheatley's 'moving back' to Silent Springs.

Chapter Eight

DIONERA

The days that followed flowed into one another as Acacia fell into her new high school routine. As her training continued, she became much more comfortable using her magic, whether it was to attack, defend, or to magically block her mind from other mages. And despite their initial dispute, AJ was more than willing to teach her how to master her power.

"You're a quick learner," the twin said one September afternoon after Acacia had cast an invisibility charm on herself. "You'll make the others jealous if you're not careful."

Acacia smiled, ending the spell. Over the past weeks, she'd learned AJ wasn't one to say things he didn't mean, and had come to appreciate his rather scarce compliments. "I guess we'll just have to keep it our little secret then."

On weekends, Acacia went adventuring with Alex, hiking through the many trails surrounding Silent Springs or swimming in Lake Prosper, a natural body of water only a fifteen-minute hike from the Swiatkowski's house. It was a pleasant routine, especially considering how resistant Acacia had been to move to Pennsylvania. And with Alex, there was never any doom and gloom talk or the feeling that secrets were being kept from her as was commonplace with both AJ and Mattes. With Alex there were no mysteries or dilemmas, just living life as a young mage in a small town.

Nevertheless, soon warm September gave way to chilly October and Silent Springs began to prepare for Halloween. Spooky decorations made their way onto the windows and porches of homes, and signs for haunted houses and hayrides were posted throughout the town and school alike.

"They're funny, actually," Alex said, gesturing toward a sign for a haunted house in the stairwell leading to the cafeteria. "They don't do justice to real haunted houses though, like with actual spirits."

But in a town like Silent Springs, the peace and calm only lasted for so long. And it seemed the peace of the past few weeks would soon come to a screeching halt.

"I'm telling you, Mattes, I don't remember." AJ's voice became audible as Acacia and Alex rounded the corner, his voice higher and more strained than usual. "It's not like it happened yesterday."

"You don't remember or you don't *want* to remember?" Mattes fired back, his tone dripping with annoyance. "You need to work with me if we want that damn vacuum to stay shut."

The two boys were standing in the far corner in the nook of the staircase, speaking in hushed tones. Both wore grave expressions on their faces, looking like they had just seen one of the spirits Alex had mentioned.

"What vacuum?" Alex asked, walking over to join them. "What're you guys talking about?"

Mattes chuckled and ran a hand through his tousled hair. "Which vacuum? Why, only the single most important vacuum in the entire country, Alexander the Not So Great."

Alex and Acacia exchanged a pair of confused glances before turning back to their companions.

"Look, forget about it." AJ picked his bookbag off the floor. "This isn't the time or the place for this conversation."

"It's never going to *be* the time or place for this conversation," Mattes groaned. "You just don't want to think about it. Even though so many lives hang in the balance."

"Can you turn down the melodramatics, please?" Acacia wrinkled her nose at her friends. "You'd think this was the latest adventure movie playing at the theatre downtown."

"Sometimes real life is more unrealistic than fiction if you think about it. As much as we might not want it to be." AJ looked towards the cafeteria, his eyes distant, and slightly out of focus before gesturing for the other to follow. Seconds later, AJ and Mattes led the way to their regular lunch table, their body language as stiff as if they'd only recently recovered from a paralysis curse.

"So . . . what were you guys talking about?" Alex asked once everyone sat down. "And why is 'the most important vacuum in the country' in danger of being opened?"

Mattes let out a lengthy sigh and dug out a small photograph from his jacket pocket, which he handed to Alex and Acacia. On it was the image of a tall woman with curly, dark red hair, crouching in the branches of an oak tree. "This woman's been hanging out in the Bloody Meadow late at night, every night this week," Mattes explained, his hazel eyes intense. This was the second time Acacia had seen serious Mattes, and she couldn't help but feel unsettled. "From what I can tell, she's been inspecting the magical locks on the seal."

"Mattes thinks she's Dionera Tartaran." AJ took a peanut butter sandwich from his bag. "One of Sisyphus's minions who escaped after the end of the war."

The dark-haired boy narrowed his eyes at his friend. "And killed your father. Details, Andrew Swiatkowski."

So, she must be one of the homicidal redheads AJ was talking about, Acacia thought, blocking her mind from the others. *Well, she does look dangerous, I'll give him that.*

AJ turned to face his best friend, his gray eyes stormier than ever. "Matthias Knight, we have discussed this. I told you I *don't* remember, so will you drop it already?"

Mattes folded his arms in front of his chest and leaned forward, looking almost menacing. "And I told you, Andrew Swiatkowski, you don't *want* to remember. There's a distinct difference between the two."

At that moment Percy arrived at the table, his face riddled with confusion. "Hey, guys? How about we take it down, say, a few notches at least?"

Mattes and AJ looked at each other, glanced at Percy, and shrugged.

"It shouldn't matter if that woman is Dionera or not." After his abrupt outburst, AJ seemed to have returned to his typical state of calm rationality. "If she's been hanging around the Bloody Meadow, we can assume she's up to no good." *And the fact that the energy readings we've been getting have been even stronger than usual support that.*

"And what would you recommend that we do about it, Captain Obvious?" Mattes drawled, his tone bored. "Since you are *oh* so full of excellent ideas."

Acacia's mouth dropped open. Keeping the existence of magic secret to non-magicals was a matter of utmost importance to most mages, or that was the perception she got from spending time with her new friends. *But if it's so important, how can they be discussing somebody breaking into Sissy Puss's vacuum in the high school cafeteria?*

Sure, nobody's said 'magic,' but it's still possible for someone to figure it out!

Well, I mean they are both crazy, Alex mind-spoke to Acacia. *Being crazy makes you do a lot of weird things.*

Mattes turned to Alex, glaring daggers at him. *How many times do we have to tell you to close off your mind before you start talking about people? You're going to get yourself killed when you do it to the wrong person.*

Matthias Knight, cool it, AJ piped in. *I get that you're nervous, but there's not much we can do about it right now.*

Mattes rolled his eyes at his friend, his expression disgruntled. *Okay, so there may be a deadly assassin mage running around the forest trying to free Sisyphus and company, but we're all content to sit around and wait because there's 'not much we can do about it'?*

Well, this is escalating quickly, Acacia thought, glancing between AJ and Mattes. *Wonder what happens if they start fighting right here in the cafeteria?*

For one, we might get to see which one of them is the better fighter, Alex replied, winking at her. *I know they used to spar a lot, but AJ would never tell me who won most of the time.*

AJ glared at them, with the intensity of one who'd heard their entire conversation. *Maybe AJ does have a point,* Acacia thought, her face burning with embarrassment. *I'll have to try to remember to block my thoughts. But when I figured out how to do this, I didn't think I would be surrounded by a bunch of mind-readers!*

"I'm no mind-reader," Mattes said, his hazel eyes dancing in amusement. "I'm not a photographer either, but I can picture you and me together."

"Knock it off, already!" Alex yelled, rising to his feet. "No one thinks your pickup lines are funny!"

"Alex." Percy's blue eyes darted back and forth. *Don't forget where we are. I know I sound like a nag, but there's no need to make a scene.*

Mattes chuckled, watching their reactions as if they were as entertaining as his favorite TV show. Then again, Acacia doubted the boy had much time for TV while keeping order in the Underground. "Oh you, guys. Always so worried about poor little Matthias." He rose to his feet, shooting AJ a quizzical look. "Anyway, there's enough time for a quick chess match. That is, if you have the guts."

AJ's eyes widened. "You have the board and the pieces?"

"Of course. To the roof!"

Acacia's mouth dropped open in shock as she watched both boys sprint out of the cafeteria, their bags thrown over their shoulders. "Did they really just go from talking about deadly assassin mages to playing chess in, what, five seconds?"

"Like I said, they're both crazy," Alex explained with a shrug. "Honestly it's more disturbing when they have serious conversations like when we saw them in the hallway."

"As you can see," Percy chimed in with a wide grin. "Even when they *are* serious, it doesn't last long."

Acacia glanced between Alex and Percy, letting out a long sigh. "Every time I turn around, or breathe, it seems like I just have more and more to learn."

"Don't worry about it too much, Acacia," Percy said. "If you didn't have so much to learn, AJ wouldn't have enough to keep him busy. Think of it as community service."

Acacia laughed and refocused her energy on her lunch, pushing all thoughts of assassination mages and evil plots from her mind.

***

Several hours later, Acacia and the twins were in a clearing in the middle of the forest, all seated cross-legged with their hands cupped on their knees. By the end of the day, Ivy was nowhere to be found, so Alex had tagged along with Acacia's lesson. Acacia and Alex were supposed to be tracking sources of magic, but given the conversation at lunch, both were struggling to concentrate on their assigned task.

"So, is it really her?" Acacia asked, opening her eyes. "Dionera?"

AJ shook his head, his expression stoic. "Acacia, focus." As Acacia had come to learn, Andrew Swiatkowski was not one to be distracted when he didn't want to be.

"But it's a good question," Alex protested. "If it's the lady who killed Dad—"

"I think both of you need to work on your tracking skills," AJ told them. "Most mages underestimate the importance of tracking, but being able to locate sources of magic might make the difference between life and death. Especially if Sisyphus and his minions are close to escaping."

Acacia rolled her eyes and let out an exasperated sigh. *Here we go again,* she thought, this time consciously closing off her mind. *Another doom and gloom speech about Sissy Puss.*

"So, when's the big day?" Acacia didn't even bother to mask her irritation. "Since he obviously forgot to give us the memo."

A sardonic smile worked its way across AJ's face, and he reached out his right hand as if to catch something. "I do appreciate the challenges, Red. It helps keep things interesting."

"What the heck are you talking ab—" Alex began, his voice laced with confusion. But before he could finish his thought, his brother jerked his hand to the right and Acacia's bookbag flew into it.

"Andrew Swiatkowski, give me that back right now!" Thoroughly irritated, Acacia bolted to her feet. "Didn't your mother teach you not to take things that aren't yours?"

AJ stood up, a flicker of amusement in his dark eyes. "Like I mentioned, you need to practice your tracking, Find me." With that, the twin conjured a bright wall of blue magic and disappeared into it, leaving nothing behind but a scattering of leaves in his wake.

Acacia leaped to her feet and whirled around, wondering what had possessed AJ to run off with her things.

"He gets like that when he's frustrated," Alex explained, scratching his head. "I mean, it's not an excuse, but my brother has . . . interesting ways of managing stress."

She sighed in exasperation. "Or he just likes to push my buttons, him and Mattes both."

"Could be." Alex pushed himself to his feet, a look of urgency on his face. "Either way, looks like you'll have to track him down to get your stuff back. It's annoying, but it's probably a more interesting way of learning how to track than this meditation thing he had us doing. I'd love to help, but Ivy's calling me so I have to go. Good luck! I know you can do it!"

"B-but I don't know how to track!" Acacia stammered. "Is it hard?"

Alex shrugged. "Just remember how AJ's magic feels. Focus on that and use your own power to search for it. Then you might be able to teleport yourself to wherever he is. Bye!"

In an instant, Alex too had disappeared, leaving only a few blue sparks in his place.

Great, Acacia thought. *I'm in the middle of these stupid woods by myself and my teacher who's supposed to be helping me get ready in case Sissy Puss comes back is stealing my stuff, and my best friend is off training with his crazy sister. What now?*

Complaining isn't going to get you your things back, Acacia, AJ's voice said clearly in her mind. *Alex gave you some excellent advice, so do yourself a favor and follow it.*

Acacia let out another sigh of exasperation. *What was Alex's advice again? Focus on how AJ's magic feels and use my magic to find it? But what does AJ's magic feel like?* She wasn't sure she'd ever noticed . . . except for the first day when AJ had used his power to keep Acacia's own untamed power from destroying her. Then it felt cool and powerful, almost like a gentle ocean wave. Racking her brain, Acacia thought back to how it had felt when she had deflected the twin's attack with her own shield spell. Remembering the blue burst plowing into her shield, Acacia noted that it again had felt cool, but also precise, as AJ never used more energy than necessary. In other words, AJ's power just felt like AJ: cool, calm, and above all intelligent. It dawned on Acacia that this was how all mage's powers could be identified. Magic clearly wasn't just the different colored flashes of light a person could conjure. It was their entire person, including their strengths and weaknesses, as well as quirks and fancies. By latching on to this, it might be possible for any mage to locate any other mage, verify that they were unharmed, and even communicate with them telepathically.

I knew you could do it! Alex said, his tone brimming with equal parts excitement and pride. *Now go get your stuff!*

Acacia grinned and set to work tracking down her teacher.

***

AJ Swiatkowski sat atop one of the branches of his favorite oak tree, Acacia's school bag propped between his back and the tree's trunk. He hadn't planned on stealing his student's things to force her to practice her tracking abilities, but Acacia hadn't been the most cooperative either. The girl had made strides in learning to control her power, but she still lacked the level of concentration AJ had hoped she would've acquired by now. In that respect, Acacia was similar to Alex, who AJ knew from experience could be distracted in the blink of the eye.

Especially when Acacia was involved.

The twin pushed away his thoughts of frustration and removed the photograph Mattes had presented him with earlier that day from his jeans pocket. At first, he wasn't sure if he recognized the woman or not. After all, it *had* been ten years since he'd witnessed Dionera Tartaran murder his father. Now, away from all the distractions and chaos of the school cafeteria, it would've been impossible for him *not* to recognize her.

It's her, AJ mind-spoke to Mattes, his voice grave yet determined. *Dionera Tartaran.*

The one escapee from our parents' great aerial prison, Mattes responded. *Well, your parents' anyway.*

As much as the others struggled to understand his and Mattes's friendship, AJ had known when they first met that they'd be inseparable. Both he and Mattes had pasts marked by darkness and a sense of determination and desire to correct the wrongs of the past. They were also debatably too clever for their own good, but then again, they *had* won Mattes's title as Underground Lord at the ages of twelve and thirteen.

I figured you'd remember if you allowed yourself to, Mattes said. *That kind of thing you don't forget.*

I've been trying to forget for ten years, AJ reminded his friend. *Unsuccessfully.*

Mattes's voice chuckled in his mind. *I don't think watching your father die is something you forget. But what does this mean for us now?*

From what I've heard, Dionera Tartaran isn't any regular mage; she's a fire mage and an assassin. Even if we did want to take her down, it wouldn't be easy. What do you think, Drew?

Mattes was the only person in AJ's life to ever call him Drew. He remembered the day they met as well as if it had happened last week.

"'AJ' isn't a name," twelve-year-old Mattes had said. "It's initials. So I'm not calling you that."

"Fine," AJ had replied, shaking his head. "Call me what you want then."

Mattes smirked, his hazel eyes dancing. "Drew it is then," he proclaimed and the two shook hands. "Matthias Knight, at your service. But you can call me Mattes."

Hello? Earth to Drew, Mattes calling! His friend's voice was insistent in his mind. *Anybody home?*

AJ shook his head, stirring himself from his daydream. *Sorry. But we're in the same place we were before I remembered. We still have someone lurking around the meadow, but now we* know *she's a dangerous murderer and could burn the town to the ground if she wanted to.*

You're not answering the question, Drew, Mattes said. *What do you think we should do?*

It *was* a good question. How were they going to handle Dionera? Or better yet, *could* they handle her? They'd grown stronger over the years; after all, it *had* been through their joint effort that Mattes had become Underground Lord. But Dionera Tartaran was a well-known assassin mage, earning a reputation in the magical community as a menace with her set of lethal, cursed knives. From what AJ had learned from his research, Dionera always wore her opponents down with her fire-based attacks and saved the killing blow for her knives. Her knives, which she was alleged to lace with poison to ensure the success of her assassinations. Dionera Tartaran had never been unsuccessful in her attempt to take a life when one was marked for death. AJ was the only surviving witness to an assassination, which was more attributable to the fact that if she hadn't departed, Dionera would've had to fight her way through the entire Swiatkowski family.

She's deadly and she might remember I'm the one who got in the way. AJ shoved the picture back in his pocket. If the two of them continued to patrol the Bloody Meadow to monitor the energy levels, there was a chance Dionera would recognize him. *I'm a decent mage, Mattes, but so was my dad. And it didn't do him much good.*

We're going to be okay; you know that right? Mattes said, a hint of softness in his voice. No one else saw this side of Matthias Knight, the understanding, sensitive side. The side that would do anything for the people he cared most about, including placing his own life at risk. The side that wanted nothing more than for his people to be safe and happy. *We're a team, and a damn good one if I don't say so myself.*

AJ snorted rather loudly, then remembered he was supposed to be hiding from Acacia. *And that's why we can't act until we're certain we're making the best decision,* he said, allowing his logic to take over. *She's most dangerous with the element of surprise, so we make sure we don't give it to her.*

So . . . we wait?

We wait, and we watch, AJ said, this time with much more confidence. The main difference between the two of them was the fact that Mattes was more prone to acting upon his impulses, where AJ was more likely to plan. Order and chaos, joined together to make an unbeatable team. *If we find out for sure she's figured out a way to force the vacuum open, we must get others involved. It's too great a risk and threat for us to handle alone.*

Sounds good, Mattes agreed after a moment of silence. *Oh, and it looks like your student finally showed up.*

Later, Mattes, AJ said with a crooked grin and looked down to see a much more irritated Acacia Wheatley staring him down from the forest floor.

"You found me before I thought you would," he said, pulling the bag from behind his back. "I was assuming at least another ten minutes."

"Andrew Swiatkowski, this is *not* funny!" Acacia roared. "Give me my stuff back, now!"

She's got quite the temper. Mattes wasn't always the most tactful, but he usually had a good point. *Might want to work on that before incorporating her into any battle plans.*

AJ sighed. The current situation had piqued Mattes's interest enough for him to observe through AJ's eyes, which was possible only through the permanent connection spell they had cast two years earlier. That spell allowed them to perceive the world through the other's senses, see what the other was seeing, hear what the other was hearing and so on. This connection had proven useful on many occasions, especially during the night Mattes had defeated the previous Underground Lord in battle. However, one drawback of the spell was that it could be very difficult to keep Mattes out once he found his way in.

"Acacia, humor me," AJ began, setting the bag in front of him on the branch. "I'm an enemy mage and I stole something of high value from you, but you managed to track me down. What do you do next?"

Ah, situational training, Mattes commented. *Of course.*

Acacia continued to glare daggers at AJ. "Why can't you just be a normal person and give me my stuff back? I need it to do my homework!"

AJ shook his head. This was going to be more difficult than expected.

"For your information, Acacia, this is exactly how I was trained," he informed her in what he thought was a reasonable tone. "It's called situational training, and it was the majority of what my Uncle Jack did with me. As you might guess from the name, in situational training you're presented with a particular situation, and you use your magic to react."

"Why were you trained by your uncle instead of your mom?" Acacia asked, the frustration billowing from her body in waves. "Do you think men are better at magic than women?"

AJ rolled his eyes. "No, Acacia. Ivy was two weeks ahead of me in getting her powers, and my mother already had her hands full with her. As you might imagine. Plus, it's not the best form to have more than one student per teacher. Percy hadn't gotten his magic yet, so my uncle offered to teach me."

"You were two weeks behind Ivy?" Acacia repeated, arching her coppery brows at him. "Isn't she like . . . three years older than you? How old were you?"

"Eleven," AJ replied with a sigh. "But that's a story for another day, and you're evading the situation, which is the whole point of situational training. Now"—he paused, flashing Acacia the most challenging expression he could muster—"react."

She looked up at him for a few minutes before she smirked. AJ had come to know Acacia well enough to know a sarcastic comment was not far behind. "Well, why would an enemy mage want my bookbag? Seems a bit odd, don't you think?"

"I'll give you two pointers, and that's it." AJ held up his index and middle fingers of his right hand to prove his point. "One: Negotiate with me, convince me that I don't want whatever I took from you."

"And two?"

"Two. . ." The twin let his voice trail off. "Attack me. Force me to return your things. But whatever you decide, get on with it. If I were an enemy mage, I wouldn't be this passive."

"You, passive?" Acacia laughed. "You have to be joking."

"Acacia!"

"Okay, I'm working on it."

Acacia remained silent for several minutes, her left hand held in a loose fist next to her mouth. Finally, she opened her mouth again and began to speak.

"Mr. Enemy Mage, don't you think a bookbag is kind of boring? I mean I sure do! You could let me take it off your hands and get something way more exciting—"

I hope she never has to negotiate for any of our lives! Mattes exclaimed. *We'll all be dead before she said something coherent!*

"Okay, let's forget the negotiation for now," AJ ordered, ignoring Mattes's comment. "So . . . try attacking."

"Do you have a thing with having me attack you or something?" Acacia tapped her feet on the ground. "And isn't it kind of pointless? Since you have, what, three years of experience on me?"

"It doesn't matter," AJ told her, leaning back against the tree trunk. "There's no telling how many years of experience an enemy mage will have on you, and experience doesn't mean everything. So go for it."

Why is she so hesitant to attack you? Mattes asked. *Hell, when we were practicing, we fought all the time.*

I think it's because she's not used to the idea of it. AJ surveyed Acacia, keeping his eyes open for any sign of movement. *Before this year, she probably never thought she'd have to attack anyone, never mind hordes of minions.*

You're not exactly 'hordes of minions,' Drew, Mattes said in an offhand tone. *And I'm guessing you're the only one she's attacked yet.*

AJ shook his head and then noticed that while he had been caught up with his telepathic conversation, Acacia had vanished.

We're attacking from alternate directions now, he thought, rising to his feet atop the branch and glancing right, then left, to get an idea where she had gone. *Not bad.*

AJ closed his eyes and inhaled deeply through his nose. Unbeknownst to many, the twin was what the magical world called a Sniffer, a mage with the inborn ability to smell magic. Most mages could track others' auras through their own powers, as Acacia had learned to do. However, the tracking ability of non-Sniffers was limited by many factors, including the strength of their magic and their level of concentration. Unlike non-Sniffers, AJ had been able to detect the smells of different auras and spells, and even Sniff out individuals with other special abilities, such as Seers and Shapeshifters, since he was a small child. AJ hadn't seen fit to tell Acacia about this yet, as she had enough difficulty staying focused the way it was. *When she's a little more experienced,* AJ reasoned. *Once I'm more confident she won't go into some type of shock from having so much information thrown at her at once.*

Acacia's magic smelled like a thunderstorm, the combination of a fierce downpour of rain and a bit of a smoky fire along with it. A complex smell for a complex girl. And right now, that complex girl was directly above him in the air.

AJ swung his right arm in a semicircle above his head, conjuring his shield just in time for Acacia's green bolts of lightning to crash into it. The girl had used her power to propel herself high up into the trees and then leaped off from wherever she had landed with her lightning spell ready. However, she didn't seem to have planned out what she would do after she attacked him. As soon as Acacia's attacks fizzled out, AJ dropped his shield and the girl began to free fall from above, barely saving herself by grabbing hold of the branch.

"You're getting more creative," AJ complimented her, tilting his head to the left. "You might want to work on your landings though."

Acacia stuck her tongue out at him and summoned her bag before letting go of the branch and falling to the forest floor below.

Maybe she's cleverer than I first thought. Mattes sounded impressed, and impressing Matthias Knight was no easy task.

Don't you have anything better to do? AJ growled. *I'm in the middle of a lesson here.*

Suit yourself. Later.

AJ shook his head and leaped off the branch after Acacia, landing on his feet a few yards away from where she was currently slinging on her bag, preparing to make a run for it.

"So, you're just going to let the enemy mage go without a fight?" he challenged. "Kind of anticlimactic for a situational training session."

Acacia's vivid green eyes shone with irritation. "What's the point, AJ? You're just going to block everything anyway. That's what happens everytime you insist on me attacking you."

AJ let out a short laugh and grinned crookedly. "It's called improvisation, Acacia. If you're trying to hit me and my shield's in the way, find a way to get around it."

Acacia rolled her eyes and charged at him, launching balls of green power in his direction. AJ dodged them, but with every flash he evaded, two more took its place.

Interesting, he thought. *Rapid assault to keep me from summoning the shield. Again, not bad. Not good enough, but not bad.*

AJ stopped dodging and positioned his feet in a solid stance. One of the flashes hit him squarely in the shoulder, but he ignored it and crossed his arms in front of his face. Acacia launched a strong lightning spell at him. However, at the precise moment before it made contact, AJ rotated both his wrists and Acacia's green lightning hit a pale blue screen, causing it to careen back at her at full force. The girl gasped and tried to summon a shield of her own but was slammed into the ground by the brunt of her own attack.

"That's called a reflective spell, Acacia," AJ informed her, as if he was doing nothing more than explaining a homework assignment. He walked over to where the girl was trying to push herself to her feet, scanning the damage he had done. To AJ's relief, Acacia wasn't too banged up, just a few burns on her arms and face. "I've found them useful over the years, especially since they can be used for—"

Acacia grabbed his left ankle with an iron hold. AJ studied her for a moment before realizing what she was doing.

"You can be an annoying know-it-all sometimes," Acacia grunted as she sent a current of green electricity coursing up through AJ's leg.

Definitely getting there, AJ thought, dislodging the girl's grasp with a single blue flash of light before the spell reached his knee. *Who knows, maybe we'll have a decent team by the time they all break out.*

One can only hope, Mattes's voice piped in again. *For all we know, that could mean next week.*

Now AJ was annoyed. While he didn't mind Mattes keeping an eye on what he was doing, there were times when AJ wished his friend would let him do his work in peace.

"Matthias Knight, I said I would talk to you later!" he exclaimed, before noting Acacia's perplexed expression.

"Everything okay up there?" she asked, standing up and rapping on his forehead like it was a door. "Is someone a little iron deficient?"

"Sorry about that," AJ said, feeling his face redden in embarrassment. He knew Acacia told Alex everything that happened during her lessons, and he wasn't in the mood for all the ribbing he would get at home. "How about you though, are you all right?"

"Oh yeah, I mean you wouldn't think a 'little lightning spell' would hurt me or anything I hope," Acacia retorted with a broad smirk. "But I'll have you know that if you ever touch my bookbag again, I will. . ."

The girl went on, describing what she would do, but AJ's nostrils were suddenly filled with a fiery smell, one much stronger than that emitted by the stormy scent of Acacia's magic. *Someone else is here. And something tells me they're not friendly.* AJ Sniffed the air, searching for a trace of whoever, or whatever the fiery scented magic belonged to, realizing with a jolt that the scent was familiar, something he had Sniffed before, a long time ago.

"Um . . . AJ?" Acacia poked him in the shoulder. "Is everything okay?"

"Sorry, Acacia," AJ replied briskly, taking a firm hold of her hand. "We have to go . . . *now.*"

With that, AJ teleported them back to the woods outside the high school, the image of his father's killer burned into his mind.

Chapter Nine

THE BLOODY MEADOW

In the days that followed her first experience with situational train-ing, Acacia thought both AJ and Mattes seemed a bit off, but wasn't certain how to broach the topic. After all, she suspected asking if they were running around chasing Dionera would result immedi-ately in them shutting down and refusing to ever open up to her about anything serious.

"Their problem is they're both crazy," Alex said one Saturday af-ternoon as they sat on the edge of the lake. Now that the temperatures had dropped, it was too cold to go in the water, but it was still a pleasant hangout spot. "The more important question is . . . what are we doing for Halloween?"

Acacia grinned. With Alex, there were no evil mages on the verge of escape or shadows lurking behind every rock. With Alex, Acacia felt like she could just be . . . Acacia. "What do you usually do for Halloween? Don't forget, I'm New Girl."

"Well. . ." Alex rubbed his chin with his index finger. "We magic folk don't go trick or treating or any of that stuff. Halloween's more of a non-magical holiday, but that doesn't mean we can't do something."

"Something like?" Acacia picked up a small stone and tossed it at the lake's surface, causing it to skip across the water. "Watching scary movies, finding a haunted house. . ."

Alex looked off into the heavens above. "Have you ever been to the Bloody Meadow? The one where Sisyphus and company are locked up in the sky?"

Acacia sat up straight as a board. "Your brother took me there once, on the first day of training. And made me promise to never go back unless I was with him."

"AJ is the most paranoid person I know." Alex stood up and offered Acacia his hand. She took it, and her friend pulled her to her feet. Alex was stronger than he looked, which Acacia assumed came from the combination of soccer and magical training. "C'mon, Acacia, I've never known you to back away from a challenge. And we won't do anything. We'll just walk up, look, and come back. What harm could it do?"

I'd feel a lot better if I knew you weren't running around here by yourself, AJ had said.

What reason had he given for not wanting her to return to the Bloody Meadow? Something about not being able to hide her power from the mages locked inside the vacuum? Well, it *had* been over two months since the day of her first training, hadn't it? Surely, she would be able to hide her and Alex's magics if she needed to. After all, everyone was always telling her what a quick learner she was, especially since she'd learned of the existence of magic on the first day of school.

"Why do you want to go, Alex?" Acacia asked, peering into her best friend's face. Alex was prone to whims, but he always had a reason behind the whim. "I mean, I'm down, but it doesn't seem like a place you go to hang out."

Alex's expression was calm and serious, his light gray eyes gleaming like small silver moons. "You probably know already," he said, scratching his head. "But everyone always underestimates me, thinks I'm either weak, scared, or silly. Mattes, my brother, even Percy and Percy never has a bad thing to say about anyone. And I'm not weak or scared or any of that!"

Acacia squeezed her friend's hand. "I know you're not, Alex. I know it's hard, but we can't care what other people think. If they have something to say, let them say it."

"I know. But sometimes you have to do something to prove yourself, y'know? Show them all that you're just as good as they are, even if you get scared and mess up."

"Alex, everyone messes up," Acacia reassured him. "Mattes, for all his 'Bask-in-my-sheer-awesomeness,' teleported yesterday and ended up outside my house thinking he was somewhere in the Underground. Nobody's perfect."

The boy smiled at her, the excitement clear on his face. "Okay, I get it. But I still want to go. I haven't been there in years, and I'm curious if it looks any different from how I remember it. So..." Alex let his voice trail off. "Acacia Wheatley, are you in?"

Acacia stretched out her neck. No one had mentioned Sisyphus or Dionera since last week. Surely if any major development had happened either AJ or Mattes would have mentioned something . . . right?

It was Acacia's turn to grin. "Well, you don't think I'd let you go by yourself, do you?" Turning back to take in the breathtaking image of the lake at sunset, she added, "Mr. Swiatkowski, it would appear we have a date."

"Sounds like it," Alex said with a nod. "I'll pick you up at eight."

***

Matthias Knight was uneasy, perhaps the most uneasy since he and Drew overthrew the previous Underground Lord. The hours before the events of that night unfurled had been racked with tension and uncertainty, but tonight seemed just as bad.

Something's going to happen . . . tonight, Mattes thought, running a hand through his hair. He knew it was a nervous habit, but most of the time, it came across as part of the self-assured façade he worked so hard to uphold. *Forces of darkness are gathering.*

Mattes stalked the hallways of the Underground, deep in thought and barely conscious of what was happening around him. So deep in thought that he walked headlong into a steel door.

"Everything all right, sir?" Lyon, one of Mattes's scouts asked from around the corner. Lyon was an excellent scout, thirteen years old and filled with youthful energy. Lyon could, however, be a bit nosey for Mattes's liking.

Mattes massaged his temples, hoping to avoid a headache. He wasn't in the mood for dealing with scouts, or anyone else for that matter. Talk had been going around lately of the possibility of a revolt, despite Mattes's fair governance and dedication to justice. *Oh well. I guess it comes with the territory.* After all, he *had* been in power now for two years, and two years was more than enough time to gain some enemies.

And gain enemies he had.

"Yes, Lyon," he replied, working to keep the emotion from his voice. "Your Underground Lord is just a bit distracted."

According to hearsay, Lyon had been as unjustly condemned to the Underground as Mattes had been. After the end of the first war, the Council had exiled a large number of mages who might have participated in some illicit dealings to the Underground. Only because of the hard work of a certain junior Council member could Mattes and the other minors in the Underground venture aboveground for school.

Mattes thought back to his father, Elias Knight, who'd been convicted of high treason and sentenced to death by the Council five years earlier. Of course, Elias had worked for Sisyphus during the war, but unlike the idiots who'd gotten themselves locked in the vacuum spell, the man kept a low profile and continued to enact acts of violence against magical society. Finally, Elias was caught, found guilty, and sentenced to death by fire. After that, the Knight family was torn apart, as Mattes and his mother Ilsa were exiled to the Underground and his little sister Emily was sent off to some foster family. The official reasoning was that in no way could Ilsa and Mattes not have known about Elias's illicit dealings, while Emily, a mere child, had to be innocent.

Still, Mattes had been a child too, hadn't he? Technically he *still* was, though most of the time it didn't feel like it.

Upon learning the truth of Elias's secret life, Ilsa turned to drugs. Ten-year-old Mattes soon realized he was on his own and learned to do what he needed to survive, creating alliances among some of the most powerful dissidents of the previous Underground Lord. Three years later, Mattes *became* the Underground Lord.

"You might want to un-distract yourself, sir," Lyon advised, skipping a stone off the floor. "Everyone's saying Nikolaos is working on a plan to overthrow you."

Mattes smiled and patted the boy on the shoulder. "You leave the worrying to me, all right, Lyon?" He made a mental note to check on the mentioned plotter when he had the chance. Nikolaos Lacken had been one of the previous Underground Lord's strongest adherents and had almost caused Mattes's plan to fail three years ago. Mattes wouldn't put it past the man to stage another coup once presented with the opportunity. "You know how the saying goes about great power and great responsibility . . . and I do have the power."

The thirteen-year-old nodded and disappeared down one of the cavernous passageways.

You feel it coming, don't you? Mattes mind-spoke to Drew, leaning against the iron doorway. *I think it's happening tonight.*

His friend didn't respond right away. They had both been distracted since Drew had recognized the strange new mage as Dionera Tartaran, but Mattes knew from experience that they'd come through when they needed to.

I mean, it's Halloween and a full moon, Drew replied, sounding a bit more somber than usual. *Is it really something out of the ordinary for these circumstances?*

I don't know, Mattes responded. *How prepared do you think your student is?*

As well prepared as she could be with only two months of training, his friend said in a flat tone. *I can only do so much with so little time. And besides, you know as well as I do that the battlefield is the most effective training ground.*

Mattes nodded in agreement. Truth be told, he *was* somewhat impressed with Acacia's skills after watching her training session through his connection with Drew. From the looks of it, they'd be able to put up a decent fight when something happened, if none of them were killed first.

I'm going to take care of something, Drew said, his tone brisk. *Keep the connection open and let me know if anything crops up.*

Same to you, Mattes replied. *Be careful, wherever you're going.*

Matthias, I'm always careful.

Sure you are.

At that exact moment, a blood-curdling scream came from one of the far corridors, chilling Mattes to the core. Wordlessly, he tore off in a mad dash in that direction, hoping that whatever awaited him wasn't as awful as it sounded.

***

Alex kept his word about picking Acacia up on Halloween, arriving at the girl's house at eight o'clock on his bike. At first, Acacia hadn't been too keen on hopping on the back of the boy's two-wheeler but soon reasoned that she'd already engaged in much more reckless behavior on a daily basis.

"We can hang out at the house for a little bit," Alex said, whizzing through the neighborhood. "Put on a scary movie or something."

"Sounds good." Acacia held on to the boy's back for dear life. "As long as I'm back by ten."

They arrived at the Swiatkowski's home within minutes and settled in the family room. The house seemed eerily silent, especially in comparison to the last time Acacia had been there, when even Ivy had ventured out of her room to socialize.

"Mom's at the Golecs," Alex said. "And Ivy's over at Jared's house again. It's just me and AJ, and I haven't seen him come out of the room in at least an hour."

Acacia raised her coppery brows. "That's kind of odd, isn't it? Isn't he usually off doing . . . whatever it is that he does?"

Alex shrugged and flipped on the television. The two of them spent a few minutes trying to find a decent scary movie, deciding on one involving a family who had moved into a house possessed by malevolent spirits. After a good half hour or so, AJ emerged from the twins' shared room looking more somber than usual and proceeded to the closet.

"Going somewhere?" Acacia asked as the boy slipped on a black fleece jacket.

"The cemetery." AJ didn't so much as glance in their direction.

Odd, Acacia thought, closing her mind off to both twins. *He's usually a bit more talkative than this.*

"And what are you planning on doing at the cemetery?" Alex looked away from the TV as five or six ghosts emerged from the little girl's ceiling. "Going ghost hunting?"

"I'm going to see Dad," AJ replied in a factual tone, as if they should've known what he was doing. "Bye." Without another word, he departed, closing the door behind him.

After the door clicked shut, Alex turned the television off. "Now that he's out of the way, you ready?"

Acacia arched her brows at him. "Were we just waiting for your brother to leave? You know we could have left from my house."

The twin shrugged. "I wanted to hang out with you here for a bit, as long as you were okay with it," he explained, pushing himself to his feet. "Now c'mon, don't you want to go now?"

She let out a particularly long sigh and shook her head. Tonight, it wasn't just AJ who was being difficult.

***

Acacia and Alex trudged through the pitch-black forest, their way lit only by Alex's blue orb. The meadow was much farther away than Acacia realized; it had taken her and AJ only seconds to teleport there from the area they had used for training, but everything seemed closer when all one had to do was teleport from one place to another. She stopped for a moment to look up at the night sky. It was a cold night, and the heavens were dark, littered with stars, with the full moon gleaming with a yellowish glow. The forest surrounding them was quiet as well, quiet as the grave.

"We're almost there," Alex said, breaking the silence. "I think."

"So, when was the last time you were here?" Acacia narrowly avoided tripping over a large rock.

Alex stepped on a twig, causing it to snap loudly. "About two years, I think. I know we have to take threats seriously, but there's no way the others aren't overreacting. Like, do they really think Sisyphus is going to escape just because a couple mages are walking by?"

He pushed a large branch out of the way, holding it until Acacia passed. From that point, the heavily wooded path opened into a wide meadow, the sky alight with flashing colors.

Well, here we are, Alex mind-spoke with a crooked grin. *The Bloody Meadow.*

They both took a seat in the tall grass on the far side of the meadow, closest to the thick forest. Acacia stared up into the vacuum spell, watching as flashes of light flew chaotically above them and crashed into an invisible wall. Acacia could feel the sheer power contained within the vacuum, just as she had when she'd been there with AJ.

Alex slid his hand under hers. "See? No cataclysmic event. Now do you believe me when I tell you they're all paranoid?"

Acacia laughed and allowed herself to lean into the boy. "I never said I didn't believe you. I just—"

"Now what do we have here?" a shrill female voice cackled from far above their heads.

Acacia and Alex spun around as fast as they could and saw a tall, slim woman with a fiery mess of red hair perched up in a tree. She looked to be in her late twenties or early thirties and appeared athletic, as if she had spent her life training for a competition. Without another word, she leaped from the tree and landed several feet away from the two teenagers with catlike grace.

Acacia and Alex scrambled to their feet.

That's her, *isn't it?* Acacia asked, her mind racing. *That woman from Mattes's picture?*

It has to be, Alex replied, stepping in front of her.

"Who are you anyway?" he demanded. "And what do you want?"

The woman laughed in a way that almost seemed psychotic. "Now *you* look familiar," she said, her voice dripping in arrogance as she studied Alex with orange eyes. "Have we met?"

"I said who the hell are you?" The combination of the yellow moon and the flashing auras cast an odd pallor on Alex's face.

"And what business do you have here?" Acacia said, stepping forward so she was even with her friend. "Or if you haven't any, get out!"

"I must say, I'm a bit disappointed," the woman said with a short sigh. "Here I was thinking my reputation preceded me . . . but clearly I was mistaken."

Acacia opened her mouth to yell something else at the intruder, but before she could, the woman moved, firing an orange blast from her outstretched hand. Acacia and Alex ducked for cover and watched as the strike passed over them and—to Acacia's horror—turned to fire and encircled the entire meadow.

"I am Dionera Tartaran," the woman said, her eyes reflecting the fire surrounding them. "And I am the mage who will restore Lord

Sisyphus to his full power. And you two will stay for the festivities. I'm positive he will be more than thrilled to have some fun after all these years."

Something about the way Dionera said 'fun' made Acacia's skin crawl.

"We won't let you!" Acacia yelled. She knew she was bluffing and was certain Dionera knew as well, but what else could she do? All she knew was the woman had to be stopped. Acacia couldn't sit by and watch as this pyromaniac freed those monsters. . .

"You think you can stop me?" Dionera laughed again, this time even more maniacally. "You must be joking!"

A flash of blue materialized in front of Acacia and Alex, adding more color to the strangely lit meadow. The light soon faded, and AJ assumed a protective stance between them and Dionera.

"*I'm* not," he retorted at the enemy mage. Turning to Acacia and his brother, AJ mind-spoke, *You two get out of here, now. I can't defeat her if I have to worry about covering you too.*

No! Acacia responded, hearing the anxiety in her voice.

We're not leaving you here by yourself, Alex added. *No way, no how.*

Well, you're not helping me fight, AJ said, without taking his eyes from Dionera for even a second. *You two don't have the battle experience.*

And you do? Acacia glared daggers at her friend.

The boy shifted on his feet and flashed her a challenging glance before turning back to face their foe. *You have no idea.*

"You I definitely remember." Dionera touched her index finger to her chin. "*You're* Swiatkowski's brat! The little boy who got in the way!"

AJ inhaled sharply and took a step backward. "I'm bigger now," he retorted, regaining his icy composure. "So, you're not doing anything without going through me first."

Dionera laughed uncontrollably for several minutes. "I drove a dagger through Joseph Swiatkowski's heart without blinking! Or did you forget about that, brat? What makes you think *you'll* fare any better?"

"I'm faster," AJ replied, bringing his right arm across his body, sparks of blue magic appearing at his fingertips.

Andrew, you can't do this! Alex exclaimed, his eyes wide with fear. *You heard her, she killed Dad, she'll kill you too!*

I know what I'm doing, Alex, AJ's voice was unnervingly calm. *And besides, Mattes is on his way.*

Dionera stared the three of them down, a broad smirk crossing her face. "Well, since you want to die, I'll be more than happy to grant your wish!"

Dionera lunged forward, the beginnings of another blast of flames at her fingertips. Within milliseconds, AJ shoved both Acacia and Alex to the ground and rotated his wrist, conjuring a solid blue shield. Dionera's orange fire beat into the shield like wildfire, but the twin showed no sign of being worried. He glanced back at his companions and communicated telepathically, *You two get behind that boulder over there*—he gestured to the large rock with his eyes—*or I'll put you there myself!*

Acacia grabbed Alex by the hand and obeyed. As much as she didn't care to admit it, AJ did seem to know what he was doing. The question was if he—or he and Mattes—would be able to defeat Dionera.

It's going to be okay, Acacia assured Alex, giving his hand a gentle squeeze.

I sure hope you're right, he said. With nothing else to do, the two peered over the top of the rock protecting them and watched the battle unfold.

"You're stronger than I thought," Dionera told AJ. "I'll have to stop underestimating you."

AJ shifted his weight to his left leg, both arms extended out in front of him, palms facing the enemy mage. Despite his initial aggressive comment, he showed no interest in engaging in a battle of wits with his opponent.

Dionera sneered. "Well, try dodging this!" she challenged, shooting what appeared to be a whirlwind of fire at the boy.

AJ froze momentarily. But as the fire whirled toward him, he tapped his right foot on the ground and propelled himself into the air using the strength of his left leg. A sphere of bright blue light appeared from his palms and grew until it was about half the size of Dionera's fire spell. Blue collided squarely with orange, and in midair, AJ pushed off his sphere with both hands and flipped over both attacks, landing on his feet. This time, he lunged at Dionera, sending a wave of magic spiraling at her.

Holy crap, he's fast, Acacia commented to Alex. *I mean, I knew he was fast, but not* that *fast.*

And she is too, Alex replied. *Neither of them has made a direct hit yet, so it's hard to say who's better. But my brother's fighting scared, which isn't good. I just hope Mattes gets here soon.*

Fighting scared? Acacia repeated, confused. *How?*

Alex frowned and tapped his head. *Remember that freaky twin thing? I can tell. Don't get me wrong, he's hiding it well, so I doubt Dionera knows. But yeah, so far, he hasn't gone into panic mode, so hopefully it'll stay that way.*

Dionera, meanwhile, seemed to be becoming frustrated that she hadn't been able to hit the boy.

"You're wasting my time, brat!" she called and, launching herself into the air, fired a rampage of orange bursts.

AJ rolled his eyes and dodged the blasts without much effort. "Could you give me a little more credit than that? Everyone knows rapid fire is one of the most—"

"AJ!" Acacia hollered frantically, watching as the fire reared and made its way for her friend again. "Those attacks aren't gone yet!"

AJ spun around and crossed his arms in front of his body, conjuring a quick shield where they intersected. But, to Acacia's shock, the rampage of attacks passed right through AJ's shield and hit him squarely, plowing him into the ground.

"Andrew!" Alex cried out. He began to climb over the boulder, and it was only with great effort that Acacia was able to pull him back.

"I gather you're not a fan of my boomerang fire." Dionera sauntered across the meadow, her movements almost like that of a predatory animal. "Though *I* wouldn't be either, if I were run down by it."

AJ let out a brief groan and pushed himself to his feet, his dirty blond hair singed and small burns apparent on his face.

AJ, stop it now, Alex pleaded. *Let's all go and let someone else deal with this. We can't handle her.*

AJ glanced over in their direction, his gaze stormy and determined. *I don't just run away from my problems. I would have thought that by this time, you* wouldn't *either.* He paused, lifting his right hand so it was level with his nose, his thumb pointed inward. A minuscule blue sphere appeared in the palm of his hand, looking almost like a tiny star. *I'm not sure this will work, but even if it doesn't, it should at least scare her.*

"What a nice little nightlight you have there, little boy," Dionera cackled, her orange eyes gleaming with malice. "Is that like the ones Daddy used to—"

AJ began to glow blue, with the center of his power coming from the tiny orb. Acacia had no idea what he was doing, but she was certain that whatever it was, it was going to be impressive.

Crap, Alex said in a worried tone. *It's a destruct—*

The entire sky lit up in blue light. Acacia and Alex were blown back several feet and could only watch as AJ's spell tore through the meadow, seemingly destroying everything in sight. Once the light had faded, Acacia noted it had bulldozed the high grass and obliterated a number of trees.

"Well," a familiar voice spoke from a flash of yellow light. "At least they won't have to mow the lawn."

Seconds later, Matthias Knight materialized in the middle of the meadow about two feet from where AJ was still standing. From what Acacia could see, Mattes too looked worse for wear, with a considerable deal of swelling around his left eye and a few bruises on his face.

AJ grinned weakly and staggered over to his friend. "It sure took you long enough, Mattes," the twin commented, looking a bit unsteady on his feet. "I hope your situation wasn't . . . oh, what—"

"I had a run-in with jolly old St. Nick. If we make it out of here alive, he's going to make himself quite a nuisance." Mattes's hazel eyes searched the meadow for a trace of the enemy mage. "I *do* hope you managed to disable that witch with that destruction spell of yours."

"Now, you I don't remember." Dionera appeared in a flash of orange several yards away. While she didn't seem to have been hit directly by the destruction spell, she hadn't dodged it completely either, given the burn marks across her face and jumpsuit. "No matter. You can join the festivities as well."

"How kind of you." Mattes snorted and cast a disdainful look in the woman's direction. Turning to AJ, he extended his hand, which was gleaming with bright yellow magic. "What do you say we finish this now?"

AJ nodded and the two linked arms. Blue magic spiraled from AJ and yellow from Mattes in ribbons of light. Acacia and Alex exchanged worried glances and sprinted to where their companions were standing in the middle of the devastated meadow, preparing to attack.

"You don't have to do this by yourselves!" Acacia yelled. "Let us help you!"

"Four is bound to be better than two!" Alex shouted.

"Why are you two still here?" Mattes demanded, stealing a fleeting backward glance at them. "Get out while you can. Tonight's not the night for your first battle."

"Why won't you guys let me help?" Acacia clenched her fists, feeling the power within her begging to be set free. "AJ, you've been telling me I'm a natural for two months now. Why are you being so headstrong?"

"We've done this kind of thing before, Acacia." Mattes voice was level but held an alarmed quality she hadn't heard before. "For three years. It's not about not having a good opinion of you—"

"We're trying to protect you," AJ said, his voice strained. "And the best way to do that right now is to get you out of here. There'll be another day for you to fight."

"I wouldn't be too certain of that, boy!" Dionera roared, lunging for the four of them.

It was obvious Mattes and AJ worked well together; in fact, they seemed to work off each other's thoughts, knowing exactly what the other was about to do and responding in the way to best complement that action. They both fired a wave of power to halt Dionera in her tracks, creating an intertwined spiral of blue and yellow. In response, Dionera launched her own blast of orange magic, and the competing sets of attacks collided with one another, filling the sky with a thunder of static.

They can't do it, Acacia thought. *Maybe if they were both feeling at their strongest, they could, but they're both pretty beat down.*

But the question was, what could she do? If she did nothing, Dionera would bludgeon them to within an inch of their lives and destroy the enchantments holding Sisyphus and his cronies in the vacuum above, freeing them to wreak havoc upon the world. If she *did* do something, it was possible the same fate would befall them. Still, Acacia felt in her heart that she had to at least try. Ignoring AJ's and Mattes's warnings, Acacia fired a single beam of green at Dionera's chest.

The moment her spell left her body, Acacia knew in her gut something horrible was about to happen. Mattes was yelling about something, but she didn't know about what, or care, for that matter. She could only watch in shock as her beam of power was sucked, as if by a black hole, into the sky above.

"How darling of you, my dear!" Dionera exclaimed, her face twisted into a vicious snarl. "Lord Sisyphus told me that he and Minos could best use Swansgrove magic to escape—and turns out, that's you!"

Acacia had no idea what the woman meant by 'Swansgrove magic' but could only watch in horror as her attack disappeared into the vacuum and a ragged hole formed dead center. Hell was about to be unleashed into the small town of Silent Springs, and no one could do anything about it.

"Mattes, cover me!" AJ yelled at the top of his lungs over the incredible whooshing sound from the widening hole in the vacuum spell. The twin sprinted through the meadow and positioned himself beneath the gaping hole, shot both arms high into the sky, and fired a stream of blue into the weakening enchantment above. Acacia watched in wonder as AJ's power flowed up and filled the jagged hole, keeping it closed for now.

"Goddamn it, Drew," Mattes whispered, his hazel eyes filled with worry. "You've no idea what you're doing."

Whatever was at the point of escape was not thrilled by this latest complication. Shortly after the hole had been temporarily sealed, something fired a current of black lightning down at AJ, electrifying him every second he maintained the spell shut.

"Sound the alarm!" The distress and pain were evident in AJ's voice as he called out to his friend. "I won't be able to hold it closed much longer!"

"Mattes!" Acacia said, her eyes staring up into the hole in the sky. It was like a horror movie she and Alex might watch on a weekend, except this was real. "What's he talking about, the alarm?"

Mattes let out an exasperated sigh, grabbed Acacia and Alex by the wrists, and took off for the center of the meadow, dragging them along with him. "This spell," he explained, the wind blowing his messy dark hair in every direction possible, "will send out a distress signal that can be seen and heard by every mage within a twenty-mile radius." The boy paused, casting a fearful glance across the field. "It might be our only chance to get out of here alive."

With that, Mattes extended his right arm into the sky, his index and middle fingers pointed upward, and shot a single stream of yellow energy into the blackness of the night. Mattes's spell continued up for what seemed like forever, until it finally stopped and exploded, creating at least ten small blasts in the sky.

"Well, that's that," Mattes said, dusting his hands off. "Now let's hope someone shows up before we're all dead."

"Guys!" AJ yelled, his voice weaker than ever. "I . . . I can't— "

"No!" Acacia, Alex, and Mattes all screamed simultaneously. But it was too late. AJ's eyes rolled back into his head as his body went limp, and he began to collapse. Alex ran forward as fast as he could and caught his brother, tears streaming down his face.

"Andrew, no," the boy pleaded, shaking his unconscious brother. "C'mon, please. . ."

Both Mattes and Acacia stared in horror at the hole in the sky above, which was now expanding at an astounding rate.

"You won't wake him that way," Mattes said in an aloof voice. "He's gone and drained himself holding that damn thing shut. Though given the present circumstances, it might not be a bad way to go."

Blue light flashed next to where they stood, and seconds later, Percy stepped from it, looking flustered. "I'm sorry I'm late," the twins' cousin said, his expression rather abashed. "I would have come earlier if I'd— Oh my god, what happened?"

Without another word, the older boy nudged Alex aside and examined the unconscious AJ. Carefully, he pulled back one eyelid at a time, murmuring something about the direction the eye was facing, and tapped his cousin on the forehead three times, the tip of his index finger sparking with his blue magic. Scarcely a second after Percy's third tap, AJ's eyelids fluttered open.

"Wha—?" Alex stared in awe at his cousin, fumbling over his words. "How?"

"Healer, remember?" Percy said, helping his disoriented cousin into a sitting position. Turning to Mattes, he added, "And you, don't think I didn't take note of that black eye of yours. Once we get home, I'm going to look at all you adrenaline junkies."

Percy, however, still didn't notice the massive hole tearing the night sky asunder. With a heavy sigh, Mattes forced the boy's head to look upward.

"Percival, focus!" he exclaimed, becoming more visibly irritated by the moment. "Sisyphus escaping! Remember, the reason you came here in the *first place*?"

Percy murmured a quick "oh, right" and stood up, positioning himself in front of his younger cousins. "So, um," he began in a daft tone. "What should we do about that?"

"Are you serious?" Mattes exploded. "If you're this worthless in combat, why didn't you at least bring someone with you?"

"Hey, I'm a healer, not a fighter!" Percy protested. "I heard the alarm, so I came, all right? You don't have to be so combative."

"We're in combat!"

"Guys!" Acacia hollered. "Do we have a plan here?"

"You won't be able to keep the vacuum closed," AJ spoke up for the first time since being revived. "They're just too powerful. We . . . don't stand a chance."

"Oh, you're still alive?" Dionera asked after countless minutes of silence. "Ah well, all of you, make way for the most fearsome mage in history, Lord Sisyphus!"

With that, the sky above them was ripped open, as if by a thousand gigantic claws. All the colors which hours ago had clashed against the vacuum now flew chaotically in all directions.

There's just one left, Mattes mind-spoke. *Sisyphus himself.*

Since the day she had learned of the existence of magic and the story of the magical war, Acacia had wondered what the infamous Sisyphus looked like. Acacia had always envisioned him with dark hair and bloodshot red eyes, but she wasn't sure that was accurate since she had never seen a picture of him. But now they were all going to find out firsthand, whether they wanted to or not.

"Well, "Mattes began in a resigned voice. "It was nice knowing you all."

"What the hell is that supposed to mean?" Alex demanded, his voice panicked. "What do we do?"

AJ groaned and tried to force himself to his feet. "We . . . we can't just give up—"

"Andrew, stay put!" Percy ordered in the first authoritative tone Acacia had ever heard him use. "You're hurt and drained. If you use any more magic, you'll be in a coma for months!"

Percy's comment had the desired outcome; AJ slumped back to the ground without a word of protest.

Acacia was aware of the bickering continuing between Mattes and Percy but had it tuned out for the most part. In what had to be a daze, she watched the scene unfold behind the two older boys: Dionera's cackling as her compatriots flew off in every direction imaginable, the fire surrounding them growing closer and closer, a massive swirling of sheer blackness. Would this all have happened if she and Alex hadn't come here? Would that gigantic hole have opened if she hadn't tried to fight Dionera? Acacia couldn't shake the feeling that *she* was responsible for the mess they found themselves in in.

"And here he comes, at long last!" came Dionera's ecstatic cry. "Finally, Lord Sisyphus returns!"

The black mist faded away, and there he stood.

Sisyphus was tall and of strong build, the definition of his muscles easily visible through his black jumpsuit. He appeared to be in his forties, with long, jet-black hair, which blew wildly in the wind along with the cape attached to his suit. His eyes were a piercing electric blue, which seemed to have the effect of freezing everyone in his path.

The mage took a few moments to stretch out his hands and arms, as if he had just woken up from a long nap. He cast an arrogant smirk in their direction and sauntered toward them.

"How lovely of you children to join my welcoming brigade," Sisyphus said in a voice that reminded Acacia of an evil count from a vampire movie. "Such a pity more of your associates couldn't be here . . . but ah well. They'll know of our return soon enough."

"What's he doing?" Acacia asked, her mind racing. "Is he going to attack us or what?"

"He's playing with us," AJ whispered in a hushed tone. "He'll want to get us as panicked as he can before he does anything, so we won't be able to react when he does attack."

"And you must be Joseph Swiatkowski's sons." Sisyphus's piercing gaze landed on Alex and AJ. A sinister smirk worked its way across the mage's face, as if he were recalling some entertaining memory. "He was quite the thorn in my side, tracking me here and there across the country. And you." He shifted his gaze toward Mattes. "You are the spitting image of my good friend Elias. How is the old bugger doing?"

Mattes's father, a friend of Sisyphus? Was he joking to get under the boy's skin?

Mattes clenched both hands into tight fists, yellow magic circling them as if he meant to attack despite their disadvantage. "Elias Knight is dead! And you're dead wrong if you think I'm anything like that dung beetle!"

Sisyphus chuckled and rubbed his sideburns. "Temper, Mr. Knight. You certainly inherited *that* from Daddy dearest."

Ignoring Mattes's empty threats, Sisyphus turned and examined Acacia. Seconds after those icy blue eyes fell upon her, her blood turned cold. Possibly all the countless warnings and horror stories about Sisyphus had finally sunk into her consciousness, but as soon as Acacia met his gaze, she knew she was looking into the face of evil.

"Swansgrove," Sisyphus remarked, pushing Mattes aside as if he were a child's plaything, coming to stand directly in front of her. With a sinister sneer, Sisyphus took Acacia's chin in his cold hand and inclined her head, forcing her to hold his gaze. "I *knew* it could only have been one of *you* who could send the energy field off the scale."

Acacia shivered, but for the first time in her life, she was frozen in fear. She had no idea what Sisyphus was talking about; she remembered AJ mentioning something about the Swansgrove family, but Acacia was a *Wheatley,* not a Swansgrove! For the life of her, she couldn't remember what her mother's maiden name was, but surely it was something normal like Collins or Sullivan. The talk of the energy field was familiar too, but Acacia still found it difficult to believe she had caused such a change. Her power was strong, but was it that strong compared to everyone else's?

"You leave her alone!" Alex's voice broke the dead silence, as he pulled Acacia out of Sisyphus's icy grasp and behind him. The twin was a mix of terror and fury, but for now, the fury had taken over, making him bolder than she'd ever seen him. "And stay away—"

Sisyphus snapped his fingers, and Alex crumpled to the ground, screaming in agony.

"Alex!" Acacia and AJ both cried out, as Mattes and Percy knelt and attempted to calm the twin's writhing body.

"Why are you doing this?" Acacia demanded, regaining her strength and her temper. "None of us have done anything to you! You're torturing high school kids!"

Dionera cackled, her orange eyes reminiscent of a large predatory cat. "Not the point, little girl. This is war."

"And that," Sisyphus added, gesturing to Alex, who was obviously being tormented with some terrible curse, "is the fate of all those who defy me."

For a brief second, time stood still with Sisyphus and Dionera standing menacingly above them about to unleash unknown horrors upon the town. And then, as if with the drop of a pin, the tide began to change.

First there was one, then another blue flash of light on the far side of the meadow that gave way to Cecelia Swiatkowski and a man with the same blond hair and blue eyes who Acacia guessed to be Jack Golec, Percy's father. Seconds later, two green flashes materialized in the space adjacent to Cecelia and Jack, from which two figures—a father and daughter both with light brown hair—emerged. Acacia couldn't place a name with either of the two latest arrivals, but she *had* seen the girl in the hallways of the high school. With one more blue flash, Ivy appeared, stepping in line with her mother.

Sisyphus let out a long sigh and relinquished whatever curse he had placed Alex under. "It's becoming a bit overcrowded for my tastes," he commented to his cohort.

Dionera smirked and nodded. "Hope you brats had a nice taste of what's to come." Dionera and Sisyphus held hands, and a swirling mist of black materialized around them. Sisyphus took one last glance at Acacia and called, "We will battle, Swansgrove. And I will destroy you, along with all your little friends."

"Don't let them—" a male voice called out as Dionera and Sisyphus disappeared into the night.

From the corner of her eye, Acacia saw a rustle of activity but was too distracted by the disappearance of Sisyphus and Dionera to notice who it was. They were gone, but surely not for good. When would they return? Tomorrow? The day after? Several months later? And why did Sisyphus call her Swansgrove? Was that come sort of secret insult she didn't understand? Was it someone else he had mistaken her for? Acacia's head was spinning with questions—or more accurately, her head itself was spinning. People were moving around her, though what they were doing or saying, she couldn't be sure. The last thing she saw before losing consciousness was her mother, in the middle of a deep discussion with Cecelia Swiatkowski.

Chapter Ten

EXPLANATIONS AND APOLOGIES

When Acacia first woke, she was disoriented and uncertain if the confrontation with Dionera and Sisyphus had truly taken place or if it had all been a dream. After all, a dream would have been preferable. However, when she studied her surroundings more closely, she realized she'd been sleeping in the twins' bedroom instead of her own. Meaning, the terrible battle *had* in fact taken place, and they'd all come to the Swiatkowskis' home afterward. Letting out a a small groan, Acacia forced herself upright and slid her feet from the bottom bunk of the twins' bed to the floor. As much as she'd love to remain in bed, the cozy comforter wrapped around her body, she knew the only way she'd get to the bottom of what was going on was to find either the Swiatkowskis or her mother. Neither of which would happen if she remained cocooned in bed.

It *had* been her mother in the meadow, Acacia was sure of it. Had she come in response to Mattes's distress signal? Was Dervla Wheatley, the woman who wouldn't even allow Acacia to read fantasy books or dress up as a witch for Halloween, a mage? If so, why hadn't she told her? If Acacia had known about the existence of magic sooner, surely it would have been less of a shock to her now. Her mother always had a rationale for everything—what was it this time?

As Acacia exited the twins' bedroom, she heard the faint sound of music coming from downstairs. She walked down the steps and into the living room, where Percy was brewing a strong-smelling potion in a pewter cauldron on the floor, Alex was sitting on the couch, and AJ was playing the piano. None of her friends looked well; Alex's eyes were puffy and a bit sunken in as if he hadn't slept in weeks, and AJ looked . . . frail, both his arms covered in bandages from wrist to elbow. Percy didn't look injured but seemed exhausted, not even glancing up from his work when Acacia entered the room.

"I didn't know you played piano," Acacia said to AJ as she sat next to Alex on the couch.

"You didn't ask." The twin looked up from the keys at her. Something about AJ didn't seem quite right. . . Acacia had never known him to sit quietly and focus on something unrelated to magic or school. But then again, what did she know about AJ besides the fact he had gotten his full powers when he was eleven? Although she spent a lot of time with AJ learning magic, she couldn't say she knew him well.

Well, I guess anything's possible, she thought.

Percy scooped a portion of the steaming green mixture into a mug and offered it to Acacia. "Drink this. It's a fortifying draft. Doesn't look the most appetizing, but it'll help you get your strength back in no time."

Acacia took the proffered mug and peered at its contents. Green, bubbly, and sticky looking. Definitely not appetizing and not the first thing she wanted to ingest after what had happened in the meadow.

"Their mom and your mom are in the kitchen talking," Percy said. "Turns out they were the best of friends all through college and after. I gather sometime after the war, your mother decided to move across the country to get away from all this. As you can imagine, Cecelia wasn't thrilled with her decision."

Acacia ventured a single sip of the green slop. It was a bit like drinking fire and tasted of intense spices she didn't recognize. *So that's why Mrs. Swiatkowski said we moved back,* she thought. *And how she knew my mom. But why didn't she say anything about it?*

"So." The draft warmed Acacia from the inside out. "What do we do now? And where's Mattes?"

It was impossible for Acacia not to notice the glare on AJ's face which could only be meant for her. She thought the boy was going to scold her, but some communication appeared to take place between him and Percy, and AJ turned his gaze back to the piano.

I guess I get a reprieve for now, Acacia thought as she swallowed another gulp. *But Percy won't be able to hold him off forever, especially if he's as mad as he looks. And it's not like I don't deserve it.*

"Matthias has his own problems to deal with," AJ responded, a touch of coldness in his voice. "But it's past curfew, so he wouldn't be allowed to be above ground anyway."

Acacia blinked. *That's interesting. Mattes has a curfew when he has to be in the Underground. I didn't realize that.*

"It would appear, Acacia," AJ said, his gray eyes stormy as thunderclouds. "There are many things you don't realize."

"And you can shut up!" Alex rose from the couch. "You think because you're better at magic, you can say whatever you feel like!"

Acacia winced, feeling the pure power resonating between the twins. AJ's magic was more powerful than Alex's, but Alex's was enhanced by his anger. As Acacia remembered, magic was often closely intertwined with its user's emotions, as was the case with her still relatively untrained power. Alex had been training longer than she had but still had the same difficulties in controlling his power that Acacia did. But no matter how fierce his rage might be, Acacia doubted Alex would stand a chance against AJ in a confrontation.

Acacia positioned herself between the twins, holding her arms up in a sort of surrender. "Guys, let's not do this. We're friends here, right?"

"If we're friends, then why didn't he tell us your power was going to get sucked up by Sisyphus when you tried to do something?" Alex demanded. "Would have been helpful, don't you think?"

It was times like these that made Acacia realize she found AJ's quiet anger infinitely more terrifying than any temper she'd ever seen.

"Actually," AJ fired back. "I specifically told her not to go there for that reason, but obviously the possibility of Sisyphus and his henchmen escaping wasn't reason enough! Do you get it now, Alex? Do you understand why I don't always tell you everything? You don't listen to me *anyway*, so what's the point in wasting my breath?"

"Okay, guys, that's quite enough." Percy looked up from his potion, his blue eyes wide with anxiety. "We've all just evaded death. There's no need—"

"There's no need?" Alex glowered at his cousin. "How can you say there's no need, Percy? How can you listen to this jerk accuse Acacia of opening the stupid vacuum spell on purpose?"

"If you would listen with your *ears*, you might notice I'm not accusing Acacia of opening the vacuum on purpose!" AJ shot her another intense glare, a hint of disappointment hidden in his stormy eyes. "Even an idiot can tell she's ignorant, not malicious."

Alex lunged, and it was all Acacia could do to grab the boy from behind and try to keep him from attacking his brother.

"Acacia, let me—"

"Both of you stop fighting right now!" Acacia bellowed, her power surging within her. Once again, she felt completely in the dark about everything going on, only now a murderer and his team of assassins were on the loose. She was aware of the consequences of her fiery temper, but at the current moment, Acacia couldn't bring herself to care. She needed answers to her questions, and she needed them as soon as possible. "Don't we have better things to do than stand around fighting each other? Now, is somebody going to tell me what the heck's going on here?"

"Perhaps if you stop carrying on like a child."

It was a statement that very well could have come from AJ's mouth, but Acacia realized the boy was silent, his dark eyes fixed on the doorway behind them. Acacia whirled around and saw her mother, long red curls framing her face like flames.

"Mom!" Acacia called out, for one moment forgetting about the mysteries surrounding her and running to her mother. She embraced her as tightly as she could, willing, for just this moment, for all the craziness to disappear. "Mom, I-I . . . why?"

"Follow me, Acacia Lynne," her mother replied, her voice stern. Without another word, the woman terminated the embrace and strode out of the room as if late for an important meeting.

Acacia wiped her eyes and followed her mother out of the house.

***

As her mother spoke, several more important pieces of the puzzle fell into place. Acacia's mother, with Cecelia and Joseph Swiatkowski and Jack Golec, had served an integral role in the previous magical war. Jack Golec, a talented combat mage, worked for the Bureau of Defense but became frustrated when the Council began to consider negotiations with Sisyphus. Determined to fight for the good of the country on his own terms, he took a leave of absence to conspire with his sister and brother-in-law to fight Sisyphus.

One fateful night, when all appeared to be lost, a group of mages including Dervla, Cecelia, Joseph, Joseph's brother and sister-in-law, and Jack took to the woods outside Sisyphus's stronghold to offer one last challenge to the forces of darkness. Stella Golec, Percy's mother, and Acacia's non-magical father had stayed home with the children: seven-year-old Ivy, the six-year-olds Percy and Dave, two-year-old Sarison, and of course four-year-old Alex, AJ, and Acacia. Two of the twins' cousin on Joseph's side had also there at the house with them, a Nathan and Natalie who Acacia couldn't remember. At the end of the battle, Joseph had frozen the sinister mages temporarily, and Dervla had single-handedly cast the vacuum spell, locking Sisyphus and his followers in the sky of the Bloody Meadow.

"So," Acacia voiced for the first time since her mother began to speak. "Alex and AJ . . . did I know them? Before we moved?"

Her mother smiled. "Yes. And little Alexander was as fond of you then as he is now. Of course, out of the two of those boys, I have to say I'm glad it's him and not the other."

Acacia felt her face flush bright red. She wanted to learn about what was happening, not be lectured on her friendship with Alex! And what had her mother meant by her comment that she was glad Acacia had chosen Alex instead of AJ? From the first day of school, she had been drawn to Alex, but that didn't mean they were dating!

"But . . . so, Mrs. Swiatkowski . . . she knew who I was from the beginning of the school year?" Acacia asked, trying to force the embarrassment from her face. "I know she said something about knowing you, but she didn't say anything about you two being best friends. Or about knowing that I'm your daughter."

"Cecelia and I may not always agree on everything," Dervla said, tilting her head thoughtfully. "But we always respect each other's wishes. When we first moved back, we did meet up, long before the evening you went over for dinner. I asked her not to tell you or her boys anything about our history. I figured you would eventually learn the truth, but I wanted you to be able to live a normal life as long as possible." Her mother paused and shook her head, a worried expression on her face. "Of course, I knew all about your little lessons with Andrew, and for what it's worth, I'm glad Cecelia didn't go to the Council when your power manifested. The less involvement with the Council, the better off you are."

Her mother went on to describe the aftermath of the war, the widespread devastation that plagued much of the East Coast, the deaths of so many of their friends and family, lost forever as a price of their freedom from Sisyphus and his forces of darkness. Dervla's brother had been killed during that final battle, creating a hole in her heart that had never healed. Silent Springs had transformed from the place of her mother's youth to a graveyard of the fallen.

"I thought if you, Sari, and Dave didn't know about the existence of magic, it would stay away." Her mother let out a long sigh. "Somehow Dave didn't inherit the gift, but I knew you and Sarison did from the days you were born. I thought there was a chance it would lay dormant and you could live normal lives. But this year, I felt our normal lives ending and realized we couldn't avoid the inevitable any longer."

"So, we moved back?" Acacia asked, feeling the pieces falling into place.

"So, we moved back."

Acacia's powers, and her sister's, had been kept hidden for all these years, to protect them from the world of Sisyphus and his minions. Despite this, Acacia still found herself faced with his fiendish icy eyes, malicious sneer, and swirling black power. She wanted to scream at her mother for making everything more difficult, but she couldn't. After all, everything would still be the same, wouldn't it? All those people would still be dead, Acacia would still have to master her magic, and Sisyphus would still be free.

Most of Acacia's questions had been answered, but a few remained.

"Mom," she began, feeling the gravity of her next question settle over her heart. "What happened to Mr. Swiatkowski, the twins' dad? AJ told me Dionera killed him, the lady who was out in the meadow tonight."

"Oh yes. Dionera Tartaran." Discomfort settled on her mother's face, manifesting in every muscle in her body. "Well, I suppose your friend didn't tell you the nature of Joseph's death, did he?"

"AJ only told me he was killed." Acacia tried to remember if the boy had given any other hints. "When they were four."

Her mother let out a long sigh. "That's accurate enough. He didn't tell you he was there when it happened, did he?"

Hadn't Dionera said something to AJ when he appeared in the meadow to rescue Acacia and Alex?

You I remember. You're the little boy who got in the way!

"It wasn't long after the end of the war, maybe only a week or two. Not all of Sisyphus's people were imprisoned in that vacuum. Some weren't at his stronghold the night of the final battle and escaped. Dionera was one of them." Dervla Wheatley looked up to the sky, her green eyes wide with apprehension. "Of all Sisyphus's agents, she was by far the most dedicated. So Dionera did a bit of research to find who had stuck Sisyphus there in the first place. At that point, we'd already moved out West, but she discovered the Swiatkowskis had been involved in the final battle. So, she decided to target them."

Her mother cleared her throat. "Joseph was always a skilled tracker and spoiled her sneak attack. He went out to confront her and was so wrapped up in the moment he didn't realize Andrew had followed him out. Of course, this didn't go unnoticed by Dionera. She grabbed him and put a knife to his throat to intimidate Joseph. He couldn't attack her with his son's life on the line or *wouldn't*. From what I heard, it was a stalemate for quite some time, until Dionera attacked Joseph with that nasty fire magic of hers. He dodged it and was about to knock her over and send the child to safety when Dionera managed to get him with one of her cursed daggers."

Acacia froze in place. Losing a parent was bad enough, but to see it happen. . .

"Jack Golec was the first on the scene. After killing Joseph, Dionera made the error of letting go of the boy. Jack got hold of him before she could grab him back, and that was it." Dervla Wheatley let out another long sigh. "Cecelia called me in quite a state when it happened. But hearing about it only solidified my reasoning to keep you as far away from this mess as I could. We came back for the funeral, but were on the next flight back west."

You say you came back because you didn't want to abandon Cecelia, and then right after her husband's funeral, you abandoned her again, Acacia thought, blocking her thoughts. *Some great friend you turn out to be, Mom.*

They turned around, heading back in the direction of the Swiatkowsis' house.

"Mom, one more thing," Acacia said, masking her irritation. "Why did Sisyphus call me Swansgrove? I know they're a magical family, but—"

Dervla placed her hand on Acacia's shoulder. "Wheatley is your father's name," she explained, the pride apparent on her face. "Swansgrove is *my* name. We're one of the oldest magical families still in existence, as well as one of the most powerful. Many of us have had abilities other mages can only dream of."

So that's why Sisyphus called me Swansgrove! Acacia realized with a start. *Maybe* that's *why everyone says my magic is so strong!*

"But hold on," Acacia began, the confusion settling in once more. "Sisyphus said something about it being Swansgrove magic he could use to escape? If my magic, Swansgrove magic, is that powerful, how did he manage to suck it up into the vacuum like he did?"

Her mother nodded. "Magic affects other magic, Acacia, and the stronger the magic, the stronger the catalyst it creates." She paused, a dark expression crossing her face. "That night ten years ago, I genuinely thought all would be lost. I made a pact with the collective Swansgrove power that I would give up my power if I could create the vacuum spell to lock Sisyphus away. It worked; the spell was strong enough to hold him all this time, but I lost my magic that night. That's why you're not just a mage, Acacia, you're the Heir of Swansgrove, the most powerful of all living members of our family. I *was* the Heir of Swansgrove years ago, but when I gave up my powers to ensure Sisyphus's defeat that night, it was passed along to you, even though you didn't have your powers yet. As for the vacuum spell, it's been weakening for years, so I think when you tried to help your friends, the spell recognized the Swansgrove aura. It was probably confused, which allowed Sisyphus to finally blast through."

Acacia's head was spinning in confusion. *So let me get this straight. I've gone from being just a regular kid, to a kid with magic powers, to the heir of some powerful magical family? Can things get any more complicated?*

As they arrived back at the house, Cecelia opened the door, a small smile on her face. Her bright blue eyes were red, Acacia assumed from crying, but she seemed happy.

"It's good to have you back," the blonde woman said, stepping aside to let them in. "I hope you'll stay the night; we always have plenty of room here."

"As long as we don't impose. . ." Acacia's mother let her voice trail off.

Cecelia grinned and greeted them both with strong embraces.

"You've imposed on me by staying away, Dervla," the woman said, leading them back into her home. "I've missed you too much already to have you leave again anytime soon."

***

Acacia woke in the same bed she'd found herself in after passing out in the Bloody Meadow. She didn't remember falling asleep, or anything after her conversation with her mother, but she decided it was much easier to let it go than spend more time obsessing over the details. Percy had left, she assumed, but they'd all see each other at school . . . school! With all the time Acacia had been sleeping, she wasn't even sure what day it was. She jolted upright, only vaguely aware one of the twins was snoring above her. She tore out of the room in search of anyone who would be able to tell her what was happening.

Acacia padded down the steps and through the living room, without seeing a trace of anyone. The snoring twin was probably Alex, but where was AJ? Was everyone still sleeping? What day was it?

No, everyone *couldn't* still be asleep. For one thing, Acacia could hear someone in the kitchen. Was it Cecelia, making coffee and waiting for everyone else to wander out of bed?

"Hello," AJ said, his voice clipped. The twin was making pancakes on a large griddle on the stove. "Did you sleep okay?"

Acacia was almost shocked by how well the twin looked. AJ's arms were still bandaged, but he had regained most of his strength, no longer looking like the frail boy of the night before.

"Yeah, I'm fine, thanks," she replied, watching the boy with cautious eyes. Acacia could tell from his tone that AJ was tense, no doubt at least in part because of the unresolved argument from last night. Every time AJ as much as insinuated that Acacia did anything less than perfectly, Alex rose to her defense, but Acacia now recognized the danger in this. She wasn't perfect and she wouldn't ever be, but that didn't mean she couldn't handle criticism. And after the events of the previous night, some criticism might be what she needed. "How do you feel?"

"Annoyed that my student would disregard my warning and go sneaking about in the Bloody Meadow on Halloween of all nights."

Okay, Acacia thought, meeting her companion's hard gaze. *I deserve that.*

"Acacia, you don't seem to understand the gravity of the situation we're in." Acacia wondered if AJ had read her thoughts or if he was just speaking his mind after the events of the previous night. "You and my brother are adrenaline junkies, but just because you want to live life on the edge doesn't mean you have to put yourselves in danger. Both of you are lucky you weren't killed."

Acacia blinked. "Oh, okay so *you're* not?" she fired back, struggling to keep a grasp on her temper. "And we 'put ourselves in danger'? What would you call what you did, challenging a murderer to a magic duel?"

"I call it trying to save your lives," AJ retorted, his tone almost as calm as Percy's. "I'm not glorifying my actions. But you two got yourselves into serious trouble, and if I wasn't a— If I wasn't as good at tracking as I am, it could have had a very different outcome."

"If you weren't a what?"

"A good tracker."

"That's not what you were going to say." Acacia returned the boy's glare with a potent one of her own. Unfortunately, AJ seemed impervious to her attempts to guilt him back, in a way Acacia thought her mother would respect.

"I don't care." AJ flipped the cooked pancakes onto a large plate and handed it to her. "Here. Have some breakfast. They're buckwheat."

Acacia sighed and took the proffered plate. Arguing with AJ was like trying to bust through a solid brick wall with her head.

"I know it's not enough, AJ, but I'm sorry," Acacia said, cutting her pancakes with a fork and knife that the twin had laid out on the table. "And what you said last night. . . you're right. I should have listened."

AJ surveyed her, his gray eyes searching hers.

It's the quiet ones you have to look out for, Acacia thought, taking a bite of her breakfast. *Especially the quiet ones with strong magical powers.*

"You had to grow up really fast, didn't you?" Acacia asked, cutting off another piece of her pancake. It was heavier than what she was used to, but tasty nonetheless. "My mom . . . she told me about what happened to your dad, and to you. I'm sorry."

"No, Acacia, you are *not* going to turn this into a sob story about my father." AJ's dark eyes flashed with quiet rage, and Acacia debated if she'd made a poor decision in bringing it up. "I don't need your pity."

"This isn't about pity, AJ!" Acacia looked back at the boy, this time searching *his* face for anything that would give away his true feelings. "This is about the fact that I'm your friend and I want to help you! Dionera tried to kill you too, right? You might have untreated PTSD!"

"Acacia, enough." AJ shot her a glare so intense, so piercing, it froze the blood in her veins. "This conversation is *over*, do you understand? I'm sorry your mother told about . . . *that*, but you are not my therapist, and you don't need to worry yourself with my baggage."

Acacia swallowed a mouthful of pancake and examined her companion. His calm demeanor of only a few moments ago was gone, replaced with what she would best describe as a heightened state of anxiety. The boy's skin had paled, not quite as much as it had after their confrontation with Sisyphus, but still enough to cause worry. With her newfound knowledge, Acacia wondered if seeing Dionera, never mind fighting her, was causing her friend to have unpleasant flashbacks.

"Look, Acacia, I'm sorry," AJ said, breaking an uncomfortable silence. "I shouldn't have yelled at you." *And you shouldn't go nosing around in my past,* his nonverbal language indicated.

"No, *you* look," Acacia replied in as calm of a voice as she could. "My dad's a psychologist. I've been around this kind of stuff all my life, not the magic, but the phobias and the subconscious. If you think it'd be weird to talk to my dad, that's fine, but he could at least help you find—"

This time Acacia could feel the fury rising from AJ's slight frame and had to marvel at the extent of his control over his power. AJ might not be as calm as Percy when it came to nerves, but the twin's self-discipline was impressive. "You don't get it, do you?" AJ asked, a hint of disappointment and sadness in his voice. "You think all these problems can be solved, just like that. Well, I hate to break it to you, but it's not always that simple."

"Maybe not, but maybe it could help. You seem like you repress a lot. It's not a very healthy defense mechanism."

"You think you know me because your mother told you the details of my father's death," AJ said, his gray eyes becoming slightly glassy. "Sorry to disappoint, but you *don't*. You have no idea."

Here we go again, Acacia thought. *He's getting defensive and paranoid just like the first day of school.*

"Then why don't you tell me?" she said. "Since I have no idea."

If I hadn't been so stupid, my father would still be here! AJ covered his eyes with his elbow and stormed out of the kitchen. *So do me a favor and stop trying to get in my head!*

"AJ! Where are you going?"

Acacia sighed and, taking one last bite of her pancake, followed the boy into the living room. He was sitting again at the piano and had started to play a classical piece Acacia had heard once at a friend's recital. Except AJ's playing was at least ten times better than any of Acacia's friends had been. And he appeared to be playing from memory.

"Andrew Swiatkowski, step away from the piano," Acacia commanded. "You're crying, and I guess you don't know this, but I don't abandon my friends when they're going through a rough time."

AJ ignored her, dedicating his full attention to the piano. He seemed to think she would leave him alone if he pretended she wasn't there. Little did he know, the chances of that happening were nonexistent.

"Fine, have it your way," Acacia said, silently marveling how AJ could continue playing while crying. "I'm just going to have to hug you."

"Don't touch me!" The boy recoiled as if Acacia had said she was going to throw acid on him. "I don't want your . . . pity-hugs!"

"What the hell is a pity hug?" Alex asked, emerging from the top of the stairwell. In a few quick steps, he descended and sniffed the air, obviously enchanted by the smell of freshly cooked pancakes. "And more importantly, what are you two doing up? It's Sunday the last time I checked."

AJ wiped his eyes with his sleeve, his face reddening, and stared at the floor. "There's pancakes in the kitchen if you want," he said in a defeated voice. "I figured you would be hungry, so I made a lot."

Alex scrutinized his brother. As the two boys exchanged grave expressions, Acacia realized they were likely mind-speaking to one another and blocking her from their conversation.

"Okay, well that doesn't explain what you're doing up so early on a Sunday." Alex yawned. "Hey, Acacia. Good to see you."

Acacia let out another sigh. Truthfully, she was still concerned about AJ after the comment he made about causing his father's death, but she didn't want to pursue it in front of Alex. Situations like these always baffled her. How could a child think he was responsible for the death of a parent because he'd been taken hostage?

AJ sniffed and rubbed his eyes again. "By the way, we're going to be questioned by the Council today. So, you might want to think about what you're going to tell them when they ask you what you were doing in the Bloody Meadow."

Acacia and Alex exchanged flabbergasted glances.

"The Council is going to do what now?" Acacia inquired, her heart rate accelerating. Her knowledge of the magical government was far from complete, but she did feel somewhat appalled that they would give up the war with Sisyphus and attempt to negotiate with him. And with everything she'd heard, the thought of being summoned by them for questioning was not a pleasant one. How much did this omnipresent Council know? They had to know that the three of them, as well as Mattes and Percy, had been involved in the battle which ended with Sisyphus's escape. Were they going to be punished for it?

AJ shrugged. "Well, it's not like I know *when* they're going to summon us. We have to wait until they do, and then go and answer their questions. In other words, you might want to eat some breakfast."

Acacia and Alex exchanged a pair of befuddled glances.

"And how do *you* know they're going to summon us?" Alex demanded, his face paling. "Haven't become a Seer, have you?

"Don't be ridiculous." AJ glanced up from the piano, and Acacia noticed the skin around his eyes was rather red. She realized with a jolt that her friend might have been crying long before she woke up. "We were right there when it happened. They would be stupid not to summon us. But who knows, maybe we're already in trouble?"

"And what's that supposed to mean, maybe we're already in trouble?" Alex asked, his tone panicked. "What are they going to do? And us, what are *we* going to do? And—"

"Zander, the fact that Sisyphus and his minions are free means we're in trouble." AJ lifted his hands from the piano and faced them. "But no, I don't think they're going to do anything to us, but they have to be dealt with in a diplomatic way, and neither of you do well with diplomacy." AJ shot both Acacia and Alex a scolding glance, looking rather perturbed. Some sort of unspoken communication seemed to happen between the twins, and after a few seconds, a look of sudden understanding crept across Alex's face.

"That's where Mom and the rest of the adults are, isn't it?" the boy asked his brother. "The ones that were there, anyway."

AJ nodded.

A flash of brilliant golden light appeared in the center of the living room. At first, Acacia thought the flash would give way to a human form as some unknown mage teleported into the room, but instead, it rotated, transforming into a small orb about the size of a baseball.

"A. and A. Swiatkowski and A. Wheatley, your presence is requested at the Gold Chamber of the Silent Springs Council Headquarters." A disembodied voice spoke from the orb in a commanding tone. "Please arrive at the above-mentioned location via portal 727 in no less than twenty minutes."

Seconds after the orb's last words had been uttered, the ball of light flashed and disappeared with a small pop.

"Well, that was sooner than expected," AJ commented, rising from the stool, and stretching out his arms. "It's not even nine-thirty yet."

"Do you really know what's going on here?" Alex was looking more worried by the moment.

AJ smirked and let out a long yawn. "Nope. And not to say I told you so, but I told you that you should have eaten breakfast. If you would have spent less time hassling me, you could have had pancakes." The boy rose from his seat, a look of deep dread settling across his face. "Now come on, you know the Council doesn't approve of tardiness, don't you?"

Every day I'm here things get stranger and stranger! Acacia thought. *Will it ever make sense?*

She had a sneaking suspicion that her question was one she didn't truly want answered.

***

After the three of them cleaned up and changed, they headed in the direction of the forest yet again. From the moment they left the house, AJ began spewing a litany of precautions about speaking to the Council members, only half of which registered in Acacia's brain. The twin appeared to have all but recovered from his mental breakdown in the kitchen or, as Acacia thought more likely, had an exceptional ability in hiding his true emotions.

"... and make sure if you do have to talk to them you address them all as 'Councilmember,' 'ma'am,' or 'sir,'" AJ was saying. "They tend to get annoyed if you address them as anything other than that."

Acacia halted abruptly and stared at her friend. "You know this all from experience? Or is this just what you think will happen?"

"Well, that's what they told Mr. Jones when he was petitioning for all those people stuck in the Underground with Mattes who've never been convicted of anything," he said. "I mean, he's on the Council now, but at the time, he was an attorney working for one of the humanitarian agencies in town. But they called him an insolent fool because they were angry because he addressed Adolphe Albergast by his first name instead of as 'Councilman Albergast.' And Mr. Jones was an attorney, not a bunch of kids like us."

"And how do you know this?" Alex asked his brother in an irritated voice, fishing out a piece of pancake he had brought with him in a plastic bag. "Let me guess, a little birdie told you?"

"Amara did." AJ's pace was at least twice as fast as usual, making Acacia think he had taken the Council's message of appearing at headquarters in no less than twenty minutes to heart. "I'm not a spymaster, Alex. Just observant."

"Not as observant as you think," Alex muttered under his breath.

They had arrived at a fork in the path. In front of them sat a large boulder, while the trail went on both to the left and right.

"Portal 727 opens right here," AJ said, gesturing towards the enormous rock. "Have either of you traveled by portal yet?"

"Like . . . teleportation?" Acacia asked. "The way everyone travels everywhere?"

"Guess that's a no then," the twin retorted, striding over to the boulder and placing his hand on it. "Portal hopping is a bit different from teleportation. You don't have to concentrate too much on where you have to go; it's more like a subway. All you have to do is enter the portal, which is usually marked on some kind of landmark like this rock here, and it'll take you where the portal's set to go."

"Are you sure this is the right one?" Alex folded his arms across his chest. "You don't use the portal system that much either."

AJ shrugged and his hand touching the boulder glowed with golden magic. The gold spiraled from the contact point and spread out, creating an intricate design on the rock's surface. The golden light gradually faded, but the design remained visible on its surface, changing in shade from blue to black. Seconds later, a golden wall of magic thundered into existence, reaching from the ground to about six feet in the air. As soon as it solidified, the numbers 727 appeared at the top of the wall, written in elaborate script.

"Oh, and also, don't lie in the Gold Chamber," AJ advised them, not taking his eyes off the shimmering wall of light. "It's physically impossible. And they'll get annoyed and say—"

Alex let out a disgruntled groan and walked into the portal, pulling both Acacia and his brother along behind him.

CHAPTER ELEVEN

THE COUNCIL OF MAGES

After several minutes of tumbling through a vortex of brilliant golden magic, Acacia, Alex, and AJ stood in the entryway of a stone passageway, which was lit by floating orbs of every color imaginable. Acacia spun around to see where they had come from, but the golden light of the portal had already disappeared, and behind them, the passage was a dead end, with only a tapestry bearing the numbers 727 indicating any type of clearance. Wherever they were, they appeared to be underground, but Acacia couldn't tell how far below the surface. On the walls hung portraits of men and women dressed in spectacular robes, who Acacia assumed were former Council members. AJ let out a brief sigh and walked off at a rapid pace, motioning for them to follow.

"So, I'm guessing you knew since last night we were going to be summoned here," Acacia inquired, struggling to keep pace with the twin. After witnessing AJ in action during the battle with Dionera and seeing how fast he could move, Acacia no longer felt as inadequate when she was unable to keep up. "Otherwise, I don't think you would have been up so early making breakfast."

"She's got a point, AJ," Alex said, a crooked grin materializing on his face. "You did take a solid beating."

AJ let out a single, false-sounding laugh but offered no other response.

As they continued along the stone passageway, it eventually opened into a large foyer, adorned with elegant tapestries, beautiful mahogany tables, and numerous red striped couches. A stream of foot traffic passed through this area, and most of the people were dressed in smart suits and carried official-looking briefcases. On the far side of the foyer was a set of golden doors, artistically molded with the same intricate design that had appeared on the boulder when AJ had opened the portal. The doors were flanked by a sculpture of a dragon in flight on each side, which also appeared to be of solid gold.

Man, they must have needed a ton of money to build this place, Acacia commented about the sights throughout the room. *And what's with all this gold? Like I know they said it was the 'Gold Chamber,' but—*

You have heard of politics, right, Acacia? AJ's voice was dripping with sarcasm.

Are you an anarchist? Acacia asked the twin, thinking back to the first time AJ had spoken about the magical government. *Because I'm pretty sure that's the type of thing an anarchist would say.*

Nope, AJ retorted, his eyes watching the individuals passing through the chamber. *I'm not even old enough to vote.*

"And you call *me* difficult," Acacia commented, glaring at him. *Maybe this was what Mom meant when she said she's glad I picked Alex to be closer friends with.*

"There you lot are," an unfamiliar girl's voice said. "I've been looking for you since the summons was sent out."

Amid all the foot traffic in the foyer, it took Acacia a moment to locate the speaker. There, a bit off to the left stood a girl with light brown hair cut in a short bob and dark, evergreen eyes. Acacia vaguely recalled seeing her at school and at the end of the encounter with Sisyphus but couldn't remember ever speaking with her.

"Acacia, this is Amara Jones," AJ remarked in a formal tone. "The presiding Speaker of the Youth Assembly and daughter of Councilman Brian Jones. Amara, Acacia Wheatley."

Amara Jones looked exactly like the politician's daughter Acacia now knew her to be. Every aspect of her—her neat, straight hair to her businesslike heather green skirt and jacket—screamed elegance and poise. Amara scanned Acacia with cautious eyes before extending her hand.

Oh great, Acacia thought. *Another know-it-all.*

"Pleasure to meet you, Acacia," Amara offered, giving Acacia's hand a firm shake. She shot both the twins a rather harsh look. "Good to see no one managed to get you lost yet. You might not be aware of this, but Swiatkowski has the habit of getting 'lost' whenever he doesn't feel like answering difficult questions." Something told Acacia the girl wasn't talking about Alex.

"Er, thanks? It's nice to meet you too," Acacia murmured, feeling taken aback. "Hey, I'm sorry for asking, but what is the Youth Assembly?"

Amara cast another particularly annoyed glance in AJ's direction and turned back to Acacia. "I thought Swiatkowski was supposed to be teaching you," the girl said, her expression somewhere between frustrated and apologetic. "The Youth Assembly, or the Youth Assembly of Mages is the organization of underage mages through which we can discuss important occurrences in our world and ensure our voices are heard by the Council." Amara brushed off her sleeves, her green eyes confident. "And I'm the Speaker, meaning I have the responsibility of raising said concerns to the Council itself. I used to have an associate who helped me with this rather challenging task, but it appears he has more important things to do than follow through with the task he began."

Okay, so there's definitely something going on between this Amara and your brother, Acacia mind-spoke to Alex, arching her brows as she glanced between them. *Do you have any idea what it is? Does she have a crush on him or what?*

Alex laughed out loud, which drew the stares of not only Amara and AJ but also a few passersby, and his face turned red.

"I didn't hear that, and you'd better be sure I don't," AJ commented, his gray eyes stormy. "Even when the two of you do block off your thoughts, you're still painfully obvious when you're talking about people."

Amara grinned and let out a small laugh. "Now, now, Andrew, what say we save the hostility for the meeting? I'm positive your friend Derek Albergast will have more than a few things to say to get under your skin."

"The meeting with the Council?" Acacia asked, the confusion settling in once more.

Amara tilted her head, appearing almost entertained by her question. "The Youth Assembly meeting. So don't any of you go having any bright ideas about trying to run off after being interviewed. We have topics of high importance to discuss."

"Of course," AJ responded. "As long as the Council doesn't lock us up first."

"They won't." Amara rolled her eyes at him. "It's illegal, for one thing. And for another, the elections are upon us and none of them will want to do anything that would jeopardize their chance for re-election."

At that moment, the ornate golden doors swung wide open and the same commanding voice that had spoken from the summoning orb called, "Andrew James Swiatkowski!"

AJ took a single glance toward the foreboding chamber ahead and turned back to Acacia and Alex, his face pale but expression resolute. "Remember what I told you," he warned, his voice high and tense. "Answer their questions, but don't offer any information they don't ask. And keep your minds as blank as you can in case they try to probe your mind."

"Wait," Acacia said, feeling panicked. "You mean they're questioning us separately? I thought—"

"Don't let them see you panic." AJ scratched the back of his neck. "Answers are the only thing you owe them."

The twin sighed and walked past the busy foyer and through the golden doors. The second he entered the room, the doors clanged shut with a loud bang and locked, evidenced by the sound of unseen gears turning.

Acacia turned to Amara, who was still standing next to them, her hands clasped in front of her and a thoughtful expression on her face.

"Why are they doing this?" Acacia asked the girl, her tone grave. "This all seems a bit much just to ask a couple kids questions about what happened last night, with all the door clanging and mysterious voices."

Amara flipped her neat bangs across her forehead with her left index finger. The girl did not fluster easily, if at all. *Or,* Acacia considered, *she's just used to all this.*

"Intimidation tactics, Acacia." Amara's voice was as calm as if they were discussing a homework assignment. "Divide and conquer as they say. I'll see you two in a bit. Do try not to panic; it'll only make you look guilty."

With that last comment, Amara turned on her heel and left Acacia and Alex staring after her.

So that's the famous Amara Jones, Acacia thought. *Fourteen years old and in charge of it all. No wonder she and AJ are friends.*

Alex reached out and touched her hand. "I'm sorry I got us into this," he apologized, staring at the floor. "I never should have talked you into going to the meadow with me. . . I— It was stupid of me, and—"

Acacia grasped her friend's hand tightly, making him meet her gaze.

"I think they would have escaped one way or another," she remarked in an attempt to console her friend. "If we'd been there or not. But we'll get through this, okay?"

A small smile crept across Alex's face, and he led her over to one of the smaller couches.

"I believe in you, Acacia," he said, his expression sincere. "Not because you're a Swansgrove or whatever, but because you're you. And I think, when the time finally comes when you do have to fight Sisyphus, you'll be ready for him."

Acacia grinned and sat next to him. "I just hope I don't let you down."

With that, the two sat in silence outside the Gold Chamber, waiting nervously to be summoned.

***

It was impossible for Acacia to tell how long it had been since AJ disappeared into the Gold Chamber. Time dragged on forever while she and Alex sat on the striped couch waiting for something . . . *anything* to happen. Acacia pondered what types of questions the Council would ask and the best ways to answer them. Surely they'd want to know what she and Alex had been doing in the meadow in the first place . . . but how *could* she answer that? There really wasn't a good explanation for why they had been there that night. What had AJ said, complete, honest answers without offering more information than was requested?

A good thirty minutes passed by the time the golden doors swung open again, this time summoning Alex to the chamber. Acacia had squeezed Alex's hand, reassuring him that everything would be okay, and watched him proceed hesitantly into the room.

With no one to keep her company, Acacia began to worry, first about AJ, then about Alex. She'd thought AJ had been joking about the Council locking them up, but what if they had? Amara had said imprisoning them was illegal, but then again, some of the other things they had done, at least according to AJ, seemed illegal to Acacia as well.

"Acacia Lynne Wheatley!"

Acacia stood up right away, her heart racing. She let out a harsh exhalation and brushed her coppery waves down with her fingertips to steel herself for what she had to do.

Well, here I go, she thought, walking up to the open doorway. Inside was an enormous chamber set up like a giant courtroom with golden gilded walls and red velvet carpets. On each side were rows of wooden pews, and in the middle of the room was a mahogany platform where the accused stood during the proceedings. In the front of the room was the Council's bench, where the seven members sat.

"Miss Wheatley, please come in," one of the Council members said in a commanding voice, and Acacia felt herself magically pulled across the room, until she was standing atop the platform. Acacia heard the golden doors clang shut behind her but was far more concerned with the mages in front of her. Five men and two women were all dressed in billowing black robes. Most of them seemed to be older, maybe in their mid-fifties or early sixties, but one younger-looking man with light brown hair and dark green eyes had to be Amara's father, Brian Jones.

One particularly stout man sitting in the center seemed to be the spokesperson for the group. He cleared his voice and spoke in the same commanding tone that had summoned them from the orb.

"Miss Wheatley, we have a few questions for you before we let you go on your way—"

"What did you do with my friends?" Acacia heard herself demand, bracing her hands on the platform, the words leaving her mouth before she had the chance to censor them. "Why didn't they ever come out of here?"

One of the other mages, a sullen man who from his pallid skin seemed to have spent most of his time in darkness, stood up, his black eyes blazing with intensity.

"Insolent girl," he bellowed. "Do you have any idea to whom you're speaking?"

Councilman Jones, who had been seated on the man's left, also rose to his feet, raising his arms in a calming gesture.

"Councilman Valhart," Jones remarked in a remarkably calm tone. "She's a fourteen-year-old worried about her friends. Let's just finish the interview and we can all go home."

The skeletal-looking man scowled at Amara's father and sat back down. Jones glanced toward the man in the middle. "Councilman Roberts, do you mind if I do the questioning this time?"

Roberts shrugged, the indifference clear on his face. "Do what you want, Jones. This one doesn't look like she knows much of anything, even if she *is* a Swansgrove."

Acacia wasn't certain if she felt more intimidated or annoyed by the Councilman's comment but made a conscious effort to keep her mouth closed. *Just answer their questions,* she reminded herself. *And don't lose your cool. Again.*

"Miss Wheatley, please relax," Councilman Jones said, walking out from the enormous tribunal bench to come to the aisle. "Both of your friends have been released in no worse condition than when they entered."

Acacia allowed herself to relax a little. It did appear to be safe to trust Mr. Jones—after all, even Amara didn't seem bad. The girl might be an annoying know-it-all, but from what she could tell, she did have good intentions. Acacia figured she couldn't ask for more than the one decent Councilmember to be the one asking the questions.

Jones cleared his throat, his dark green eyes empathic. "Trust me, Miss Wheatley, I understand your concerns about your friends, especially given the dire consequences we find ourselves in. With your cooperation, we will have you in and out in no more than fifteen or twenty minutes."

Acacia nodded, her anxiety somewhat abated.

"Miss Wheatley," Jones said. "Were you aware prior to the event of last night that you are, in fact, the Heir of the Swansgrove magic?"

Of all the questions Acacia had been expecting the man to ask, *that* certainly had not been one of them.

"The question surprises you?" The stocky man in the middle of the group inquired, obviously having read her mind. "Did you not think being descended from one of the most powerful magical families in existence might be of interest for us?"

Just focus on the question, Acacia thought. *Focus on the question and how to answer it.*

"No, I didn't know I was," she said, forcing a neutral expression on her face. "I only found out last night when my mom told me about what happened ten years ago."

The stout man let out a large, throaty laugh. "What kind of ignorant child doesn't know her own heritage?"

Jones turned on his heel and faced the haughty Councilman. "Mister Hodgedallins, I will remind you that I am conducting this interview," the younger man stated, the irritation clear in his voice. "And as such, you will do your best to not aggravate the interviewee."

Acacia noted the similarity between the attitude of Councilman Jones and his daughter but reminded herself not to allow her mind to wander.

"Can I say something?" Acacia raised her hand as if she were in school. After Jones nodded, she continued, "I just want to say I don't know what my friends told you, but there's a lot I don't know. And I mean, that doesn't make it right, but I didn't know about this—any of this—until the first day of school this year. I'm trying to catch up and figure out how to . . . really be this Heir of Swansgrove like everyone says I am."

The row of mages exchanged curious glances. If only she could read their minds the same way they could read hers!

Councilman Jones cleared his throat. "We are aware of the struggles you face because of your mother's decision to keep you unaware of the existence of magic. In fact, Mr. Andrew Swiatkowski explained the situation to us earlier today, advocating quite strongly on your behalf. But we must continue with the discussion at hand."

And of course, I didn't get to see that, Acacia thought with a sigh. *I only get to hear Andrew Swiatkowski yell at me for being ignorant.*

"Our concern is that Andrew Swiatkowski's family has not proven themselves loyal to the Council or its decisions," the one called Valhart said. "As you are undoubtedly unaware, both Joseph and Cecelia Swiatkowski were well known as rebels with little respect for governmental authority. The boy has obviously inherited his parents' inclinations."

Acacia thought back to the conversation at dinner the first time she had been to the Swiatkowskis' house. What was it Cecelia and AJ had been saying? Things tended to work out for the better when the Council wasn't involved?

"Councilman Valhart," Jones retorted, this time not bothering to turn around, his face contorted in pure frustration. "You dislike the Swiatkowskis because they have a tendency to question authority, whereas you believe tradition should be followed to the fullest extent possible, no matter how antiquated said tradition happens to be."

Valhart sneered, though at whom Acacia couldn't be sure. "Councilman Jones, forgive my interruption," he declared with a smirk. "But you've hardly been involved with our prestigious organization long enough for you to truly understand the importance of loyalty to one's government."

Jones rolled his eyes and refocused his attention on Acacia. "Miss Wheatley," he said, his voice tense. "As you might imagine, we have entered a stressful time. The dark mage Henry Moore has escaped, along with many of his compatriots. They will soon be gathering their forces, regaining their strength, and preparing to launch an attack against us."

"All due in part to your magic!" one of the female mages, a blonde with brown eyes screeched, bolting to her feet. "If you hadn't been so foolish, Moore wouldn't have been able to harness it upward and free himself!"

One of the other women with billowing black curls stood up, just as irritated as the blonde had been. "Nonsense, Iselda! She's a child and was trying to save her friends! Any of us would have done the same!"

"Any of us would have known better than to go there in the first place!" the blonde woman hollered. "She and that Swiatkowski boy are fools!"

Valhart sneered again, obviously entertained by the women's argument. "Ladies and gentlemen of the Council," he began in a condescending tone. "I hear you commenting on the disruptive, rebellious nature exhibited by the Swiatkowski family, yet you are hesitant to label them as they are—political enemies and traitors of the most dangerous sort."

"Mister Valhart!" Jones roared, spinning on his heel and confronting the man face to face. "You will stop making empty accusations without a shred of evidence. I cannot allow you to continue your bizarre path of attempting to defame upstanding citizens who have done nothing but support and defend our community!"

Acacia looked nervously between Jones and Valhart. If she had noticed anything since entering the chamber, there was definitely tension between the more traditional members of the Council—namely Valhart and the blonde woman—and the more progressive ones, particularly Jones and the woman with the dark curly hair. And although she didn't understand much about this magical government, one thing she *did* know was she didn't want to get thrown in the middle of an argument between politicians. Adapting to this whole new world, never mind learning how to master her magic, was difficult enough without making an array of powerful enemies in the very government which exerted considerable control over her life.

"Sir," she said, clearing her throat and looking directly at Jones. "I'm really sorry for what happened. I did try to attack Dionera to help my friends because I didn't think they were going to make it on their own. But I had no idea my magic was going to get sucked up like that."

"Ignorance!" the blonde woman screeched, pointing her finger accusingly.

Councilman Jones rolled his eyes. In the short time she had known both him and his daughter, Acacia marveled at how similar the two were, in terms of general attitudes and the way in which they presented themselves. The Joneses were diplomatic to a fault, but at the same time refused to tolerate disrespect from others.

"Miss Wheatley, we have no more questions at this point," Jones replied in a calm yet restrained tone. "You are free to leave."

Acacia studied their faces for a moment, as if waiting for one of them, perhaps that blonde woman Iselda to protest or demand she be thrown in the dungeon. When none came, she stepped down from the platform.

"Oh, don't worry yourself, Swansgrove," Valhart commented once Acacia had almost reached the door. "You and your friends will be back, mark my words."

Acacia turned her head, giving the man one last glare, and exited the room, allowing the door to slam behind her.

***

"C'mon let's go," AJ said, pulling Acacia by the wrist down a dark, stone corridor. Acacia had been wandering along the hallway leading into the foyer where they'd been waiting earlier, but before she could figure out where she needed to go, found herself being pulled by her wrist in the direction of the underground tunnel where they'd entered through the portal stop. Acacia didn't have the best sense of direction, but she was certain they were no more than a few minutes walk from the exact spot where they'd entered the Council Headquarters via portal spell.

Acacia did the best she could to keep pace with her friend, flabbergasted at how he'd managed to find her in the first place. "Did you put a tracking device on me or something? I swear, you seem to know where I am better than I do."

"I told you already, I'm a very good tracker," AJ replied in a factual tone. "I got it from my father. Alex, on the other hand, inherited his likability. Both have their uses."

"So, what did your family do to that Valhart guy to make him dislike you so much?" Acacia asked. "You should have heard him going on about how you're all a bunch of traitors who hate the government, like you guys tried to overthrow it or something."

AJ appeared to be avoiding her eyes, his gaze fixed on the path in front of them. "We're not its biggest fans, no. But I'd steer clear of Johan Valhart if I were you. He's a bit of a relic from the old days when it was considered best practice to interrogate people with a hot poker."

They continued down the passageway until they arrived at a large set of steel doors, adorned with grotesque knockers in the shape of deformed gargoyles.

"Here we are," AJ said, glancing at Acacia. "Well, are you ready for your first Youth Assembly meeting?"

"Am I ever ready for any of this?" Acacia let out a deep sigh, feeling the gravity of the past twenty-four hours seep into her bones.

AJ shrugged, a hint of understanding apparent in his dark gray eyes. "Don't worry about it too much," he assured her, acting like the skinny fourteen-year-old that he was. "I wasn't ready for people trying to kill me either. None of us are. We just have to make sure we're able to adapt and improvise. And we keep surviving."

Acacia studied the boy carefully. Frank honesty was not AJ's typical modus operandi. "Well, we're doing well so far on that. Wouldn't you say?"

AJ gave her a halfhearted grin. "Survival is part skill, part improvisation, and part luck," he explained, ticking each mentioned part off on his fingers. "You can be the most talented mage in the history of the world, but if you can't improvise, you'll be dead seconds into a fight. And you can't control luck, so you make up for it with the other two."

Acacia had always shrugged off the twin's constant nagging about the need to react and improvise as part of his desire to control everything, but maybe he *was* looking out for her best interests. After all, to her knowledge, AJ had experienced some vicious bad luck in his life but always seemed to be able to overcome it. Conversely, the twin *was* a bit jaded and reluctant to trust, so it wasn't that he had passed through it all unscathed. But still . . . for AJ to have survived everything he had . . . he *had* to be doing something right.

"Well maybe I have the luck of the Irish," Acacia said, playing with a lock of her red hair. "Couldn't hurt, right?"

AJ let out a long sigh and pushed the giant doors open. "Here's to hoping."

Inside was another large chamber, though neither as large as the Gold Chamber nor as ornate. While the previous room had been covered from one side to the other with gold, this one was rather plain in comparison, made of stone and decorated with only a few purple tapestries and a row of wooden benches arranged in a large circle. When they entered, the room was almost full with the other young mages of the town. Glancing around, Acacia recognized Percy talking to some girl with long brown hair on the other side of the room and Ivy sitting with a tall boy who Acacia figured to be her boyfriend.

"There you guys are!" Alex called, emerging from the sea of people to greet them. The boy looked well, although a bit quieter than his usual cheery self. "We all survived then, and without getting locked up!"

"What a pity, I'd say." A boy who looked to be in their grade with dark brown hair and blue eyes had walked up next to them, a haughty smirk on his face. "God knows it'd be a relief for all of us if you all would just disappear."

AJ took a step forward and folded his arms across his chest. The twin had to be a good four inches shorter than the newcomer, but then again, did not intimidate easily.

"Pleasure as always, Derek," AJ remarked, his gray eyes stormy. "Can we help you with something?"

Derek Albergast, Alex told her. *His family's one of the most powerful and richest magical families around. Oh, and his dad's on the Council too. That guy to the far left with the black hair?*

Acacia nodded, remembering the man. *He didn't say much of anything when I was there. Mostly Jones tried to ask me questions, Valhart instigated him, and the two women argued.*

Iselda Abramov and Eramina Belacourt, Alex replied, scratching his chin. *That must have been interesting.*

"Swiatkowski, you never cease to frustrate me," Derek was saying, blue eyes dancing in entertainment. "The Council had the opportunity to get rid of you traitors once and for all, and instead of being thankful to see the light of day again, you have the nerve to speak to me so rudely. You haven't forgotten who my father is, have you? After all, it'd be quite a pity if that miserable little institute where your mother works just happened to be shut down."

AJ showed no signs of being intimidated by the boy's remarks. "And I suppose your father is far too important to help a couple of mages try to keep Sisyphus from escaping into the night. After all, he must have been pretty busy not to respond to an emergency signal."

"My family does not respond to signals from lowlifes," Derek retorted, his glare equally fierce. "If you had an ounce of sense in you, you'd have sent out the alarm yourself, instead of having that worthless Knight boy do it."

AJ raised his brows at the newcomer, as if daring him to say more.

Once again, Acacia thought, glancing between the two boys, *it's the quiet ones you have to watch out for.*

"I say back to West Virginia with the lot of you," Derek continued, glaring disdainfully at both twins. "You're all a bunch of inbred hillbillies anyway."

"Hey!" Alex hollered. "You shut your stupid rich boy mouth, Albergast!"

"Alex, relax," AJ said, a curious expression creeping across his face. "Derek is clearly one of those people who thinks everyone from south of the Mason-Dixon Line is a backwoods hick." The twin blinked and turned back to Derek. "You know that's classist, right?"

A spasm of rage flashed across Derek's face. "How *dare* you speak to me in that way! You're nothing more than an idiotic hick and you know it!"

AJ shrugged, clearly unaffected by the other boy's threatening demeanor. "Then my 'hick' comments shouldn't bother you at all, should they?"

Derek growled and made a move to grab AJ by the collar, but Amara Jones pushed her way through, placing more space between the two boys. "Gentlemen! If you could both stop quarreling like children, I'd like to call this meeting to order."

Acacia turned to Alex, a grin forming across her face. *I didn't realize your brother was such a good instigator. I mean, I knew he was with us, but I had no idea he did it with everyone else too.*

It was Alex's turn to shrug. *It's not everyone, believe it or not,* he replied. *But rich boy here is a huge pain. And since it's not good to punch him in the face with his dad being on the Council and all, it's a good thing AJ gives him a hard time for all the crap he tries to get away with. My brother is a pain too, but he doesn't let people talk crap on our family.*

Acacia ventured a side glance at AJ, who was currently too preoccupied with Amara and Derek to pay them much heed.

"I apologize, Amara," Derek said. "But it's so hard to concentrate with some of. . ." He cast a disdainful glance at the three of them. "*These* people around."

AJ let out a harsh laugh, his dark eyes particularly stormy. "Mr. Albergast. Maybe we should recall who accused whom of being a, what was it, an 'idiotic hick' before we start—"

"Enough, both of you!" Amara shouted, glaring at both boys. With that, the room fell silent, and the girl glided between the rows of young mages, taking her place in the center of the bench in front of them. "Now, if we can all put our differences aside, I'd like to call this meeting of the Youth Assembly to order."

Derek rolled his eyes and stalked off without another word, joining his friends on the right side of the chamber.

"Amara can be a bit forceful at times," AJ acknowledged to Acacia and Alex, as if noting some scientific fact.

Alex shook his head at his brother. "And you can be blond sometimes. Seriously, AJ?"

AJ shrugged. "You'd be a bit forceful too, if you were in her position. Trying to keep all the mages under eighteen in line and bringing all the concerns to the actual Council? It's no easy task, you know."

Acacia recalled that Amara had previously made some remark to AJ about having to do everything now after her cohort had decided to resign but figured she would have to leave *that* mystery for another day.

Amara cleared her throat and spoke in an assertive but not quite commanding voice. "First, I'd like to thank everyone for being here today, though I know for some of you it wasn't by choice. But as all of you know, we are now faced with the greatest threat of both our as well as our parents' generations."

The chamber was filled with the hushed whispering of the young mages trying to piece together why they had been summoned to the meeting.

"It's true then."

"I can't believe it."

"My colleagues," Amara said. "Sisyphus and his associates have escaped."

The girl remained silent for a few moments, allowing the effect of her announcement to settle into the room.

"It is only a matter of time before they launch their first attack," Amara continued. "This is the reason I've called you here today. I believe once Sisyphus has regrouped, he will lay siege not only to the Council and the adult mages but us as well. As such, I'd like to hear your thoughts about what we can do to prepare."

The room fell utterly silent for a few minutes after Amara's request. Mages exchanged nervous glances, each hesitant to be the first to respond.

"Well, so much for the famous Youth Assembly," Ivy sneered, pulling herself to her feet in a standoffish manner. "I sure hope at least one of you has some idea of what to do when Sisyphus and his minions come to kill you."

"We'd be more than happy to hear your brilliant plans, Ivy," Amara retorted, her green eyes grave. "We're all open to suggestions."

Ivy let out a loud, derisive laugh. "You want my suggestion, Jones? Stay alive and don't get caught. If they catch you, you'll wish you were dead."

With that, the blonde strode out of the room, closely followed by her boyfriend, letting the doors slam shut behind them.

Amara sighed and rubbed her temples. "Somehow, I find it hard to believe no one has anything to say. You realize the entire reason for forming the Youth Assembly is to give all of us under eighteen a voice in the political process? What's the point of having a voice if none of you are willing to speak up?"

"My sister does have a point, you know," AJ said. "Not the most tactful one, but she never was one for tact."

"And why should we listen to either of you?" Derek crossed his arms over his chest. "Everyone knows your whole family deserves to be locked up, particularly you, you unhinged headcase!"

Alex pushed himself between Derek and AJ, his face marked with sheer fury. "Don't you *ever* talk to my brother like that again! You think just because your dad has money you can say whatever you want—"

"Zander, down." AJ placed his hand on his brother's shoulder. "It's not worth it."

What the hell do you mean it's not worth it? Alex asked. *Did you not hear what he said? He can't get away with saying crap like that!*

AJ inhaled deeply through his nose, shooting both Alex and Acacia a conciliatory glance. *You have to pick your battles with people like Derek,* he explained, gray eyes a bit tired. *Some people will just say whatever they think will bother you, so you do your best to not give them what they want. And besides*—AJ gazed up at the ceiling for a moment—*it's not like anything he's said today was the worst he's ever said to me anyway.*

Alex sighed and dropped his aggressive stance.

What was the worst then? Acacia asked. *If that wasn't bad enough. . .*

An imagination is a horrible thing to waste, Acacia, AJ replied tiredly. *Do use it.*

The twin took one small step forward and cleared his throat. "Amara's right," he said in a grave tone. "They won't hesitate to attack and kill us if we're in the wrong place at the wrong time. Those of you who think they'll have mercy on us because we're kids—you need to get this idea out of your head, the sooner the better. They'll stop at nothing to get what they want and destroy everyone in their way."

A wiry boy with light brown hair sitting on one of the benches to the left raised his hand.

"But if they . . . want to . . . kill us or whatever," he said after Amara's nod. "W-what are we going to do? I-I mean, I know we can't just w-wait, but . . . I don't want to g-go looking for them either. . ."

Alex's hand brush against Acacia's, and she couldn't help but notice the deep red of his face.

I guess that was me, he commented in an embarrassed tone. *Looking for trouble and all.*

It was both of us, Acacia assured him. *It wasn't like I tried to talk you out of it.*

"No, we can't wait around," AJ responded to the wiry boy. "But we *can* prepare." It was obvious the twin was no longer speaking only to the anxious boy but to the Assembly as a whole. "Those of you who do have battle experience—which I'm guessing is not many of you—get more, even if it's just with your friends. Practice all you can—and practice with mages who you know are stronger than you. Think about what you'd do if the unthinkable were to happen to you, because it can. Work on your weaknesses, whatever they might be, because you'll never know what you might have to do."

Acacia raised her coppery brows. *Have you rehearsed this by any chance? Or are you that good of a public speaker?*

AJ winked in response. *I might be an anemic with a warped personality, but I do have some redeeming qualities.*

An older girl with curly blonde hair rose from her bench, her blue eyes icy.

"And just why should we listen to you?" she demanded, crossing her arms in front of her chest. "I know you managed to not be obliterated by Dionera Tartaran, but you're a kid. What can you possibly know about battle?"

AJ shrugged. "I know enough. But that's not really the point. My father knew plenty more about battle, and in the end, they still killed him. Knowledge won't save you, but improvisation might."

Amara nodded and rose to her feet. "Unless there are any other closing comments, I declare this meeting adjourned," Amara remarked curtly. "Everyone stay safe, and travel in groups if possible, especially when going into the forest."

Little by little, the crowd dissipated from the room. Acacia was glancing around, trying to memorize the faces of all her fellow teenage mages as best she could, when suddenly, she felt a burst of magic surface next to her.

"I do hope last night will be the last impulsive escapade from you lot," Amara commented. "You do realize you *all* could have died, right?"

"Amara, enough." AJ was beginning to look more drained by the moment. "I think we've all heard it enough for one day."

The girl folded her arms across her chest. "And *you* of all people should know better, Andrew. I need you to not get yourself killed with war upon us. Try not to do anything stupid."

"Worry about yourself, Amara," AJ said, rolling his eyes at her. "You're going to have enough of your own problems keeping everyone else in line."

The girl shrugged indifferently and walked off.

I guess they're not that buddy-buddy, Acacia commented to Alex. *That's funny. At first, I was almost wondering if there were—*

Acacia, Amara and I are more allies than friends, AJ mind-spoke in an irate tone, obviously having overheard her. *And we're* not *together if that's what you're thinking.*

Acacia shot her friend a curious glance. *Well, someone's a bit touchy! What happened to not letting people get under our skin?*

AJ glared daggers at her and rolled his eyes. Alex let out a brief sigh and stepped between them.

"Come on, guys," the twin said, his eyes pleading. "Can we save the hostility for the bad guys, please?"

"Well, well, well," a familiar voice sneered. Much to Acacia's surprise, Derek Albergast had joined them again, a large smirk evident on his face. Turning to AJ, the boy said, "So you did fight Dionera, Flopsy. When I first heard that, I figured someone had to be lying, since I thought you're far too cowardly, but then I remembered, you're more of an idiot than a coward."

Rage flashed across AJ's face but disappeared almost as quickly as it had appeared. "Goodbye, Derek," he commented flatly, turning away. "Next time, try to agitate someone who doesn't know your games quite as well as I do."

Abruptly, the twin strode toward the giant door at a brisk pace. Acacia and Alex exchanged a pair of flabbergasted glances and followed him, unsure of exactly what was taking place.

"She'll be back for you, you know!" Derek hollered after them. "Everyone knows Dionera Tartaran doesn't just let people go after she's tried to kill them!"

AJ froze and glanced over his shoulder at Derek, his gaze stormy. "Let her come. Next time I'll be ready."

Without another word or glance behind, AJ led them both out of the chamber, letting the doors slam shut on the way out.

Alex protested, "AJ, how can you just—"

"Walk away?" AJ interrupted. "It's easy. Much easier than standing and arguing until you look like a fool."

Acacia halted and placed her hands on her hips. "AJ, *stop*. What's going on here? And why did that creep call you 'Flopsy'"

"Anemia occasionally makes you lose consciousness if not properly treated," AJ replied, his tone cold. "As for what's going on, you two are going home. There are more enemies afoot than we first realized."

This time, it was Alex's pale brows that shot up. "Then where are you going?" he demanded. "It's no more dangerous for us than it is for you!"

AJ shrugged, clearly not caring. "I have some errands to run. Just take the same portal back and I'll see you later."

"What the heck do you mean you have some errands to run?" Alex grabbed his brother by the back of his shirt. "What am I supposed to tell Mom? 'Oh, AJ's not with us because he had some errands to run?' What the hell could be so important that you can't come home with us?"

AJ whirled around, shooting his brother a particularly stormy glare. Acacia blinked and noticed that for a second AJ's eyes had turned a deep blue before quickly changing back to their typical dark gray.

Am I that tired that I'm imagining things now? Acacia thought, blinking several times to clear her head. *It's been a long day, but I didn't think I was* that *confused!*

"I'm fine, Alex," AJ retorted coolly, shrugging off his brother's grasp. "So do me a favor and mind your own business."

"You idiot, what happened to 'we share ninety-nine percent of our DNA, your business *is* my—'"

But AJ stormed away from them, walking up to a wooden door with a deep purple tapestry with the number 732 suspended above its stone arches and reached out to touch it with his right hand. Bright golden light emanated from the point where AJ's hand touched the door and flowed over the door's surface, creating an intricate symbol similar to the one that had been formed on the boulder a few hours earlier. Acacia watched in awe as the golden design spread until it covered the entire door and faded to black. Before she or Alex could move to halt AJ's actions, the blue magic faded to black and another golden door appeared directly in front of him. AJ turned to shoot them one last glance before stepping into the wall of golden light. Seconds later, the golden magic vanished, leaving no trace of the sarcastic teenager. Acacia stared at the space where he'd been mere seconds earlier and let out a shallow sigh.

"Both your brother and Amara are pains in the butt all right," she said. "But I give them credit, they *do* have style."

"Well, AJ better enjoy that 'style' while he can," Alex said, shaking his head. "Because once I get my hands on him, he's not going to be able to sit for weeks."

Acacia laughed, beginning to feel truly at ease for the first time all day. Alex might not have AJ's tracking ability, or legerdemain with magic in general, but when given the option, Acacia would pick Alex's jocular nature and sense of humor any day.

Shaking his head again, Alex held out his hand, which Acacia took immediately. "Well, Acacia, let's get you home."

Acacia nodded, rubbing her friend's hand. "And Alex?" *There's no one else I'd rather face sure death with.*

The twin's face went bright red as he turned to lead the way towards the portal entrance 737.

Chapter Twelve

AFTERMATH

I t was almost four o'clock in the afternoon when Acacia and Alex arrived at the Wheatleys' residence. As soon as she opened the door, Acacia's mother darted up from the couch and smothered her in a tight embrace. Her father got up as well to greet them, and both he and her mother thanked Alex profusely for bringing her home.

"N-no problem," Alex said in a shaky voice. Acacia had never given much thought to when or how she envisioned her family meeting her new best friend, but *this* hadn't been what she'd expected. "Acacia, I'll... see you tomorrow?"

Acacia nodded. *Good luck tracking down your brother.* In the past few months, Acacia had come to realize AJ could be rather difficult to find when he didn't want to be found.

Thanks. But Acacia? I don't know how to tell you this but . . . I like you. A lot.

Alex turned to face her parents, his face turning a brilliant shade of red. "Sorry to run, but I should be getting home! Bye, Mr. and Mrs. Wheatley, it was great meeting you!" Without another word, Alex disappeared into a flash of blue light, leaving Acacia with her family.

"Seems like a nice kid." Acacia's father walked back over to the couch and sat down. "High energy too. He'll need it, to keep up with our Acacia."

Acacia's mother winked at her, as if to say, "I told you so."

Dave rolled his brown eyes and flicked off the television. "So, it's true. All this stuff about magic and bad guys trying to take over the world?"

Acacia nodded. She was always the serious one, out of the three Wheatley children, but she knew Dave was more mature than he let on. As frustrating as he could be when he was picking on her or refusing to give her a ride, Dave was a good older brother.

"And they're back, the bad guys," Acacia explained. "As of last night. And the leader, Sisyphus, told me I'll have to fight him someday."

"Oh!" Sari jumped up from her seat, her brown eyes wide with enthusiasm. "I want to fight him too!"

"Sarison," both Acacia and her mother chided.

"You don't even have your powers yet, Sari." Acacia pointed out.

Acacia's mother let out an exasperated sigh. "That's not the point, Acacia. None of my children need to be running around fighting Sisyphus!"

"But, Mom, he said—"

"I don't care what he said, Acacia," the woman said in a forceful, no-nonsense tone. "You are my daughter, and if I say you're *not* to go chasing after Sisyphus, you're not to do it!"

Acacia scowled. "But, Mom, I have to train and get stronger. And besides, even if I don't go looking for trouble, it might find me anyway."

"Acacia Lynne Wheatley," Acacia's mother warned. Acacia knew she was in trouble when her mother used her full name. "I tried to keep magic from you for fourteen years. Obviously, I was not successful, but under no circumstances are you to involve yourself with any plots of taking down Sisyphus."

"Mom, I didn't say—"

Her mother was unrelenting. "I know you didn't say, Acacia. You don't have to. But I know how Joseph Swiatkowski operated, and your friend Andrew is the same. He's a schemer, Acacia, and you'll steer clear of his schemes unless you want to be sent back to California."

Acacia felt as though she had been stabbed in the chest. She couldn't go back to California now—she couldn't! She wasn't sure what she could contribute here, but there *had* to be something she could do. If she went back west, she'd be powerless to do anything to help her friends *or* the magical community in general. She would lose her mind.

"Mom, this isn't even about AJ," Acacia protested. She wasn't exactly sure how her mother had reached her conclusion about the boy, though she figured something could have come up in one of her conversations with Cecelia. "This is about me. If I really am the Heir of Swansgrove like you say I am, doesn't that mean I have a responsibility to make sure he's defeated?"

"*Acacia Lynne Wheatley.* I told you about that so you could understand why your magic was affected the way it was last night, not so you could develop a messiah complex! To think, a child facing off against a dark mage who brought the Council to their knees!"

An awkward silence followed, which Acacia's mother broke by clearing her throat.

"I'm sorry to be so brusque, dear," she said. "But this is all for your own good. Let the Council solve the Council's problems. Let Andrew teach you how to control your magic if that's what you want, but don't worry about saving the world. Enough Swansgroves have been sacrificed for the good of the Council already."

Without another word, Acacia's mother kissed the top of her head and walked out of the room. Dave shot her a confused glance, and their father took Acacia's hand and led her to the couch.

Acacia sniffed, upset by her mother's intense ultimatum. "Dad, I only wanted—"

"Shhh," her father replied, his brown eyes serene as he gave her a hug. "You just do what you have to do. You're not going anywhere."

Acacia and her brother glanced at each other, their expressions equally puzzled. *Parents.*

***

The following morning, Acacia woke early, threw on a change of clothes, and gulped down her oatmeal in record time.

"Would you relax, Achy?" Dave arched his coppery brows at her as he sipped his coffee. "I'll give you a ride today."

Acacia dropped her spoon on the table. Ever since her brother had gotten his license, he refused to be seen anywhere in public with her, as if it would forever taint his reputation.

"Seriously?" Acacia asked. "You *never* give me a ride!"

"That's . . . generous of you, David," their mother commented, glancing up from her newspaper. "What's the occasion?"

Dave rolled his eyes, his expression scandalized. "Jeez! Am I not allowed to give my kid sister a ride to school or what? I'm not mean, I just don't like to do things like this all the time because then people expect it!" Turning to Acacia, Dave set his cup down on the table. "We *do* have to get going, though. If we get there early enough, they won't even see you with me."

"You were the one who was just telling me to slow down!" Acacia protested. "Which one is it?"

"Go now." Dave rose to his feet. "Do you want a ride or don't you?"

Acacia scowled, picked up her bookbag, and followed her brother out the front door.

***

David didn't utter a single word the entire drive, which surprised Acacia, since she assumed he'd offered her a ride to talk in private. Once they arrived at the school, her brother parked in the student lot and they both exited the vehicle.

"Why did you drive me today anyway?" Acacia asked, slinging her bag over her shoulder. "I mean, I appreciate it, but it's . . . a bit out of character."

Dave shrugged. "Believe it or not, Achy, occasionally, I do like to do something nice. Besides, it sounds like you're going to need some allies, including ones who can't shoot fireballs out their fingers."

Acacia grinned and gave her brother a quick hug before he could manage a protest. Dave rolled his eyes while muttering under his breath, and the two of them headed toward the school.

They arrived at the front doors within five minutes. Since David had insisted on leaving the house so early, the doors wouldn't unlock for a while, though a small crowd of students had gathered outside the building.

It's kind of bizarre, Acacia thought, as her brother disappeared into the crowd. *It's only been two days since the last time I was here, but so much has changed. With Sisyphus and his buddies on the loose, people are way more worried than they were last week. I just hope nothing else happens until I get better control over my powers. I thought I was getting better, but there's no way I'm ready to take on Mr. Sissy Puss. And something tells me that I am going to have to face him again, whether my mom wants me to or not.*

"Hey there, bright eyes." Acacia cocked her head and saw that Alex had joined her, a concerned expression on his face. "How're you holding up?"

Acacia shrugged, thinking back to the conversation with her mother the day before. "Okay, I guess. Except for the fact that my mom threatened to send me back to California if I get involved in any kind of 'save the world' plans."

"Well, that's . . . *interesting*," Alex responded, adjusting the straps on his backpack. "Think she'll do it?"

"Anything's possible. It was her who moved us out there after the end of the war. Though I think my dad would stick up for me if she tried to send me back there." Acacia let out a long sigh and pulled her braid over her shoulder. "So, what happened at your house last night? Did you ever find out what AJ's 'errands' were?"

Alex shook his head, a hint of disappointment on his face. "Nope, but the Golecs came over and we had a family conference. Nothing too exciting, but we're trying to be more careful now since the Council thinks we're a bunch of wannabe government traitors."

Acacia nodded, remembering Valhart's comments during her interrogation. *From the conversations with AJ I've had over the past month about the government, I've picked up on a political agenda, though what that political agenda is, I'm still not sure,* she thought. *But between everything my mom and Valhart said, he might come by it naturally.*

Still, that doesn't explain the reason for it, and if the whole family has a reputation for opposing the Council, there must be one.

The throng of students had begun to make its way into the school, and Acacia realized the entry bell must have rung. Alex grinned at her and tapped her on the top of the head with his index and middle fingers.

"C'mon now, Acacia," the twin commented in his usual bright tone. "Don't start worrying about us. We don't look like it, but we're pretty tough. And besides, you've got a lot more to worry about, with training and staying out of trouble with your mom and taking down Sissy Puss."

Acacia chuckled. "Just don't say any of that to my family!" There would be time to delve into the Swiatkowski family history later, perhaps when she wasn't about to be late. "C'mon, Alex, race you to homeroom!"

The two of them laughed and took off, oblivious to a pair of ever-green eyes watching their entrance with interest.

***

Percy Golec sat in his fourth period English class, unable to concentrate on Mrs. Davis's lecture on Shakespearean literature. After all, a war was brewing, a war with the power to throw the entire magical community into shambles. The events of the past few days had Percy worried, far more worried than he typically allowed himself to become. After all, AJ worried enough for the whole family without anyone else's help. But then again, Sisyphus's escape and the additional pressure from the Council was enough to put even the calmest mage on edge.

It was bad enough that he'd had to endure the Council's interview and Amara Jones's Youth Assembly, but when Percy arrived home, his parents rushed them all over to the Swiatkowskis for an impromptu family meeting. It wasn't that Percy didn't think the meeting was a good idea, but family conferences were usually more effective when all members of said family were present.

AJ had shown up late, which Percy didn't find surprising given the boy's disappearance after the Youth Assembly meeting. What Percy did find curious was his cousin's dejected mood, which did not improve throughout the evening. Ivy, the oldest of the cousins, was nowhere to be found.

"This is no laughing matter," Percy's father had said in a cold, disgusted tone. Percy wondered if his father realized no one had been laughing in the first place. "If Sisyphus is allowed to roam free again, we'll have another war on our hands."

"Now, Jack," Percy's Cioci Ceil, the twin's and Ivy's mother replied. "I hope you didn't come here to repeat what we all know."

Jack Golec and Cecelia Swiatkowski were an interesting pair. Percy's father was a skilled Justice Enforcement officer who was responsible for the capture of hundreds of dark mages throughout his career. Conversely, Cecelia was a researcher first and a stealth operative second. Jack's strength was his offensive magic and skill in battle, where Cecelia was more talented conducting analysis and finding minute flaws in the enemy's strategy. Despite their differences, the two had been equally feared by the enemy in the previous magical war and still had reputations as mages most did not choose to cross.

"Whether you know it or not isn't the issue, Celia," Jack retorted, his gaze fixed on the twins. "The issue is that both your boys were at the scene of the crime, right as Sisyphus blasted himself free into the world. Some might talk about your parenting."

Cecelia shrugged, not perturbed in the slightest. "In that case, 'some' might do better to talk about why the Justice Enforcement Officers weren't the first ones to arrive at the scene of the crime instead of a couple of teenagers."

It's interesting just how different they are, despite being raised the same way, *Percy thought.* Every time anything strays from the plan, Father goes on the offensive with anyone in sight, and Cioci Ceil calmly takes the time to plan her next move, reflecting before reacting. I guess it's no surprise they did such different things during the war.

Not quite so different. *AJ shot him a brief despondent glance.* They just have their own preferred methods of killing people is all.

Percy raised his brows at his cousin. At first, he had assumed AJ's 'errands' had something to do with Mattes, but Percy was aware his cousin's most melancholic moods usually had something to do with Ivy. In years past, AJ and Ivy had been very close, sharing things with each other that most brothers and sisters would never tell one another, but a few years ago, the two suffered a drastic falling out. Percy never found out what had happened, but he figured it had to be substantial to cause AJ and Ivy's relationship to fall apart as it did.

Yeah, AJ, because you know oh-so-much about killing people, *Alex retorted, jumping into their conversation. Alex had made it no secret he was peeved at his brother for refusing to come home with them, though Percy was certain AJ had done so to try and talk some sense into their sister.* How many people is it now that you've killed?

Those are some big words coming from someone who's not finished with their training.

Well, those are some big words coming from someone who got their butt handed to them! *Alex's face turned a deep shade of red, but Percy doubted AJ even noticed. The twin seemed to be blocking them all out, completely immersed in his own thoughts. Percy had told his cousin on more than one occasion he would be much better off letting people know what he was thinking instead of shutting everyone out, but AJ hadn't taken his advice to heart, at least not yet.*

No matter, *Percy thought, this time careful to block his mind from the others.* They'll all be a good team someday—Alex, AJ, Acacia, and Mattes—when the time comes. *Sure, it'd be nice if that time was now, but you know what they say about good things coming to those who wait.*

Percy didn't consider himself to be part of the team because he didn't consider himself a fighter. He had been turned away from martial arts at an early age, having witnessed firsthand the consequences of war in the infirmaries where his mother Stella worked. Percy remembered with vivid accuracy the mangled bodies of the injured as they were brought in, sometimes with badly burned skin and sometimes on their deathbed after being subjected to powerful curses. Percy had spent hours with his mother during these years, watching with fascination as she was able to reduce suffering with the combination of spells and potions at her disposal. From that point on, Percy knew he too wanted to be a healer and use his power to help others. His father, a warrior who had desired a strong son to follow in his footsteps, had been less than thrilled to learn that Percy had more interest in following in his mother's footsteps. In fact, more than one heated discussion had taken place in the Golec household about Percy's desire to become a healer. Percy didn't mind compromises, but this was one area in which he refused to negotiate. This wasn't to say he hadn't learned a considerable amount of fighting magic as well, for as his mother always said, even the most skilled healer was worthless when shot down, dead on the floor of their own infirmary.

"Mr. Golec? Mr. Golec? Would you care to comment on the character of Hamlet in Act II?" Mrs. Davis's voice abruptly stirred him from his reverie.

"Sorry?" Percy asked, trying to pull himself together. Truthfully, he hadn't heard a thing the teacher had said from the moment he sat down. Percy didn't usually have much trouble staying focused in school, but prior to today, he hadn't been concerned about the fate of the world in English class.

Mrs. Davis was scrutinizing him with suspicious eyes. It was obvious the woman knew Percy had no idea what she was talking about but wanted to make him sweat before letting him go.

"Well, Mr. Golec, I do hope today's lecture hasn't kept you from more important things," she commented in a wry tone. "Since it's been so dreadfully boring—"

At that moment, the bell rang, and the class began to tear out of the room.

"Make sure you finish reading the play by tomorrow, the lot of you!" the teacher exclaimed after the fleeing students. "And Mr. Golec," she added, giving the boy a final harsh glance. "Make sure you're present tomorrow, am I understood?"

Percy nodded obediently, gathered his things, and headed out the door.

***

After Sisyphus's escape, Acacia expected her training to take on a more aggressive approach, with hours of practicing different spells to prepare her for their next encounter with the dark mage and his minions. What Acacia didn't expect was to be sitting behind a solid pewter cauldron in the Golecs' basement, trying to follow Percy's handwritten instructions on how to brew a Revitalization Solution, a potion to help recover from light to moderate injuries.

"Make sure to follow the right sequence while mixing," AJ told her from the other side of the room. The twin's eyes were closed, and he appeared to be deep in thought. "If you put something in at the wrong time, it'll go bad, and we'll have wasted a batch of quality ingredients."

Acacia checked the recipe before stirring in the rest of the scales. The potion was turning a light shade of green, which according to the description in the book meant she was doing well with following the directions so far.

"So, what are you doing, anyway?" Acacia asked, stepping back from her cauldron and wiping the sweat from her brow. "Not keeping you awake, am I?"

AJ opened his eyes and cast a challenging glance in Acacia's direction. Her mind held no doubt the boy had been paying close attention to what she'd been doing, but she was also certain he was doing something else as well.

"I'm not sleeping, Acacia. Occasionally I do need to multitask."

"But you can't tell me what it is?" Acacia scowled at him. "I must say, I'm disappointed in you. Here my mom was all concerned you have all these super-secret schemes you're trying to get me involved in, and instead you're making me cook up healing potions."

AJ studied her for a moment, his gray eyes searching, and he shrugged and pulled a geometry textbook out of his book bag. For whatever reason, AJ's emotional reactions seemed more strictly controlled than usual.

"Sorry to disappoint," he said, not giving much away. "But if I'm going to be the one responsible for your education, you're going to be as balanced of a mage as possible, and that means being able to attack, defend, and do other things like potion-making. I'm not convinced I'm the most qualified to be teaching the Heir of Swansgrove, but I'm doing the best I can."

Acacia shook her head and turned back to her potion, which was bubbling. She still wasn't sure what being the Heir of Swansgrove really meant, aside from her magic being incredibly strong. Did it mean she would have to defeat Sisyphus in battle as her mother had ten years ago? Even if she *was* the Heir of Swansgrove, what needed to happen for her to become powerful enough to live up to her name? "Actually, I was more curious what you and Alex are fighting about this time."

AJ raised his pale brows and shrugged. "My brother and I disagree about any number of things. It comes with the territory of sharing ninety-nine percent of your DNA. And speaking of Alex, it looks like he's decided to join us."

Acacia blinked and whirled around as the basement door was flung open. Alex stood in the doorway, his soccer clothes spotted with grass and mud stains from practice.

"And *what* do you think you're doing?" Alex yelled, glaring daggers at his brother. "Sisyphus is on the loose, and you're teaching Acacia how to clang a bunch of pots around? What kind of teacher are you?"

"For one, you don't need to slam your uncle's doors." AJ rose to his feet in a motion fluid enough to make Acacia jealous. "For another, as someone who hasn't finished their own training yet, I'm not sure you're the best judge of what a magic teacher should and shouldn't be doing."

Alex was down the stairs in less than five seconds. *Oh boy,* Acacia thought with a sigh. *Here we go again.*

"I've had enough of your stupid comments, Andrew!" Alex yelled, his cheeks crimson with frustration. "How many times are you going to remind me I haven't finished training yet?"

"That depends. How many times are you going to tell me how to teach my student?"

"Guys," Acacia said, standing up and forcing herself between the twins. "What about saving the hostility for the bad guys? You know, the ones who tried to kill us the other night?"

Alex shook his head and took a deep breath. "Oh, come on, Acacia. You're the Heir of Swansgrove, not some apprentice potion-maker. Don't tell me you don't think it's kind of odd that your first lesson after Sisyphus broke loose, this joker has you playing with lizard tails and—"

"She is learning how to brew beginner's level potions, Alex, not 'playing with lizard tails,'" AJ fired back, an annoyed expression visible on his face. He flicked his wrist and a leather-bound planner appeared in a small flash of blue magic. The book opened to a particular page when AJ reached out to grab it, which he handed to his brother. "I honestly don't feel the need to justify my training schedule to you, but since you're so concerned, take a look."

He has a training schedule for me? Acacia thought, watching as Alex's light gray eyes skimmed through a few pages of AJ's planner. *AJ really is trying his hardest to train me well.*

"Monday, November second," Alex read aloud. "Seven to two-thirty, school. Two-thirty to four-thirty, teach Acacia potions. Four-thirty to five-thirty, long run. Five-thirty to six, make dinner." The boy let out an irritated sigh and tossed the book back at his brother. "You have got to be kidding me, AJ. What kind of fourteen-year-old plans out every single day of every single week?"

AJ shrugged and with another flick of his wrist, the planner disappeared in another flash of blue magic. "In case you've forgotten, I don't make fun of you when you manage to forget what you're supposed to be doing on a daily basis. How about you lay off my planner?"

"Are you guys seriously fighting about a schedule?" Acacia shook her head. "And I thought I was bad for getting mad at Sari for stealing my hairbrushes!"

"Acacia, you should pay more attention to your potion," AJ told her. "It's going to go bad and we'll have to throw the whole batch out."

Alex rolled his eyes and let out a long, disgruntled sigh. "And what are you going to do with a potion when Sisyphus shows up at the front door, Andrew? Toss it in his face and see if he runs away?"

"You were here when I told you I don't feel the need to justify my training schedule to you, right? I planned it weeks ago, and I'm not about to change it because you don't think it's good enough."

Acacia was quickly losing her patience. She had grown fond of all her new friends in Silent Springs, but she often found herself astounded how fast a mild disagreement could turn into a battle. And to be fair, it wasn't *all* attributable to AJ's often difficult temperament. She could understand Alex's anger, but there were enough real problems around that it wasn't necessary to get upset over things as simple as an afternoon potions lesson.

Alex was not pleased with his brother's response. "How's Acacia supposed to reach her full potential if all you're doing is teaching her stuff that's *not* going to help her defeat Sisyphus? You were the one who was trained by Uncle Jack, AJ. I'd think you'd want her to be ready for a fight!"

"Why don't you focus on your own training instead of telling me how to conduct mine?"

"Why don't you focus on not being such a crappy teacher and I'll think about it?"

"Stop it, both of you!" Acacia yelled, her own temper beginning to fray. "What's the point of standing around fighting about how I should be trained?"

The room was getting warmer, though Acacia wasn't sure how or why. She was aware the cauldron behind her was continuing to bubble, making her think she had added something out of sequence or missed a step, but she didn't care. *What if Alex is right?* she thought. *It makes more sense for AJ to be teaching me attack magic with Sisyphus on the loose, doesn't it? But even if he is right, it doesn't mean he needs to insult AJ like that. Does everything have to be a fight?*

"Watch your temper, Acacia," AJ warned, his dark eyes taking note of the bubbling cauldron. "You're going to make something explode."

"Mr. Swiatkowski!" Acacia pointed her index finger accusingly at the twin, her patience expired. "I don't know who taught you manners, but you *cannot* walk around telling people they're going to make things explode!"

And what if Sisyphus showed up at her house in the middle of the night? As powerful of a mage as her mother had been, due to the events ten years ago, she no longer had a trace of magic. Could Acacia protect her non-magical father and brother, as well as her mother and sister?

Taking note of a disturbing scratching noise, Acacia whirled around, and to her shock, saw the cauldron rocking back and forth on the cement floor. Even from across the room, she could tell its contents had turned from a light green to an unsettling purple. And it *did* look like it was about to explode.

"Hey!" Acacia exclaimed, feeling her stomach drop. "What?"

"You didn't happen to use the powdered earthworms instead of the chopped ones, did you?" AJ didn't even bother to hide the disappointment in his voice. The twin walked past his brother, the discussion of not even a minute ago all but forgotten, as he knelt next to the increasingly dangerous-looking cauldron. "And besides, you do remember that everything you put your magic into can be affected by your emotional reactions, don't you?"

"You know it's gonna blow in like five seconds, right, AJ?" Alex retorted sharply. "So why don't you stop complaining and do something about it?"

AJ sighed and, without another word, made a complex hand movement above the cauldron, bathing it with the blue aura of his magic. Within seconds, the spell disappeared into thin air, the bubbling cauldron along with it.

"I thought having you brew potions would help you concentrate and work on that temper of yours," AJ commented, his tone more disappointed than irritated. "I guess I was wrong."

"Hey, what the heck did you—"

"I just sent it outside, Alex," AJ said, rising to his feet and glancing between his brother and Acacia. "Come on, let's go check the damage, shall we? After all, that was Percy's old cauldron that was just destroyed."

Acacia and Alex exchanged a brief set of curious glances, and without another word, they followed AJ upstairs and out the front door.

***

AJ hadn't been joking when he said the cauldron had been destroyed.

"Holy crap, Acacia," Alex voiced, gaping at the mess of melted pewter that had scorched a noticeable crevasse in the Golecs' backyard. "The next time I tick you off, remind me to not."

Acacia knelt in the grass beside what only minutes before had been a functional cauldron. *I wonder what caused more damage,* she thought. *The actual potion or my magic mixed in with it and made to boil over when I lost my temper.*

"I wouldn't worry too much about that if I were you, since it's destroyed either way." AJ blinked and glanced back at Acacia. "Honestly, I *would* be annoyed, but I'm too impressed at the moment."

Acacia! Alex mind-spoke, the shock palatable in his tone. *I think this is the closest anyone has come to making AJ speechless! Anyone who wasn't trying to murder him, anyway.*

"Well, what are you two standing around waiting for?" AJ raised his brows at them. "I'm not going to be the one to tell Percy we wrecked his cauldron and didn't bother to replace it. And besides"—the twin shot a backward glance in the direction of the half-melted mess—"that's still too hot to clean up right away." Without another word, AJ walked off toward the road, a determined expression on his face.

Okay, there is something weird going on here, Acacia mind-spoke to Alex, making a conscious effort to block her thoughts. *I haven't known your brother for too long, but I've never seen him this distracted. And I'd have thought for sure he'd give me a stern talking to about destroying the cauldron, not just saying 'oh well, let's go replace it.'*

Alex shrugged as the two of them followed AJ to a large tree, which emanated immense stores of power from within. Something told Acacia it was another one of the portal stops in town, just like the enormous boulder had been. *I don't know, don't you think he just was impressed you managed to explode it as bad as you did? He seemed honest to me.*

AJ touched the tree with his right hand, causing it to alight with an intricate, golden design. Acacia allowed herself a smile, pleased that she'd been correct about it being another stop in the portal system. AJ shot them both a piercing glare, clearly aware of at least some of their conversation.

"For future reference, if and when you two do have to fight some-one." AJ quirked his brows at them, every ounce of distractibility vanished from his pale face. "You might want to do a better job of communicating discretely than you do when you're talking behind my back. It might save your lives."

Alex let out an exhausted sigh, glaring back at his brother. "Let it go, AJ," he growled, as the three of them stepped into the portal. "You're worse than Mom."

Acacia let out a sigh of her own as they tumbled through the golden magic of the enchanted portal system, still unable to shake off her concern that there was something important AJ wasn't telling them.

***

Minutes later, Acacia and Alex stood next to each other in the apothe-cary, which to her surprise was squeezed between an old bookstore and a small café downtown. As with many of the other magical stores, Acacia undoubtedly had passed the shop numerous times throughout her time in Silent Springs, without a clue as to what it was.

"Hey Acacia, look at this thing!" Alex remarked in an excited tone, pulling her over to one of the aisles of the shop, which was lined with strange, bottled substances. "This one looks like a brain!"

Acacia gazed at the bottles with fascination. She found the brain jar without too much difficulty, along with several other bizarre sub-stances, including eyeballs floating in a greenish liquid, a number of claws and fangs, and tiny five-legged rats.

"Do people use all these things for potions ?" Acacia picked up a vial of small, slimy tails, examining it for a moment before placing it back down on the shelf. "This makes me want to never make potions, ever again."

"Some do." Alex shrugged. "Percy knows how to make a lot more potions than either me or AJ, so I guess he's the better person to ask. Most of us know how to make a few potions and that's about it. No offense to the potion-makers out there, but it's not the most exciting. I'd rather learn how to fight than sit around mixing a bunch of stuff together to see if it might turn out to be something useful."

Can you two at least try to be slightly more respectful of the art of po-tion-making in an apothecary? AJ asked, his telepathic voice dripping with annoyance. *I'm no potion-maker, but I don't insult people who are.*

Well, if you're no potion-maker, why are you trying to teach Acacia how to make potions? Alex demanded, placing a jar filled with some kind of purple liquid back on the shelf. *Seems weird if you ask me!*

Acacia sighed and walked to the end of the aisle to investigate what AJ was doing. He had picked up a cauldron about the same size as the one Acacia had wrecked and placed it on the wooden counter and appeared to be in the middle of a discussion with the shopkeeper about it.

"So, it was about this size, made of pewter, maybe with a little bit of iron mixed in," AJ was saying. "The only problem is I'm not sure if this will be strong enough for what I need it for."

"That cauldron's strong enough to withstand third-degree acids, any kind of potion that the likes of you could ever dream of brewing, and magical fire up to four hundred degrees in temperature." The shopkeeper, a man in his forties with a head full of sandy brown hair, was studying AJ, his expression a mix between disbelief and annoy-ance. "What in the name of all creation are you planning to do that a Grade A cauldron like this wouldn't be strong enough?"

"It's not what I'm planning to do with it as it is who will be using it," AJ responded. "My . . . friend has a talent for destroying things."

With that, Acacia placed her hands on her hips and walked over to the counter. "Mr. Swiatkowski. What do you mean by 'a talent for destroying things'?"

AJ and the shopkeeper turned toward her, both visibly stunned by her outburst. Much to Acacia's surprise, the shopkeeper leaped over the counter and covered the distance between them in one long stride. Blinking in shock, Acacia took a single step backward.

"Surely *this* cannot be the Heir of Swansgrove?" the man asked, his dark eyes wide with amazement. "Acacia Swansgrove, the child destined to defeat the forces of darkness for good?"

Acacia's mouth dropped open in shock. Was it possible she had that much of a reputation in the magical community? *Sure, Sisyphus and those Council members knew who I was,* Acacia thought. *But I've never even met this guy before. How could he possibly know who I am?*

"You bet it is!" Alex exclaimed, emerging from the shop aisle, his gray eyes looking just as excited as the shopkeeper's did. "And you said it, she's gonna kick Sisyphus's butt like it's never been kicked!"

Out of the corner of her eye, Acacia could see AJ roll his eyes, but she was far too shocked by the shopkeeper's reaction to her appearance to care.

"If this is for Acacia Wheatley, consider it a gift from one member of the resistance to another!" the man said, clapping AJ on the back hard. "It's the least I can do."

Acacia's mouth fell agape again. *Did he just give us the cauldron for free?* she mind-spoke to both of her friends. *Is this happening right now?*

It would appear, AJ replied, glancing between Acacia and the shop-keeper. *You have more friends that we first realized.*

Moments later, the three teenagers were again walking up Main Street, Acacia's gift as well as a replacement for the cauldron she had destroyed magically shrunken and tucked away in what to the normal eye looked like nothing more than a cloth grocery bag. Acacia was vaguely aware of Alex chatting beside her as they approached the portal stop but still found herself far more concerned by AJ's silence. Normally, AJ would have said something to her about the shopkeeper's gift and Acacia's luck, a warning about not wrecking this cauldron, something! Acacia had no doubt something was going on, and AJ had at least an idea of what it was but, for whatever reason, wasn't telling them.

Acacia's nerves had reached their breaking point.

"Okay, look," Acacia began, halting and grabbing AJ by the shoulder. "I want to know why you're so spacey today. You're never this quiet except when you're thinking of doing something sneaky, and in case you didn't realize, it's too dangerous for that!"

AJ's eyes turned from blue to gray as they focused on her, something Acacia realized she had observed before. The boy blinked and studied her, as if surprised she had decided to confront him. "I'm going to ask you nicely to let go of me," AJ said in a calm tone. *I would think learning you have friends in high places would put you in a good mood. Not to mention getting your own cauldron for free.*

"And I'm going to ask *you* what's going on," Acacia retorted. "There's something you're not telling us about, and I want to know what!"

AJ shrugged and slipped out of Acacia's grasp, seemingly unperturbed by her outburst. *Both of you need to learn how to deal with your problems without having temper tantrums,* he remarked, continuing along the sidewalk. *It's more befitting of toddlers than teenagers.*

"Well, our tempers wouldn't be so short if you didn't act like such a—"

Oof.

Acacia had no time to react before the newcomer, a small but athletic girl with light brown skin crashed sidelong into the three of them. Acacia opened her mouth to yell but froze in shock as the other girl glowed orange.

No, don't! Acacia mind-spoke, feeling the familiar sensation of another mage's powers whisk them away. *There's too many—*

The last thing she saw before the orange light enveloped them completely was the sight of the girl staring wide-eyed at her, looking just as shocked as Acacia herself.

Chapter Thirteen

ONAWA

The teleportation spell faded away, and both Acacia and Alex were thrown roughly to the ground. Opening her eyes, Acacia realized they were in a grassy meadow, though one she didn't recognize. Not wanting to be taken by surprise again, she pushed herself to her feet and turned to give Alex a hand.

C'mon, we've got to hurry! she mind-spoke. *What if she's working for—*

Acacia whirled around and saw the last of the orange magic vanish in the middle of the meadow, and as it did, two figures emerged, landing on their feet with catlike grace.

"And who," AJ asked, crossing both arms in front of his chest. He paused, allowing the entire situation to settle in. Acacia couldn't help noticing that as he looked at the girl, AJ's defensive manner disappeared. "Are you?"

The girl smiled and took a small bow. She was shorter than Acacia, but every inch of her body was filled with exuberant energy. Her straight black hair fell to her shoulders, and her eyes were the color of mahogany.

"Onawa Mescal, at your service." Her brown eyes glanced between AJ, Alex, and Acacia with curiosity. "What a ride! We've all got our talents, I guess, and teleportation isn't mine. My mom says it's because I don't have the concentration for it, and maybe she's right. Whatever, I'd rather spend some quality time with a dragon than play around with silly charms or enchantments!" Onawa said all this very quickly.

Okay, Acacia thought. *Maybe she's not evil. A little crazy, but not evil.*

A lot of mages are like that, Alex told her, glancing between Acacia and the newcomer. *Passion can make you a bit . . . eccentric.*

Acacia shook her head, not willing to make up her mind about Onawa quite yet. *Maybe I'm worrying about nothing*, Acacia considered as she walked over to where AJ was standing. *After all, AJ's the paranoid one. If he's not worried about this girl, I guess I shouldn't be either.*

"But anyway, who are you guys?" Onawa asked, her tone curious. "I wasn't trying to bring you along with me, but I'm not sorry I did. It's been a while since I had regular people to talk to."

"Oh, yeah." Much to Acacia's surprise, AJ's face was flushed as he clasped his hands in front of his body. "My name is AJ—Andrew Swiatkowski." He turned and gestured toward Acacia and Alex. "This is my brother Alex and our friend Acacia Wheatley. Welcome to Silent Springs."

A joyous expression filled Onawa's face, and without warning, she jumped into the air and gave AJ a rather vigorous hug. "This is Silent Springs! You're serious, right? If this is Silent Springs, I'm finally here!"

Acacia and Alex exchanged a pair of glances, both their brows raised in confusion. *Okay, Alex, do you know what's going on here?* Acacia mind-spoke, befuddled by the scene unfolding in front of her. Onawa had let go of AJ but was still standing close to him. *How is your brother not freaking out? This is the same kid who freaked out at me for trying to give him a hug when he was having a mental breakdown. And now he has no problem with hugs from strangers?*

Alex chuckled and glanced at Acacia, a look of understanding on his face. *I never thought I'd see the day*, he commented, watching AJ and Onawa with newfound interest. *Looks like little brother is growing up.*

Huh? What do you mean by—

But before Acacia could finish her thought, AJ turned around and shot them a fearsome glare. *Enough, both of you. You're as mature as a couple of second graders.*

Takes one to know one! Alex flashed his brother a crooked grin. *Now, don't let us take you away from your new best friend.*

"You've been looking for Silent Springs?" AJ asked the girl after turning away from his brother. "Do you mind if I ask why?"

Onawa beamed at him and clapped him on the shoulders in enthusiasm. "Of course not! Do I look like someone afraid to share about themselves?"

And she touched him again, Acacia mind-spoke to Alex in disbelief. *So, I guess human touch doesn't make him explode.*

Alex laughed. *Who would've known? Learn something new every day.*

Acacia half expected AJ to turn around again and start yelling at them, but he appeared to be too absorbed in his conversation with the newcomer to care what they were saying. Onawa glanced between the three of them and smiled, obviously ready to tell her story.

"See, I'm from the Jicarilla Apache Nation in New Mexico, but with all this happening here, about a week ago, I told my parents I was leaving." Onawa tucked a lock of black hair behind her ear. "They weren't happy about it, but they knew I was bored, and a bored

Onawa is never a good thing. Okay, they told me, but only if I stayed with my Uncle Nantan who lives in this little town in Silent Springs, Pennsylvania. So, I left with S'feirra, looking for the place. I didn't think I was ever going to find it, but here I am!"

Acacia blinked and examined the girl with newfound curiosity. *Is this girl for real? What kind of teenager tells her parents she's leaving home because bad things are happening on the opposite side of the country?*

If Onawa heard her thoughts, she gave no sign. "But sometime last week, these weird guys start chasing me, and then, the prison in the sky opens and all of these auras start going all over the place! And then S'feirra gets spooked and takes off so then we're off course—"

"Hey sorry," Acacia interrupted, scratching her head. Onawa's rushed manner of storytelling was a little hard to follow. "But what's S'feirra?"

"Oh!" Onawa exclaimed, fishing out a silver whistle from underneath her jacket. "I forgot!" Without another word, she blew into it, creating a high-pitched screech. Acacia and Alex exchanged confused glances and searched for any sign of activity.

What the heck was that about? Acacia asked. *Do you think that's her dog?*

Alex shrugged, looking every bit as lost as Acacia felt. *I'm hoping it's just a dog and not some monster. She seems the type to have weird pets, don't you think?*

Acacia heard a soft swooshing sound off in the distance but didn't think much of it. Was this how her life was going to be now, her friends acting more bizarre than normal and random strangers telling her their entire life story? Acacia had just come to terms with the fact that life as a mage didn't make sense, but she'd been hoping for a bit more clarity than this.

"But anyway." Onawa stretched her arms in front of her. "We ended up in this place where everything was just black and dead looking and crawling with these nasty sprites. I know not everyone loves dragons, but I'll take a dragon over a sprite any day."

The swooshing noise was considerably closer now. Acacia looked off into the distance and could see the figure of a giant winged reptile closing in on them.

"Alex, AJ!" she screamed at the top of her lungs, pointing at the shape with her index finger. "Dragon!"

Both twins looked up at the creature barreling toward them.

"What the hell is *wrong* with you!" Alex bellowed, turning on the still-ecstatic Onawa. "Did you just sic a freaking dragon on us?"

"Oh, relax." Onawa waved her hand about, as if dispelling Alex's concerns. "It's just S'feirra, and I've been looking for her. We got separated after the horrible sprite place. See, we ran into the guy with the dead eyes, and he kept wanting me to sell S'feirra to him, and I told him no, she doesn't belong to me, so how could I sell her? He just kept saying 'Oh, Henry will love this beastie,' so I sent her off and then I got out of there as fast as I could."

The dragon was now right in front of them, hovering with an occasional flap of its leathery wings. It was a beautiful creature, its body covered with sky blue scales, except for its underbelly, which was protected by silver ones. It was about fifteen feet long from its nose to the tip of its tail; not quite as large as Acacia had first anticipated, but it was still the largest living creature she had ever seen.

"S'feirra, down," Onawa commanded, and without another word, the dragon flapped its wings one more time and landed behind her.

Don't panic, AJ warned Acacia and Alex, his tone calm. *It might be friendly.*

S'feirra let out a single fearsome roar, glaring at the three of them with its large yellow eyes. Acacia grabbed Alex's arm, pulling herself closer to him, her eyes absorbing the sight of the fantastic yet terrifying creature in front of them.

Friendly? Alex repeated, his tone incredulous. *AJ, if that's what you call 'friendly,' I'd hate to see what you call unfriendly!*

Onawa rolled her dark brown eyes at the dragon and, without another word, rapped it on the head.

"S'feirra!" the girl hollered reproachfully. "What have I told you about yelling at friends?"

The dragon looked at Onawa with what seemed to be a sad expression on its face. It then uttered a low-pitched whine and bowed its head, looking like a dog that had been scolded by its owner.

"She says she's sorry," Onawa explained, stroking the creature on the head. "She thought you were the people who were chasing me before."

S'feirra laid her head down and the ground and looked up at them, wagging her tail with excitement. Despite the creature's fearsome appearance, she did seem to act more like an overexcited puppy than a legendary killing machine.

"Um, Onawa?" Acacia spoke up, still recovering from the shock of a dragon roaring at her. A fearsome creature, which prior to a few moments ago, she'd only seen in movies. "I don't mean this in a bad way, but if you're coming to live in town, I don't think you can bring her with you. Maybe your family didn't tell you this, but there is a decent population of non-magicals that would all have heart attacks if they saw a dragon walking down the street."

The girl stroked the creature's muzzle in a loving manner, similar to the way a pet owner would pet their cat or dog. *Okay, I can't say I know much about typical mage-dragon relationships,* Acacia thought.

But I wouldn't guess that most mages are comfortable being up close and personal with something that big.

We're not, Alex noted in a tense tone. *Those of us who aren't insane, anyway. I've only seen a dragon once before, and it was miles away. And it was scary enough when the thing wasn't right in my face!*

"Oh, I know," Onawa said. "We're going to find S'feirra a nice little cave where I can come visit her after school, and we can see about finding the woodland dragons, won't we, girl?"

The dragon crooned and rubbed her head against Onawa's hands. Acacia scratched her head and let out a brief sigh. She wasn't irritated, but sometimes she did wish things made more sense. This girl had appeared out of nowhere and teleported them all in plain daylight from a busy street to a random meadow. Had anyone seen them? And what were Onawa's intentions for coming to the sleepy little town of Silent Springs? Maybe she wanted to help, but did she really want to jump into the middle of a magical war? Acacia also couldn't help but feel confused by AJ's uncharacteristic behavior. The boy had made it clear to her that he wasn't comfortable with people touching him, particularly those he didn't know well. But how could AJ be uncomfortable with Acacia touching him after knowing her for several months and be okay with Onawa doing so after just meeting her? Could Onawa have something to do with how distracted AJ had been all day? Acacia had known for quite some time that something was going on in her friend's mind; perhaps this energetic dragon girl had something to do with it.

You have no idea how long I've been waiting for something like this to happen. Alex looked pleased with himself. *Me and Percy both. But it looks like Mr. No Emotions has met his match.*

AJ shot his brother a piercing glare, making Acacia wonder if he had managed to blast through Alex's mental defenses. Alex's amused expression vanished as a cluster of blue sparks appeared in the middle of the twins' locked gazes. Within seconds, they vanished, as if they had never been there in the first place.

Crap, that was close! Alex told Acacia. *He came this close to reading my mind that time. I guess we do need to practice blocking our thoughts.*

Acacia grinned and shook her head. That seemed more like the AJ she knew. But could it be possible? If what Alex was saying was true . . . could AJ have . . . a crush on this girl? Did AJ even get those?

"We'd better get going now before it gets dark," AJ remarked, shooting his brother one more sidelong glance before turning back to Onawa. "Or before your friends come looking for you again."

"Works for me!" Onawa rubbed S'feirra's muzzle one last time before the creature took to the sky once more. "I'm glad I tumbled into you guys after all! Now, where are we again? All these forests look the same to me."

AJ grinned sheepishly and walked toward the edge of the meadow. "It looks like you sent us about five miles away from the town limits. There should be a portal stop over this way that will take us back to Silent Springs. It shouldn't be too difficult finding your uncle's house from there."

Acacia giggled, glancing between AJ and Onawa with amusement. *Maybe things don't make sense,* she thought. *But at least things have gotten more exciting than a boring potions lesson!*

***

AJ knew Acacia had been perplexed by his behavior for much of the day but couldn't bring himself to care. Sure, he had been more distracted than usual, but he hadn't been neglecting her training. And besides, it wasn't like AJ wasn't occasionally distracted with something else during their lessons anyway. It was just that today he wasn't doing quite as well with hiding it.

"Wow," Onawa marveled as the four of them emerged from the portal stop, located on the top of a hill overlooking the outskirts of Silent Springs. "I would have been wandering around for hours looking for that!"

The girl was beaming, no doubt ecstatic to have reached her destination after long days of travel. There was something about Onawa Mescal that AJ couldn't quite put his finger on, something that drew him in like a moth to fire. The question remained, however, just how badly he would get burned.

Alex rolled his eyes at the girl. "I believe it. Since you've been flying around lost for two weeks now?"

But Onawa's attention was focused on examining the town before her. The green forests of Pennsylvania had to be a foreign sight for the girl, if she'd lived her entire life in the dry deserts of New Mexico. And what reason would she have to lie about it?

"I think my uncle lives over there somewhere." Onawa pointed toward the eastern part of town, where the suburbs of Silent Springs gave way to forest. "I don't remember the exact address, but it's off a dirt road. Once I get settled, I can whistle for S'feirra, find her a little cave space nearby, and I can go visit her every day after school!"

"True," AJ said, shooting the girl a crooked grin. "Would you like some company on the way? Something tells me that you could benefit from an abbreviated walking tour of the bustling metropolis of Silent Springs, Miss Mescal."

Onawa smiled back, an amused glimmer in her brown eyes. "Your bustling metropolis doesn't have anything on me, Swiatkowski." She dusted off some dirt from her shoulders. "But I won't say no to a tour.

And besides, as much as I like roughing it, for once I think sleeping in a bed will be nice."

Onawa reached out and interlaced her fingers with AJ's, her grasp strong yet not overpowering. The girl's hands were warm, in comparison to AJ's cold ones, which always seemed to lose the ability to hold heat from mid-October through most of March. Maybe, just maybe the two of them were imbalanced enough to create some sort of bizarre equilibrium.

Come on, Andrew, AJ thought. *Now you're being ridiculous.*

"Oh!" Onawa exclaimed and turned around to Alex and Acacia. "Sorry, I almost left without saying goodbye! I'm glad I got to meet you guys too! I'll see you tomorrow at school?"

Alex and Acacia glanced at each other and looked back at Onawa. They were both much more extroverted than AJ could ever be, but neither was a match for Onawa's wealth of energy.

"Nice to meet you too." Acacia scratched her head, her expression thoroughly puzzled. "Sure, come sit with us at lunch if you're in sixth period."

"Same," Alex said, picking up the cloth bag containing the two shrunken cauldrons. "I guess I'm taking these home, AJ? Since you're tour guide for the day?"

AJ nodded. "Acacia can take her cauldron home with her. If you don't mind dropping the other one at the Golecs, I'd appreciate it." AJ sighed, thinking of the molten mess he had left in the Golecs' backyard. "And since you'll be over there, let Percy know I'll be over to clean up." He certainly didn't want Percy getting in trouble for a mess he didn't make in the first place.

"Awesome!" Onawa said, a broad grin on her face. She turned back to Acacia and added, "I'll see you then! I think we're going to be great friends!"

"You two have fun." Even from a cursory glance, AJ noticed his brother was amused by the situation. *I'll talk to you about this later, bro.*

You can talk to me all you want, AJ retorted, shooting Alex a quizzical expression in return. *That doesn't mean I'll talk back.*

Without another word, AJ and Onawa started down the trail toward town, leaving Alex and Acacia far behind.

***

"You're different, you know?" Onawa said as they turned down a narrow alleyway leading away from downtown Silent Springs.

AJ grinned, paying close attention to the uneven cobblestones lining the pathway. "Oh? In what way?"

"Well for one you're not afraid of my dragon," Onawa replied with a playful grin. "Do you know how many people can't even look at me because they're so terrified of S'feirra? Your friends were afraid of her. So why aren't you?"

AJ shrugged, trying to act normal. "It's not that I'm not afraid. I'm afraid of plenty of things, but I just try not to let my fear dictate what I do."

"That doesn't explain why you weren't afraid of S'feirra."

He laughed. Unlike many people AJ knew, Onawa was straightforward in her communication.

"Well, she was with you, wasn't she?" AJ said, hoping this explanation would suffice. "Somehow I didn't think you'd let her turn us all into smores."

"That's passable, I guess." Onawa raised her right brow at him, her brown eyes wide with inquisitiveness. "But on a different note, I also picked up that you don't exactly like being touched."

AJ scratched his ear, trying to keep his discomfort hidden. "You're more observant than you look, Miss Mescal."

"I'd be stupid to not notice," Onawa retorted, flicking AJ's forehead with her index finger and thumb. "But I'll admit, it's your friends who give you away. I thought your brother was going to bust out into laughter when I hugged you."

"Yes, but Alex also thinks everything is hilarious. So, he's not really the best judge."

Onawa smirked back at him and halted, placing both hands on her hips. "Then who *is* the best judge? After all, before I jump on board the save-the-world train, I think I should at least have a chance to judge the judger!"

"Well, I don't think I'm fit to judge which judger has the best judgment." AJ felt more at ease than he had for quite some time. "Seems to me that would be a little judgmental, don't you think?"

Onawa laughed and shook her head. "If I hear any form of the word 'judge' one more time today, I'm going to slap whoever says it offside the head so hard they wake up in a different time zone."

"Besides the one you just said?"

Onawa rolled her eyes and let out a long sigh. "You're lucky I didn't make S'feirra come with us," she retorted. "Otherwise, you'd be in big trouble right now."

Talking to Onawa was easy, almost so easy that it seemed too good to be true. Speaking with Alex and Acacia was always a challenge since they both seemed to have a perpetual need to question him. With Alex, it was always something to do with Acacia, how he dare say something like that to her, how he dare include this in her training and not that . . . the list was endless. Acacia, on the other hand, had a fascination with forcing her way into matters that didn't concern her. But with Onawa it was different. Even in the short time that AJ had known her, he felt like he didn't have to censor himself, at least as much as he usually did. Though why exactly, AJ wasn't sure. After all, personality-wise, Onawa was as different from him as possible. AJ was a planner, and Onawa was a doer. After all, how many teenagers would pack up their bags to go stay with their uncle on the opposite side of the country? And for all their discussion, Onawa hadn't made it clear what had prompted her to leave her home behind. But something deep down, something inexplicable to his logical senses, made AJ think despite Onawa's spontaneous behavior, something very serious had caused her to make her decision.

Several minutes later, they had left the cobblestone sidewalks of Silent Springs's historic district and entered the dirt paths and grassy fields of the outskirts of town. According to Onawa, her destination lay between the row of houses they were now passing and the heavily wooded area farther east.

"AJ, look!" Onawa pointed at a skinny dark gravel trail to their right, which led to a quaint, two-story wooden home. The girl took off at a sprint up the path, no less ecstatic than when S'feirra had come flying to greet her. "Uncle Nantan!"

Sure enough, a tall, lanky man with long, jet-black hair and a pair of warm brown eyes emerged from the house, his mouth upturned in a small smile at the sight of his niece. Onawa laughed and ran to her uncle and threw her arms around his shoulders.

"Uncle Nantan, I'm so glad to see you!" Onawa exclaimed and stepped back. "I didn't think I was ever gonna get here!"

The girl's uncle chuckled and patted her on the shoulder. "Silly child, of course you were going to arrive," he said, his tone almost lyrical. "You couldn't be here now if you didn't, could you?"

Onawa grinned and turned to face AJ, her expression beaming. "Bye, AJ! See ya tomorrow! Oh!" The girl glanced back at her uncle and added, "Uncle, this is my friend AJ. He helped me find where I was going. AJ, this is my uncle Nantan."

"It's good to meet you, sir," AJ said as politely as he could, waving toward the man. "Have a good evening."

Both Onawa and her uncle waved goodbye and disappeared into the house. AJ let out a long sigh, thinking of the conversation that awaited him at home. *Well, I guess it's time to stop delaying the inevitable. Time to play twenty questions with Alex.*

So, you're more afraid of your brother than a dragon? Onawa laughed. *You're right, you don't have the best judgment!*

AJ shook his head as he summoned the blue magic of his teleportation spell. *Onawa Mescal,* he thought, blocking his thoughts. *You have no idea.*

Chapter Fourteen

A Strange Vision

Acacia sat cross-legged in the high grass of the meadow, fiddling with her long, coppery braid. With all the recent changes, it was becoming increasingly challenging to keep track of everything, from rogue mages set on taking over the world to strange teenagers with an intense affection for dragons.

"Are you okay?" AJ asked, looking away from the old spell book and glancing over his shoulder at her. "You're not usually this deep in thought."

Meaning you don't think I usually think, Acacia thought, shaking her head. *Or not much, anyway.*

Since Onawa's arrival, AJ's distracted behaviors had all but disappeared, along with many of his mercurial moods. In less than a week, the twin had helped Acacia to all but master the teleportation spell, control her lightning magic to an extent she first deemed impossible, and even learn how to brew several basic potions.

"Well, duh he's in a better mood," Alex had told her one Saturday afternoon as they hiked once again to Lake Prosper. "He's gone and fallen in love with the Dragon Girl."

Acacia laughed, thinking back on that day when all they had meant to do was replace a badly mangled cauldron. None of them had been expecting the appearance of a girl who treated a majestic dragon like a young puppy.

"Do you think so? I wasn't sure your brother could do that."

"Don't tell me you're questioning the freaky twin thing!" Alex said, his light gray eyes playful. "How dare you!"

"Acacia. Acacia!" AJ's voice pulled her back to the present. "You do realize that in order for me to teach you, both of us have to be awake, correct?"

Acacia shook her head, forcing the last of the daydreams from her mind. As calm and forgiving as AJ's demeanor had been lately, she didn't want to push her luck in case he *was* able to tell what she'd been thinking about.

"Must be my narcolepsy again," Acacia said in a joking tone. "You should make these lessons a little more interesting, Mr. Swiatkowski, and you wouldn't have to worry about me falling asleep."

AJ shot her a curious glare, his dark gray eyes as stormy as ever. "Need I remind you of the dangers of being ill-prepared for your next encounter with Henry Moore? I doubt he'll go easy on you, narcolepsy or no."

Acacia laughed, hoping to smooth their conversation over as soon as possible. "Oh, come on, AJ. Don't you think it's far more likely you'll be the one fighting Mr. Sissy Puss? That makes way more sense to me."

"Acacia," AJ said, looking like he was weighing his words with care. "You are the Heir of Swansgrove. I am the heir of coal miners and fishmongers. Who do you think Sisyphus is going to want to face in battle?"

"Well, I don't know. You do pretty well for the heir of coal miners and fishmongers."

AJ wasn't as amused as Acacia had hoped he would be. The twin crossed his arms in front of his chest and stared at her, his dark eyes piercing her soul "That's because you've never run into a fishmonger at a street market," he said in a flat tone which made it difficult for Acacia to tell if he was joking or not. "But talking about the tenacity of my ancestors isn't going to prepare you for Henry Moore. Learning how to create protection circles might."

Back to business, I see, Acacia thought with a sigh. *Though I'll take that over him interrogating me about what I was thinking about.*

"AJ, listen," she began, rising to her feet. "Don't get me wrong, you've been a great teacher, and I appreciate everything you've done. But there's no way I'll be able to go face to face with Sisyphus. Maybe I'm getting to be a better fighter, but I'm not close to being as good as you. So what if I'm descended from a powerful family of mages? Who you're related to doesn't make a difference when it comes down to talent." Acacia paused for a moment and brushed off her shoulders. "Heir of Swansgrove or not, I'm nowhere as powerful as you are."

After long months of training, Acacia had finally succeeded in making her teacher laugh.

"Well, I'm glad you find my lack of expertise entertaining!" she exclaimed, feeling her brows twitch with irritation. "At least one of us does!"

"I'm not laughing at your 'lack of expertise,' Acacia," AJ informed her, his expression still amused. "I'm laughing at the fact you think I'm that powerful."

"I'm missing the joke."

AJ shrugged. "What I'm trying to tell you is I'm *not* that powerful, at least when it comes to sheer strength, not that your talents are lacking. My saving grace is I'm fast and can think on my feet." The boy paused and tilted his head thoughtfully. "You might not be the strongest yet, but you're getting stronger by the day."

Acacia felt her eyes widen in shock. Stronger by the day?

"I'm still not certain what all you can do," AJ admitted. "I've tried to do some research in my free time, and it seems that Swansgrove mages often have abilities that other mages do not, things that set them apart as a truly gifted family. With how quickly you've been able to learn after years of your magic being repressed, I do think you probably have some special abilities, though I'm not sure exactly what they are yet."

It was Acacia's turn to laugh. "Special abilities?" Acacia repeated, almost dumbfounded. "The only special abilities I have are blowing things up and making bad decisions."

"Acacia, you know that's not true," AJ said in a grave tone. "You've learned in three months what most mages learn in six. I won't argue that you've made some mistakes, but I think you're learning from them. Besides, no one can deny the extent of your power is impressive." The twin's somber expression faded, and his lips lifted up at the corners slightly. "It won't happen today or even tomorrow, but I think with enough practice and motivation, you'll stop Sisyphus."

Acacia's face flushed with embarrassment. Was it true? Had she *really* been able to learn so much more than most mages in a short amount of time? Sure, it did seem like she'd managed to learn a lot, but Acacia figured that was just because the magical world was so new to her. Could she do this, could she become strong enough so the next time she crossed paths with Sisyphus she could fight him and not freeze in fear as she had the night of his escape?

"Regardless," AJ continued, his face all business. "Before you do that, you should probably learn to make protection circles, since you may find yourself in the position of protector, whether you're protecting a few people or the whole town of Silent Springs."

The twin waved his hand, causing a ribbon of blue light to circle his wrist and hand. Taking a step closer to Acacia, he drew a circle over their heads with his hand, leaving in its wake a shimmering ring of magic.

"Making protection circles is one of the most ancient of our arts. You can use them to prevent creatures from entering an area or fortify a building from disaster. The circle itself is a conjuration." AJ flicked his wrist again, and blue light sprang from the ring above, creating an impenetrable barrier of blue magic around them. "And once it's cast, it works like a shield, only it can hide the trace of magic as well, so even if someone tries tracking you, they won't be able to."

Acacia studied the shield in fascination until the barrier separating them from the outside world was all but transparent. The magic was still there, but from what Acacia could tell, they would be completely invisible to the naked eye.

"But hold on." Acacia faced AJ. "It's magic to shield magic? Doesn't the fact that it's magic make it traceable?"

AJ shrugged and snapped his fingers, causing the semicircle to flash one final time and dissolve into nothing.

"Not if you make sure it's a solid protection circle," he explained. "Now, there are exceptions to the rule. Sn— I mean . . . mages who are very skilled trackers might be able to find you, protection circle or not. But if your spell is strong, they won't be able to penetrate it, no matter how well they can . . . well, sniff you out."

Okay, so there's something he isn't telling me, Acacia noted. *He did the same thing after we were questioned by the Council, and he knew where I was even before I did. Is AJ one of these people who can . . . sniff people out through a protection circle?*

"So why don't *you* give it a try?" AJ asked, his voice jarring Acacia back to reality. "You saw how I did it, right?"

Acacia nodded. Shoving all thoughts of secrets and magic sniffers from her mind, Acacia rolled her wrist like she had seen AJ do, and a ribbon of her magic furled around her hand and wrist. She waved her hand, and the ribbon curled farther up on her arm.

"Excellent," AJ commented, the suspicious expression on his face traded for one of approval. "Now, draw the circle and activate it."

Acacia obeyed and imitated AJ's movements, drawing a circle in the air above them with her hand. Once she completed the motion and created a ribbon of green overhead, she raised her hand into the sky, conjuring a barrier of magic, a circle of protection, around them. After a few moments, the light faded, leaving them protected and almost untraceable from the outside world.

Impressive, AJ told her. *Once again, you're a natural.*

Does that mean I'm an heir of fishmongers too? Acacia teased. *That must be why I used to be so good at selling Girl Scout cookies!*

Hilarious. Now take it down and practice putting it up again.

Acacia laughed and flicked her wrist and hand again, disbanding the spell. Shooting AJ a toothy grin, she moved again to summon another protection circle, but before she could finish drawing the shape, her vision became flooded with green light.

Weird, Acacia thought, shaking her hand to terminate whatever spell was forming. *Is that my magic? I don't remember doing anything other than trying to get this circle up.*

The world around her was changing, the bright colors of the forest darkening and becoming even colder than the typical chill of a November day. Acacia could feel a power overtaking her, flooding her vision, making it impossible for her to concentrate on anything other than the dark images appearing before her.

"Acacia! Acacia!" AJ's worried shouts barely registered in the girl's mind as she dropped to her knees. "Acacia Wheatley! Can you hear me?"

Well, I wasn't expecting this, Acacia thought, as her world faded into darkness.

***

Acacia was in a stone chamber filled with cases of books and a scattering of well-worn tapestries hung upon the cold walls. A beautiful mahogany desk rested in the center of the room, cluttered with an assortment of documents. A tall, ominous figure stood behind the desk, his back turned from Acacia's line of vision. Even so, Acacia could tell she'd seen him before. Could it be . . . was it Sisyphus? If it *was*, how was Acacia seeing him now? Was it anything more than a hallucination? Was it really happening?

A knock sounded at the door.

"Enter!" the man barked, jerking his head and looking in the direction of the knocking. "What have you to report?"

Two figures entered the study, confirming Sisyphus's identity. The first was Dionera, her hair as fiery and wild as it had been the night of the escape. The other was a man Acacia did not recognize. He was about the same height as Sisyphus, but with longer brown hair, which he wore tied back in a neat ponytail, and harsh black eyes.

"Lord Sisyphus," the other man began with a bow. "I regret to inform you of an unfortunate turn of events. Our operations did not go as planned."

"What do you mean 'our operations did not go as planned,' Minos?" Sisyphus demanded in a caustic tone. "Were you successful or not?"

Minos looked at Sisyphus, his expression grave. "The girl escaped, my lord. We thought we had her and her dragon, but when we were about to snatch her, she got away."

Sisyphus's face contorted in rage. "We have been out of commission for ten long years! Ten years! The idiotic Council has clearly forgotten what we are capable of and the time for action is now! Many of them now show no fear for me and will defy us without a second thought! We must give them something to be afraid of!"

The study fell silent at Sisyphus's words, as both Minos and Dionera looked to their master, awaiting their orders.

"Dervla Swansgrove gave up her magic to lock us in the damn vacuum years ago and thus won't prove much of a problem to us," Sisyphus continued. "But her daughter, young Swansgrove, is another story. If she is allowed to reach her full potential, she will threaten all our aspirations of seizing control once more. For our goals to become a reality, she must be eliminated. But the time is not right. We must first place fear in the heart of every mage still obedient to the Council."

Dionera smirked, her orange eyes gleaming with anticipation. Something about the mage made Acacia's skin crawl. Of course, she was a powerful mage, but her passion for Sisyphus's cause intimidated Acacia as much as her magical capabilities. It was obvious Dionera would do anything to ensure Sisyphus's return to power, no matter what the consequence in human life.

"That can be arranged, my lord," the woman said. "Our dungeons are ready and lie in wait for those who would defy us."

Sisyphus glanced at her with perceptive blue eyes. "Dionera, you plot revenge on the Swiatkowski boy. But remember, you underestimated him once and were almost obliterated."

"That brat didn't—"

"That brat *also* must be eliminated for our plans to come to fruition," Sisyphus said, his tone chilling. "But he is far cleverer than you think. If allowed, he and Swansgrove will destroy us, with the help of their little friends."

Fire rose from Dionera's athletic frame. "I will not allow it! I will kill him, I swear it!"

Sisyphus was indifferent to the woman's sudden outburst. "You both are my two most trusted vassals. I want every mage in this town in terror for their lives, and I care naught for how you do it, as long as it's done. Am I understood?"

Dionera and Minos glanced at each other and nodded.

"As you command," Minos said. "If you will be so kind as to excuse us, sir, Dionera and I will make our departure. We have much work ahead of us."

The last image Acacia saw before the scene faded into nothing was Sisyphus nodding, his expression surprisingly mild, as the other two mages turned on their heels and exited the study without another word.

***

"Acacia! Acacia Wheatley, wake up!"

Acacia was vaguely aware that someone was shaking her, but only regained consciousness when a rush of shockingly cold water was dumped on her. Acacia coughed and sputtered, pushing herself up-right, as she tried to mop the liquid from her face.

"Ugh." The combination of the cold water and the November air had left Acacia feeling quite chilled. "Because I was so hoping something else weird would happen today."

It wasn't until then that Acacia remembered all of what she had just seen. Sisyphus, Dionera, and Minos, all plotting how best to eliminate her and terrorize the magical world!

"AJ!" Acacia exclaimed, abruptly grabbing her companion by both shirt sleeves. "I don't know how I saw it, but I did. Sisyphus, Dionera, and this other guy Minos—they were talking about— They said they have to eliminate us!"

The twin knelt next to her, his dark gray eyes concerned yet oddly calm. "You saw Sisyphus and his minions? Could you tell where they were?"

Acacia shook her head. "No," she confessed, the worry knotting in her stomach. "Didn't you hear what I said? Dionera, she has it out for you, big time! And Sisyphus, he said both of us need to be destroyed for his plan to work! Me because of being a Swansgrove and maybe being able to stop him, and you because they think you're too clever. And they said they're going to attack the town because people aren't scared enough of them!"

AJ nodded, his eyes filled with understanding. "Acacia, breathe. I'm sure whatever you saw was upsetting, but we must keep our wits about us—"

"But how could I even see it?" Acacia asked, her mind racing. "Was it real? Am I . . . am I a Seer?"

AJ shook his head, and Acacia couldn't help but notice flecks of blue appear in his gray eyes. But with everything she had just heard, Acacia couldn't bring herself to worry too much about it.

"You're not a Seer," the twin informed her. "I would have known if you were. There's a possibility it could be one of those special abilities I mentioned before. And as for whether what you saw really happened, I think it might be in our best benefit to assume it did so we can be prepared."

Acacia narrowed her eyes at him. "And just how do you know I'm not a Seer? I didn't think most mages got visions."

"They don't. But you're not most mages either. Trust me on this one."

Without another word, AJ rose to his feet, and Acacia followed his lead. Every time she came close to figuring something out, every time things began to make sense, something else came up, some piece of information threatening Acacia's world. If she *wasn't* a Seer, how could she peer into Sisyphus's world as she had? And what did AJ mean by saying he would have known if Acacia was a Seer? Most importantly, what were they going to do about the impending doom threatening to destroy not only themselves and their friends, but also the rest of the magical community?

Acacia felt a sudden change in the energy field surrounding them. Another mage was here, she was sure of it . . . but who? The rush of magic energy was familiar, but not dark like that of Sisyphus's or any of his allies. . .

"Hello, Onawa," AJ said, a small smile spreading across his face. "Come to join the festivities?"

Sure enough, Onawa stepped out of the brush, her clothes covered with minor burns and scratches. "I'm telling you what." Onawa shook her head as if AJ had told a particularly bad joke. "I've never met anyone with a weirder idea of what 'festivities' are. Most people think birthday parties and weddings, not abandoned meadows and girls passing out on the ground. Though I suppose if they have too much to drink at the parties and weddings, there could be some passed out girls at those too."

Acacia liked Onawa well enough but found something odd about her. There had to be some other reason she would travel across the United States other than the fact she had been bored. Acacia also imagined Onawa had to be the girl Minos had mentioned in her vision.

Onawa and AJ seemed to be in the middle of some sort of unspoken communication until the twin nodded at the two girls, his expression a bit more resolute than it had been moments before.

"I'm going to tell Amara about what you saw, Acacia," he said, a thoughtful tilt to his head. "There's a possibility it didn't really happen, but I'd rather err on the side of caution."

Acacia let out an exasperated sigh. She didn't have a problem with being cautious, but she didn't see why they had to go running to Amara Jones. "Yeah, because we're all best friends with Little Miss Council. I'm sure she'll be thrilled when you tell her Acacia passed out and started hallucinating—"

AJ's pale brows twitched, but he made no other sign of acknowledging her comment. "Onawa, I trust you'll take good care of Acacia?"

The dark-haired girl grinned, a mischievous set to her mouth. "Better care than you, no doubt."

Without a moment's notice, AJ disappeared in the blue magic of his teleportation spell. *Well,* Acacia thought. *This should be interesting.*

"Here we are," Onawa commented. "It looks like *I'm* on Acacia duty now. I'll admit, I'm nowhere near as conscientious as AJ. Do you want to go feed S'feirra with me?"

"Onawa," Acacia said in as calm of a tone as she could muster. With everything she had to worry about, the thought of going to befriend a deadly dragon was not high on the list of things she wanted to do. "Look, it's not that I don't like you, or S'feirra, but. . . " How could she say what she was trying to say without coming across as mean? After all, from what she could tell, Onawa was a good kid . . . she just found her story a bit odd. "Why did you really come here? I'm having a hard time believing it's just because you were bored—"

Onawa looked at her with bright brown eyes. "So *that's* what you've been weird about, is it? You see, part of it is that I was bored. But the other part of it is we've all been following what's been going on over here, but of course no one wanted to do anything about it. I'm not okay with just sitting around waiting for someone to do something, so I decided to get up and do something about it." Onawa shot Acacia a toothy grin and pushed lock of dark hair out of her eyes. "If we're going to be friends, Acacia, you should know I don't wait around. I do what needs to be done and worry about who doesn't like it later."

Acacia nodded. She was beginning to like Onawa more by the minute.

"That makes two of us," she said. *She and AJ are completely different in some ways*, Acacia considered. *But then again, they do both take matters into their own hands. Maybe they are better matched than I first thought.* "So, do you still want to go feed S'feirra?"

Onawa made an excited squeal, and before Acacia could change her mind, the two girls disappeared in the bright orange of Onawa's teleportation spell.

Chapter Fifteen

PREPARATIONS

The following months passed without any further earthshaking incidents like those of October and early November. Acacia grew fond of Onawa, and the two girls spent a good deal of time together, exploring the deep forests of Silent Springs and visiting S'feirra. Acacia enjoyed having a girlfriend to do things with, especially since Onawa's sense of adventure often surpassed her own.

As time went by, Acacia became more and more curious about what was transpiring between Onawa and AJ. They didn't seem to be dating, but something about them clicked. With Onawa around, AJ was less uptight, quicker to laugh, and much less stressed. Acacia knew her friend was still concerned about Sisyphus's plots, but for the most part, AJ was behaving like a regular fourteen-year-old.

Fall nights soon gave way to winter ones, signaling a change in the weather Acacia was unprepared for. The temperatures plummeted and every so often snow would drop from the sky.

"You mean you've never had a snow day?" Alex asked her one day on their way to lunch. "That's the best part of winter!"

Acacia shrugged. "I lived in Sacramento, Alex. The coldest it ever got there was about forty degrees. You don't have to deal with snow when it's that warm."

"Poor Acacia," Alex said, poking her shoulder playfully. "Forced to relocate to this horrible winter wasteland, where it's colder than forty degrees every day from November to March—"

"Is there ever a moment when you're not running your mouth, Alex?" AJ asked as he and Onawa sat down at the table. "I would think your jaw would tire from time to time."

Alex looked at his brother and arched his pale brows. "Nice of you two to show up, eh? Sixth period lunch started fifteen minutes ago."

Oh boy, Percy mind-spoke to Acacia, shooting her a tired glance. *Alex has been on the offensive for a good week now. He appears to be trying to make AJ 'fess up.'*

He probably is, Acacia agreed. Although she didn't know Percy quite as well as the others, she'd grown to see him as a bit of an older brother. *He's convinced AJ's madly in love with Onawa.*

Percy laughed brightly. *And what do you think, Acacia? Out of all of us here, you spend the most time with AJ, except for Onawa. What do you think? Has my cousin been smitten by the love bug?*

Acacia shrugged. *Maybe,* she replied. *Though I'm not sure what AJ madly in love would look like. He hasn't been distracted like some people get when they have a crush. And if anything, he's less obsessive than usual. The only difference is that he's hanging out with a girl besides me.*

"Your point being?" From what Acacia could tell, AJ wasn't annoyed yet, but if Alex continued to bait him, he would be soon.

A wide grin crept across Alex's face. "My point is that you and Mescal must have been up to something!" Alex's voice was triumphant, as if he had won some great prize. "C'mon, AJ, you know it's true! So, tell us already, what were you guys doing?"

"The only thing I know to be true is that you ran away from a raccoon this past weekend screaming 'Bigfoot!'"

Acacia couldn't help but giggle under her breath. *Poor Alex,* she thought. *No matter how hard you try, I don't think you'll be beating AJ at a battle of wits anytime soon.*

"You idiot, you were the only one who was there!" Alex rose from his seat, his muscles tense with frustration. "You were *supposed* to keep it a secret!"

"Oh, was I? Sorry, Zander, it must have slipped my mind."

"AJ, I'm going to kill you!" Alex roared, nostrils flaring.

This time Acacia could feel the surge in power as Amara Jones approached their table. Of course, the girl couldn't teleport in plain sight, but she moved almost as quickly as AJ did.

"I'm afraid you'll have to get in line for that, Alex." Amara glanced from Alex to AJ with narrowed eyes. "Though you might be waiting for quite some time."

Alex let out a sigh of exasperation and fell back into his seat, his rage dissipated. Acacia fidgeted nervously in her chair and took a bite out of her sandwich. Maybe it was the fact that the girl was so composed, no matter what the circumstance, or perhaps because she was so closely connected with the Council, but Acacia couldn't help but find her unnerving. Amara was also analytical to a fault, and even short conversations with her left Acacia wondering if everything she said would be kept on file until Amara found a way to prove her guilt later.

"Tell me about it." Alex sighed, rolling his gray eyes. "Anyway, what brings you over here, Jones? Not enough excitement for you at the band geeks' table?"

”No. ” Amara's voice was annoyed, her expression a perfect match. "Unlike you, I don't aspire for my lunch to be as lively as a football game."

AJ shot the girl a curious look, clearly perplexed by her entrance. *So, what is it that you want, Amara? It's not every day you decide to grace us with your presence.*

What I want is for all of you to stay out of trouble, Amara told them all, her tone as sharp as a dagger. *As much as I don't like to believe secondhand visions from people who aren't even Seers*—she stole a quick glance at Acacia. *My father thinks any sign of Sisyphus launching an attack against us merits caution.*

Bugger caution, Mattes remarked, his hazel eyes bored. *If I got scared every time someone threatened to kill me, I'd have been living under a rock for the past five years.*

Amara rolled her eyes. *I'm not telling you to live under a rock, Knight. All I'm asking is that—*

We watch out for the shadows behind every rock? Onawa asked, a mischievous look in her brown eyes. *Not going outside should* definitely *get rid of the whole Sisyphus trying to murder us thing.*

Oh dear me. Mattes was pleased to have someone just as contrary as he was. *Have we entered an alternate universe where Sisyphus is a good old boy and we're the ones scheming to destroy this dinky town?*

Acacia laughed out loud despite herself and noticed that even AJ and Percy were chuckling under their breath. She had been trying to keep a straight face, but with Mattes's and Onawa's sarcastic remarks, it was becoming more difficult than ever. *Oh no,* she thought. *Now Amara will hate me even more than she did before!*

Amara's face had turned a shocking shade of red with Mattes's words. *Yes, how very clever you all are,* the girl retorted as she turned to abandon their table. *Do me a favor and when you're being chased down by Sisyphus and the fire-witch, don't coming crying to me.*

"Amara, hold on for a minute, would you?" AJ said, a twinge of remorse in his voice. *I'm sorry for laughing at you, but you don't need to be so hissy.*

If Amara had been a dog or wolf, her hackles would have raised. "If you want to see hissy, Swiatkowski. I will be more than happy to oblige."

Both Percy and AJ sighed, and Acacia was stricken by the similarity between the two boys. They had quite different personalities and interests, but AJ and Percy were both introverted, more likely to sit back and process a conflict than jump into action.

"Remember where we are." Percy glanced between Amara and his cousins, his face blanching with concern. *There's no need for any more brawls in the cafeteria, especially since none of your names are Ivy Swiatkowski.*

Too bad, eh? Mattes mind-spoke. *That would make things more interesting. Shall I invite her over?*

You will do no such thing! AJ replied, as Alex said, *Don't you dare!* The twins glared briefly at each other and looked back toward Amara, both of their faces flushing in embarrassment.

"Amara, look." AJ's left leg began to bounce up and down. "I'm sorry. Why don't you have a seat with us? You obviously came over here for a reason—"

"So why don't you tell us what that something is?" Mattes finished AJ's thought. "Since you clearly know something the rest of us don't."

Amara's temper appeared to have cooled, at least somewhat. *Even if I do, Matthias Knight, why should I tell you?* The girl's tone was irate, but not enraged as it had been moments earlier. *It's not like any of you are forthcoming with the information I need.*

Excuse me? AJ questioned, rising to his feet. *And just how can you say that after I told you—*

Save it, Swiatkowski, Amara retorted. *But do us all a favor and keep your little friends out of the forest. In case you didn't notice, fewer people are there to run to the rescue if Sisyphus and his cohorts happen to show up.*

With that, the girl stalked away in the direction of the exit stairs.

"Well, she was nice." After a few moments, Onawa pulled a container of some kind of beans and a piece of cornbread from her lunch bag. "I wonder what she's got stuck in her behind."

"She seemed worried," Percy commented, his blue eyes tired. "Something tells me that conversation might have gone differently if you hadn't patronized her, Mattes."

Mattes shrugged. "Bugger if I care. If you've got something to say, spit it out or don't say it at all, as Father used to say. Right along with 'Death to the progressive bas—'"

"Matthias, *enough,*" AJ interrupted, shooting his friend a stormy glare. "You do realize that staying on decent terms with Amara is difficult enough without you complicating things, right?"

"Yes, but you do oh so well with complicated situations. You do remember, of course, that portal we found last summer that sent us all the way to—"

"All of you have a lovely lunch." AJ cut Mattes off again and walked off in the direction Amara had departed, his book bag and food forgotten at the table. "I'll see you later, I'm sure."

"And where the heck are you going?" Alex asked, his eyes wide with surprise. "And besides, aren't you forgetting the most important part about lunch? The lunch?"

"Well, someone has to try to smooth things over with Amara," the boy explained in a clipped tone. "And it isn't going to be Matthias."

Onawa let out a small 'oh' and leaped to her feet. "Hey, hold on a minute!" She picked up her bowl with one hand and spooned its contents into her mouth with the other. "I'm coming too!"

"Onawa. . . " Acacia scratched her head in confusion. "What?"

I made her mad too, Onawa said, her eyes remorseful. *So maybe I can help!*

AJ looked back at Acacia and the others, shrugged, and departed, Onawa not far behind.

"*Now,*" Alex said, his expression as serious as the grave. "Do any of you doubt me when I say they're in the process?"

Acacia thought back on the comments Alex had made the day of Onawa's arrival. As she let her mind wander, she felt something—or someone—catch her attention. Acacia stood up and scanned the cafeteria with her magical gaze, trying to find the source of the energy. Acacia could hear Alex talking to her, but in her sense of heightened consciousness, the boy's words were far away, like he was speaking to her from a different dimension. The image of the cafeteria too seemed to slow and fade around her.

There, a mysterious boy with a head of hair as fiery as her own and odd golden eyes, gazed back at her from across the room. *But who was he?*

"Acacia!"

Alex's holler shocked her back to the present. Acacia shook her head and looked again across the room. The redheaded boy had disappeared.

"Sorry about that," she apologized, rubbing her forehead. "I thought I saw something."

Percy looked at her, a curious smile fixed on his face, but remained silent.

"Not Sissy Puss, I hope." Alex smirked and took a bite of his sandwich.

"Not today," Acacia replied in what she hoped was a joking voice and pushed the image of the redheaded boy from her mind. "At least I hope not."

***

AJ seemed to think Acacia had progressed far enough in her training to be trusted with some independent reading. Much to her surprise, over the next few days, AJ entrusted Acacia with a variety of his own books, assigning her to read several chapters a day. Acacia had first assumed all the boy's books would be dry, historical accounts of the evolution of magic, or changes in the structure of the government, so she was pleasantly surprised to find most of her assignments were engaging reads about a number of subjects, some historical, some theoretical, and some dedicated to new spells and enchantments. After Acacia finished with a particular reading, AJ tested her knowledge, either by quizzing her, giving her tests that Acacia could tell the twin had written himself, or having her demonstrate some of the magic she'd learned about. Given AJ's previous reaction when he had found Acacia going through his bookcase back in September, Acacia was shocked the boy would willingly let her borrow his books, but reasoned he must now know her enough to consider her trustworthy with his prized possessions.

"Glad to see you doing your homework," AJ remarked, walking into the Swiatkowskis' living room one afternoon as Acacia digested her latest assignment and Alex focused on his math problems. "Both of you."

"I like this one," Acacia replied, closing the text with a snap. "It's not as dry as I thought, especially for a history book."

The twin shrugged, his gray eyes vacant, as if his mind were elsewhere. "Just because everyone thinks I'm a walking encyclopedia doesn't mean that's *all* I read." Turning to his brother, AJ asked, "So how long has it been since you had a lesson with our dear sister?"

Alex laid his pencil on the floor and studied his brother's face. Judging by the twins' expressions, Acacia could sense a serious conversation was on the way.

"A couple weeks I guess." Alex frowned. "Why does it matter?"

AJ's gaze darkened, though with anger or irritation, Acacia couldn't be sure. "It matters because Ivy has an ethical obligation to you."

"Yeah well, she's Ivy."

"One can't shrug off ethical obligations no matter what one's name happens to be."

Alex let out a sigh of exasperation. "AJ, when are you going to realize that nobody cares about your stupid ethical obligations?" he demanded in a cross tone, his homework forgotten on the floor. "Just because you think the Protocol is important doesn't mean anybody else does."

The Protocol? The term was familiar enough, even if Acacia couldn't remember exactly what it was. *Oh, that's right, I read it in one of my assignments. The Protocol is the set of rules and regulations that say what mages are supposed to do, like once a mage starts teaching another mage, they've got the responsibility to finish.*

"As ineffectual as the Council is, *they* would be quite interested to know," AJ replied, his expression devoid of emotion. "In fact, they might be interested enough to investigate."

Without warning, Alex leaped to his feet. "You are *not* going to make a report on Ivy. I don't know what kind of crack you're on, Andrew, to think that's a good idea—"

"I would go with 'adherence to an ethical code' as opposed to crack," AJ retorted. "You know, as much as Uncle Jack may have been the bane of my existence during my training, he did beat mage ethics into my head very well."

"Well, ethics aren't what Ivy's going to beat into *my* head if you snitch on her!" Alex's voice was more panicked than Acacia expected. "If she gets in trouble, it's me she's going to come after, not you! So, stay of out of my business!"

Acacia felt like she had walked into a family feud she had no right to observe. Of course, she had been spending a lot of time with Alex the past few weeks, but it had never occurred to her that Ivy had stopped her friend's training, even if it *should* have. And if it was true . . . AJ probably wasn't out of line in threatening to report her, but at the same time, Acacia couldn't help but think Alex was right that whatever fallout from said report would come down on him. Didn't AJ realize that?

"I'm going to give her a warning, of course," AJ said. "It's only fair. But if she doesn't resume your lessons, I will go to the Council. Ivy might be annoyed at you, but if she's going to come after someone, it'll be me."

"And that doesn't bother you?" Acacia was half curious, half impressed.

AJ shrugged, an indifferent expression on his face. "I honestly couldn't care less. My sister isn't so great a mage that she's been able to beat me in a fair fight. And besides"—he glanced between Acacia and Alex—"fully trained mages are ethically bound to uphold the Protocol. And in case both of you didn't know or managed to forget, the Protocol states that mages are not only required to fulfill their ethical responsibilities to teach their students, but also to act when another trainee's education is neglected."

Acacia blinked. From the sound of it, if AJ followed through with his threat to report her, Ivy could get in serious trouble. *Would AJ really do that?* Acacia thought. *I know AJ and Ivy don't get along, but tattling on her to the Council seems pretty drastic.*

"This is all because you're mad about what I said about you and Dragon Girl, isn't it?" Alex demanded, pointing his finger at his brother. "You don't like it when someone figures you out! Well, guess what, Andrew? Being twins means you can't keep anything from me, not even—"

"That Dragon Girl, as you've so eloquently put it, has a name, Alexander," AJ said, his tone much sharper than it had been moments earlier. "So, if you're going to talk about her, I suggest you use it, as endearing as your nicknames may be."

See what I mean, Acacia? Alex rarely had any information he could use against his brother and seemed to be making the best of his current suspicions. *He's—*

"No, Alex, I can assure you this has nothing to do with Onawa." AJ's pale brows twitched, a sure sign of his irritation, however mild. "Or any other conclusions you've jumped to."

"Oh?"

AJ shook his head and grabbed his left shoulder with his right hand as if he had a muscle spasm. "This isn't about you, Alex, this is about our sister's belligerent lack of respect for—"

"Okay, okay, AJ, we get it," Acacia said, beginning to feel a bit annoyed herself, though at whom she wasn't certain. "Ivy's not doing her job. Is something wrong with your shoulder?"

"You both have more important things to worry about than my shoulder," AJ told her, crossing his arms in front of his chest. He glanced again between Acacia and Alex, this time more apprehensively, almost as if he expected them to attack. "Anyway, I'm off in search of Ivy since there's always a chance she might decide to start working with us without forcing her hand. Can the two of you be trusted to behave yourselves for an hour or so?"

Acacia laughed and shook her head. *Weird,* she mind-spoke to Alex. *This is the first time since Sisyphus's escape that your brother has seemed concerned about us getting in trouble.*

That's because he's trying to make nice with Amara, Alex replied. *She doesn't want any of us running around in the woods, remember?*

"Yes, Andrew, I think we can handle it," Alex retorted, shaking his head. "And let me add how honored I feel that you don't let my feelings get in the way of your quest to save the world." *Acacia, don't freak out.*

Why would I?

Much of what happened next was a bit of a blur. AJ turned to leave, his expression a mix of irritation and apprehension. As he did, Alex lunged and grabbed his brother from behind, forcing him into some kind of arm lock.

"Alex!" AJ hollered, in one of the most furious tones Acacia had ever heard him use. "What are you doing?"

AJ struggled against Alex's grasp but, to Acacia's surprise, was unsuccessful in breaking free. *So much for thinking AJ couldn't be defeated,* she considered. *Though that was a bit of a sneak attack.* "Alex, don't you think that's a little . . . extreme?"

"Ow, get off me, Alex—"

"Just hold still, you bugger—"

"Hey guys!" Acacia stepped in, ready to pull the two boys apart. "Is this neces—"

A resounding ripping of fabric sounded, as Alex tore AJ's sleeve. Acacia threw herself between the twins, separating them before they could start arguing again. *Of all the things I don't need right now, getting in the middle of a Swiatkowski family brawl has got to be far up on the list.*

Acacia looked up and, much to her surprise, saw that AJ's left sleeve had all but fallen off, revealing a pale arm almost entirely covered with bruises.

"Ha!" Alex pointed triumphantly at his brother's arm. "I knew you were hiding something! How about telling us where that came from, AJ?"

"Oh my gosh," Acacia said, feeling much more concerned than she had been moments earlier. "What happened? Did—"

AJ let out a sigh of exasperation and made a quick hand motion over his sleeve where it had been ripped.

"Do yourself a favor, and don't worry about it," he replied, as the blue sparks of his magic repaired his shirt. "It's nothing either of you need to concern yourselves with."

"But—"

"Whenever my brother doesn't want to tell me something, it usually has something to do with Matthias Knight," Alex said, appearing to speak only to Acacia. "Helping Mattes with this or that, running around the Underground with murderers and thieves—"

AJ rolled his dark gray eyes. "Not everyone needs to know what I'm doing. Including the two of you. What I do in my free time is none—"

"So, were you helping Mattes or hanging out with Dragon Girl?" Alex demanded. "I think Mom would want to know why her youngest is running around either with homicidal maniacs or giant fire-breathing monsters. Pick your poison, I guess—"

Alex! Acacia warned her friend, becoming annoyed herself. *Do you really need to be so aggressive? AJ is frustrating, but you don't have to bait him.*

"What I was doing, Alex, falls under the category of none of your concern." AJ walked over to the closet and pulled out his blue winter jacket and scarf, shrugging both on. "I don't go around demanding to know what you're doing in all your free time, which has been a lot of time, since you haven't been training now for at least a solid week. So, I don't think you have much of a right to go around nosing in my business." AJ took one last look at them, his dark gray eyes stormy. "Anyway, I'm off to have a chat with our dear sister. Stay out of trouble, the both of you, or I'll know about it."

With that, AJ walked out the front door, his pace rushed, as if he were late for an important meeting. Acacia exchanged a curious glance with Alex, shaking her head in confusion.

"You know," Alex said after an awkward silence. "Some people joke about having an evil twin . . . I actually have one." Shooting Acacia a quick grin, he added, "Come on, let's go for a walk while it's still bright out. I'd rather not be around when AJ finds Ivy and gives her hell."

Acacia smiled back at her friend and extended her right hand, summoning her winter coat with her magic. A look of surprise crossed Alex's face; he clearly hadn't been expecting her to agree quite so easily.

"If there's the slightest sign of trouble, we come back," Acacia ordered in what she found to be a surprisingly authoritative tone for herself. "Somehow I think both of us have enough to deal with without getting on your brother's bad side."

Alex laughed heartily, pulling on his jacket. "My brother, a bad side?" he repeated. "Surely you must be joking! Now come on, before you give yourself the chance to change your mind!"

Chapter Sixteen

THE VIRSEYEH

Within minutes, Acacia and Alex found themselves once again in the dense woods of Silent Springs. Acacia glanced in wonder at the forest, amazed its appearance could change so much with the passing of a few months. While in the fall it was filled with vivacity and color, now all the plants were barren and covered with snow.

Still concerned about the vision showing her Sisyphus's insidious planning, Acacia was determined to avoid any chance of putting herself or anyone else in danger. She scanned the surrounding area for any sign of a threat, pushing aside the thought that she was, in fact, picking up a bit of AJ's paranoia.

"You're getting pretty good at scanning spells." Alex paused to ball up a handful of snow. "I guess you did manage to learn something from that crazy brother of mine."

Acacia snorted and studied her friend's face. Alex was grinning at her, a mischievous glimmer in his light gray eyes, and tossed the snowball up in the air.

"Alex, I'm warning you. Don't even think about it."

"Think about what?" An innocent smile had formed on her friend's face. "I'm not thinking about anything."

"Alexander Swiatkowski. I do not want that white junk in my face."

Alex chuckled and winked at her before launching his snowball ammunition. Acacia yelped and ducked, narrowly dodging the cold projectile.

"Alex, this isn't fun—"

Out of the corner of her eye, Acacia saw him form another snowball.

Without another word, she sprinted off into the woods, hearing her friend's footsteps chase after her in the snow.

***

After about fifteen minutes of fleeing from Alex's snowballs, Acacia collapsed on top of a large snow pile, her arms outstretched to her sides.

"See?" Alex commented, flopping down beside her. "I told you 'that white junk' isn't so bad."

Something about Alex made Acacia want to spend as much time with him as possible. She was hesitant to say she was in love with him, but she felt a connection with him she didn't have with the others. Acacia was the most at ease when she was with Alex—even if he *was* pelting snowballs at her—and felt like she could truly be herself. But . . . did that mean they were dating or soon would be? Acacia had never dated anyone before and had no idea how. Besides, Acacia never had a friend like Alex, who she could go on adventures with without being judged and talk to about everything. Would dating change all of that forever?

"You're so serious today." Alex reached out and touched the side of Acacia's face. He had hugged her plenty of times; this kind of touch seemed different somehow, more meaningful. "Are you okay?"

"No, I—" Acacia began but, picking up on a strange aura, dropped off midsentence. "Hey, where are we?"

They were in a section of the forest Acacia had never seen before. The dense trees of the woods had thinned out, giving way to a slight clearing. This area was different from most places she and Alex had traveled to, darker, less full of life. Acacia couldn't shake the feeling that something was wrong with this place, something sinister she couldn't quite understand. She knew in some cases if a location boasted of a dark history such as a murder or battle, the aura could be affected in a negative way. Was it possible this place had a dark history Acacia was unaware of?

"Good question," Alex said, his face paling. "I don't think I've ever been here before. It's got a weird aura though."

Alex pulled himself to his feet and walked around the clearing, casting a scanning spell. Feeling rather unsettled, Acacia followed him. The longer she remained here, the stronger she could feel it, an aura of darkness, not quite the same as Sisyphus's, but, if possible, even darker.

"Alex, I think we have to go." Acacia's heart pounded in her chest. Could the dark aura have something to do with Sisyphus? Had he created some sort of creatures of darkness to send after Acacia and her friends? Was that part of his plan to ensure the magical community came to fear him once more? "I don't know what's going on here, but I don't like it."

"No complaints here," Alex said, his face blanched with apprehension. He shook the worry from his face as he turned back towards Acacia, shooting her a crooked grin. "My dear brother will be so proud of us. I can hear it now, 'Acacia, Alex, I underestimated you. From this day forth, I'm going to trust you.' Oh, and don't forget, 'Yes, Alex, my wise and handsome older brother, you've been right all along. Onawa is my one true love, the peanut butter to my toast, but the good, homemade peanut butter like you get at the market, not the cheap overprocessed garbage they sell at the grocery store next to the jelly in the tube—'"

Acacia couldn't help but laugh. "Somehow I have a hard time imagining AJ saying anything like that." Acacia grasped her companion firmly by the hand. "It seems a bit . . . much."

"Maybe it is." Alex flashed her an infectious smile. "But I did get you to laugh, didn't I?"

Acacia opened her mouth to speak but felt a sudden burst of energy materialize behind her. She whirled around in time to see a swirling black mist several yards away.

"What the heck is—" Alex's question was cut off as Acacia took off at a mad sprint, pulling him along with her. *I should have listened to my gut from the beginning before the dark magic had the chance to try and kill us,* she thought. Was it too late already? Or did they still have a chance, a chance to escape before whatever had created that mist could catch up to them, and—

Acacia, stop! Alex froze, halting their progress. *Look!* It didn't take Acacia long to realize what he was talking about. Another sheet of black mist had appeared in front of them and spread through the air, enclosing them in a globe of dark energy.

I still might not be as good as AJ or Mattes, Acacia thought, preparing to attack before whatever it was had a chance to attack them. *But there's no way I'm going to stand around here until whatever that is tries to kill us!* She thrust both arms to the sky and shot a shaft of bright green light into the mist above them. Something let out a shrill screech, causing Acacia to take a step backward in surprise.

Not bad, Alex commented, conjuring a sphere of blue magic in his hand and positioning his back against Acacia's. *I take it we're fighting our way out of here?*

Unless you have a better idea.

Alex launched the ball of energy into the sky. It soared a couple feet above their heads, levitated for a few moments, and then broke off into many smaller spheres, which flew like a set of missiles into the mists. Within seconds, the balls went off like small explosives, successfully dispelling the mist.

And there they were, the creatures whose magical force Acacia had felt only moments earlier and whose appearance was enough to give any child nightmares.

Acacia counted twelve of them total. Their bodies looked like the top half of skeletons, from the skull to the bony rib cage. Though Acacia couldn't identify what these creatures were, she could tell they weren't *just* skeletons. They floated in the air, suspended by dark magic, and wore the same golden amulet around their necks and purple cloaks on their skeletal frames.

"Really?" Alex said. "Did it have to be skeletons? I hate skeletons!"

One of the creatures let out a shrill cry, and its eye sockets lit up with an eerie purple glow. One by one, the monsters lifted a bony hand and emitted a low growling sound. To Acacia's horror, their bony hands glowed the same shade of purple.

"Did I mention that I hate skeletons?" Alex groaned. "All dead and—"

"I don't think they're regular skeletons." Acacia twisted her wrists so they were both positioned horizontally in front of her face. "I'm not an expert, but I don't think regular skeletons float around in the air glowing purple. But how about this—I'll take these six and you take those six, and maybe we can get out of here alive."

Alex still looked unsettled by the creatures floating above but nodded. "Sounds good."

The first of the monsters that had begun to glow let out another piercing screech and conjured a swirling purple sphere. One by one, the others followed suit, and soon the sky above them was filled with purple orbs. Sensing danger, Acacia grabbed Alex by the hand, keeping her other hand positioned in front of her.

"Quick!" she said, hearing the panic in her voice. "Let's make a shield. With both of us powering it, it should be strong enough to hold them—"

But before she could finish her thought, the first of the skeletal creatures threw its ball of purple light at her, which hit her in the stomach and knocked her into Alex with considerable force.

"Acacia!"

"Alex, focus!" Acacia brought her right hand across her body, sending a wall of green power into the beasts. Her attack sent them flying several feet backward, but to her dismay, they flew right back, seemingly undamaged. Alex stole a concerned glance in her direction but launched another blue sphere into the horde of skeletons. The twin's spell exploded midair, causing the skeletons to be jostled to pieces, but they again reconstituted themselves.

"I don't get it!" Alex cried. "Nothing we do sticks to these guys! What are they, *invincible*? What do we have to do to get rid of them?"

Acacia forced herself to her feet. She could feel the pain in her stomach spreading, as if the attack had been poisonous. Acacia didn't want to show any sign of being hurt, since it would make Alex worry, but she knew if they didn't do something soon, she wouldn't be able to remain standing for much longer.

Why does this always *have to happen?* Acacia thought, willing herself to attack with all her power. *We weren't even doing anything bad this time! And what's the point of being the Heir of Swansgrove if I can't even take out some creepy skeletons!*

Alex grasped her hand again and gave it a small squeeze. *We got this, Acacia,* he remarked in a tense voice. *Now let's kick some skeleton butt.*

Acacia threw her free arm straight up into the sky and shot a tendril of green lightning into the horde of skeletons. As she maintained the spell, Acacia noticed Alex's blue magic intertwining with hers, strengthening her attack. Acacia watched in amazement as the green and blue spirals soared into the sky and electrified the creatures one by one.

"If that doesn't get rid of them," she said, feeling her body weaken. "I don't know what will."

As the spell coursed through the creatures, the air was filled with a shrill, unearthly screeching so loud Acacia was certain her eardrums would burst. Finally, she could no longer continue channeling the energy and let go, sinking to her knees on the cold snow.

"Acacia!" Alex yelled, kneeling on the ground beside her. "Are you o—"

"Alex, look!" Acacia pointed upward. The creatures had stopped screeching and convulsing with the power from their attack and appeared to have regrouped. A low humming noise filled the air as the skeletons flew in a circle above them. They moved faster and faster, a swirling purple haze surrounding them at a concerning rate.

Oh bugger, Acacia thought, feeling the end was near. *So much for defeating Sisyphus, I guess.*

"Amach-ni-nae, vryan, eryu chineyu, vram!"

Acacia did not recognize the voice speaking in an unfamiliar tongue. At first, she believed the eerie words came from the skeleton creatures spiraling above them, but to her surprise, they began to screech again in agony and receded into the forest.

Alex helped Acacia to her feet, the confusion obvious in his eyes. "Any idea what that was?" he asked. "Not that I mind the dead nasties disappearing, but I thought we were goners!"

"It was me," that same voice said.

Acacia and Alex turned around and saw a boy with bright coppery hair and golden eyes emerge from the woods. Acacia studied the newcomer's face with great interest. She couldn't identify him, but she *knew* she had seen him before . . . somewhere. "I'm Patrick, Patrick Delaney. I was passing through, and it looked like you two were in a bit of trouble . . . so I took the liberty of stepping in."

"And good thing you did!" Alex stepped forward and shook the boy's hand. "I'm Alex Swiatkowski, and this is—"

Acacia walked over to greet Patrick herself. "Acacia Wheatley. Thank you so much for helping us! Alex is right, we would've been goners if you hadn't."

Patrick's golden eyes flashed with strange magic. Acacia couldn't put her finger on it, but something was different about the boy. He was obviously a mage, and a powerful one at that, but without even casting a scanning spell, Acacia sensed something unfamiliar about his magic.

But he did save us, Acacia thought. *So, he can't be bad, right?*

"Well, what a surprise," a familiar voice said before Patrick could respond. Acacia turned and saw AJ, the magic of his teleportation spell vanishing into thin air. The twin looked beyond irritated, his eyes darker than usual and narrowed at Acacia and Alex. AJ walked through the snow with purpose, his pace not slowed in the slightest by the fluffy white stuff. "Silly me, I was expecting to see you two at the house. You know, the probability of being attacked by creatures of dark magic tends to be a bit lower there. In the house, the creatures of dark magic have to break in."

AJ cast a suspicious glance in Patrick's direction, his gray eyes calculating as ever. Acacia could see the cogs in the twin's mind turning, as she could feel herself weakening, the pain in her stomach spreading like wildfire. *AJ, please don't be rude,* she pleaded. *Patrick helped us. If it wasn't for him, those horrible things would have killed us.*

"Good day, Wrin." Patrick glided through the snow toward AJ. The redhaired boy did not appear to be perturbed at all by AJ's comment. "How ironic that my path brings me right to the fox itself."

The fox itself? Acacia thought, clutching her stomach. *Is he . . . calling AJ a fox? What does that even mean?*

AJ studied the newcomer meticulously, as if he could find out what was happening from looking at the boy's face alone. It almost seemed to be a stand-off of sorts: AJ's quiet intensity testing the waters of Patrick's mysterious, and potentially dangerous, power.

"Andrew Swiatkowski," AJ said after a long silence, his gray eyes flashing blue. "Thank you for helping my brother and my friend. You must be quite the mage to defeat a swarm of such creatures with ease."

AJ had a point. How had Patrick, a boy as slight in appearance as AJ, been able to rid the area of those monsters? Ever since she'd received her full powers, Acacia had always thought AJ to be the epitome of a good mage. He was fast, clever, and always seemed to know just what to do to get himself, and whoever else was around, out of a bad situation. But AJ didn't exude the boundless power as Patrick Delaney did. And Acacia had to wonder what AJ would have done if *he* had arrived instead of Patrick. Even with his years of experience, Acacia wasn't certain AJ would have been able to stop those cursed, floating skeletons.

From the looks of pure terror on your faces, I think it's safe to say you've come face to face with some kind of creatures of dark magic, AJ told her, his tone neither angry nor annoyed. *Which we will discuss when there's not such a crowd.*

A crowd? But—

Patrick let out a laugh, which for whichever reason resonated in Acacia's mind as rather harsh, even biting in tonality.

"Oh, Wrin," the redhaired boy said, as if AJ had just told a particularly clever joke. "Surely you of all people understand the importance of improvisation. After all, you would have to, being as . . . unassuming as you are. Looking as breakable as you do has proven to be a gift in disguise. That, along with that deer in the headlights expression on your face, has given you plenty of opportunities to keep everyone around you from asking too many questions that might have kept you from playing with too much fire."

AJ still didn't appear to be intimidated by Patrick's remarks, but he did seem to be unsettled by the accusations. Grasping Alex's hand again, Acacia watched the scene unfold with curiosity. Even in her exhausted state, Acacia could tell Patrick's comment was much more than just a simple remark made to get under AJ's skin. The air was heavy, the challenge laid fastidiously by the mysterious Patrick Delaney in the hopes that AJ would react in some way. In Acacia's experience, AJ wasn't one to particularly care about challenges, unless he felt intervention was of the utmost necessity. From the look on the twin's face, now didn't appear to be one of those rare instances.

"Pleasure to meet you, what did you say your name was? Patrick, right?" AJ retorted, his expression of slight confusion replaced with one of innocence. "Thank you again for helping my friends. And welcome to Silent Springs."

"I am known as Patrick Delaney, Wrin." Patrick's mouth twisted into a dangerous smile. "I wish you and your friends all the peace you *deserve.*"

Something about the way Patrick said 'deserve' made Acacia feel even more uncomfortable than she already did. Was the boy trying to wish them well or warn them they deserved every bad thing that came their way?

AJ shot Acacia a backward glance that seemed to communicate, 'well, that took you long enough,' and turned back to Patrick.

"Well, Patrick, good day," AJ said. Turning back to Acacia and Alex, he gestured toward the town with his gaze. *Have the two of you had enough of an adventure for one day? I'd like to get going before your new friend decides to get more specific about whatever he knows about me or the sun sets. Whichever comes first.*

What do you mean before he gets more—

But the three of them were already vanishing in the blue haze of AJ's teleportation spell. *Great, here we go again,* she thought. *Back to detention.*

***

Much to Acacia's surprise, AJ didn't appear to be angry or even annoyed at them, despite their near-death experience. The twin teleported them right outside the Swiatkowskis' front door and rushed them inside the house and into the study in a manner not all that different from a dog herding sheep. The room was small, maybe only a little bigger than the twins' bedroom, and lined with wooden shelves, stocked to the brim with books of all sizes. A beautifully crafted oak desk and chair took up much of the space in the room, but with just enough room, two additional chairs were positioned in front of the desk. AJ motioned for Acacia and Alex to sit, though in Acacia's mind, the boy's movements might have been better described as sitting them down.

"I need you two to tell me exactly what you saw," AJ said, as he perched on top of the desk like a nervous cat. "For the time being, I don't care about your new friend or what he's doing in Silent Springs. We can worry about him when we figure out what kinds of . . . *things* are running around the woods trying to murder people." AJ's face was paler than it had been minutes earlier and his expression was somber.

If I'm remembering correctly, AJ didn't look this frazzled the day after Sisyphus escaped, Acacia thought, careful to block her thoughts. *What about Patrick or whatever attacked us has him so worked up?*

"Jeez, AJ, would you chill?" Alex rose from his seat. "Okay, we screwed up, going off out there—"

"I don't care about that right now, Alex. Somehow, the idea of creatures of darkness running amok in the forest is a bit more upsetting to me than your lack of caution, which doesn't ever change," AJ said. He gave Alex a good, hard look and turned to Acacia. When his dark eyes fell on her, his manner changed almost instantly. "Acacia, I'm sorry, you're hurt. You were hit by one of them?"

Acacia nodded, holding her midsection. The pain did appear to be subsiding, though she wouldn't go so far as to say it was a full recovery.

"They were . . . skeletons, I guess you could say," she said. "But just the top half. And they just . . . floated in the air. They first showed up in this weird black mist—"

"And had purple magic." Alex reached out and squeezed Acacia's hand in reassurance. "Hey AJ, have you ever heard of skeletons that all wear the same medallions and cloaks? Because that's what I would say these guys looked like."

AJ frowned and hopped off the desk, standing in front of Acacia, his intelligent eyes wary. "Wounds inflicted by dark magic have a tendency of seeming to get better and then take a turn for the worse, if untreated," he told her, his eyes grave yet sympathetic. He turned toward the door. "I'll go get you something to put on it."

AJ closed the door behind him, as if subliminally warning Acacia and Alex not to even consider leaving the room.

He seems . . . different, Acacia mind-spoke to Alex, scratching her head. *I have to say, I don't get it. It's not like we haven't been in bad situations before. Sisyphus being on the loose must be worse than a bunch of weird skeleton things, right? But from the way your brother's acting, you would think today was the end of the world.*

Alex shrugged. *Yeah, but don't forget about Patrick. I think something about Patrick threw him off. Maybe he didn't like that pet name or whatever Patrick gave to him. What was it, Wrin or something?*

True, Acacia agreed with a nod. To herself, she thought, *Somehow Patrick seemed to know way more than he should about how to get rid of those monsters and about how to get under AJ's skin. I wonder what else he knows?*

The door creaked open again, and AJ handed Acacia a small glass vial of a white gelatin substance and approached one of the bookshelves. Without wasting a moment's time, he pulled an ancient-looking text from the stacks.

"That's a healing ointment, Acacia," he explained, flipping through the pages of the book, his eyes focused on the task at hand. "You should apply it to the wound site as soon as possible, and it'll heal the effects of the dark magic. Ah, right." AJ laid the book on the desk with caution, as if afraid to damage its binding. "The Virseyeh."

"The what now?" Alex leaned closer to get a better look at what his brother had found. "What the heck's the Vir—"

"Virseyeh, Alex. Vir-say-eh," AJ said. Pocketing the small vial, Acacia joined her friends at the desk and peered into the book that had them so enthralled. Surely enough, it was opened to a page entitled "The Virseyeh," depicting what looked like an exact image of the creatures Acacia and Alex had met earlier that day. "Creatures of darkness, begotten only with a blood sacrifice from the summoner. Which is illegal, of course. The last Virseyeh sighting was probably . . . ten years ago during the war. Though I suppose Henry Moore and his associates don't care about the law."

"So, when you say 'blood sacrifice,'" Acacia said, swallowing a bit nervously. "You mean like . . . cattle, sheep . . . that kind of thing?"

AJ shot her a quizzical look, his pale brows raised. "Sure, cattle, sheep . . . people. Dark mages tend to use whatever's around. Though the power of said Virseyeh tends to be correlated to the strength of the blood of whatever the mage killed, so if they want their Virseyeh to be able to do some serious damage, the preference tends to be other mages. So, if the Virseyeh you two ran into were really that strong, I'm guessing the sacrifice was human."

Holy crap, Acacia thought, staring in wonder at the image of the Virseyeh decorating the page in front of her. *Someone . . . killed someone to send those things after us?*

"You think. . ." Acacia began, looking away from the book and examining AJ's almost bizarrely calm countenance. "It was one of Sisyphus's people? Trying to eliminate us?"

AJ shrugged, his expression noncommittal. "Could be. But don't forget, there's also a possibility someone else conjured them. An enemy yet to come out of the shadows. Which brings us back to your new friend Patrick Delaney."

"I know what you're going to say, so don't bother," Alex interjected, folding his arms in front of his chest. "'That boy's dangerous, don't trust him.' AJ, he saved us, something you wouldn't have been able to do, if you weren't too busy running around trying to get me in trouble with Ivy dearest—"

"My point exactly." AJ closed the book with a snap and returned it to its proper place on the shelves. Turning back to them, he tilted his head and continued. "Something about Patrick is . . . different. He is not a mage like you or me. He is more powerful, or at least, he is differently powered. "

Alex rolled his eyes and shook his head. "Andrew, of all the ridiculous garbage I've heard come out of your mouth—"

"It isn't garbage, Zander," AJ interrupted, beginning to scratch the back of his left hand. "You know as well as I do that I can pick up on these kinds of things. How did he banish the Virseyeh, with just a few spoken words?" AJ didn't appear to be angry, annoyed perhaps, and increasingly worried, but not angry. "I know it's been a while since you had a lesson, Alex, but even *you* know that most mages wouldn't be able to banish creatures of darkness that easily."

Acacia cleared her throat, glancing between the twins. *AJ does have a point,* she thought, careful this time to block her thoughts. *It's not like Alex and I aren't trained, at least somewhat, and we couldn't touch those things, even with our strongest attacks. And for as good as he is, I don't think AJ would have gotten much further with them. So, Patrick's got to be super powerful. Either that . . . or he was up to something.*

"So, AJ," she said. "Any idea why he called you Wrin? Or whatever it was."

"None." The longer they talked about Patrick, the more visibly concerned AJ became, which made Acacia more ill at ease as well. Typically, the boy did a phenomenal job of hiding his emotions, so when it was obvious he was worried, Acacia could only assume something was wrong. "But speaking of Patrick—"

"AJ—"

"Look, I know the two of you aren't going to listen to me," AJ said, shooting them a grave expression. "You're going to do as you like, no matter how much I warn you that dark magic is afoot. But would you at least *think* about what you're doing, about the potential consequences of your actions?" He paused for a moment, studying their expressions with calculating eyes. "To be honest, either you both were lucky that Patrick happened to show up at the right time or he unleashed the Virseyeh himself. I don't know about either of you, but I don't think either of those options are fantastic."

Alex let out an exasperated sigh. "So what, AJ? Don't ever trust anyone again, don't leave the house? We can't just stay cooped up in here waiting for the war to be over!"

"Would you let me finish, Alex?" AJ asked, his tone becoming higher and tenser with each passing moment. He shot them a fierce glare, one Acacia guessed might make his mother proud. "I'm not asking you to live in exile the rest of your life. All I'm asking is for the two of you to put a little more thought into what you do." Genuine fear was reflected in his eyes, though fear for exactly what, Acacia didn't know. "No matter who summoned the Virseyeh, the fact they were summoned is very serious. And this Patrick character, I can't tell you not to trust him, but at least consider the possibility he might not be trustworthy. His arrival, right after the appearance of the Virseyeh . . . well, it could be a coincidence, but I don't know if it's a good idea to make that assumption yet."

But if Patrick had summoned the Virseyeh, why would he waste his time saving them?

Sensing another outburst from Alex, Acacia placed her hand over his. *Alex, don't,* she requested. *Please, no more fighting. He's just worried, and to be honest, I am too.*

After a long pause, Alex sighed in defeat. *Fine,* he replied. *No more fighting.*

"Okay, Captain Paranoia," Alex said to his brother, his own brows raised. "We won't start inviting Patrick to our unchaperoned home-work parties until we know if he's trying to kill us or not."

If AJ was offended by his brother's remark, he showed no sign of it. "And that, Zander, is all I ask for," he said, rubbing his bruised shoulder. "And Ivy asked me to tell you that your next training session will be tomorrow at five. It would appear she's not quite as incorrigible as you think."

Without another word, AJ walked out of the study, his mission accomplished.

What a year this is turning out to be, Acacia thought, sighing deeply. *I wonder what'll be next, a pack of werewolves?*

I'll take whatever comes our way, if I still get to be with you, Alex said, grinning at her. *C'mon, let's get you home before Mommy freaks out.*

Acacia grinned and shook her head at her friend. *Watch yourself, Alex,* she warned him. *Your chivalry is showing.*

Chapter Seventeen

UNCERTAINTY

In no time, midterms ended, and winter break began. A few months ago, Acacia would've been thrilled to be freed from the responsibility of school, but now the sudden freedom caused only unease. More free time gave her more time to ponder what Sisyphus and his cronies were up to and the connection between Patrick Delaney and the Virseyeh.

What had the boy been doing there in the first place? Given the weather, Acacia doubted he'd been out for a hike. What if Patrick *had* summoned the Virseyeh? What purpose did it serve, then, for him to save them from sure death? Maybe he was trying to gain their trust . . . so he could manipulate or capture them later. Could he be working for Sisyphus?

But then again, maybe it *was* a coincidence, and Patrick really was trying to help. He had behaved . . . oddly toward AJ, but as Acacia had learned firsthand, the twin didn't make the best first impressions. Patrick seemed observant, so it reasoned he would have noticed AJ's distrusting, suspicious attitude. Acacia didn't know why Patrick had called her friend Wrin, and it didn't seem AJ did either. Was it possible

Patrick knew something about him, or even about the rest of them, that they weren't aware of yet? And if it was, what was it that he knew?

"Acacia? Acacia? Anybody home?"

Acacia blinked. Once again, she'd been caught in a daydream, though instead of pleasant walks on the beach, her ponderings were filled with thoughts of Sisyphus, Dionera, the Virseyeh, and Patrick Delaney. Pushing these thoughts from her mind, Acacia shook her head and reoriented herself to her surroundings. She was sitting with Alex on the floor of the twins' bedroom, crouched over a well-used checkerboard. To her dismay, she appeared to be losing, and quite badly at that. Acacia couldn't help but let out a shallow sigh. On a typical day, she could thrash Alex in checkers without much difficulty. That she was losing was proof enough this business with Sisyphus and Patrick had her distracted.

"Sorry, Alex," she said as she rubbed her eyes. "I've just been thinking about . . . well, everything. There's so many things going on and none of them make any sense."

"You *do* know it's my brother who's supposed to freak out over every little thing, right?" Alex asked her. "Don't tell me you're getting paranoid too, thinking Sisyphus and company are watching our every move!"

Acacia rolled her eyes. She knew she'd been more distracted since the confrontation with the Virseyeh, but with the knowledge that Sisyphus was plotting her demise, she couldn't help it. Alex might be annoyed at her, but Acacia preferred her friend's annoyance to doing something foolish and ending up either in Sisyphus's clutches or dead. After all, wasn't it better to be cautious when she was certain someone was trying to kill her?

"That's it, isn't it?" Alex's eyes filled with understanding. "Acacia, AJ's paranoia is contagious, and I think you've caught it!"

As if on cue, AJ poked his head in the doorway, his brows arched in curiosity. "What are you two doing in here?" he asked, looking more cheerful than he'd been in weeks. "And what's contagious, Alex? I hope you're not getting sick again. I really don't feel like catching it this time, so if you could keep your germs on your side of the room, it would be much appreciated."

Alex sighed and shook his head. "No, Andrew, it's your paranoia that's contagious. And now you've gone and given it to Acacia."

AJ leaned against the doorway and shrugged, casting a flippant expression in his brother's direction. "You mean you're thinking twice before running off getting yourself in trouble?" AJ shot Acacia an amused glance. "I *must* be cleverer than I was giving myself credit for."

"Well, you're in a good mood today," Acacia commented, tilting her head. "What's up? I'm not used to seeing you *not* look like you think the world is about to end."

AJ combed his fingers through his hair in an almost Mattes-like gesture. "Allegedly Sisyphus has been spending time away from his headquarters, in search of some great black dragon," he explained. "I don't know why, but there's a rumor he hopes to use it a sacrifice for some horrific dark magic ritual. It seems they've given up on hunting S'feirra, which isn't a bad thing. I don't know too much about dragon magic, but Onawa says there's major differences between the magics of different breeds."

"Oh, look at you knowing what Onawa says," Alex chimed in, smirking at his sibling. "What else does Dragon Girl say, brother dearest?"

"Alex." AJ was looking considerably more exasperated. "Shut up, please."

Acacia felt her own curiosity mount. *So, Sisyphus is looking for a black dragon,* she thought, the gears in her mind turning. *But why?*

What can he do with a black dragon that he couldn't do with a blue one? And what does he want to do anyway? Is this all about getting rid of me? This seems . . . bigger somehow.

"So how exactly do you know about this, AJ?" Acacia asked. "It doesn't sound like something that would be on the evening news. . ."

The boy shrugged, an indifferent expression on his face. "I hear a lot of things. People talk in this town if you have the patience to listen."

Meaning he's been hanging out in the Underground with Mattes and they've been snooping around, trying to get information on Sisyphus's old supporters, Alex mind-spoke to her, his light gray eyes alight with interest. Winking, he added, *And to think, my dear brother's always telling us about not getting into trouble.*

Acacia shook her head. *Not now, Alex. AJ obviously knows something about what's going on, but he's not going to tell us if we annoy him too much.*

"That's . . . odd," she said, focusing her attention on AJ. "When I had that vision, it seemed like Minos and Dionera don't get along. Sisyphus must know that too. Why would he leave the two of them to take care of his lair, fortress, whatever while he goes off looking for a big, black dragon?"

AJ studied her for a few moments and rubbed his chin, a thoughtful expression on his face. "Good point." He walked over to his bookshelf. "So, I suppose the question is why Sisyphus would leave his headquarters under the supervision of two officers who are more likely to pick a fight with one another than to attempt any further planning to bring about the destruction of Silent Springs."

"I can think of a better question," Acacia retorted, twirling her long braid between her fingers. "Who knows you're spying on them and is giving you bad information on purpose?"

She couldn't tell if AJ was more amused or intrigued by her comment.

"A double-crosser so to speak," he said, looking rather impressed with her reasoning. "Fascinating."

"Paranoid, not fascinating," Alex piped in, standing up and crossing his arms in front of his chest. "Like I said, your paranoia is contagious."

AJ rolled his eyes and, kneeling by his bookshelf, moved a book from the bottom shelf to the second. "So have the two of you seen more of your friend Patrick Delaney? It's odd for someone to show up when the two of you are in mortal danger and then disappear."

"You would think Patrick did something to you," Alex retorted, bristling. "Yeah, I get it, AJ, the kid's . . . well, weird. But he saved us, and to be honest, you're kind of weird too!"

If AJ was disturbed in the slightest by his brother's comment, he showed no visible sign of it. *Then again,* Acacia thought, *something tells me Alex has called AJ weird on more than one occasion.*

"That might be true, Zander, but at least I don't run around in the woods searching for Virseyeh to play with." AJ rose to his feet and glanced at Alex and Acacia in turn, looking pleased with himself. "You also might be interested to know after doing a bit of research, I think I may have figured out what it is about him that gives me a nervous tic."

"AJ, everyone gives you a nervous tic!" Alex exploded, losing whatever calm he still had. "Me, Acacia, Mom . . . you probably give yourself a nervous tic!"

AJ laughed. "No, well not *yet* I haven't. Actually, Alex, it seems to me your friend may be Woodsfolk. Think about it, supernatural magical abilities, using names that are Woodsfolk in origin—"

"Woodsfolk?" Acacia asked, taking a step forward. She knew she had heard the term before but couldn't quite remember from where. "They're what again, a secret society?"

AJ shot her a rather annoyed glance. "As we discussed three weeks ago, the Woodsfolk are a specific race, human in appearance, but not truly human. Very powerful magic courses through their bodies different from that which resides within human mages."

"Different how?" Acacia scratched her head, feeling confused. "And how can they be human and not human at the same time?"

"Woodsfolk are *not* human. They appear human, but they are a different race." AJ tilted his head. "Their magic comes from nature, and is often much stronger than human magic, more destructive. Woodsfolk also don't see a problem in the use of blood to perform spells and enchantments, which most human mages look down upon." AJ met Acacia's gaze directly, his dark gray eyes challenging. "And by blood sacrifice I mean *human* blood, not deer or rabbits. They're not a people to be trifled with."

Acacia blinked, trying to wipe the incredulous expression from her face. "You think Patrick is one of them? Why exactly?"

"For one, he called me 'Wrin,' which is a Woodsfolk word for fox," AJ explained in a flat tone. "For another, he smells Woodsfolk. I, ah, I mean he feels it. It's a different aura."

"He smells Woodsfolk?" Acacia repeated, dumbfounded. "What's *that* supposed to mean?"

"Nothing. It means nothing." AJ's face was flushing, possibly the reddest Acacia had ever seen it. "Just a slip of the tongue is all."

He definitely meant to say 'smells' not feels, Acacia pondered. *No matter how straightforward he seems to be most of the time anymore, there's still something AJ's hiding from me, and maybe the others too. I don't get it. We're in the middle of a war, multiple bad guys are trying to kill us, but he still feels like he has to keep secrets from me? Does he still not trust me? Does he trust anyone?*

"Okay, fine then, Mr. 'Slip of the Tongue,'" Alex said, a suspicious look on his face. "Say you're right and Wrin means fox. Why would Patrick call *you* that?"

"Zander, please don't ask me to understand the thought processes of rogue Woodsfolk." AJ shook his head, walking past them toward the door. "I can't even understand my own thought processes most of the time. Anyway, I'm sorry to have interrupted your . . . checkers match. I'll leave you two to your own devices. Oh, and Acacia? Don't forget about training tomorrow, at two o'clock. You might want to review some of your attack spells beforehand since it seems as though your memory is not quite as good as it once was."

AJ turned to leave as Merlin, the twins' black cat, slinked in the door and rubbed his head against the boy's ankles. He seemed to temporarily forget what he was doing, dropping to his knees to pet the animal.

"Okay, fine, I forgot about the Woodsfolk," Acacia replied. "But that doesn't mean I've forgotten about everything!"

"Time will tell." AJ picked up the cat and headed out the door. "Anyway, see you later! I have to take Merlin to the V-E-T. Bye!"

"Well, that was weird," Alex said, his expression truly befuddled after his brother's abrupt departure. "I've had some pretty bizarre conversations with him, but that one had to be at least top five."

Acacia nodded. "I believe it. But what do you say we forget this stupid game and lighten up with some snow soccer? I haven't played in forever."

Alex grinned at her and picked up his soccer ball. "It would be my pleasure," he said with a bow. "Prepare to be annihilated, Wheatley."

Acacia shook her head and followed her friend outside, still trying to push thoughts of Sisyphus's dragon hunt and the Woodsfolk from her mind.

***

Henry Moore leaned back in his armchair, allowing himself a single sigh of exasperation. His plans hadn't been going as planned, and he had to wonder if he was making the correct tactical decisions, including the placement of his lair. He had meticulously selected this location after days of scouring the thick forest outside Silent Springs, unable to turn down an abandoned Woodsfolk castle. Moore estimated it had been decades since the structure had been occupied by the Woodsfolk, but a residual aura remained.

The castle was a complex labyrinth of passageways, designed to confuse any mage who wandered inside. It was possible to spend days, weeks searching for an exit. Meanwhile the inhabitants of the castle could watch in entertainment as the person walked around in circles and either close all egresses on them, leaving them to their doom, or drop them into a dungeon cell.

Moore rose from his seat, exited his study, and headed for the throne room, where he knew his officers awaited him. Both Minos and Dionera had performed their roles well; Minos, or Lionel Wrently as he had been known in a previous life, was his closest advisor and a brilliant tactician, while Dionera Tartaran had been trained from birth to be an assassin. And to be honest, Dionera was not only an assassin, but a good assassin. After all, it had been she who'd killed off Joseph Swiatkowski, and if she had been a bit smarter, she would have been able to eliminate his son as well. But as was common among fire mages,

Dionera was . . . hot under the collar. While men like Henry Moore and Minos saw the world as an intricate game of chess, Dionera saw a lengthy list of people to obliterate.

Pushing the massive entryway doors of the throne room open with the power of his magic, Moore sauntered in, looking at each of his officers in turn. Minos looked as calm and collected as ever, his long, dark hair pulled back in a neat ponytail, clad all in black. Dionera, in contrast, could have passed as some kind of fire elemental, her red locks falling wildly in ringlets around her face.

"Good evening, Lord Sisyphus." Minos bowed his head with respect. "Our plan to spread fear in the town is well underway. It will not be long until all mages dwelling within a twenty-mile radius of Silent Springs will be whispering your name again in fear, their sleeping hours filled with the horrors that once were and again will be."

Dionera made an indignant "pah!" noise to illustrate her disgust. "Nightmares! How terrifying, Minos! Anything but that! Unless of course, you want to consider *doing* something!"

"Dionera, enough," Moore commanded, shooting the woman an icy glare. "Ours is a multistep process; it does not suffice to run around killing everyone in sight. From my experience, those types of plans rarely work as well as anticipated. As I remember, even your insidious plan to wipe out the entire Swiatkowski family fell short of your expectations."

Out of the corner of his eye, Moore saw Minos allow himself a triumphant smirk. It was no secret that Minos had a less than favorable view of Dionera Tartaran. Clearing his throat, Moore continued, "Nevertheless, if the intimidation stage is as underway as the two of you claim, I believe we can progress into the next stage. We shall give young Swansgrove a true taste of war."

"Sisyphus?"

Moore raised his gaze to see both his officers surveying him with curiosity. Minos's dark brows were arched sharply toward the center of the man's forehead, as they always did when he was trying to understand something. Dionera looked lost, but then again, she was trained to kill, not to understand.

"Sir, would it not be more profitable to finalize our plans against the Council rather than some novice girl?" Minos asked. "Her rashness has much cooled within the past month, possibly due in part to the influence of the one Swiatkowski boy—"

"Who I will destroy!" Dionera yelled, flames appearing at her fingertips.

"But one girl cannot pose a greater threat than the entire body of magical government," Minos continued as if he had not heard Dionera's outburst. "Surely—"

Moore hardened his gaze and tented his fingers thoughtfully. "Minos, Dionera, Swansgrove will remain standing, along with her little friends long after the Council has fallen. The Council will fall, of this much I am certain. But the Council is an archaic institution whose legitimacy has been contested for generations! If left alone, it might collapse all by itself! But this girl is a figure and a figure who it is alleged will bring about my downfall!"

"Lord—"

"It has been Seen, and so it will be so!" Moore raised his eyebrows. "Unless we can stop this figure from becoming a figure at all!"

A small smile crept across Minos's face, reminding Moore very much of a crocodile. "And how do you hope to achieve this, Henry?"

Minos might not consider Moore's strategy to be the best, but ultimately, he would do whatever his commander asked of him. Fifteen years had already passed since Lionel Wrently came before him, bent on vengeance for the death of his beautiful fiancée. Back then, Moore had been an idealistic scholar and researcher who worked to make conditions better for mages under the Council's governance, but those days were long gone. Moore doubted that many mages remembered these aspects of their past. The Council had made sure of that.

"The answer is quite simple, Minos," Moore said, rising from his seat. "To prevent the girl's destiny from coming to pass, we must break her spirit. And to do that"—he looked once again between his two officers—"we must take from her what she holds most dear."

Minos clucked his tongue in approval. "Very well, my lord. It will be so."

***

Alex Swiatkowski deftly kicked the soccer ball past Acacia and watched in amusement as she went tromping after it in the snow. It was obvious Acacia still hadn't become accustomed to the white stuff even after a solid month of winter. True, she had stopped ranting in frustration quite so much every time her feet sank into the packed snow or when Alex caught her off guard with another well-placed snowball, but it was still another aspect of life in the Northeast Acacia was struggling to adapt to.

"Having trouble there, are we?" Alex teased as Acacia nearly slipped on the snow in hot pursuit of the ball. The girl huffed in that slightly arrogant way of hers and sent the ball flying at his face with a strong kick. *Temper, temper,* Alex thought, as he headed the ball, sending it back in Acacia's direction. She fared much better this time around, managing to hit it well past Alex's range. *There's fire in her,* he thought, making sure to seal his thoughts off from her as he permitted himself a moment of silent admiration. *Not like Dionera's fire, all full of hate*

*and death . . . more like a glowing star, brighter and more dangerous
than all the wildfires in the world—*

"Do you plan on getting the ball, Alex?" Acacia asked, her vivid
green eyes bright with amusement. "Or do I need to get your balls
too?"

Alex felt his face redden and turned to search for the lost ball.
Acacia wasn't mad; in fact, she didn't seem to get angry all too much
anymore except when she thought she was being underestimated. But
she was always passionate, putting everything she had into whatever
she decided to do, whether it be soccer, magic . . . friendship. . . Since
the day they had first met, Alex and Acacia had become fast friends,
chatting easily about any number of things, working on homework,
going off on adventures together. . .

Alex nudged the ball out of the snow and dribbled it over to her.
Here she was, smart, brave, talented—not to mention gorgeous—*and*
she liked hanging out with him! Percy told Alex he needed to work on
his self-esteem, but his cousin never seemed to understand that every
time he turned around, he was surrounded by people who were always
better than him. Alex wasn't a natural at magic like his brother and
sister were, and to make matters worse, whenever he had to train with
Ivy, he became so nervous he couldn't think straight. He wasn't bad
at magic, but he didn't like to ask questions, since Ivy would turn the
question around to make him look stupid. And as for his brother, AJ
was never cruel, but he tended to put his nose in things where it didn't
belong, which rarely improved the situation.

But Acacia was different. From the beginning, she understood
things that others missed, and was always happy to see him. Of course,
that wasn't to say they always agreed on everything. The two of them
had plenty of disagreements, but they were never particularly bad

ones. And Acacia did tend to be a bit on the proud side. But no matter what, Alex could never stay mad for long, especially with her.

"Don't worry, Wheatley," Alex commented, grinning as Acacia sent the ball back to him, this time much more gently. "I'm pretty sure I can be trusted to catch a ball."

Acacia returned his grin, her coppery brows raised in a challenge. "Are you sure about that, Alex? You had me wondering there for a minute. . ."

I want to protect her, Alex realized, not taking his eyes off hers. *I'll train and get stronger so she won't have to worry about creeps like Sisyphus touching her again, ever.*

"Oh, no worries." He kicked the ball between his feet. "I've been doing this for a while."

"You're showing off, Swiatkowski," Acacia accused in a playful tone. It never ceased to amaze Alex just how quickly they fell back into this, the casual chatting, the occasional flirting, right after a discussion about the imminent danger everyone was in due to Sisyphus's evil plots. Was it possible to have two separate lives without having some kind of multiple personality disorder? "You know I can't move in this stuff."

Something wet touched Alex's nose. Glancing upward, he noted, *More snow. Well, this is ironic.*

"Snow, again?" Acacia voiced, the white flakes contrasting with the bright red of her braid. "Does it ever stop?"

Alex bent down, picked up the soccer ball, and walked over to where Acacia was standing, barely noticing the delicate crunch of the snow beneath his feet. He really liked her, that much was certain, but he had never been sure how *she* felt. That was what bothered him the most—not knowing.

"Acacia, I just think you should know," he said, dropping the soccer ball on the ground. "You're beautiful in the snow."

He leaned forward and kissed her, cupping the side of her face in his hand. And she didn't pull away.

It was as if time had decided to stand still. For a moment Alex froze, almost unable to believe what was taking place. When he did, Acacia tilted her face upward, her expression one of the most contented he had seen in quite some time.

Alex, she said. *I—*

But Acacia never said what. Before Alex could tell what was happening, they were kissing again, only this time he couldn't tell who was kissing who. Acacia ran her hands through his hair, until one ventured downward, exploring the skin on the back of his neck. Unable to ignore the pleasant shiver down his spine, Alex dropped his hands to Acacia's waist and held her gently. He didn't dare touch her any more than that or let his hands wander. He had waited this long; there was no need to rush things *now.*

Alex wasn't sure how long they stood there, kissing in the snow with their bodies partially intertwined. When their lips parted, he looked at Acacia for a moment, then, feeling his face redden, looked at the snow coating the ground.

"I guess we should probably go home," he said, scratching his head. "Before it gets dark . . . or something."

Acacia pushed his chin back in her direction, a demure smile on her face. "Let's go with 'or something.'" If anything, she seemed happy, relieved by the events of the past few minutes. "I'll talk to you later?"

Alex's face burned, but he merely nodded and watched as Acacia disappeared in a flash of bright green magic.

Well, that was interesting, whatever that was, he thought. *I wonder how long it'll take for everyone to find out.*

You should worry a little less about your adventures in kissing and a little more about what you have to do to ensure no more lives are lost, a familiar voice said in his mind.

Alex scanned the surrounding area carefully using his magic. Other than a few of the neighbors, no other source of magic was nearby.

Patrick? he asked, thoroughly confused. *Is that you? Where are you? And what are you talking about?*

There is no time for explanations. Patrick's voice was clipped and harsh in tone. *You must come now or your brother will die.*

Alex's heart seized in his throat. Could it be possible? Could his paranoid to a fault brother be in grave danger, and at that, not more than an hour after he saw him last?

But the others. . .

You know as well as I do if you take the time to gather the rest of your friends it will be too late. Patrick's tone was resolute and final. *Now, Alexander, what is your decision?*

Alex took one last glance toward the town of Silent Springs, thinking of all his friends and family there, his brain struggling against his heart.

All right, Patrick, hold on, he said at long last. *I'm coming.*

***

"So this is your cat?" Onawa Mescal asked, peering into Merlin's carrier as the two of them sat in the back of the enchanted bus traveling back to Silent Springs from the nearby town of Havenwood, where the veterinarian's office specializing in magical creatures was located. The girl smiled and stuck her finger in through the carrier door, petting the cat's nose. "Figures. He acts like you."

AJ let out a single laugh, raising his pale brows at his companion. "Oh? How so?"

"He plays hard to get." Onawa pulled her finger back out of the carrier and folded her hands on her lap. "But once he figures out you're a decent person, he warms right up to you. And doesn't act like a complete arrogant prick."

"So, what, you think *I'm* playing hard to get?" AJ asked, shooting Onawa a curious look. "With whom? You?"

"Maybe not hard to get." Onawa leaned back in her bus seat and looked up at the ceiling. "Defensive, I guess. You don't like to be petted, just like the cat."

AJ couldn't help but roll his eyes. "Onawa—"

"Don't 'Onawa' me," the girl retorted. "I tell it like it is."

"I can see that." There had been something . . . different about Onawa, from the first day AJ met her that made him *want* to trust her. AJ trusted few people, particularly those he wasn't related to. Mattes had been an exception, as they had both been lost and alone when they first met. But when he met Onawa, AJ had tossed his usual rules aside. Of course, his anxiety had been warning him since the beginning that something would go terribly wrong, but so far AJ had been able to ignore these thoughts. "Anyway, what are you doing the rest of today?"

"Oh, you know," Onawa said. "Visiting S'feirra, maybe watching a movie with Uncle." The bus slowed to a stop, and the girl rose to her feet. Flashing him a mischievous grin, Onawa leaned close to AJ's face and whispered, "If you want to hang out with me, you should say something instead of beating around the bush. You must know by now I don't do subtle."

"Bye, Onawa," AJ replied. "See you tomorrow."

Waving, the girl winked again and exited the bus.

People were hard to understand, which was why AJ usually didn't bother trying. It was much easier to not think about it, what people were thinking, how they felt about you, freeing the mental energy for other things. Figuring out new and more effective ways to use magic for instance. Or playing the piano.

A few stops later, AJ got off the bus and walked the block to his house. Maybe someday he would figure out the mystery of human connection, but today wasn't going to be that day.

"Hey, is anybody home?" AJ called, walking in the front door. Even before he asked, he could tell the house was deserted. Truthfully, AJ hadn't expected to see either his mother or sister. Cecelia Swiatkowski had been working long hours for the past few weeks, and Ivy had been avoiding him since he had confronted her about Alex's training, but he had been expecting to at least see Alex. It was almost five o'clock, and with their mother still at work, Alex would usually come poking around to see what was for dinner. Lately AJ had been doing most of the cooking, and he always made enough for four, just in case. Sometimes AJ thought setting the table for all of them was a waste of time, and a depressing waste of time at that, since it reminded him that his family was isolated and fragmented, possibly beyond repair. At the same time, he recognized it as a sign of hope—hope that someday they would all be together again. AJ sighed, closed the door behind him, and released Merlin from the carrier.

Something felt eerie about the empty house that AJ hadn't sensed in a long time. Unlike his brother, AJ didn't mind being home alone, but for some reason, he couldn't help but feel uncomfortable, as if he was being watched. Scanning the house with his magic, AJ could pick up on something . . . an aura with an earthy scent, familiar but not comforting.

"Hello? Is someone in here?" AJ glanced behind himself and walked into the living room. Trace magic littered the house, but from what he could tell, its original source was long gone. AJ hadn't noticed anything broken or stolen, so why would anyone bother breaking and entering, unless it was an act of intimidation. *Alex? Did you let someone in the house?*

No response.

Where would Alex have gone? Ever since the incident with the Virseyeh, neither Alex nor Acacia had been wandering around much, which had been a great source of relief. Maybe Alex had gone to Acacia's house for dinner? He was usually pretty good at letting AJ know he was going somewhere. . .

He found nothing suspicious in the living room. Everything was in the same place as it had been when AJ had gone to take Merlin to the vet. Scanning the room with his peripheral vision, he sniffed the air and picked up the same scent again, this time noticing it had left a trail leading upstairs.

Alex, can you hear me? AJ asked, trying to reach out again to his brother through their connection. He couldn't shake the feeling that something was wrong, horribly wrong. Even if Alex didn't feel like talking to him, he would always respond, if not on the first attempt, on the second. *Alex, come on, what's going on? Are you okay?* If something had happened to Alex, AJ would have felt it, just as he'd felt a crushing pain in his arm when Alex had broken his during a soccer match. If he wasn't responding, something had to be seriously wrong or his connection blocked somehow. . .

A note was nailed to their bedroom door with what looked to be some kind of iron throwing star. AJ pulled the object free with a bit of difficulty, holding the door in place with his foot, and cut his hand on one of the star's sharp edges in the process. Wincing, he placed the star on the floor and opened the note.

"Wrin,

You would do well to keep a better eye on that brother of yours, as it appears he tends to make bad decisions when left to his own devices. I would advise you to start using your brain sooner rather than later, as time is not on your side."

AJ tightened his grasp on the note, watching it shake in his quivering hand. *Oh my god, Alex,* he thought, forcing himself to take a deep breath to avoid a panic attack. He could stand here staring at the note—which could only have been left by Patrick Delaney—for hours, days, but that wasn't going to change the fact that Alex was in grave danger. That AJ had told his brother to show caution with the newcomer and, as usual, Alex had neglected to listen didn't change things either. It was far easier to sit back and ruminate about the past than it was to do something. AJ knew he couldn't let himself think too much about what had happened, or his imagination would get the best of him.

Hey Acacia, AJ mind-spoke, sensing the girl's surprise and confusion as he reached out to her through their telepathic connection. *We have a problem.*

Chapter Eighteen

Hard Decisions

No more than half an hour after Acacia's world was flipped upside down in the best way possible, she received the chilling message from AJ that Alex was missing. She'd been at home with Sari and David watching television, and her main concern had been trying to hide the fact she'd just had her first kiss. Their parents were out on a date night, so it posed little challenge to slip out. While David could be a protective older brother when he wanted to be, tonight was not one of those times, as he was more interested in fighting with Sarison over the remote than Acacia's pitiful excuses for why she had to leave the house. Her mind overflowing with worry, Acacia teleported to the Swiatkowskis' house and greeted AJ with a strong hug.

"Let's go," he said, pulling away from Acacia's embrace in a rather cold fashion. "We have a lot of figuring out to do."

Acacia considered arguing with him—after all, he *had* to be upset too—but ultimately decided against it. She had her way of dealing with stress, so AJ was entitled to his own. Closing the door behind her,

Acacia followed her friend into the dining room where Percy, Mattes, and Onawa were clustered around the table, each of their faces fixed in concentration.

"Patrick Delaney was kind enough to stop by and leave me a note telling me I should keep a better eye on Alex since he has a 'tendency for making bad decisions when left to his own devices.'" AJ placed a piece of paper and a small metal object in the middle of the table. "Acacia, do you have any idea of where Alex may have gone?"

Acacia shook her head, trying to hide the pain from her face. "After you left, we played soccer. We took his ball and went around the block to the field across the street. But it was getting . . . cold, so I went home. I assumed he did too."

"Acacia, it isn't your fault," Percy assured her, his blue eyes serene. "It probably isn't Alex's either. Andrew, this Patrick fellow—"

"Looks to be a complete snake," Mattes interjected, his hazel eyes blazing with irritation. "Can you remind me why the hell you guys even *considered* trusting him?"

Acacia let out a sigh of exasperation. Of all the things she wasn't in the mood for, a pointless argument with Matthias Knight sat high up on the list. "Look, Mattes, *enough.* In case you weren't aware, Patrick did save Alex and me from a swarm of Virseyeh." Acacia glared at the boy, determined not to allow him to get the better of her. "Worrying about who we shouldn't have trusted isn't going to change the fact that Alex is missing and some Woodsfolk kid has something to do with it."

After a moment of silence, Onawa clapped, as Percy looked with nervous eyes between Acacia and Mattes. Shaking his head, AJ cleared his throat.

"Well spoken, Acacia," he said, shooting her an appreciative look. "What do *you* think we should do?"

"What do I think we should do?" Acacia repeated, feeling quite confused. "Why are you asking me? Aren't you the genius mastermind?"

AJ rolled his eyes, the impressed expression of moments earlier replaced with one of annoyance. "Hardly. And the last time I checked, you're the Heir of Swansgrove, not me."

An uncomfortable mix of frustration and fear filled Acacia's core, causing twisting knots to form in her stomach. "AJ, we've been through this. I don't care who I'm related to or what alleged great magic I'm destined to have. I'm just . . . normal!" She stared at him, willing the boy to come to his senses once again. AJ couldn't seriously think Acacia, who had only been training for about four months now, could lead them on some suicide mission! "You want to know what I think? We need to call the cops—Justice Enforcement, right? Isn't it their job to investigate crime and disappearances and things like that?"

"We don't have *time* for Justice Enforcement, Acacia!" AJ protested, anxiety flashing across his pale face. "Do you know how long it would take for them to send someone out? They'd put us under surveillance the second we made the report, and we'd be powerless to do anything to help Alex." He paused, his dark eyes every bit as scared as they'd been the night of Sisyphus's escape. "You know the Council doesn't like us; just how much urgency do you think they'd place on finding a missing Swiatkowski?"

"Well, what do you expect *me* to do?" Between the stress of worrying about Alex and feeling pressured to act, Acacia was losing her temper, and fast. "Maybe I've gotten better over the past four months, but I still barely know what I'm doing—"

"You are the Heir of Swansgrove!" AJ yelled, his eyes welling with tears. "You are the most powerful mage I have *ever* met, including Sisyphus and Dionera!" He paused and wiped his eyes dry with his hands, forcing a neutral expression on his face. "Don't you *get* it, Acacia? You summoned lightning magic your first day of training. That's unheard of. I know you don't—we don't—completely know what you being the Heir of Swansgrove means, but knowing that you have this power, can you really sit by knowing Alex has been lured to Sisyphus's lair?"

Acacia felt her brows shoot up in surprise. "Excuse me? *What?*"

"Patrick lured Alex into Sisyphus's lair. It's the only logical explanation," AJ said, as Onawa tiptoed over and squeezed his hand reassuringly. The two locked eyes for a moment, and AJ turned back to Acacia. "No matter the reason for his betrayal, Alex is in grave danger, and we have to do something about it."

Onawa let out a short sigh and turned to Acacia, her brown eyes kind but fierce. "Acacia, AJ's right. It's time to stop being a student and start being a leader."

Acacia swallowed nervously and glanced between each of her friends in turn. "It's not that I don't want to help Alex. Maybe I am as powerful as you guys say, or will be, but I still don't think I can beat Sisyphus."

"You don't *have* to," Mattes pointed out, a crooked grin on his face. "All Drew's proposing is a rescue mission, not an end the war mission. I think we can push that back until at least spring break."

Acacia prepared herself to protest, but a lightbulb went on in her mind. "Hold on one minute." She turned to AJ and narrowed her eyes suspiciously. "How do you *know* Alex is in Sisyphus's lair? As soon as you told me about Alex going missing, I tried to figure out where he was with my own tracking spell, and I couldn't pick up a thing! It's not like I haven't practiced—"

"Practice doesn't have anything to do with it," Mattes interjected, an amused expression on his face. The boy raised his dark brows at AJ in an almost challenging fashion. "You seriously haven't told her yet?"

"Haven't told me what?" Acacia pulled herself up to her full height, feeling frustration pulse through her body in waves. "You haven't told me *what*, Mr. Swiatkowski? What could be so important that you have to keep it a secret, even though I've never done anything to—"

AJ and Mattes exchanged glances, AJ's nervous, Mattes's amused. Mattes shrugged and cleared his throat while Percy let out a particularly long sigh.

"He's a Sniffer," Mattes explained, glancing first at AJ and then at Acacia. AJ glared at him, but if Mattes was at all disturbed, he certainly didn't show it. "And to be honest, a pretty good one."

"And what the heck is *that* supposed to mean?" Acacia demanded, looking between AJ and Mattes, unsure which boy she should be more frustrated with. Truthfully, she wasn't surprised AJ had been keeping something from her, as he always seemed to be hiding something, but she also couldn't help but be annoyed. Acacia had done everything AJ had asked her to do for the most part; what did she have to do to earn his trust?

"It means he can smell magic." Mattes looked entirely too pleased with himself for Acacia's liking. "Thus, the Sniffer part."

Acacia rolled her eyes. "Magic doesn't—"

"Just because *you* can't smell magic doesn't mean other people can't," AJ argued, shooting Acacia a reprimanding glance. "But we can discuss it later, when Alex isn't in grave danger." He turned, looking at Mattes, Onawa, Percy, and Acacia in turn. "Anyway, from what I can tell, there's some kind of aura blocking enchantment wherever he is, which explains why you can't sense him. It's a strong spell, but no spell, no matter how strong, can throw a Sniffer off the trail."

Acacia studied her friend with curiosity. In retrospect, she realized the signs of AJ's Sniffing ability had been there, but she hadn't been paying enough attention. How AJ had been able to locate her so quickly on multiple occasions, being able to tell that Patrick was one of the Woodsfolk from the first time he'd met him. . .

"So, you *can* find him," Acacia remarked, feeling all the anger and frustration receding. After all, what did it matter that AJ had kept his Sniffer status a secret from her? Even though Acacia had only known AJ for a few months, she could easily tell all his actions were calculated, premeditated. If he'd decided against telling her about his ability, Acacia could only assume he had a very good reason for doing so.

AJ nodded. "Sisyphus's lair is in the deep part of the forest, maybe about another twenty-minute hike from the Bloody Meadow. We can set up a campsite close by to finalize our plan."

How am I going to do this? Acacia thought, feeling the hot stares of all her friends. *I'm getting the hang of my magic, but I'm no expert. But what other options are there? AJ's right, the Council doesn't like the Swiatkowskis to begin with, so going to them isn't an option. And besides—* She glanced at each of her friends and took a bold step forward. *Maybe they're right. Maybe the time has come for me to put my skills to the test and teach Sisyphus a lesson about messing with us!*

"Well then, what are we waiting for?" Acacia asked, placing her hands on her hips. "Enough standing around, let's go rescue Alex!"

Onawa let out a squeal of excitement and hugged Acacia with a surprising amount of strength given her size. Percy and AJ nodded at her, looking equal parts pleased and anxious. Mattes shrugged and gave her a thumbs up.

"That's what I'm talking about!" Onawa exclaimed, squeezing Acacia even harder. "We'll show Sissy Puss who's boss!"

Acacia squeezed her friend back and thought of Alex. Alex welcoming her with open arms on the first day despite the disaster it had been, Alex standing by her even when she made terrible decisions. . .

There's no one else I'd rather face sure death with, she thought, remembering their mind-spoken conversation after Acacia's first experience with the Youth Assembly. *And there's no one else I'd rather face sure death for, either.*

"Well, everyone," she began, peering into each of her friend's faces in turn. "We're not going to save Alex standing around. Let's go!"

***

Acacia stared off into the distance from their camp in the direction where Sisyphus's lair was supposedly located. Not surprisingly, AJ had been right; the dark mage's hideout wasn't too far away, particularly with the help of a teleportation spell. Sisyphus appeared to have selected an old castle for his headquarters, with foreboding tall towers encircled by a perimeter wall, all constructed entirely of stone. Acacia couldn't help but think the building looked a little out of place, like something out of an Arthurian legend thrown into the modern United States. The entire edifice exuded an aura of doom and dread, making Acacia second guess herself, her plans, and the likelihood that she and her friends would be able to find their way in and out with Alex in tow.

"Hey," Onawa said, sitting next to her by the fire, a bowl of some kind of soup in hand. "Eat something. Don't want to go around passing out in there, do you?"

Acacia glanced up from her silent reverie and accepted the food from her friend. "Thanks, Onawa," she remarked, taking a spoonful of the steaming mixture. Acacia could make out the distinct taste of beans, peppers, and chilies. "How are you doing?"

Onawa shrugged, her brown eyes flickering in the firelight. "I'm fine. Ready to kick some butt."

Acacia snorted into her soup. Compared to Onawa, Acacia was a careful planner, especially over the past few hours. It was due to Onawa's spontaneous personality that Acacia had suggested she be the one to create a diversion so the rest of them could slip inside the building.

"Are you sure you're okay with this?" Acacia asked. "I don't want to put you in danger—"

"Acacia." Onawa rolled her eyes. "I put myself in danger. If I didn't want to do it, I'd have knocked you unconscious and been out of here before you could say 'dragon's egg.' Which you wouldn't have been able to say since you'd be unconscious."

Acacia grinned. To say that Onawa was direct was a bit of an understatement.

"And besides," her friend continued. "I know how important Alex is to you. What kind of friend would I be if I wouldn't help you save him?"

Alex. Acacia had been doing her best not to think about him since the impromptu meeting in the Swiatkowskis' kitchen, choosing to focus her attention on figuring out a way to retrieve Alex and get out of Sisyphus's lair.

"Does everyone else here know my feelings better than I do?" she whispered to Onawa in the lowest voice she could muster.

"Yes!" Mattes called from the other side of the camp. "Yes, we do!"

AJ, who had been in an involved conversation with Mattes and Percy, rolled his eyes and walked over to Acacia and Onawa, a mildly annoyed expression on his face.

"Don't worry about him," the twin said. "Matthias has the unfortunate tendency of running his mouth when he's anxious."

"Why don't you come over here and say that?"

AJ ignored his friend's comment. "I'm sorry Acacia, but do you mind if I steal Onawa from you for a minute? Before operation rescue mission commences?"

Acacia shrugged. "Sure, why not? And besides, Onawa's her own person. You don't need *my* permission to talk to her."

Onawa jumped to her feet and stuck out her tongue. "Darn *right* we don't need your permission!" She grabbed the boy by the hand and the two walked off toward the other end of the camp. Acacia couldn't help but shake her head. *Maybe Alex was right about those two,* she thought. *Normally I wouldn't assume holding hands was a big deal, but for AJ, that very well might be 'fallen in love'*—

Acacia's inner monologue was interrupted as Percy took Onawa's spot next to her by the fire.

"You know, Acacia, you should give yourself a bit more credit," he said. "You may *think* you're not getting anywhere, but what you've accomplished in four months is extraordinary, Heir of Swansgrove or not."

Acacia let out a long sigh. In her time in Silent Springs, she'd never had a lengthy conversation with Percy, and she wasn't sure she wanted to have one right before breaking into Sisyphus's fortress. Percy always seemed nice enough, but she didn't know much about him, except he was Alex and AJ's older cousin and was by far the quietest of all their group.

"Percy, I haven't done anything." Acacia poked a stick into the still roaring fire. "Even if I will be a great mage someday, that's the future, not now. Now I'm just some girl—"

"'Some girl' who is well on her way to mastering her power while learning about a world she never knew existed," Percy corrected her, his blue eyes reminding her a bit of Cecelia Swiatkowski's. "And besides, you're in high school. So, unless you're completely different from every other teenager, you're also in the middle of figuring out who you are."

Acacia raised her coppery brows at him. "And just who might that be?"

"You're seriously asking me that?" Percy asked. "You're a strong girl, Acacia, I hardly think you need a boy to tell you who you are."

Acacia shrugged and shot her friend an annoyed expression. "Do we *really* have to have this conversation right now, Percy? I get it, knowing myself is important, but being a good mage is what's going to save Alex, not being self-aware or being a good person."

"And what makes you think the two don't go hand in hand?" the older boy replied in a reflective voice. "After all, do you think it's possible to be a 'good mage' without being a good person first?"

Acacia sat back and studied Percy's face, allowing his words to sink in.

"I guess it depends on what you mean by a 'good mage,' doesn't it?" Acacia tilted her head thoughtfully. Percy did have a point. Sisyphus had to be a skilled mage, but with all the destruction and death he'd caused, Acacia didn't think he could be qualified as 'good.'

"Acacia, tell me this," Percy said with a grin. "What's more important, being able to do incredible feats of magic or being able to improve people's lives in some way or another?"

Acacia grinned back at him. "Alex told me a while ago that you want to be a healer. That's why, isn't it, so you can try to make people's lives better without getting caught up with all the politics?"

"Healing is what I love, what makes me happy. And I'm not just talking about the magical type of healing. You're a healer as well, Acacia, although a different type."

Acacia scratched her head. "Me? A healer? But *I* don't know how—"

"You might not be able to mend broken bones, but you're still a healer," Percy explained. "After all, of what use is a healed body, if the soul remains broken?"

"Golec, what the hell are you even talking about?" Mattes demanded from the other side of the camp. "I swear no one in your whole family makes any sense!"

Percy winked at Acacia and rose to his feet. "It's not the magic, Acacia, but what you *do* with it. Whether you affect people's lives for better or for worse. The choice is yours, so just be sure to decide carefully."

With that, Onawa and AJ reappeared from the woods, followed closely by the majestic S'feirra, the dragon's golden eyes gleaming in the firelight.

"Well, everyone?" AJ said in a bright tone. "Are we ready?"

Acacia almost leaped to her feet in anticipation, winking back at Percy. "Mr. Swiatkowski. I thought you'd never ask."

***

The dragon soared through the black night sky with an occasional flap of its magnificent blue wings. Acacia watched from behind the tree as Onawa clutched S'feirra's back as easily as if she were horseback riding. *I still can't believe how she does that,* Acacia thought. *You would think I wouldn't be surprised anymore, but. . .*

S'feirra swooped down and breathed fire on one of the castle's high towers. Of course, no one was on that tower when she did, but the creature's sudden appearance had the desired outcome. The night air was filled with the shrieking of Sisyphus's minions, and within minutes, about ten of them flooded out of the building's front gates and followed the dragon in hot pursuit.

"Do try not to worry your pretty head off," Mattes told Acacia. "This won't be the first time Onawa's ever given those idiots the slip."

Acacia glanced back at the boy and nodded. It would be difficult to keep herself from worrying about her friend entirely, but she did trust Onawa to protect herself.

"There, do you see it?" one of Sisyphus's men hollered. "This is the second time we have encountered this dragon! This time, it cannot escape!"

Acacia scanned the crowd of cloaked figures until she located the speaker. Dark hair, cruel eyes . . . *Minos,* she thought. *Sisyphus's right hand.*

Good point, AJ replied in her mind. *With him gone, we might have a much easier time of it.*

All right, everyone, Acacia began, speaking to all her friends. *Do we all know the plan?*

Duh. Mattes looked at her as if she'd asked him if he remembered his name. *Percival and I stroll in through the front door and beat any eggheads that come our way while you geniuses slip in the back, grab dear Alexander, and get out before someone decides to kill us.*

Acacia gave the boy a gentle shove. *Do* not *do something stupid and get captured, Mr. Knight. Do I make myself clear?*

Crystal, captain, Mattes replied, examining her with admiration. *Well, Perce, shall we go?*

Percy nodded, and the two boys took one last cautious look for sentries and made a run for the giant set of doors. Percy reached for the door, but he was too slow; Mattes extended his right arm, his palm open in an aggressive posture.

"Team Redhead!" he cried as he blasted the door in with an impressive flash of yellow magic. Once the smoke settled, Mattes looked back at Acacia and winked. "And *that* is how you open a door!"

Percy grasped Mattes by the arm and hurried into the castle, pulling his mission partner along behind him. Acacia shook her head and glanced over at AJ. He had two fingers at his left temple, staring incredulously at the hole Mattes had created in the front of the building.

AJ, we need to get going, Acacia reminded him. *That wasn't what I was thinking of when I said 'distraction,' but it* is *Mattes.*

Her friend nodded and let out a long sigh. *You're right. I hope you don't mind if I don't blow open the back door screaming like an idiot.*

I'd much prefer it if you didn't, actually.

The two walked around the castle grounds, keeping a careful eye out for any additional sentries. Within a few minutes, they came to the back of the building. The only way in was a single wooden door with a bit of iron plating around the edges.

Well, here we are, Acacia said. *It looks legitimate at least.*

It looks like a trap, AJ replied, a hint of anxiety in his voice. *Though I guess we don't have a choice.*

Acacia walked over to it and, taking a breath, reached deep within herself into her power and forced the door open. Inside all she could see was darkness. AJ followed her, as silent as a cat, and conjured an orb of bright blue magic to guide their way.

Well, in we go. He took the first step into the dark passage, gesturing for Acacia to follow. *I've told all the others, but I figured I would wait to tell you until now; this place is built on Woodsfolk ruins.*

Meaning?

"Meaning our magical connections, our telepathic ones for instance, are compromised," AJ explained out loud, pausing in the darkness for Acacia to catch up. The door slammed behind them, and Acacia forced herself to keep moving. "And the walls move on their own and most likely will try to ensnare us in a trap."

Acacia swallowed. The thought of the walls and corridors closing in on them as they went forward had worried her since AJ and Mattes had discussed the possibility of traps inside the castle. But the plan was simple, and hopefully easy. Onawa and S'feirra were distracting most of Sisyphus's minions, Percy and Mattes had broken in through the front entrance and were creating a distraction inside the fortress, and finally, Acacia and AJ would find Alex. Once they found him, one of them would send a signal to the others, and they all would escape as quickly as possible.

The two teenagers traveled down the dark, stone corridor, lit only by AJ's orb. Acacia tried not to pay too much attention to the sights and smells surrounding them, but out of the corner of her eye could make out some dreadful sights, some skulls, blood smeared on the walls. . .

"Acacia, I want to apologize," AJ said, glancing over at her with wide eyes, which to Acacia's surprise glowed with the blue of his magic. "For not telling you about being . . . a Sniffer. I was planning on telling you soon, but I should have told you from the start." He let out a sharp sigh, and Acacia would have bet his face was red with embarrassment. "The truth is . . . you're going to think I'm dramatic, but you *are* one of the most trustworthy people I've ever met. It's just. . ."

Acacia let out a sigh of her own. Truthfully, she had been wondering about the whole Sniffing thing—what it was, how it worked, why

AJ had been so hesitant to talk about it—but during a rescue mission didn't seem like the best time. *But hey,* Acacia thought. *Who knows if we will get out of this alive? Better late than never.*

"It's fine, AJ." She narrowly avoided stepping on a piece of bone. "But why does it matter? So, you can smell magic. It's not like you killed someone."

"Sniffers have a bit of an . . . unsavory reputation in our world," AJ continued in an anxious voice. "There's always been Sniffers who sell themselves as mercenaries to dark mages, despite the terrible cost of human life." AJ paused, and Acacia debated reaching out to touch his shoulder reassuringly but decided against it. "We're exceptionally skilled at finding people, particularly people who have other magical abilities like Seers and Shapeshifters. Many of these mercenary Sniffers are the ones responsible for the near extinction of the Seers and the massive hunting and capture of countless mages during wartimes. Sniffing is a rare gift as well, but to think that we caused so much pain and death . . . it's enough to make you feel . . . dirty."

Acacia thought back to what Percy had told her moments earlier—it's not the magic, it's what you do with it.

"So, you didn't tell me because you didn't want me to think that you're . . . dirty?" Acacia asked. "Andrew Swiatkowski, do you *not* know me better than that? You're a good person, no matter what kind of weird powers you have. If you can't see that, then I guess you're not as perceptive as I first thought."

"I'm probably not," AJ confessed, the light from his orb causing an odd sheen across his face. "But I thought you deserved to know the truth."

Acacia shook her head. Was it possible there was such blatant prejudice in the magical world? That people hated Sniffers based on an ability they were born with? That seemed to be AJ's rationale for keeping it from her, but how many of her friend's fears were plausible and how many were misguided? AJ *did* tend towards paranoia . . . but then again, he'd also been proven to be correct about many things, including the danger of Acacia venturing to the Bloody Meadow and Patrick Delaney.

"There *is* something I wanted to ask you," Acacia said, thinking back to the conversation they'd had before departing the house. "In private."

"Oh?"

"Is it true what you said before, about me being the most powerful mage you've ever met?" Acacia asked, studying AJ with inquisitive eyes. "That's a big statement to make to someone who's only had their magic for a few months."

AJ shot a quick glance in her direction. Maybe it was Acacia's imagination, but it certainly looked like his face had flushed in embarrassment. "Of course it's true, Acacia. Why would I lie about something like that?"

"There's just no way," Acacia argued. "How could I possibly be more powerful than the other mages you know, Sisyphus included—"

"Sometimes things just are the way they are." Her friend scratched the back of his left hand so rigorously Acacia wouldn't have been surprised if it bled. "I really don't know what else to tell you. You have great potential, which to this point has been untapped. Maybe you don't have the experience yet, but I've always thought we learn best in the real world, when we're faced with real problems. As much as I'd rather Alex didn't go missing, maybe this is the opportunity you need to come into your power."

Acacia chewed on a fingernail, considering AJ's words carefully. "You think I have this power because I'm . . . the Heir of Swansgrove? Too bad I don't know what that actually means. "

"Not yet, but we will," AJ assured her, a rather gentle expression on his face. "Trust me. I just haven't been able to do as much research as I wanted to with everything going on the past few weeks. But we *will* figure it out, Acacia, I promise."

They had arrived at a fork in the corridor. Acacia could feel traces of Alex's aura extending from the right and a deep, raw power from the left.

"Well, this is where we part ways," AJ said, glancing first to the passageway to the right and then to the left.

"Excuse me?" Acacia turned and faced her friend head on. "We're in this together, AJ. It's insanity to split up in this enormous labyrinth—"

"It's insanity to *not* split up, Acacia." AJ retorted. "You can pick up on Alex's aura now, right? The spell shielding him is weaker now that we've passed through the major fortifications of this, well, fortress. I know how strong your tracking skills are; you should be able to find him now without any difficulties."

Acacia froze and arched her coppery brows in confusion. They had been over this plan multiple times, so why would AJ try to change it now?

"AJ, what the hell makes you think splitting up is a good idea?" Acacia roared, placing both hands on her hips. "We're wandering around a dark mage's lair crawling with bad guys, the walls themselves are trying to seal us up into an early grave, and *now* you decide we're going to split up?"

"Sisyphus is doing this to get to you, you do know that, right?" AJ asked, undisturbed by her outburst. His eyes were still bright blue, which Acacia assumed was a result of using his Sniffing magic. "He convinced Patrick Delaney to lure Alex here, but no matter how much they may explain it away as part of their efforts to scare the mages of Silent Springs, this is all a ploy to get to you, Acacia."

"And yet you think it's a good idea for me to wander around this place by myself." Acacia glared at her friend, still confused by his thought process. "Besides, I *told* you that Dionera woman has a vendetta against you."

AJ laughed, glancing at her with interest. "Acacia Wheatley, you really should have a little more faith in yourself, and in the rest of us as well." He gestured toward the left-most tunnel with his eyes. "This passage will take me to the magical core, where the Woodsfolk and dark magics converge. I'll go there and figure out a way to prevent the fortress from, as you said, 'locking us up in an early grave.' You don't need me to rescue Alex. I'm sure he'd rather see you, anyway."

"But. . ." Acacia grasped for the right words, unsure of how to best talk sense into her friend. "That magic is too strong. There's no way you'll be able to—"

AJ cleared his throat, shooting her a particularly sharp glance. "Acacia. When I tell you I can do something, you need to trust me on it. Not having the walls close on us will make our escape less complicated."

"Okay, but what about Sisyphus?" Acacia demanded, feeling her anxiety rise in her chest. "You said he did all this to lure me here. What am I supposed to do when he tries to kill me?"

AJ studied her, a resolute expression on his face. "You don't let him," he replied, as if surprised Acacia hadn't thought of this herself. "Acacia, I know this isn't easy, and honestly, I don't think it's going to get any easier. But I learned a long time ago that when life becomes . . . trying, we must become even more trying to fight back. Even when we're surrounded in darkness." AJ looked at her, tilting his head thoughtfully. "We must light the fire inside ourselves to light the fire inside others. It's the only way to purge the darkness from our world."

Could it be true? Acacia thought. *Can I really beat Sisyphus, stop him from taking over and whatever other insidious plans he has?*

"You and your cousin have a knack for delivering passionate inspirational speeches," Acacia replied, shooting her friend a crooked grin. "Maybe it should be you two in charge of the Youth Assembly."

AJ rolled his eyes and let out a brief laugh. "Hilarious, Acacia. Anyway, we're wasting time. Percy and Mattes can't hold Sisyphus's minions off forever."

"You're right," Acacia agreed. "But before we split . . . I want you to promise me something this time."

"Oh?"

Without a moment's notice, Acacia hugged him, and much to her surprise, AJ didn't recoil. If she wasn't mistaken, the twin even seemed to be hugging her back, at least a little.

"Be careful, okay?" she said, disentangling herself and tugging on her braid. "And don't do anything stupid. Alex and I do enough of that for all of us."

AJ shrugged but made no refusal. "Good luck, Acacia," he said, much of the tension gone from his face. "You have the skill and the ability to improvise, so luck is the only thing you need."

Acacia nodded and conjured her own orb of light to lead her way as she watched AJ disappear down the passageway to the left.

Oh AJ, she thought. *If you would just drop that wall for more than five minutes at a time, people might realize you're not as cold as you come across.*

Shaking her head, the girl held the orb high above her and turned to the right, letting the trail of Alex's magic guide her through the dark corridors of Sisyphus's stronghold.

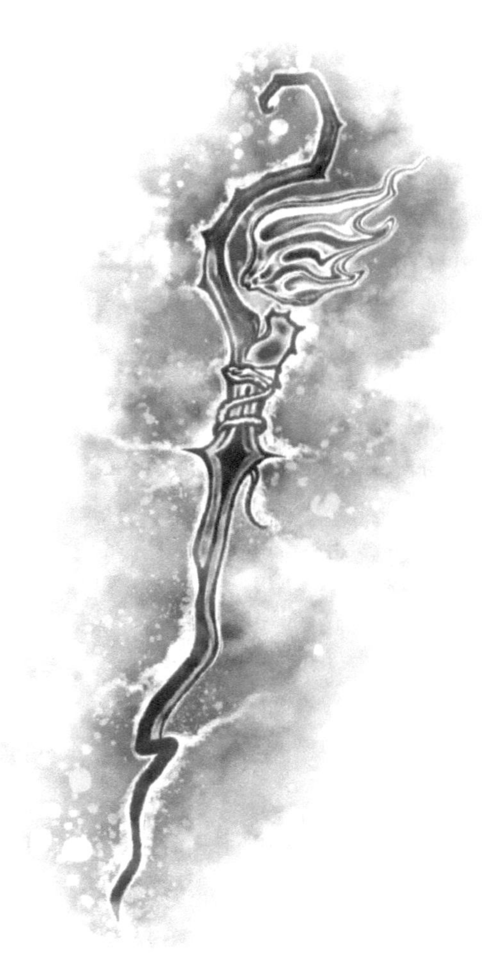

Chapter Nineteen

THE STAFF

Percy took one more cautious glance down the hallway and motioned to Mattes that all was clear. Of course, Matthias Knight was too preoccupied with blasting open yet another door to notice, and Percy had to walk over to the far side of the corridor to collect him.

Oh Matthias, Percy thought as he pulled Mattes away from whatever chaos he was set on creating. *One might think you're trying to get us captured.*

Percy really didn't have a problem with Matthias Knight. Of course, Percy and Mattes had rubbed each other the wrong way on occasion, but it was usually because they were so different. While Percy was calm and collected, Mattes was rash and impulsive. Over the years, Percy also noticed that Mattes rarely disclosed much personal information, instead distracting everyone with his standoffish façade. All of it, the exaggerated attitude and excessive flirting, was . . . so artificial and forced. Mattes had something behind all his theatrics he didn't want others to know about, but Percy hadn't yet figured out what it was.

"Matthias Knight," Percy began, keeping his voice as low as possible. "If you keep this up, we are going to be caught."

"Percival." Mattes yanked his arm free. "Can you please explain to me how we are supposed to create a diversion if we can't blow stuff up?"

Percy let out a sigh of frustration. Fortunately, they hadn't encountered many of Sisyphus's guards, but he couldn't shake the feeling their luck was about to change, particularly if Mattes continued his assault on every door in sight.

"Mattes," Percy said in what he hoped was a grave tone. "We are here to make sure Acacia and AJ don't run into more trouble than necessary. How well do you think we can accomplish that from one of Sisyphus's holding cells?"

"That sounds like a challenge."

"It isn't one. Don't be an idiot."

"And *that* sounds like another challenge."

Percy let out another long, aggravated sigh. He knew Mattes was acting that way to cope with the stress of being in enemy territory, but Percy was losing his patience.

"Look! Hey you! Stop right there!" a man's voice called from the far side of the chamber in front of them. "Who do you think you are?"

Mattes rolled his hazel eyes. "I think I'm the one who blew your front door in," he responded in a factual tone. "I'm quite dangerous actually; you might want to get a few of your friends first."

The man lunged at them, but Mattes showed no sign of being intimidated. He merely lifted his right hand and fired a wave of yellow magic at their attacker, causing him to fly backward into the stone wall.

"If Sisyphus is anywhere near as horrible a fighter as these jokers, we might as well kick his butt while we're at it," Mattes remarked, watching the man struggle to rise to his feet.

Percy walked over to the mage and placed two fingers on his forehead.

"Hey! What're you—"

With a shallow inhalation, Percy sent a shock of his power into the man's head, knocking him unconscious and wiping away whatever memories he might have from their encounter.

"You see, Percival," Mattes said, taking a step forward. "Absolutely nothing to worry—"

The stone he had stepped on sank down, well past the grade of the rest of the floor, and the door to their rear closed with a slam. To Percy's horror, the wall behind them inched forward, propelled by some unseen trigger.

"Well, that was unexpected."

Percy shook his head. He had assumed the lair would be filled with traps and had been trying to get his companion to show a bit more caution for the past fifteen minutes. However, Mattes was extremely strong willed and did what he wanted, which didn't make him the easiest mission partner, at least from Percy's perspective.

"It wouldn't be so unexpected if you paid attention every once in a while." Percy scanned the chamber with his magic. At first, he'd been hesitant to believe the walls of the building pulsed with powerful Woodsfolk magic that could ensnare them. He could no longer doubt it.

"You worry entirely too much, Percival," Mattes replied, leaning against the wall. "Of all the tight squeezes I've been in, this is nothing."

And people wonder why my cousin looks about ready to strangle someone most of the time, Percy thought with a sigh. He ran his hands along the walls of the chamber, searching for something to help them escape, trying not to focus on the walls closing in on them. What would happen if they couldn't find a way out in time? Would the walls crush them, or would they stop once he and Mattes were rendered immobile? What would become of them if they were captured?

Forcing the thoughts out of his mind, Percy flicked his wrist and pushed his magic against the wall closing in on them, preventing it from creeping any closer. He could feel the power within the fortress walls pressing against his own, its power hot, immeasurably potent. Before he could blink, Percy felt another aura joining his, Mattes's yellow magic, evening out the force that sought to harm them. The wall was stopped in its tracks for now, but how long could they last against such a power?

"Wouldn't worry about it too much, Percival," Mattes said through gritted teeth. "We'll be out of here in no time."

As if on cue, the magic of the walls abruptly receded, disappearing deep into the building. Percy let go of his spell, blinking in shock. Did the magic that had been trying to kill them only moments earlier just disappear into thin air?

"Told you," Mattes said, a smug expression on his face. "So what do you say, Percival, shall we believe Matthias the next time he tells us everything's going to be all right?"

A long wooden door with an intricate stone archway appeared at the far end of the room and opened, revealing yet another cavernous corridor, lit with a handful of floating torches. Mattes shot Percy a look that seemed to say "I told you so" and headed for the door, conjuring an additional orb of yellow light to guide their way.

"But how—" Percy began, feeling flustered. "Why?"

"Why ask why?" Mattes proceeded through the threshold of the open door. "Well? Are you coming, Percival, or are you going to stand there practicing your question words?"

Just go, Percy told himself, shaking his head. *Mattes is right, we can worry about why all this happened later, when we're not all in mortal danger.*

"In all seriousness, Percy," Mattes said, "you need to trust me. Drew and I—we've done this kind of thing before. No, it's not the most fun thing in the world, messing around with dark mages, but it's what we have to do if we want to stop Sisyphus and his goons from taking over the world, or killing everyone, or whatever else he wants to do." He paused, shooting Percy a somber glance. "But to do that, we must trust each other. So, do you trust me?"

Percy met Mattes's gaze and grinned. "I don't always understand you, Matthias Knight, but I do trust you. I've always wondered about you a little, wondered what it is you think you have to hide, but I respect your reasons for hiding it."

Mattes raised his dark brows, clearly confused by Percy's thought process.

"I always knew there was a soul in there somewhere, no matter how hard you tried to hide it," Percy continued. "And it might become more evident to everyone else, sooner rather than later."

"Not at all," Mattes argued, turning from him to look straight ahead down the corridor. "You don't yet comprehend the depth of my depravity."

"There they are! Seize them!"

Percy glanced over his shoulder at the sound of a group of Sisyphus's agents rapidly approaching. This time there had to be at least ten or twelve of them, making a bit of an entertaining sight, each struggling to be the first to emerge from the narrow passageway.

"Come on, this way," Mattes said, trotting down an even narrower corridor. "Let's give them a roundabout, shall we, Golec?"

Percy laughed and followed his companion down the hallway.

***

AJ padded down the narrow stone corridor, Sniffing the air to track the scent of powerful magic. Over the years, being a Sniffer had created more problems than solutions except in situations like this. After all, being able to smell all auras meant AJ was often overwhelmed and on edge trying to keep his power a secret. Then again, being able to sniff out a missing person's aura did prove useful during a rescue mission like this.

Proceeding farther into the tunnel, AJ held up his orb of blue power and focused his attention on the aura of the castle's core. AJ knew his brother's magical scent, so he'd Sniffed it without difficulty. AJ had been apprehensive once he'd realized Alex was in an old Woodsfolk fortress, but he'd tried to hide said apprehension from the others. After all, it wasn't necessary to *be* calm in a crisis, but it helped if you appeared calm.

I want to know what Patrick's role in all this is, AJ thought, the earthy smell of the Woodsfolk magic growing stronger with every step. *I get the feeling he saved Alex and Acacia because he was there, not because he cared about them. But the way he was calling me Wrin was . . . creepy. And what does it even mean? Most people don't just go around calling people foxes.*

AJ paused to clear his thoughts. He would have time to worry about Patrick Delaney once they escaped from this hellhole. Besides, AJ hadn't sensed the boy's aura since leaving the house. What had Patrick done to lure Alex here? And why had he bothered to do it? Was he in league with Sisyphus? Or was he merely trying to teach them a lesson?

The passageway came to an end, bringing him to a plain wooden door. Pushing all questions about Patrick Delaney aside, AJ inhaled deeply and gave the door a strong push. Inside sat a chamber from which he could sense the castle's magical core.

The chamber wasn't a big one, only a little more spacious than his family's living room. Like the rest of the castle, the walls were carved from stone, but here they were covered with shimmering golden runes. As AJ had learned from his reading early in his training, these kinds of runes were a sign of Woodsfolk magic and possessed the power to move walls and activate traps. And the only way to neutralize the Woodsfolk runes was to force the transformation of the symbols. To accomplish this, one had to be familiar with the ancient runic script and possess enough power to alter the runes. Despite what he'd told Acacia, AJ wasn't sure if his abilities were strong enough to force such a transformation, but he knew he had to try.

AJ walked across the chamber with trepidation until he reached the opposite wall. Letting out a sharp breath of air, AJ raised his right hand, conjuring a wave of his magic and launching it at the blazing symbols on the wall. The runes absorbed his magic as if he had dumped a pail of water on them, but AJ didn't give up. He lifted his hand higher and shoved his magic once more against the ancient power of the runes.

Pulled at the Woodsfolk magic within, *willing* for his power to reign victorious.

After what felt like an eternity, the runes flashed bright blue and fell neatly under AJ's control. He allowed himself a small grin and rotated his wrist, effectively scrambling the symbols across the stone wall. *I did it,* AJ thought, feeling almost giddy with accomplishment. *I'm not sure how, but I did it.* Now the castle wouldn't be able to trap them from the inside. All that was left was for Acacia to retrieve Alex and they could get out of this miserable place.

"Well," a familiar voice spat. "What do we have here?"

AJ spun around, his heart leaping into his throat. Leaning against the wooden doorframe stood Dionera Tartaran, her bright red hair tumbling around her angular face. The woman's orange eyes glowed with feral intensity, almost as if they belonged to a hungry lion instead of a human being.

"Dionera," AJ said, feeling quite stupid. It wasn't exactly that he was surprised; after all, Dionera had made it clear in both their previous encounters as well as in Acacia's vision that she wanted him dead. But then again, one never expected to turn around and see their worst fear standing right behind them.

So why didn't I smell her coming? AJ scolded himself as he watched Dionera for any sign of attack. He wouldn't be able to forget Dionera's stench of sulfur and smoke, even if he wanted to. *How could I let myself become so absorbed in tracking this stupid core that I didn't notice this psychopath following me?*

Dionera reached into one of her pockets and drew out an obsidian hilted dagger, her orange eyes glinting with anticipation.

"You won't get away this time, brat," she told him, running a finger down the length of the blade. "I'm going to kill you, just like I killed your idiot father."

"You'll have to catch me first," AJ challenged, his voice steady. "If you haven't noticed, I'm faster than you."

"Insolent child!" Dionera thrust her free hand forward, launching a torrent of fire in his direction. AJ had been expecting it and darted out of the way with plenty of time to spare. As he'd observed when he had fought her before, Dionera was ruled by her anger, which made her easy to read.

All right, no messing around this time, AJ thought, inhaling sharply to clear his mind. *She got me on Halloween with that boomerang fire, but I know her tricks better now. And there's no way she or Sisyphus are getting their way tonight.*

Dionera charged at him, her dagger glinting maliciously. AJ spun, bringing his right arm around him in an arc, launching a blast of blue power at her. His attack made contact, but Dionera swerved at the last moment, saving herself from the brunt of it.

AJ didn't wait for her to recover. He crossed his wrists in front of his face and quickly rotated them, channeling two tendrils of magic at his assailant. One of them was aimed too wide and missed her, but the other shot true, wrapping itself around Dionera's dagger-wielding hand. With a flick of his wrist, the spell constricted around the woman's hand until AJ heard the sickening crack of bones breaking.

Dionera let out a piercing shriek of pain. "Obnoxious whelp!" She reared back as a wall of orange flames encircled her. "Now you go to hell!"

AJ wasted no time in conjuring his shield. He wasn't sure what Dionera was doing, but he could tell it was no small volley of fireballs coming at him. He crouched low and extended the shield in a perfect circle around his body, closing his eyes to protect them from the brightness surrounding him. The wall of fire. . .

This is no good, he thought desperately, feeling the heat of the fire through his magic. *I can't beat her by like this—*

Oof.

Before AJ could react, something, some blast of magic came flying from below, where his shield was the weakest. It tore through his spell and sent him careening into the wall. Fortunately, the flames were gone now, but that didn't prove much of a consolation as he was slammed into solid stone, his head hitting the wall with a loud, resounding crack.

"What was that you were saying, brat?" Dionera cackled as she strode at a leisurely pace toward him. "That I would need to catch you? Look around, you're caught."

Come, on, move! AJ fought the cloud of dizziness and confusion fogging his mind. *Get it together or it's over!* He struggled to gain his bearings, raising his right arm to defend himself.

"Oh, I don't think so!"

He barely saw the blades until they were flying at him, and an instant later, they had him pinned to the wall by his left sleeve, collar, and several places on his shirt.

Dionera reached into another pocket and pulled out an identical obsidian hilted dagger.

"You won't be so fast once I've clipped your wings," she remarked, placing the point of the blade at his throat. A malicious smile crossed the woman's face as orange flames circled her hand, inches from his face. "You don't know how long I've been waiting for this moment. No one gets away from me, especially not some child who makes a fool out of me in front of Lord Sisyphus himself!"

"I think," AJ retorted, fully aware of the surge of pure hatred rising in his chest. Never, in his relatively short life had he hated anyone as much as he hated Dionera Tartaran, his father's murderer. If life had been fair, he would have at least been able to repay the favor. "You're giving me too much credit for that one."

Idiot, are you out of your mind? Mattes's voice demanded. Now that AJ had taken control over the runes, telepathic communication was once again possible. Until Dionera killed him, that was. *That witch is about to kill you, and you're instigating her?*

What do you want me to do, Mattes? AJ glared into Dionera Tartaran's confused face. *She's going to kill me anyway.*

Well, don't let her!

"I don't know what you're so distracted by when I'm about to kill you," Dionera remarked, tracing the blade across his throat, lightly enough to avoid drawing blood. "Pathetic little creature. Goodbye."

And then, something in AJ snapped. His magic surged around him, forming a blazing half circle of power and forcing Dionera away from him. AJ channeled his magic through his arms and sent each of the daggers that had him pinned flying across the room. From the look of shock frozen on her face, Dionera hadn't been expecting him to be able to escape. For the first time, she was on the defensive.

And what now? AJ thought, weighing his options. *Killing is wrong, but if she gets away, she'll be back another day. And it might not even be me that she comes after...*

"Stupid child!" Dionera cackled after a brief pause. "You, who have never taken life before, think to kill me? I can see it in your eyes! You waste our time! We both know you haven't the guts!"

"War isn't fair," Uncle Jack *had told him several years ago. "If you want to win, you need to do what's necessary to ensure victory. That could mean killing people in battle or taking them out from afar, to make sure they never come back to haunt you in your waking hours."*

AJ had taken his uncle's words to heart, carrying them with him throughout his and Mattes's mission in the Underground. After all, it was fine to say something, but when it came down to it, words didn't mean anything if you couldn't follow through with them.

"It's not the guts that count." AJ raised his right hand as he looked upon a cluster of runes on the ceiling. "Everyone has guts. It's someone's will you have to look out for."

With that, AJ pulled on the power of the runes on the ceiling with his magic, willing them to obey his command. The runes flashed an odd combination of blue and gold, and before he could change his mind, a pile of immense stones fell from above, crushing the shrieking Dionera underneath them.

And then . . . all was silent. AJ stared blankly at the pile in front of him, unable to believe what he had done. Trying to regain his composure, he walked toward the exit, and pain he hadn't noticed before set in. AJ's head swam, and he looked down to see that his left arm was dripping with blood. Not only had he been wounded when he'd been pinned to the wall by Dionera's daggers, but wounded badly.

No, he thought, his world spinning wildly in front of him. *Alex, Acacia—*

Onawa.

Unable to steady himself, AJ collapsed on the cold stone floor, inches away from that awful pile of stones he had created. Blood continued to pool beneath his arm, and almost right in front of his face, AJ could make out a flash of red hair, a lifeless hand. . .

Mattes was saying something to him through their telepathic connection, but AJ couldn't understand it. He had passed out before, but never from this kind of blood loss. This time, he wasn't certain if he was even going to wake up.

Sorry, Onawa, he thought as his vision went black. *At least we got to say goodbye.*

***

Acacia ran down the dimly lit hallway, her sneakers gliding over the uneven stone. She was close, so close she could almost smell Alex in front of her. It couldn't be more than a few more yards and she'd be there. She could see it, the two of them fleeing from this cursed castle, meeting up with the others in the forest, running together with their fingers intertwined. . .

Unfortunately, she did not see the jagged stone sticking out, and she tripped over it, falling facedown onto the hard, cold floor.

"Ow," Acacia whined, pushing herself up to her feet. She'd been able to break her fall with her arms, but she wouldn't be surprised if she found a bruise tomorrow. Then again, if she got out of there with only a few scratches, Acacia would consider herself lucky. Brushing herself off, she started down the hallway again, this time paying more attention to where she put her feet.

Within minutes, Acacia arrived at the end of the cavernous corridor, but much to her surprise, she found herself face to face not with another wooden door, but a solid stone wall. Could she have taken a wrong turn and gotten lost?

No, I didn't, Acacia assured herself with confidence. *I followed Alex's aura all the way here, and I know what he feels like. And I still feel him, right through there.*

Acacia stared at the wall in front of her, carefully scanning it with her magic. *There,* at the very top, was a small golden symbol, a sign of the Woodsfolk magic pulsing through the castle. Shaking her head, she drew back, preparing to summon her magic to blast through the wall. Surely it would require a decent amount of power, but she didn't care. At this point, she wouldn't allow anything to get in her way of rescuing Alex. *Well, here goes nothing. . .*

The gold on the symbol faded and turned to blue. Acacia took a step back, almost expecting it to explode, before remembering AJ's side mission. A section of the wall receded, exposing a clear entrance into the next chamber. Without another thought, Acacia grinned and ran through the newfound entrance in search of Alex.

AJ, Acacia thought, feeling the grin creep across her face. *I guess I should believe you when you say you're going to do something.*

The chamber she found herself in was vast in comparison to the series of tunnels she'd traveled through to reach this point. Acacia guessed it to be at least as large as the school cafeteria and was much better illuminated than the previous areas of the castle. The chamber was constructed of stone but was adorned wall to wall with torches and a variety of weapons, from nasty-looking knives and daggers to regal swords and staves. At the far end of the chamber, examining the wall for a way out, was Alex.

"Alexander Swiatkowski!" Acacia hollered, her heart getting the better of her head.

Alex jumped, and spun around. When he saw her, Acacia knew she wasn't imagining his eyes lighting up or the wide grin spreading across his face.

"Acacia!" Alex sprinted toward her. Acacia smiled in return and ran toward her friend. They met somewhere in the middle of the vast room in a warm embrace, and Alex kissed her on the forehead. "It's *so* good to see you."

Acacia put her hands on the boy's shoulders firmly, looking into his eyes. "Thank god you're okay, Alex," she said, feeling relief in her chest for the first time in hours. "We were so worried. *I* was so worried—"

"Acacia, what are you talking about?" Alex asked, a perplexed expression on his face. "It's *AJ* who's in trouble. C'mon, we've got to find him."

He turned to walk away, but Acacia grabbed his wrist, halting him.

"What do you mean it's AJ who's in trouble?" Acacia demanded, her coppery brows arched in surprise. "It was AJ who told me you went missing."

Alex scratched his head, looking as confused as Acacia felt. "That doesn't make any sense. Right after you left to go home, I was about to go home, but Patrick showed up and told me AJ was in danger and there wasn't much time."

"Alex," Acacia said in a grave voice. "Patrick tricked you. He made up some story about AJ so you'd come here alone, and he left a note stuck to your bedroom door saying you make bad decisions so we better come find you."

Alex studied her face for several minutes, his confusion gradually transforming into shock. "No. It can't be true; it just can't be. . ."

"It is, but we can talk about it later," Acacia replied, taking a nervous glance behind her. She could feel something coming and didn't want to find out what it *was*. "Let's go before some bogeyman decides to show up."

Fwoom.

Acacia felt the surge in energy before she saw it, swirls of black magic gathering in the center of the chamber. She wanted to run, to get out of this horrible place before anything more could happen, but her legs were frozen in place. She couldn't avoid what was about to happen, but Acacia was determined to make sure she was victorious this time.

"An interesting choice of words," Sisyphus said as the black light faded around him. The man was just as Acacia had remembered, tall and muscular, but this time, his black hair was cut much shorter. His cold blue eyes examined her and Alex with mirth. "For indeed I am a bogeyman of sorts."

Acacia glared daggers at the mage. *He may be some all-powerful wizard,* she thought, rage building inside her. *But now he's messing with my friends.*

"Well then, crawl back under the bed," she spat, her fingers tingling with magic. "I stopped being afraid of bogeymen years ago."

Sisyphus laughed heartily, as if she had just told some great joke. "You are a foolish little girl, as I thought from the beginning. After all, you walked right into my trap, didn't you?"

To Acacia's surprise, Alex stepped forward, almost shaking with rage. "How long has Patrick Delaney been working for you?" he demanded, the angriest Acacia had ever seen him. "My brother was right this whole time! I bet he did conjure those stupid skeletons after all!"

"Alex," Acacia began, a bit tiredly. "They're Virseyeh, remember?"

Sisyphus laughed again. "And *you*, boy, are particularly inept. Besides, even if that troublesome brother of yours was correct, it's not like you listened. "

"Don't you call my brother—"

"I will call your brother what I want." Sisyphus rolled his icy eyes. "After all, bogeymen are not obliged to take orders from insolent children."

"Hey!" Acacia yelled. "Look here, Mr. Lord Sissy Puss or whatever you call yourself! I'm sick and tired of you running around threatening my friends!"

Sisyphus raised his dark brows and stalked over to her, his pace slow and determined. "Miss Swansgrove," he remarked in a menacing tone. "Do you honestly believe I will drop everything I have strived to achieve in the past ten years because you are tired of me threatening your pathetic little friends?"

"My friends are *not* pathetic!"

Acacia's magic leaped from her fingers as she lunged at Sisyphus, sending a volley of green spheres flying at him. He'd either been expecting her attack or was very fast and dodged them easily. He snorted and walked over to the wall, picking up a longsword with a jeweled hilt.

"Like I said," Sisyphus said, as swirls of black magic began to circle the sword. "Pathetic."

Acacia was aware that Sisyphus was charging at her, barreling down the length of the chamber, but it almost seemed that everything was moving in slow motion. One minute she was standing there, preparing to raise her shield, and the next she was sprawled on the floor, looking up in wonder at Alex who had forcibly knocked her to the ground. Sisyphus had leaped over them but landed and lunged for them again. Pushing herself to her feet, Acacia brought her right arm across her in a wide arc, conjuring her shield. Sisyphus crashed into it and went flying in the other direction but landed on his feet. Alex wound his arm back and made a throwing motion, launching a blue orb of power that divided into three smaller bursts in midair. The bursts went after Sisyphus, exploding in his face.

"You must be joking," the mage commented once the smoke cleared, casting spiteful glares at Acacia and Alex. "Do you children really think you stand a chance against me? I have annihilated mages with twice, if not thrice, your skill! I brought your idiotic Council to its knees!"

"But why?" Acacia demanded, her coppery hair coming free of its braid. "What's the point of all this?"

Percy Golec's wise words echoed in her memory. *It's not the magic, Acacia, but what you do with it. Whether you affect people's lives for better or for worse.*

"Magic isn't for making yourself feel powerful, Sisyphus!" Her confidence rose like a tidal wave. "We don't have powers so we can oppress others, we have them so we can accomplish something great that could never be accomplished otherwise!"

"I take it you think your High and Mighty Council is set on its task of accomplishing all of these 'great things'?" Sisyphus demanded. "You don't have to talk to me about that, you silly girl, just ask the Knight boy if you haven't already. If you knew anything about that cursed institution, you wouldn't be standing around calling *me* the depraved one!"

Acacia reared back and studied Sisyphus with fresh eyes. Truthfully, she didn't know much about the Council's history, but was Sisyphus seriously trying to justify his actions against innocent people based on the corruption of the magical government?

"You can't blame the Council for what you've done, Sisyphus. All those people *you* killed—"

"Enough of this endless moralism!" The mage roared and aimed the longsword directly at her. Black fire shot from the sword, like it was a pointed flamethrower. "You will not defeat me, Swansgrove!"

Acacia crossed her arms in front of her, her wrists meeting in front of her nose. The flames hurtled toward her like wildfire, but at the last possible moment, Acacia rotated her wrists, and a green shimmer formed before her and Alex. Sisyphus's attack crashed into her reflective spell and flew back at him.

Well, there's something he wasn't expecting, Acacia thought with a grin as the black flames bit into Sisyphus and threw him backward several feet. *Maybe I can do this. . .*

"Ouch!" Alex cried, grasping his left arm as if he had been stabbed by some invisible force. "What the heck?"

"Alex, you weren't hit." Acacia raised her brows at him. "What are you—"

Her friend pulled back his sleeve, revealing a large, angry-looking red mark on the inner part of his forearm, extending from his wrist to his elbow. A look of rage crossed Alex's face, and he charged toward Sisyphus with newfound determination.

"What did you do to my brother?" Alex demanded, his tone furious. The boy sent another one of his exploding orbs flying in Sisyphus's direction, but the dark mage was prepared, blocking the attacks with a black shield of his own.

"Ask Dionera," Sisyphus replied in a sly voice. "Oh right, she's probably busy killing him. Tell me this, boy, when one twin dies, does the other one die as well? Though I suppose we could just wait and find out. . ."

Alex was yelling something back at the man, but Acacia had blocked it all out. If bickering with Sisyphus was going to get them out of here, surely it would have worked by now. To defeat him, to win the battle, she'd have to incapacitate him, at least for a few moments. There had to be some other way to do that than the constant back and forth they had been engaging in since Sisyphus's arrival in the chamber.

"If you're trying to hit me and my shield's in the way, find a way to get around it," AJ had advised her during one of their practice sessions. If doing something one way wasn't working, it didn't mean the task couldn't be accomplished; you just needed to try doing it a different way. Acacia couldn't help but grin. It was almost funny how much more sense all of this made *now,* as she confronted one of the deadliest dark mages in mortal combat.

Acacia walked to the wall and looked at the range of weapons lining its surface. Knives, swords, staves, maces, and hammers . . . maybe just maybe something here could be her way around. . .

As if on cue, a rather elegant staff fell from the rack and flew directly into her right hand. Acacia blinked and studied the strange object. The wooden staff, which measured about four feet in length, was crafted from hickory and adorned with a silver swan at the top.

Well, this is interesting, Acacia thought as she ran her fingers lightly down the weapon's smooth surface. *Maybe this is our way out.*

Acacia's magic appeared to think so as well. As she brought the staff up toward her face, rays of green light swirled up the staff's length, awaiting her command. *Here goes nothing.*

"Sisyphus!" she called, rotating the glowing staff in front of her in a small circle. "This is for my friends!"

The staff served as a vessel for her magic, helping her focus it into a single beam of bright green light. Acacia took careful aim and fired at Sisyphus, knocking him roughly to the ground.

"You. . ." the man sputtered as he struggled to his feet. "How could you possibly—"

Acacia swept her weapon in an arc and fired again at the mage, plowing him into the hard stone floor. *How is this possible?* she thought. *I'm not even that good! I mean I know everyone's been saying Swansgrove this, Swansgrove that, but—*

But that wasn't the time to figure all of that out.

"Acacia!" Alex dashed toward her, his face pale with worry. "We have to go! AJ—"

Yes, little girl, run, Sisyphus's harsh tone resonated in her mind. *Take your little toy and run as fast as you can; it makes no difference. You will not escape from us, you, or your little friends. You will not stop me, and you will not achieve your destiny, I assure you of this.*

Acacia glared daggers at the man who had caused them so much trouble over the past three months. He was so angry and full of hate . . . there had to be a reason for him being the way he was. Not that it mattered; he had proven himself as an enemy, and a dangerous one at that, but still . . . to Acacia's knowledge, most people were not simply born evil. *And who knows?* she thought. *Maybe if I had a better idea of why he is the way he is, I'd have a better chance of defeating him.*

"Think what you want, Sisyphus!" Acacia retorted, taking Alex by the hand. "You were defeated once before, you'll be defeated again!"

You and I are not that different, Swansgrove, Sisyphus told her. *You'll see.*

Acacia shook her head angrily and tore out of the chamber with Alex as fast as her legs would allow, leaving Sisyphus to cackle to himself alone in the dark.

Chapter Twenty

A CONVERSATION WITH THE SPEAKER

Acacia sprinted down the hallway as fast as her legs would carry her. *Something's happened,* she thought, her mind racing with worry. *Something went wrong. Why else would Alex have a nasty mark on his arm when he wasn't even hit?* Acacia had always had her doubts about the existence of a supernatural connection between twins, but the events of the night had removed just about all of them.

Acacia and Alex ran through old chambers and past foreboding rows of dungeon cells, rushing to reunite with their friends. Fortunately, they had yet to come across any of Sisyphus's other operatives, but Acacia wondered how long their luck would hold.

They entered a foyer, decorated with a single, red carpet and a matching tapestry. Percy and Mattes stood at the far end of the room, both marked with a few scratches and burns, but relatively unharmed. Acacia looked around furtively for AJ, until she realized he was there as well, his slight frame hanging from Mattes's shoulders.

"Well, hello there," the dark-haired boy said as Acacia and Alex crossed the room. "Fancy meeting you here." Acacia had expected Mattes to give Alex an earful for sending them on this avoidable mission, but he didn't seem perturbed in the slightest. "So, what do you say, Alexander the Not So Great? Have we had enough adventure for one night?"

Almost afraid to look, Acacia glanced at AJ's limp body. Her friend was unconscious, looking much worse for wear than the last time she'd seen him. His skin was ashen, and his left arm was bandaged tightly with what upon closer inspection, Acacia realized were several strips of fabric from Percy's sleeves. With a start, Acacia noticed the twin's magical aura was surprisingly weak, as if he'd expended a great deal of energy. It appeared AJ had run into Dionera Tartaran and had been gravely injured in the encounter.

"I take it the two of you had a change in plans." Percy looked at Acacia with kind eyes. "Don't feel guilty, Acacia. Andrew would have gone to the core if you wanted him to or not. When my cousin's mind is made up, there's not much you can do to change it."

"B-but," Alex sputtered. His light gray eyes were wide, filled with fear. "P-Percy, you— AJ—"

"Not to worry, my dear Alexander," Mattes interjected, his hazel eyes dancing with amusement. "For you see, after freezing the magic of the Woodsfolk runes threatening to seal us all in an early grave, your daring brother also managed to subdue the fearless pyromaniac Dionera Tartaran, not taking note of his grievous wounds. But, fortunately for him, Percival and I rushed to the rescue, and our resident healer had the opportunity to show off his talents—"

Percy smiled at them and placed his hands in the pockets of his jeans. Something about Percy was so calming, so peaceful it was almost impossible for Acacia to feel nervous or afraid when she was around him, no matter how bad the circumstances were.

"What Matthias means to say is that I healed him," Percy said. "Dionera managed to cut him with one of those cursed daggers of hers. I'd guess the same kind that killed Uncle Joe. AJ lost a lot of blood, but we got there in time for me to extract the poison, heal up the brachial artery, cauterize the wound and bandage it up." He was obviously excited to share his success with them, and it became clear to Acacia that he hadn't been exaggerating when he told her healing was what he did best, what he loved. "But there's no need to worry. He'll be fine with some rest. AJ lost a lot of blood, which would be bad enough, but he's anemic too. So, recovery will take a bit longer."

Acacia's head was reeling with all the information Percy had given them. "AJ's . . . going to be okay?" she asked, glancing between Percy and Mattes. "This is my fault. I shouldn't have let him go off alone—"

"Relax, would you, Wheatley?" Mattes piped in as he shrugged, readjusting his grasp on his friend's wrists. "I speak from experience when I say it's not an adventure without Andrew Swiatkowski trying to get himself killed."

"Hey, hold on just one second," Alex said, his gaze set on Mattes. "What do you mean AJ 'subdued Dionera'? Where is she?"

Mattes and Percy exchanged curious expressions, clearly debating how to best explain what happened.

"Subdued," Mattes remarked, while Percy said, "She's gone."

"What the hell is *that* supposed to—"

"When we arrived at the castle's core, your brother was lying in a pool of blood, right next to a pile of large stones." Percy's cheerful expression vanished within seconds. "At first, we thought the chamber had collapsed, but upon closer inspection, we saw Dionera had been crushed under the stones themselves."

"Yes, Percival, subdued." Mattes rolled his eyes with feigned annoyance. "Do I have to spell everything out for you?"

Lying in a pool of blood, Acacia thought. *What have I done?*

"Not to be that person, but now might be a good time for us to leave." Acacia forced the unwanted images of her friend bleeding out on the cold stone floor from her mind. "I'd rather *not* run into Sisyphus and his friends again tonight."

The three boys nodded and followed her lead. Within minutes, the five teenagers were once again outside in the frigid December night. Acacia never liked the idea of winter; it was too cold, too wet, too dismal. But now, with almost all her friends clustered around her, she had all the warmth she needed.

"Acacia!" She barely had time to react before she was thrown back with considerable force, as Onawa Mescal threw her arms around her in a tight hug. A moment later, Onawa took a step back and Acacia could see her friend was covered with small burns. "You did it! Did you kick Sisyphus's butt?" The girl's dark eyes glanced over at AJ's limp frame. "Oh . . . oh no. What—"

"He'll be all right, Onawa," Percy said. "It's a long story, but there'll be plenty of time for it once we've all gotten some sleep. But don't worry, AJ will be back to his usual sarcastic self in no time."

Acacia looked at each of her friends in turn. Despite Percy's promise, Onawa *did* look distressed, the excitement from her face replaced with shock and preoccupation. Mattes glanced toward the sky, his expression every bit as serious as it had been prior to breaking into Sisyphus's lair. Percy was as calm as ever but shivered in the frigid winter breeze. AJ was still unconscious, hanging limply on Mattes's back, his head resting on his friend's shoulder. And Alex, Alex who was always there to defend her, to support her, stood at her side, his fingers intertwined with hers.

"Well?" Acacia took one step in the direction of town and looked back to meet her friends' gazes. "Let's go home."

***

Acacia had never been so happy to arrive back home, even if she was greeted by her parents at the door. She wasn't sure how long her mother shrieked at her for disappearing without leaving a note, how worried she'd been, and so on. After some time, Dervla Wheatley had enough and sent Acacia to her room for the night, and probably the rest of her winter break. Acacia didn't regret running off to save Alex, but it *was* a relief to be home, with a roof over her head.

Finally, Sarison fell asleep, leaving Acacia alone with her thoughts. Had they really infiltrated the lair of one of the most powerful dark mages of the century? Acacia had resigned herself that things in her new world didn't always make sense, but she wondered if they would ever be less . . . chaotic. Would she ever feel comfortable using her magic like she had that night, tracking auras through mysterious corridors and battling evil? Would she ever really know what it meant to be the Heir of Swansgrove?

And what was the deal with Patrick Delaney? She could kick herself for not taking AJ's warning more seriously, but wasn't it normal to want to trust someone who saved your life? Maybe AJ was right after all, maybe it had been Patrick who summoned the Virseyeh, sending them after Acacia and Alex only to pose as their savior. Acacia preferred to think the best of people, but perhaps her new world was too dangerous for such niceties?

And what about her friends? Alex made it through the night unscathed, but the same wasn't true of the others. Percy, Mattes, and Onawa had all acquired scratches and bruises though they managed to avoid any grave injuries. But what about AJ? When her group parted ways, he'd still been unconscious, hanging from his best friend's shoulders. Acacia couldn't help but wonder what had happened when AJ found his way to the core of the fortress. He *had* managed to prevent the castle walls from trapping them inside, though how, Acacia wasn't sure. And what had Mattes and Percy said? That AJ 'subdued' Dionera under a pile of rocks? Was it possible her friend had killed the maniacal fire mage? And more importantly, what had happened to AJ in the encounter to leave him lying in a pool of blood? Percy was confident the boy would recover, but would he? Everyone told her not to worry, that it wasn't her fault, but Acacia couldn't bring herself to believe them. She was supposed to be a leader, supposed to protect her friends, not let them wander into a death trap!

And what about the staff that helped her deflect Sisyphus's attacks during their confrontation? Was there something special about her that caused it to fly into her hands? The small silver figure of a swan on it—now stowed in her closet— did it have something to do with the Swansgrove family she knew nothing about? If so, could it help her uncover the mysteries of her family's past and reach her full potential?

Acacia tossed and turned in bed, her attempts to sleep thwarted by images of redheaded Woodsfolk boys, magical staves, and dark mages. She had swung her legs over her bedframe, prepared to go to the bathroom to get a glass of water, when she noticed she had a visitor.

Turning to the door, Acacia peered into a familiar face, a familiar pair of evergreen eyes.

Acacia Wheatley, Amara Jones began, her tone as fierce as her glare. The girl stood in the doorway with her arms crossed in front of her chest. *I see you've just about killed Andrew Swiatkowski. You do realize I've been trying to prevent that, correct?*

Acacia rose from her bed and walked over to meet Amara. *Is there something I can help you with, Amara? Most people don't go around breaking into other people's houses in the middle of the night.*

Amara rolled her eyes and glared again at Acacia. She could feel the power in her visitor's petite frame, rolling off her body in waves. Sensing a challenge, Acacia crossed her arms in front of her chest as well, mimicking the girl's posture, and glared back at her. *I've faced Sisyphus, one of the most powerful dark mages of the century,* she thought. *I'm not about to let little Amara Jones scare me!*

I will need to speak with you in private, Amara told her in a flat tone. *Fortunately, there is an office available at headquarters that we can use. Get changed and meet me outside, and I'll take us there. And bring that stick with you.*

Of all the people to come looking for me, Acacia considered. *I wasn't expecting it to be Amara Jones. Okay, we trespassed on Sisyphus's territory and barely escaped with our lives, but if the Council has a problem with it, wouldn't they send someone . . . official? Mr. Jones, Albergast, even Valhart. Amara might be the Speaker of the Assembly, but are they really going to listen to her?*

Amara raised her light brows. *I'm not here on Council business, Wheatley,* she said, her green eyes flashing dangerously. *I'm trying to make sure this doesn't go further than it should. I daresay you'd rather deal with me than Councilman Valhart. But no, be my guest, refuse to talk to me and you can deal with him, and the rest of the Council. And then, when they're finished with you, maybe they'll let you watch as they interrogate your friends. Do you think they'll care that Alex feels guilty about leading you all into a trap? Or that Andrew evaded death by the skin of his teeth? Or—*

Acacia glared daggers at the girl and, lifting her right hand, summoned her winter jacket from the closet and her staff from the floor.

"Enough dramatics, Amara," Acacia whispered, slipping into her jacket. "Let's go."

***

Acacia half expected Amara to haul her into the Golden Chamber, but instead, she found herself in a small office which she assumed belonged to Amara's father. The room was sparsely decorated, with a single desk, stacked high with paperwork and lined on three sides with bookshelves. Amara took a seat behind the desk and tented her fingers in front of her face.

"Have a seat," the girl said, gesturing to the wooden chair in front of the desk. "I won't have you telling everyone I lack courtesy."

Acacia sat down, studying the girl with interest. For whatever reason, Amara seemed much more amiable now than she'd been at her house. Was it possible the girl wasn't as bad as she seemed? After all, it had taken Acacia some time to get used to AJ's biting attitude but she now understood it was part of the walls he created to protect himself. And why wouldn't Amara have a similar defense? She was only fourteen and in charge of the Youth Assembly. Many of the Assembly's members were considerably older and more experienced than her, and it wouldn't help her to show weakness in front of them—at least if she wanted to retain her position.

"Amara." Acacia chose her words carefully. "You showed up at my house and dragged me to Council headquarters at three in the morning. Since when are you concerned about courtesy?"

"I did not drag you. In case you forgot, you came on your own accord. With some prompting." Amara tapped her fingers together and cleared her throat. "Acacia Wheatley. You have *no* idea of the danger you placed everyone in tonight."

"Alex went missing," Acacia replied, her temper rising. "What did you expect me to do, wait around until Sisyphus decided to *kill* him?"

"Henry Moore seized your little boyfriend because he knew it was the best way to get to *you*," Amara spat, fury flashing across her face. "What is it going to take for you to get it through your thick skull*?*"

Acacia glared back at Amara. She had been expecting this type of conversation from the start, so it was silly to be surprised by the girl's attitude. It had been hope, Acacia realized, a hope that Amara was nicer than she thought, that she *was* on her side. Acacia opened her mouth to yell back but stopped, remembering all the times she had let her temper get the better of her. She had no intention of letting Amara see her upset. *She's stressed out,* Acacia told herself, studying Amara's tense body language.

"Isn't it odd that of all the names he could pick for his villain's name, he picked 'Sisyphus'?" Acacia asked, trying to lighten the mood. "Every time I hear 'Sisyphus,' I just think of Sissy Puss—"

"I did not bring you here to discuss Henry Moore's choice in pseudonym!" Amara hollered. *"We are here to talk about your embarrassingly poor life choices!"*

"Excuse me?" Acacia arched her coppery brows challengingly at the girl. "But how can they be 'embarrassingly poor life choices' when I was successful?"

Amara slammed her fist on the desk, scattering a handful of papers. "I knew you weren't the brightest bulb, but I wasn't expecting you to be this stupid!" Amara yelled. "Don't you understand every one of you could have died, just because you thought it would be a grand idea if you all just strolled into Sisyphus's lair to save your idiotic boyfriend—"

"You have *no right* to call Alex an idiot!" Acacia shouted, rising from her chair. "He didn't know—"

"And neither did you! The two of you were far too busy running around getting into whatever trouble you could find to consider the possibility that everything might not be as it appears!"

Acacia sucked in a deep breath and forced herself to sit back down. "Hindsight is always perfect, Amara."

Amara followed her lead and sat back down, her hands still visibly shaking. "In case you haven't noticed. You are destined to be a leader, and you need to learn to practice caution and restraint. There are others, more than you know, who look to you for guidance."

Acacia blinked again. Sure, she had led her friends to rescue Alex, but no one else had been directly affected, at least to her knowledge.

Amara let out a long sigh and stared up at the ceiling. Inspecting the girl more closely, Acacia noticed the dark circles under her eyes and the way the skin around her right eye twitched with a nervous tic.

"Acacia, you must understand, this is *not* a game." Amara turned and met Acacia's gaze again. "This is no game of cat and mouse between you and Henry Moore. When the time comes, you must act without hesitation. If you hesitate, he will crush you, take away everything you know and love, and watch as you fade into nothingness."

"Can you tell me," Acacia said, "why it is that when I hesitate, everyone yells at me to accept my destiny and make a decision, and when I make a decision, everyone yells at me to think things through?"

"You will not get pity from me. My path has not been easy either, but when destiny calls, I act."

"How has your path not been easy?" Acacia glared daggers at the girl. "You're nothing more than a spoiled brat!"

Amara jumped to her feet again. "I have worked hard for everything I have achieved, Wheatley! I started the Youth Assembly for God's sake! Do you have any clue what it's like to do something like that, with almost everyone against you?"

"Well, who did you have to step on to get there?" Acacia asked, and immediately wished she hadn't. For the first time in their conversation, Amara looked as if she wanted to hit her.

"Before you start taking a leaf from Andrew Swiatkowski's book, you should know that most of the time he has his nose too far up his father's old political philosophy books to find his way out, even if he wanted to," Amara spat. "You'd do well to consider your words a bit more carefully if you want to stay on the Council's good side long enough to fulfill that destiny of yours."

Acacia yawned. She had no idea what time it was or how long she'd been in this claustrophobic office with Amara, but she was fading fast. Though she was curious about AJ's political leanings, she didn't think now was the right time to discuss them.

"Let me see that staff, Acacia," Amara ordered, and Acacia handed it over, hoping her obedience would bring calm. Amara ran her hand up the length of the object, grasping it toward the top. "You don't even know what this is, do you?"

"I know it's how I got away from Sisyphus, or Henry Moore, or whatever other names he might have."

Amara clearly was not pleased with her answer. With a fluid motion, she swung the staff around and bopped Acacia on the head with it.

"You fool, this is the staff of the family Swansgrove, your family in case you forgot," the girl explained. She glared once more at Acacia and walked over to a wooden cabinet. "An object of great power and might. But you're nowhere near mature enough to handle it."

Acacia hopped out of her seat again. "Hey! What do you think you're doing?"

"I'm going to keep it somewhere safe until you're ready," Amara replied, placing the Staff of Swansgrove inside a vault within the cabinet and locking it with her magic. "And not a minute earlier."

"Amara! I never would have gotten out of Sisyphus's lair without it! You have to give it back!"

"I will when you're ready. *Now*, I'd say our conversation is over. Good night."

Acacia leaped into action, hoping to reach Amara to shake some sense into her. To her dismay, Amara flicked her wrist, conjuring a dark green mist, which enveloped Acacia completely. Acacia called out but was helpless to do anything as the mist swirled around her, whisking her out of the office before she could summon her own magic.

Damn you, Amara Jones, she thought, as the magic faded, depositing her in that long, dark corridor that had been her first introduction to Council Headquarters. Portal 727 stood immediately before here, gleaming with golden power. Part of Acacia yearned to turn around and search out Amara once more, but she knew it was late, or rather, *early*, and she longed for nothing more than to be with her friends and family. Letting out a deep sigh, she reached for the portal stop with her fingers, envisioning exactly where she wanted to go.

I will *get my staff back.* Acacia stepped into the golden magic of the portal, doing her bet to push her anger to the side. *Just you wait.*

CHAPTER TWENTY-ONE

SHOOT FOR THE MOON

Once the golden magic faded and her eyes adjusted to the darkness, Acacia found herself outside the Swiatkowskis' house. Perhaps another portal would have taken her closer to her house, but at least she *knew* where stop 727 went. She let out a long sigh and glanced over her shoulder, noticing the sun was beginning to rise, gradually pushing the shadows of the night sky aside.

Well, she thought, twirling a lock of coppery hair between her fingers. *I need to start trusting my judgment of character. I thought Amara was nasty, and I was right.*

Acacia shook her head and looked up at the familiar red brick house in front of her. *Well, I am here*, she thought. *I might as well go inside, just to make sure everyone's okay.*

As she took a step forward, Acacia felt a warm surge of power behind her.

"Well, look who decided to show up," Onawa Mescal said in an amused tone. "Can't keep you trapped at home for long either, can they?"

"Of course not." Acacia smiled, feeling the tension dissipate from her body. "But what are you doing here? I figured you'd be at home. It looked like you and S'feirra had a bit of a wild ride."

Onawa laughed and clapped a hand on Acacia's shoulder with surprising strength. "A 'wild ride'! Acacia, come on! Is a wild ride supposed to tire me out? If a ride isn't wild, what's the point of taking it?"

"Point taken," Acacia said with a grin. Onawa was perky this morning, her entire body filled to the brim with energy. As she thought about it, Acacia realized her friend was right—she would've expected anyone else to be thoroughly exhausted after the night they'd had, but Onawa wasn't anyone else. "Anyway, what are you doing here, Onawa? Are you here to see AJ?"

Worry flashed across Onawa's face, so quickly Acacia might not have noticed it if she hadn't been paying attention. *It's true, isn't it?* Acacia thought. *Onawa* does *like him like that. Now if we can find out if AJ feels the same way. . .*

"I saw him already, actually," Onawa replied, her face reddening as she dug into the snow with her foot. "He's okay. But I also wanted to see you, and I figured you'd be coming over to...check on things. So I decided I'd just grab you before you headed in."

"You wanted to talk to me?" Acacia tilted her head thoughtfully. She was sure much had happened since she last saw Onawa, but she hadn't been expecting the girl to seek her out to discuss it. "Everything all right?"

Onawa nodded, her expression uncharacteristically grave. "Yeah, I'm fine, it's not anything like that. What I wanted to talk to you about is more . . . personal."

"Oh?"

Her companion closed her eyes and let out a long sigh. "I guess," she began, meeting Acacia's gaze. "I wanted to thank you. For accepting me, even though I'm weird. I was always too loud, too energetic, too outgoing for people." Onawa laughed, her face brightening. "Mostly too loud though."

"You're not—"

"I didn't fit in back home," Onawa continued, without missing a beat. "Not with my classmates, my friends . . . I got along with my family, but I was always more interested in finding dragons to talk to than . . . well, just about anything. I knew I was a Dragon Speaker, and the time would come for me to have to use my gift. In a way, the whole Sisyphus escaping gave me that chance."

Acacia nodded, allowing herself to fully absorb her friend's words. Onawa had never spoken at great length about her past or her home. Truthfully, Acacia wasn't surprised to hear that Onawa hadn't felt she 'fit in' with her classmates where she had grown up. For that matter, the girl didn't really fit in with most kids in Silent Springs either. Over the past few months, however, Onawa had found her place within Acacia's eclectic group of friends.

"I remember the day when you came to Silent Springs," Acacia said, shooting her friend a broad grin. "When you teleported us all to that meadow in the middle of nowhere and S'feirra came and scared the living crap out of us. I thought you were completely insane."

Onawa shrugged. "Most people do. The thing is that I don't care. But when I tell people that, they always get offended."

"I think we're all a little crazy," Acacia said. "You, me, Alex, AJ, Mattes . . . though Percy might be okay. Our last hope, I suppose."

"Percy, our last hope?" Onawa repeated, her expression feigning incredulousness. "Don't tell me our last hope's a nerd with a cauldron!"

Acacia laughed aloud, feeling much more at ease. "I guess not. Though on the bright side, we wouldn't have to worry about anyone getting hurt!"

Her friend grinned and kicked the snow beneath her feet playfully. "Hey, wait a minute," Onawa began, turning to Acacia with wide eyes. "You still have that butt-kicking staff from Sisyphus's lair, right? That thing seemed . . . important."

"Um, about that." Acacia let out a sigh of defeat and scratched her head. "Amara showed up at my house earlier this . . . morning I guess and dragged me off for questioning, she made me bring the staff, and then . . . she grabbed it and locked it up." Her face heated with embarrassment thinking about how easily the girl had outmaneuvered her. How stupid had she been, to allow Amara to make a fool out of her and take from her the only thing that had allowed her to subdue Sisyphus and escape from his fortress in the first place? "She said it's a Swansgrove family heirloom."

Onawa blinked, her expression befuddled. "But . . . Amara isn't a Swansgrove. You are. And the way those family heirlooms work is you can't use them unless you're, y'know, part of the family. Why would she take a butt-kicking staff she can't even use?"

"She yelled at me, saying I could have gotten everyone killed and I don't know what I'm doing." Acacia shook her head. "And since I'm not mature enough to use it now, she's not going to give it back until I am."

"Well, that's stupid!" Onawa exclaimed, her face contorted in indignation. "Sure, you could've gotten everybody killed, but you didn't! What's the point of getting all worked up about something that could've happened?"

"I don't know. Because she's an egotistical control freak?" Acacia offered. She paused and took a deep breath to calm her nerves. She knew Onawa was more impulsive than she was, and despite being angry with Amara for making her a fool, Acacia didn't want to get her friend more frustrated than she already was. "But whatever. I'll get it back from her. After facing Sissy Puss, it's hard to be intimidated by Amara Jones."

"All right!" Onawa cheered, raising her fist triumphantly. When Acacia didn't share the same level of excitement, the girl cocked her head. "Well, what are you waiting for? Are we going to go get your staff back or not?"

"Not right now!"

Onawa let out a long sigh and shook her head, looking as dejected as if Acacia had just uninvited her from a party. "You're no fun at all."

"Didn't you have enough fun for one day?" Acacia asked. "Oh right. You can never have too much fun, can you?"

Her companion laughed. "Now you're starting to understand me." All the girl's fury was gone, as if it had never existed. Onawa flashed a toothy grin and gave her a quick hug. "I'm glad we're friends. See you soon!"

"Onawa, wait!" Had Onawa come all this way, just to thank Acacia for accepting her? "Aren't you—"

Acacia blinked. Her friend had vanished in the orange waves of her magic.

Oh, Onawa, she thought, shaking her head. *What are we going to do with you?*

Taking a deep breath, Acacia knocked on the front door. She had barely drawn her hand away when the door swung open and a familiar voice called, "Come in!" Acacia walked in, no longer quite as anxious as she had been a few moments before.

***

"Hi Acacia," AJ said as Acacia walked through the doorway, closed the door behind her, and entered the living room. Much to her surprise, the twin was sitting cross-legged on the floor in front of the couch, skimming a book of piano music. As she entered the room, AJ closed the book and placed it on the floor beside him, looking up at her. "Sleep well?"

Acacia studied her friend with trepidation, unsure how to reply. Of everything she expected to see upon entering the house, the sight of AJ Swiatkowski looking through a pile of sheet music would have ranked low on her list. She would have expected to see him passed out, still recovering from their nighttime escapades, but not completely alert and oriented, asking her how she slept. Though Acacia realized her friend didn't look particularly bad, weak perhaps, but she guessed an average passerby would never guess the boy had been grievously injured only a few hours ago.

"Hey there." Acacia felt a grin make its way across her face. "I see you survived the night."

"I guess you could say that," AJ said, his dark eyes flickering with amusement. "Turns out my cousin's as gifted with his healing spells as he claims to be."

"Lucky for us," Acacia said. *I'll have to start giving Percy more credit. The last time I saw AJ, I wasn't sure if he was going to make it. I guess healers* are *more important than I realized.*

AJ grinned and pushed himself to his feet, with a bit of effort. "I don't know about luck—" He moved to take a step forward but lost his balance. His expression dazed, AJ swayed for a moment and abruptly dropped to his knees.

"AJ!" Acacia called out, her eyes widening in shock. She knelt beside her friend, planting her hands on the ground. AJ had seemed okay. What had happened so suddenly to make him fall? Had Percy missed something? "Are you all right? What's going—"

"Relax, Acacia, please," AJ remarked, looking up at her with a weak smile. "No cause for alarm. I'm just a little more . . . anemic than usual today is all." The twin shifted his body so he was sitting again, leaning back into the arm of the couch. "I should have known better than to get up so fast. I just didn't want to be rude."

Acacia let out a long sigh, though out of relief or exasperation she wasn't sure. "Don't be stupid. Why would I think you were rude? You're injured, and people who are injured should be resting, not worrying about offending someone. I don't know what happened last night, but it looked like Dionera did a number on you. And Percy told us he found you in a pool of blood—"

"Which is why I'm more anemic today than usual," AJ explained, his eyes a bit unfocused. "This kind of thing has happened before without all the blood loss. I'll be fine once I get my strength back."

Acacia shook her head. *I'm too high strung,* she thought. *If I start getting upset about every little thing* now, *how am I going to keep it together the next time Sisyphus hatches some evil plan?*

"Sorry, I don't mean to snap," she said. "I was just worried about you. You were almost killed doing . . . whatever you were doing, and I was supposed to make sure everyone got out safely. If I hadn't let you go off on your own, you wouldn't have gotten hurt."

"So, what you're telling me is it's your fault I convinced you to let me stop the Woodsfolk magic from trapping us, and it's your fault Dionera tried to kill me while I was doing what I told you I was going to do?" AJ's expression was amused, as if he had just told a particularly funny joke. "Sounds like you're letting Amara Jones get to you. You shouldn't. Trust me, this time I'm speaking from experience."

Acacia's coppery brows shot up in shock. "But— How did you—"

"Know she came to pay you a house call? Let me guess—she gave you the whole 'you could have gotten everyone killed' speech?" Even in their silvery haziness, AJ's eyes were filled with understanding. "Let's just say I've known Amara for long enough to know her style. She *does* mean well, but she lets her outrage get the best of her."

"I guess I trust you," Acacia said, sitting down next to her friend on the floor. "After all, you did keep your word with whatever you did back at Sisyphus's lair. You're not bad—for a Sniffer, anyway."

AJ laughed. "Thanks for the vote of confidence, Commander Wheatley. The next time I'm contemplating using my powers for evil, I'll be sure to think of you before doing anything."

It was amazing to Acacia how much her world had changed in the past few months. On the first day of school, she had thought of AJ first as her nemesis and then as a reluctant, sarcastic know-it-all, who was only teaching her because he felt obligated to do so. But so many things had happened since then: Sisyphus's escape, the arrival of the Virseyeh and Patrick Delaney, and now their successful infiltration and escape from Sisyphus's lair. Despite their friendship's rocky beginning, they'd managed to become closer than Acacia believed possible. Although she would never have the same feelings for AJ as she did for Alex, she had come to love him as a brother, just as she loved David. Prior to moving to Silent Springs, Acacia had made friends, but now she had acquired a sort of chosen family. And she would stop at nothing to protect her family, even if that meant confronting Sisyphus until she managed to defeat him for good.

"So Dionera's gone?" Acacia asked, never one to avoid taboo topics. "Percy said—"

"That I killed her?" AJ averted his gaze and flipped through the book of music again. "I did. I moved the runes on the ceiling around so it dropped on her. No one could have survived."

"She would have killed you if you hadn't," Acacia pointed out. "If Percy and Mattes hadn't reached you in time, you might have died anyway."

The twin sighed and met her gaze again. His eyes seemed to have lost the disoriented haze, brought into focus by the gravity of their conversation.

"Sure, Dionera wasn't about to win any humanitarian awards, but it doesn't change the fact I killed her. It's not that I regret it, it's just . . . I guess we all have to come to terms that we're in a war, and sometimes we have to do the unthinkable if we want to protect . . . what we care about." He blinked, looking at her with inquisitive eyes. "I think you've learned that lesson well."

Acacia swallowed, thinking back upon the events of the previous night. She had placed all her friends in grave danger by leading them into Sisyphus's lair, but she would do it all over again, for Alex as well as for any of the others.

"There *is* one other question I've been wanting to ask you for a while," Acacia said. "But how did you convince . . . whoever you could train me? I know in the beginning of the school year you told me when a mage . . . well, finds a mage who doesn't have anyone to teach them, it becomes the trained mage's responsibility, but I would have thought that after it all came out about me being the Heir of Swansgrove, the Council would have appointed someone, whether it was you who 'found' me or not."

AJ smiled and tilted his head. "You really come up with some fascinating questions sometimes, Acacia Wheatley," he replied, an appreciative look in his eyes. "I wasn't going to tell you, because I thought it would make you feel bad, but they wanted to, back when Sisyphus escaped. They—well, Valhart, Roberts, and Albergast—tried to say it was my fault for not knowing how to handle a student. I really had to beg them not to reassign you, though so did my mom and Uncle Jack."

Acacia's brows rose in shock. How could the Council try to blame AJ for what had happened in the Bloody Meadow when it had been her and Alex who'd run off there in the first place? Though that wasn't even the most surprising of her friend's confession. Hearing that AJ had begged the Council to not pawn Acacia off to another teacher was nothing short of shocking, let alone that Cecelia Swiatkowski and Jack Golec had also petitioned on his behalf.

"Excuse me?" No matter how hard she tried, Acacia couldn't keep the surprise off her face. At the time, AJ had to have been beyond frustrated at her; surely it would have made his life much easier if her education had been passed along to some adult mage. "You begged for them to not reassign me? And your mom and uncle did too? Why?"

"Let's just say the Swiatkowskis and Golecs have always found that everything works out for the better when things are kept . . . in the family so to speak. And besides, as silly as it might sound, I do take my ethical obligations seriously. Plus, I knew I could handle it." A crooked grin crossed his face, a look not all that different from the one typically worn by Matthias Knight at his most mischievous. "Anyway, enough of the serious stuff. I take it you and my brother are finally hitting it off. Congrats! Mattes and I were wondering how long it would take.

I figured before the end of the year, but Mattes didn't think either of you would 'have the guts' until summer."

Acacia felt her face flushing bright red in embarrassment. How did their conversation go from serious to teasing in a matter of seconds? "Spit it out, AJ. What are you getting at?"

"Nothing really. But due to certain circumstances, Mattes has to give Merlin a bath. You can come watch too if you want. It should be quality entertainment."

"Andrew James Swiatkowski!" Acacia exploded. Did AJ just tell her that he and Mattes had been betting on when she and Alex would start dating? "You jerk, you can't just bet on when people—"

"What the hell is going on in here?"a familiar voice said from the top of the staircase. Acacia glanced up at a bedraggled Alex, squinting at them in the early morning light. His hair was sticking out in all directions and his pajamas were beyond wrinkled, but Acacia couldn't help but smile as she looked at him. "It's not even six yet, why is anyone—" Finally his light gray eyes rested on Acacia, and he blushed, clearly forgetting whatever he had been about to say.

"Good morning, Alex," Acacia said, her disagreement with AJ forgotten. "Sorry if we woke you up."

Alex bounded down the stairs, taking a seat next to her. "Acacia, I'm so sorry. Everything with Amara . . . I mean all of this, it's all my fault. If I had just—"

"Listened to me?" AJ offered hopefully.

Alex acted as though he hadn't heard his brother's comment. "I never had the chance to tell you before." His gray eyes met Acacia's green ones. "But you were so amazing, tearing in there and kicking Sisyphus's butt—"

"Will you at least give the anemic kid enough time to leave the room before you start the fond embraces?" AJ asked, pushing himself to his feet again, this time holding onto one of the chairs for support. "Seriously, it's rude."

Alex rounded on his brother with lightning speed. "What, now you have intimacy issues?"

"Zander," AJ retorted. "Everyone here knows I have intimacy issues. Now, can you two be trusted alone together, or shall I send a chaperone?"

"Andrew!" Both Acacia and Alex hollered simultaneously. AJ laughed once more and disappeared up the stairs.

"Idiot," Alex commented, rubbing the sleep from his eyes. "He may be a genius, but he's an idiot."

Acacia laughed and leaned into him. "Aren't we all? You, for running into that lair to try to save him, and all of the rest of us for doing the same for you?"

Alex let out a long sigh. "I guess," he agreed in a reluctant voice. "Acacia, you know I can't believe it, how stupid I was."

"You're not—"

"I am." Alex averted his gaze and stared into the carpet. "You know, it was right after I kissed you. I-I guess I wasn't thinking clearly. I should have known Patrick was a no-good, lying—"

Acacia patted him on the back. She too hadn't been thinking clearly after he had kissed her. Everything had seemed so perfect, as if she had been floating around in a bubble, watching as everything happened around her. Acacia had never been kissed before, and before Alex, she had no hopes it would happen anytime soon. Back in California, boys had always considered her a bit too tomboyish to be of any romantic interest. She was always more interested in riding her bike by the river, going mountain climbing, or—her own personal favorite—kicking her classmates' butts playing soccer. Acacia had plenty of male friends, but all of them ended up going out with her more feminine girlfriends and then coming to her for relationship advice. Fortunately, she had never developed any strong feelings for any of them, so it had never bothered her. But with Alex, it was different, and it had been from the beginning. He liked to do the same types of things as her and never got offended if she was better at them. She loved Alex's impulsive nature, even if it got them into trouble. While someone like AJ or Percy would spend hours deliberating about how to deal with something, Alex did something, even if that something was a horrible idea. He was a risk taker, but he lived life to its fullest.

"I was so worried," Acacia said, her voice a bit unsteady. "When AJ showed up at my house telling me that you were missing. I was so scared to do anything at first . . . I was just so . . . afraid I wasn't ever going to see you again."

She was only vaguely aware she had started to cry. Before she knew it, Alex had her in a tight embrace, his strong arms keeping her safe and warm.

"Acacia, it's okay," he consoled her. "I'm here now, and I'm not going anywhere, I promise."

For a few moments, Acacia was content to cry on Alex's shoulder, feeling the gentle thudding of his heart in his chest. She wasn't typically much of a crier, but with all the stress of the past twenty-four hours, she wouldn't have been able to hold back even if she wanted to.

"You know," she said, pushing the tears from her eyes. "The thought of facing Sisyphus was terrifying and facing him was even worse. But I would do it all over in a heartbeat."

"Acacia—"

"Alex, you make me feel like I can do this," Acacia said. "The magic, the defeating Sisyphus, even just high school in this little town where everyone looks at me like I'm a freak or something."

"Acacia." Alex touched the side of her face. "Have you ever thought that people stare at you because you're strong and beautiful?"

She shook her head. "I'm not—"

"Yes, you are." Alex looked upon her fondly. "This might sound cheesy, but you remind me of something I remember my dad saying when I was little. 'Shoot for the moon, 'cuz even if you miss, you'll land among the stars.' But with you, I think I shot for the moon and found the sun instead."

There was no passing flurry this time, no gentle breeze blowing through her hair, but when Alex leaned forward and kissed her, it was just as magical as the first time. Acacia kissed him back, as passionately as a fourteen-year-old with no relationship experience could, digging her fingers into his messy hair.

"Alex," she said, once they separated. "I don't really know what love is, but I think I love you."

"Acacia—"

"Well, hello there," a familiar voice called from the kitchen. To her horror, Matthias Knight strode into the living room, looking very pleased with himself. "It appears to me the two of you are getting along quite swimmingly if I don't say so myself."

Acacia and Alex sprang apart as Mattes walked over and sat on the chair next to them.

"You don't have to stop on my account," he told them brightly, folding his arms across his chest. "I would loathe to be the one responsible for disrupting your lovebirds' reunion."

"Mattes!" Alex leaped up from the couch in sheer fury. "You—"

"Please go with 'egotistical prattle-box,'" Mattes requested. "That's what your brother called me when he was sleep-talking. It's my new personal favorite."

"I am *not* my brother!"

"Clearly, because your brother is not making out with the Heir of Swansgrove in his pajamas. Really, Alexander, you might want to start planning these things out a tad better. Lucky for you she's low maintenance—"

Acacia opened her mouth to reply to Mattes's snarky statement but froze in shock as Cecelia Swiatkowski glided into the room. The woman wore what looked to be the same clothes she had worn to work the previous night and her ash blonde hair was tumbling out of her bun.

"Acacia Wheatley," she said, her blue eyes exhausted. "Your mother and I have been looking for you for two hours. Having your daughter go missing twice in the same night can be a shock for the calmest mother. Which Dervla Wheatley is not."

"B-but, Mrs. Swiatkowski," Acacia began, fumbling for words. "I just . . . um—"

Cecelia smiled and gave her a strong hug, looking at her with pride. "Acacia, I can't say I know exactly what you did, but whatever you have done, you have done well," she said. "But today is a new day, and it's time for us to get back to our normal lives."

Acacia nodded and brushed off her shoulders, preparing to follow Cecelia out of the house. Taking one last glance behind her, she mind-spoke to Alex, *I'll talk to you later, I promise.*

Awesome, Alex replied. *Oh, and Acacia, one more thing.*

Huh?

Does this mean you'll be my girlfriend?

Acacia grinned broadly and nodded. *I wouldn't have it any other way.*

"Acacia Wheatley! Do you *want* to give your parents another panic attack?"

With that, Acacia sprinted outside to meet Mrs. Swiatkowski, her heart the lightest it had been in months.

CHAPTER TWENTY-TWO

HAPPY BIRTHDAY, ACACIA!

Acacia's mother didn't send her on the next flight back to California, but she did ground her, indefinitely. To Acacia's surprise, Dervla Wheatley didn't even ask many questions about what had happened the night of her abrupt disappearance. *She has to know we ran into Sisyphus,* Acacia considered, flopping onto her bed. *But it's like she doesn't really want to know.*

"Well," Sarison said to Acacia one day after dinner. "Mom was a young mage once. I'm sure she did a ton more stupid stuff than you have, so she's just punishing you for all the stupid stuff you could have been doing when you didn't have your magic yet."

"Thanks, Sari." Acacia closed her eyes. "I'll have tons of time to think about stupid stuff to do while I'm grounded."

Her sister smirked at her. "I guess it'll make you think twice before you go running off after some boy."

"Sari!"

For the next few days, Acacia expected some Council representative to show up unannounced at her door to haul her off for another round of interrogation, but they never came. *Well, Amara did say she was going to try to keep this from going further than it should. Maybe she's more effective than I thought.*

Nevertheless, the weeks faded into months, and the academic year flew by. Sometime in early March, Acacia's mother ungrounded her and she was able to spend time with her friends outside school. Having been stuck at home for so long, Acacia was unsure of what to do with her newfound freedom. She had no intentions of getting into trouble again, which she explained to Alex the first time they hung out together as an official couple. He had nodded silently, his gaze serious. For whatever reason, Alex did listen to her better now, and she doubted he would do something she asked him not to.

In May, Acacia was allowed to invite her friends to her birthday party.

She woke up early on May seventeenth to help her mother with the final preparations, as did Sari. Since she had spent much more time at home, she had grown closer to her little sister. Acacia had come to realize aside from Sari's occasional whining, she wasn't bad for a fifth grader.

Acacia's family arrived at around eleven o'clock. As she made conversation with one of her aunts, Acacia wondered why she never thought it was suspicious that no one from her mother's side ever came to any family functions. Or for that matter, why she couldn't remember seeing them in years.

But Acacia didn't dwell on the subject. It was her birthday, and she didn't want to waste energy thinking about her mom's reasons for keeping her ancestry from her.

"Acacia!" Onawa leaped over the picket fence and gave her an enormous bear hug. "You're old!"

Acacia laughed and rubbed her knuckles into her friend's scalp. "Ha-ha, Dragon Girl. In a couple months, you'll be old too."

Onawa giggled and turned to the group behind her, who had stopped to open the gate.

"AJ! When am I going to be old?"

"September tenth," the twin responded as he and Alex caught up with her, both carrying small packages. "Happy birthday, Acacia."

Matthias Knight came flying out of nowhere, pulling up to Acacia's fence on a yellow dirt bike. He faked a cough, unsuccessfully disguising the words 'ball and chain.'

"Can I help you get something out of your throat, Matthias? Your voice box, perhaps?"

While Mattes and AJ bickered, Alex approached Acacia and kissed her forehead.

"Happy birthday, Acacia," her boyfriend said, his light gray eyes excited. "Thanks again for inviting us."

"Of course." Acacia felt her cheeks redden. "Why wouldn't I?"

Percy rounded the corner, holding the hand of a younger girl who could only be his sister, a small child with bright blue eyes and dirty blonde hair tied back in neat braids.

"Hello, Acacia," Percy said, slightly out of breath. "Sorry we're late. My mother had me run to the grocery store right when we were getting ready to leave. You did say it was okay to bring my sister, right?"

"Certainly," Acacia replied. "Hi there, uh—"

"Izabel." The child's blue eyes were reminiscent of her brother's. "With a 'z.' I'll be nine in June."

Mattes hopped off his bike, leaving it parked next to the fence. "Well, can we go in now, or are we partying here?"

Acacia shook her head at her friend's comment and led them to the backyard.

Wow, AJ mind-spoke to her as they sat down in the grass. *It's attack of the gingers.*

Andrew Swiatkowski, Acacia fired back, arching her coppery brows. *Enough with the bigotry against redheads.*

AJ shot her a crooked grin. *Well, one redhead tried to kill me, and another tried to get us all killed. Your people aren't representing themselves well in my book.*

Read a different book then.

AJ stuck his tongue out at her. As she glanced at him, Acacia noticed that months after the episode in Sisyphus's lair, a light scar was still visible on his arm. Acacia wondered if it was *ever* going to disappear.

"Stop harassing my girlfriend, AJ," Alex complained, putting his arm around Acacia's shoulders. "If you have to harass someone, can't it be someone else?"

"Acacia was my student long before she was your girlfriend," AJ reminded his brother with mischievous eyes. "In other words, no."

Alex opened his mouth to reply, but Acacia beat him to it.

"Twins," she remarked, bopping them both on the head. "This is not what I expected when I envisioned boys fighting over me."

"You envisioned boys fighting over you?" Mattes's hazel eyes danced with amusement. "Should Percival and I start fighting over you too so your dream becomes a reality?"

"Mattes!"

"Well," the dark-haired boy retorted. "You can take the boy out of the Underground, but you can't take the Underground out of the boy."

At that remark, AJ let out a long sigh, shooting his friend a stormy glare. "Must you broadcast the fact—"

"AJ," Onawa interrupted, jostling the twin's shoulder. "Can you get me a soda?"

He nodded and rose abruptly, disappearing to do as asked. Mattes poked Acacia in the side, whispering, "See? Ball and chain."

"I heard that!"

Sometime after lunch, Acacia opened her presents. Most of the gifts from her family were articles of clothing, which Acacia appreciated since the winters in Pennsylvania were much colder than they had been in California. Alex gave her a new soccer ball, AJ a book about the history of magic, Mattes a pair of arm guards, Onawa a fireproof purple T-shirt, and Percy a potion manual disguised as a chemistry book. Acacia realized one envelope had been left unopened.

"Hm," Alex commented, as she brought the envelope over to where they were sitting. "I feel like I've felt that aura before."

"Because you have." AJ glared at it as if he thought it might explode. "Acacia, I suggest you burn that."

"Ooh give it to me," Onawa said. "I can have S'feirra—"

"You idiots, it's her birthday," Mattes argued. "Let her do what she wants with it."

Acacia studied the envelope and broke its seal. She half expected some serpentine creature to emerge and attack her, but nothing happened. Acacia slid out the note inside and read it.

"Swansgrove,

Go to the Pool of L'gwin and what was taken from you shall be restored.

Al'lryn Fwein."

"Acacia," AJ said. "Where do you think you're going?"

Acacia showed her friend the note. "I'm just going to see. Maybe one of my family members dropped this."

"Acacia," he scolded. "You don't even know what the Pool of L'gwin *is*. Or what 'Al'lryn Fwein' means."

"Or what language it is," Mattes added. "Or who delivered it in the first place."

"But you two do." Acacia headed toward the gate. "Are you coming or not?"

She popped her head into the house to tell her mother she and her friends were going on a short walk and minutes later was tromping through the woods in search of the mysterious Pool of L'gwin.

About fifteen minutes later, Acacia and the others—minus Percy who hadn't wanted to leave his sister unattended—had found a small lake she had never seen before. The water was still, and Acacia could feel the magic emanating from it.

"Well, nothing here," AJ said in a sing-song voice. "Time to go."

"Andrew, "Acacia and Alex said at the same time. They glanced at each other and laughed. The two of them had been spending much more time together.

And then, the water *spoke* to her, though in *feelings,* not in words. Acacia closed her eyes and felt its great power pulling her in. . .

It was three forty-five in the afternoon, exactly fifteen years after Acacia had been born. She stepped forward toward the Pool of L'gwin. . .

And the Staff of Swansgrove shot up, out of the water and into her outstretched hands. Acacia gasped, and a surge of her green magic emanated from the staff and flew up like a rocket into the sky. Acacia looked back at her friends. Alex and Mattes both stared at her, their mouths agape in shock. Onawa was ecstatic, jumping up and down in excitement, and AJ looked as if he had seen a particularly horrifying ghost.

Acacia walked over to her friends, clenching the object in her hands.

"AJ," she said. "Those last two words on that note, what do they mean?"

"Al'lryn Fwein," AJ replied, "is a traditional Woodsfolk greeting meaning 'I wish you peace.'"

All was quiet. Acacia looked to the sky, hoping it would give her some idea of what was happening, but the clouds merely continued their crawl through the heavens above. The note, the staff appearing out of a lake...

"Ladies and gentlemen," Mattes said after a long silence. "It appears that Patrick Delaney has not yet departed."

Acacia had been thinking the same thing.

Chapter Twenty-Three

SNEAK PEAK

Woodsfolk's Dilemma, The Reluctant Lord

The stifling heat of the day lingered over Silent Springs like a smothering blanket. The town was in the middle of a July heat wave with temperatures reaching into the nineties. In the past week, there hadn't even been much of a breeze to provide relief from the heat, causing most of the town's residents to venture to one of the nearby lakes to cool off. The non-magicals flocked to Oak Hollow Lake, which was the easiest to find, accessible via one of the main roads. Conversely, the mages frequented Lake Prosper, hidden away deep in the forest and shielded with an assortment of enchantments.

Neither the non-magicals nor the mages of Silent Springs ventured to the Pool of L'gwin. From ancient times, the Pool of L'gwin had been part of the legendary Woodsfolk stronghold closest to the territory of human mages. But Patrick Delaney was not a non-magical nor a human mage. He was a Woodsfolk, a member of a magical bloodline rooted deeply in the natural world.

The boy stared into the waters of L'gwin. It was difficult to believe six months had passed since the most recent incident between the two opposing factions of human mages: Swansgrove and her friends, and the dark mage Henry Moore and his associates. The eventful night had been spurred on by Patrick's actions.

Patrick sighed and gazed into the water. He'd only acted as he did to ensure the Staff of Swansgrove fell into Swansgrove's possession. However, Amara Jones later seized the object and locked it within the Council Headquarters. Patrick had been tempted to teach the meddling girl a lesson but decided instead to return the item to its rightful owner. After all, if Acacia was to fulfill her destiny, she would require the Staff.

Acacia Swansgrove was powerful yet flawed in her predictability. Patrick had known the girl would run to the rescue if anything happened to Alexander Swiatkowski, prompting his decision to send the boy on a false mission in Moore's lair. He hadn't done it to be cruel but rather to help Acacia embark on her path toward her destiny. For both she and Wrin had roles to play if the world was not to be plunged into dark magic.

From the day Wrin had arrived in the meadow where the Virseyeh had emerged, Patrick could tell the boy possessed abilities he was yet unaware of. To stop the cycle of darkness set into motion the night of Moore's escape from the vacuum spell, Wrin would need to not only become aware of this ability but master it.

I have my work cut out for me, Patrick thought. *Wrin must remember what happened to give him that power, and Swansgrove needs to start using that Staff. I might even have an idea of how I can accomplish both in one visit.*

Acknowledgements

Wow! This adventure in the often magical, often technical world in indie publishing has certainly been a wild ride. But as our favorite Dragon Speaker Onawa Mescal would say, "If a ride isn't wild, what's the point of taking it?" And what is creating a special edition of a book than a wild ride?

This special edition of *The Heir of Swansgrove* would not have been possible if not for some very special people in my life. And without further ado...

First, I would like to thank my parents who always encouraged me to follow my dream and write. I know the notebook collection was a bit ridiculous, but as it turns out, I did need all of those notebooks to get all the ideas out. Turns out, the constant scribbling for the past twenty years did amount to something!

Second, I would like to give a HUGE shout out to Ali Collins, who created the special edition cover and the inside illustrations. I love how you were able to take my chaotic ideas and turn them into art that's both a little spooky and a lot magical. This release would not have been the same without you and I'm honored to have the opportunity to work with such a talented artist.

I would like to thank my editor Karen Robinson, who edited *The Heir of Swansgrove* for its original release. This book would not have been the same without her careful editing, and for this I am thankful.

Also, I would like to thank all my close friends who provided the support and encouragement that helped me to see this project through. Jackie, Ada, Armando, Steve, as well my inner circle of author and reader friends. Some of you have been with me from the beginning, and some I've met more recently. I would also like to give a big shout out to my fellow author pal Adrielle, who connected me with Ali and helped bring this special edition to life.

And last but certainly not least, I would like to thank you, the reader, for taking a chance on Acacia and her friends. I earnestly hope you enjoyed Acacia's journey from clueless high schooler to budding heroine. Our girl's certainly got a way to go until she truly realizes her destiny, and I'd be honored if you decide to stick around for the ride.

Thank you all again and stay tuned for the next project!

9 798989 650477